THE SEA OF SILENCE

BY NIEL HANCOCK

POPULAR LIBRARY

An Imprint of Warner Books, Inc.

A Warner Communications Company

For C.E.U., a.k.a. Toasty—
remembering the times

POPULAR LIBRARY EDITION

Popular Library®, the fanciful P design, and Questar® are
registered trademarks of Warner Books, Inc.

Cover illustration by Tim Hildebrandt

Popular Library books are published by
Warner Books, Inc.
666 Fifth Avenue
New York, N.Y. 10103

 A Warner Communications Company

Printed in the United States of America

First Printing: December, 1987

10 9 8 7 6 5 4 3 2 1

THE RISING OF THE MOON

FIRE AND DISASTER

DUST AND ASH

FOOTPRINTS IN THE SAND

A TEST OF TIME

THE SAILING

THE
RISING
OF
THE
MOON

The Horse-riding

The delightful small eels that curled and wavered in the tiny glass cages filled with seawater drew large crowds of the well-wishers who roamed the grounds, and the marvelous musicians from all points of the compass played and sang until late into the night on the day the minstrel Emerald and the Lady Elita were readying for their marriage vows. It had been rumored throughout the Line, and all the surrounding countries that bordered it, that the Elboreal would be there to set the feast, although most of those who heard this story put no credence in it, for it was a well-known fact that the Dreamers had all gone over the Boundary after Famhart and Linne returned from the bloody battle at the Fords of the Silver Mist, near Rogen Keep in Trew. Still, it was a wonderful thing to think upon, and when the preparations were made for the banquet, there was space left in all the kitchens for provisions for the Dreamers, and everyone talked as though they would not be surprised by the arrival any day of their absent guests.

The fall air was still warm and echoed the heat of the passing summer. The rebuilt shelters of Sweet Rock all stood with doors and windows open, and there was much coming and going among the dwellings, and many conversations held from the path through the open door, and much clamor and noise from outside, where the carpenters and

3

decorators set up the arena for the sporting events, and the pavilion for the bands, and the covered arbor where the ceremony of the wedding would take place.

Owen Helwin found Emerald leaving a band of roving musicians who had traveled a great distance to be a part of the festivities.

"Do you have a spare second to spend with me, Emerald? I feel as though I haven't had a talk with you since we've come home from the Fords of Trew."

The minstrel laughed, clapping the young man heartily on the back.

"This isn't the easiest thing to talk about, Emerald. I thought I could ask my father, but he and my mother have been spending a lot of time together, and I never get a chance to catch him alone."

"Aha! So you've tabbed poor Emerald a second choice, have you? Now we get down to the grist of the matter!"

"I want to know what I should do," said Owen, hesitating. "I mean, since Deros is here with us and all, I can't very well go to her father and state my intentions to him!"

"Whoa, my buck." Emerald laughed. "Back up! Your intentions?"

"Of course," snapped the youth peevishly. "This isn't easy to say, Emerald! I didn't think you would be so hard to talk to, since you and Elita are to be married."

The minstrel grew more serious but still smiled.

"I begin to see how it is, lad, and you have to forgive me my jesting with you. You know I mean it well, and it's only my long friendship with you that allows me the liberty to laugh."

"What am I to do, Emerald? Deros says she can't think of anything but gathering help for her father, and that time is a long way off. We have promised to help her, and my father says he will send a squadron of the Line to escort her home, but she fears that may not be enough."

"This is not the best time, Owen," said Emerald quietly.

"How do you mean? I think I have been slow in everything. At least it seems that way. Deros treats me now as if I were her baby brother!" Owen's agitation had grown, and he blushed a deep crimson.

His friend laughed heartily and called out to Elita, who had just emerged from one of the many shelters where the bakers worked, carrying fresh loaves wrapped in cloth.

"Come here and help us out! Owen has a terrible problem, and we need a woman's advice."

"I don't want to spread this about," hissed Owen, looking angrily at his companion. "If you shout so, I may as well tell Stearborn about it!"

"He deserves his bit of gossip, lad. There's not much that gives the old war-horse pleasure, but it's well known that he enjoys swapping bits of news now and then."

"He's noisy with any secret you lay to him," argued Owen.

"You know he would do anything for you! Your father and Stearborn are old friends. He teases you, and you react to him like a fish to bait."

"He teases on subjects that are tender," insisted Owen. "I am a good sport on most accounts, and you can attest to that!"

"This is different, is it?" teased Emerald.

"You know it's different! Now tell your intended that I just need to know what I should wear on your wedding day."

Emerald laughed and gathered Elita into his arms, careful not to spill her fresh loaves.

"What is it that could be so serious as to give these sour looks to Owen? Are you discussing a wake?"

"Nothing of the sort." Emerald laughed. "We're talking of matters of the heart."

"Then why so downtrodden, Owen? I would think you'd have a smile for us!"

Owen was blushing and looking away.

"He is hooked on the horns of the oldest dilemma," explained Emerald, taking Elita's arm. "He feels too much, and he doesn't understand why it's returned to him in such a strange fashion."

"How so?" asked Elita.

"You wenches always have the best of us when it comes to these matters," chided the minstrel. "We lads aren't equipped to play at all those subtle games. We don't recognize the tender trap until we've been snared, and the minute we respond, you heartless ladies have no mercy at all and act as though you are indifferent to our predicament."

Elita smiled knowingly and joined the men in their walk, putting her arm through Owen's and teasing him to try to cheer him up.

"It's always hard," she said, tugging at his ear. "You have to remember that we have little to save us from heartbreak. If we can't be sure of our man, then we go on to the next candidate. We have to try our little wiles and tests to make sure you are going to be our steadfast champion."

"I don't see any reason you have to be so cruel in all of it," said Emerald. "After all, how plain could it be? What must we poor fellows do to convince you ice-hearts that our intentions are honorable and that our feelings are true?"

"You won't know any of that until you've passed muster," replied Elita. "There is no way to explain how a woman tests the one she loves. But I can tell you this, Owen. If you are being put off and given the long way around, then you are most assuredly well regarded by your sweetheart."

"That makes no sense," said Owen. "Why would you say one thing when you mean another?"

Elita's laugh rang like a silver bell on the morning air. "Now you press for answers that I cannot give, my young friend. These are things that you will come to find out for yourself someday. They have been mysteries for as long as there have been men and women."

"You see? There is nothing quite so dark and murky that can't be made even darker and more confused by a woman." Emerald sighed. "And I think half the songs I know are about love and its happiness, and the others are of love lost, and the sadness and grief it brings in its wake."

"I care nothing for your songs," snapped Owen hotly, feeling as though he were being made fun of. "If you can't be civil to me, then at least tell me you don't know an answer and let it go at that!"

Emerald raised his eyebrows. "I can see this is serious. There is every indication it may even be fatal!"

"Stop your jesting! I have to go!" Owen wrested himself free and strode away angrily, his cloak flying out behind him in the wind.

Elita and Emerald watched the agitated young man until he passed from sight among the bustling crowds of people who were preparing for the great celebration. As the two stood taking in all the busy activity, Famhart and Linne appeared, greeting the younger couple warmly.

"Well met, my good fellow! Not too much longer and you'll be tied to the stake of wedded bliss like myself," laughed Famhart, clasping hands with the minstrel.

"He talks this way to try to get me stirred up," explained Linne. "I don't recall his fighting too hard to escape me."

Famhart's face softened, but his tone was still teasing. "This woman will do anything to hold her man! I've never seen anyone go to greater lengths."

"Hush, you two!" Linne said. "Go find something to amuse yourselves! Elita and I have something to talk over."

"I think we've gotten our marching orders, Emerald. Come on! There's a horse-riding come the night before last, and some of the troop mentioned knowing you."

"A horse-riding? By what name?" asked Emerald after kissing Elita.

"They call themselves the Gortland Fair, but I have seen some other colors in their stalls."

"Gortland Fair," mused the minstrel, frowning. "I don't think I knew it by that name, if I ever knew it at all."

"We shall find out presently. Here is one of the riders now. Come, lad! Here's Emerald the minstrel, who is known to some of your company."

A short, stout man in his late twenties, dressed all in shades of blue, approached, walking with the rolling gait of a horseman. He had red hair, a slight beard, and green eyes that seemed to crackle with a light of their own. "McKandles is the handle, sirs, and horses is my main affair in this here vale of life. Born and bred to the brutes, and born and bred to perish with my boots on! I has the liberty of saying I ain't never met the gent, sirs, but if you'll bear with me long enough to stroll down to our corrals, we'll has an end to our mystery soon enough."

McKandles bowed low to his new acquaintances with the wide flourish of a showman used to performing before crowds, and set off at a brisk pace.

As they went, Emerald suddenly remembered Owen. "Your son has been beached upon that rock we call the heart," he said. "He just left me in a state I would describe as frantic, although I don't think too serious."

Famhart nodded. "He has touched on the subject more than once. I remember how desperate it seemed when I was almost his age and Linne and I were first met."

"I wonder how it is that we haven't heard more from the lass's father? It seems we should have had some reports from that direction by now."

Famhart's mood changed, and a worried frown darkened his face. "I have thought as much myself, and I don't like the silence. We sent ten good men to the coast to search for any news of her people. They were well prepared to survive such a trip, and yet we have no word of them."

"Deros said it is a long journey."

"If it were in other times than these, I might agree," said Famhart, shaking his head. "Since we've returned from Trew and seen the end of Bern and Largo, I can't help having an uneasy feeling that we aren't to be let off so easily. The Dark One is not so strong as she once was, but that cycle is turning. I could sense that when Largo came back to haunt us further."

"These are strange times," agreed Emerald. "I have lived to see things that I never would have dreamed, and there doesn't seem an end to it yet." He laughed suddenly. "And here I am on the eve of being married! I never would have thought it!"

"It happens to the best of us, lad. Just when we least expect it."

"Always when you least expects it," piped up McKandles. "Begging pardon, sirs, but that's what my old pap, what used to sit a wild-eyed brute from the Wastes of Leech without no saddle, used to say. He were hitched to my dear old mammy when the two of them wasn't no more than colts, and they has given me twelve solid brothers and a loving sister that's a season less than me. I never would have been a-goin' in for it like my pap has, but he lives in a shed with two corrals and ten horses, and they waits on him like he was a hootin' king of the Eastendin. My luck ain't never held, though—not yet."

Famhart and Emerald laughed at the man's speech. They found they had arrived at the corrals of the horse-riding called Gortland Fair. It was a bustling mass of animals, and their trainers were near stained and weathered tents that had once been bright gold and blue.

The three men leaned against the corral fence and watched as a rider dismounted at full gallop, then sprang onto the animals's back into a standing position, balancing himself lightly on the speeding beast.

"That youngster would be a great asset to our squadron," said Famhart after watching for a time.

"That gent there is the pride and wonderment of the whole Gortland Fair," put in McKandles. "His name is Ulen. You won't see any other to ever match him. We put to and taken the wagers of many a poor sod that thought they could do the likes of Ulen and his brave Terrier. There ain't no other horse anywheres that can match their likes."

"Where does he come from?" asked Emerald, a faint memory disturbing his thoughts.

As Emerald watched, the horse and rider made a wide, graceful turn and galloped back toward where the three waited at the edge of the corral, and just as the animal neared, the young man tumbled off backward, landing on his feet.

"There you are, you worthless dog, lagging about with these two worthy gentlemen when you should be seeing to the mounts. Forgive him," said Ulen breathlessly. "He hasn't had much of a proper seeing-to when he was being bread-and-buttered. All his other brothers got the brains and left the poor devil in a fine kettle. He does sit a horse well, though, and thankful he can be for that!"

The youthful horseman gave McKandles a hearty slap.

"You may be a high master of the horse, Ulen, but you is nowhere near the art I has with my fists! You keep up that line of prattle, and dog that I is, I is a-goin' to wager I'll unseat you in a battle of scuffle-and-tug."

Ulen laughed again, his face full of mirth, although his voice carried a hidden edge to it that Emerald did not miss.

"We might see to that, my lad, but I don't think these gentlemen came out to witness that spectacle. I would think they had other business afoot when they were waylaid by you!"

"They was a-lookin' for anyone in the horse-riding that would know this gent," growled McKandles, who was still ruffled by the teasing of the young horseman.

"And who might I have the honor of addressing?" asked Ulen, raising his eyebrows questioningly.

"I am Famhart, and my friend here is—"

"The minstrel Emerald at your service," said Emerald, bowing.

Ulen bowed in return, sweeping his leather riding cap from his head as he did so. "Then I am indeed honored to have two such worthy gentlemen come calling. It's not often the Gortland Fair plays before such heroes."

"We are fortunate to see such an accomplished horseman as yourself. I may try to recruit you into my squadron if you don't watch yourself," replied Famhart.

Ulen bowed again. "That would be an honor I could never earn. It is my small talents that keep this horse-riding afloat in these troubled times, and I don't wonder that McKandles and his like would soon falter without me. No, I shall have to resist your invitation to ride with so famous a squadron of the Line."

A party of horsemen had come into the training arena and now trotted about in precision drills, drawing Emerald's attention away for a moment. When he looked back, he found Ulen staring at him.

"We shall have the opening clan-riding tonight after supper," the rider said, extending his hand again. "I shall have a ringside pavilion set aside for you and your party. It begins at dusk!"

At Ulen's orders McKandles handed Famhart a brass token that had the likeness of a horse's head engraved upon it.

"This here will get you to the best seat," he explained. "It's always the best if you gets there early, what with all the bash and scuffle." Ulen bowed low once more, his young, handsome face a riddle of emotions.

"Well, we shall have some good entertainment tonight,"

said Famhart, throwing his arm around the prospective bridegroom.

As Famhart and Emerald walked away, the younger man remarked, "I can't say exactly what it is, but I don't trust this horseman."

Famhart laughed. "I believe you're jealous, you old hawk! This youngster makes us all look like a sack of rags when we sit a horse! Come on, lad, look to the good side! He can't hold a candle to your yarn spinning, and I doubt he can carry a tune at all."

Elita and Linne found them before the minstrel could reply, and the two men were pressed into service carrying bundles of supplies for the festivities. The lovely smile of his bride-to-be took Emerald's mind off the disturbing thoughts of the young horseman and the vaguely disquieting way he had made an almost open threat in delivering his invitation to come to the grand opening of the clan-riding of the Gortland Fair.

Ulen Scarlett

A light south wind had been blowing all afternoon, and Deros watched a large hawk soaring and sliding up and down the blue afternoon's back for some time before she was aware she wasn't alone. It wasn't exactly a feeling of fear so much, but there was an element of uneasiness that made her wish she hadn't wandered so far from the others as she thought about Owen. Deros had seen him earlier and been quite surprised by his rudeness and abrupt departure. Her feelings had been badly hurt, and while she had concealed this from Owen by becoming cool and indifferent, she wondered if he liked her as much as she thought he did.

Deros looked about apprehensively and instinctively put her hand beneath her crimson cloak to clutch the knife that Stearborn had given her. Then she saw the reason for her alarm—the handsome young rider from the Gortland Fair, who went by the name of Ulen Scarlett, and she let go of the hilt. She had seen his amazing skills and thought that he was almost as fair in his appearance as Owen, and that he had a marked boldness to him that Owen didn't have.

"Good day, fair one! It is a kindness of the gods that I have chanced across you here. I have been searching for you to deliver an invitation to sit with me at the opening of the great clan-riding tomorrow!" He bowed low to her, sweeping his cap across the toes of his shining boots.

Deros blushed and could not find her voice for a moment. "You are thoughtful. I thank you for your kindness, but I am one of the wedding party and I must be at Elita's side."

"They could get by without you," urged Ulen. "With all the doings, no one will miss you. It will be exciting to sit with the riders of the Fair! We have a wondrous grand time, and we can show you all the magic of the horse-riding."

Ulen had opened his riding cloak, revealing a brilliant red tunic that was decorated with intricate stitchwork, which wound around the cuffs of his sleeves and across the shoulders in a bright gold-and-blue pattern of prancing horses with tiny gemstones for eyes.

Deros blushed, shaking her head. "It's not so easy! It's kind of you to ask me, but you see—"

Ulen interrupted her with a wave of his hand. "It's nothing you can't find a way out of, my lovely one. You are bound too close to your precious rituals and ceremonies. It would do your heart good to let it be free to soar for once."

The young woman blushed and looked away, suddenly finding it impossible to look at Ulen.

"I see no need to stand on so much ceremony," he went on. "My family has always lived by the law of the horse, and our ways are not so far removed from all that's right and natural."

"How do you mean?" asked Deros, standing and walking away a few steps. "I don't understand what you're saying."

Ulen laughed, throwing his head back and slapping his riding crop loudly against the top of his high boots. "You are so burdened with all your upbringing that you cannot even understand plain speech! That's what I mean! You are trapped in a lock-house, along with all the rest."

A flush of anger spread over Deros's face and she began to walk away, but Ulen caught her and held her arm.

"Let me go! I have to be back! They are waiting for me!"

"When you give me your answer," Ulen replied, his dark eyes meeting hers with a slight mocking expression.

"I gave you my answer already. I shall sit with my friend Elita! Now let me go!"

"Not until you agree to sit with me at the clan-riding."

"You're hurting my arm!"

Ulen smiled faintly, without humor. "Pain is a wonderful thing, once you've made it your friend. I sometimes sit at night with my hand in the hot coals of the fire to keep up my nerve. If you lose your concentration, you will be burned."

Deros clutched the handle of her knife, and she was on the point of bringing it out when a rider came noisily through the wood very near them, whistling and singing a merry song. It was a tune that Deros was familiar with, and it was sung by her old friend, the minstrel.

Emerald pulled up in surprise and dismounted.

"Well, what have we here? How fare you, good horseman? What brings you so far from your friends, Deros?"

The girl blushed, turning a fiery red. "I came out for the air and met this young man here. We've had some cross words and I don't wish to speak with him any further. Can you come back with me, Emerald?"

"Of course. I think Owen has been looking for you."

Ulen Scarlett bowed stiffly and spoke in a guarded tone, never taking his eyes off Deros. "You will honor me if you attend the clan-riding, my lady. Remember what I said about setting your heart free. You will grow old and ugly if you don't."

"There's a topic fit for a long discussion over a winter fire, my young friend," offered Emerald, hoping to put an end to the topic without offending Ulen.

"Perhaps not, good minstrel, for I hold by no bounds but my own good time and skill. You shall find more to Ulen Scarlett than you may bargain for. Good day!"

The bold youngster strode away, his boots gleaming in the sunlight, and Emerald and Deros watched as he mounted his horse, which had been left to graze in a small clearing not far away.

"Are you all right?" asked Emerald, holding the shaken girl to calm her.

"Yes, I think so."

"He may be a wondrous horseman, but by the spurs of Windameir, if he's done anything to cause you alarm, I shall see him hided and thrown out on his ear."

"No, Emerald, he did nothing." Deros suddenly found herself wishing it were Owen who had found her and come to her aid, and the disappointment she felt made her even more angry at him, because it was not so. "I'll be all right now," she said, trying to hide her agitation. "Where have you left Elita? I should find her now."

"She and Linne were concocting some scheme when I left them. Famhart had to look to a dispute among the bakers, and I came out this way to try to find that duffel-headed young friend of mine."

"I'm glad you didn't find him," snapped the girl. "He's rude, and I hope someone can teach him a little about how to treat his friends."

Emerald's eyebrows shot up at the suddenness of the attack. "Treating his friends without a proper kindness, is he? I shall have to have words with the pup. I thought after all we'd been through, he would have had some idea of how it's all done."

Deros blushed a deeper red and began walking rapidly back toward the settlement.

"Wait! I'll walk back with you."

"No need, Emerald. I was just upset for a moment, but Ulen's gone now and I'd like to walk back alone, if you don't mind."

The minstrel studied the fair features of his young friend and smiled. "I did come out this way on an errand. I'll go ahead and finish it, if you promise me you'll go straight back and tell Elita I'm on my way to the weavers to pick up the tunic."

"I'll tell her." Deros reached out and touched his arm, then turned and quickly walked toward the lazy white smoke from the many fires that burned in Sweet Rock, all signaling the preparations of the feast day on the morrow.

As she walked, she pretended that it was her wedding day and that she and Owen were to be wed, but then she remembered she was angry at him. "I should go and sit with that brash young horseman! That would stir up my high-and-mighty Owen Helwin!"

"Who are you talking to?" asked a voice from behind her, which frightened her badly, for she hadn't heard anyone since Emerald rode away.

She turned slowly, dreading the thought that it might be Ulen again.

"I'm sorry to have startled you, but I thought you were someone I knew from my old settlement."

It was a young man, clean-shaven and dressed in the uniform of a Line Steward. "My name is Jeremy."

"I am Deros," replied the girl, trying to recall if she had seen his face before among the many Stewards that filled the camps and settlements.

Jeremy bowed to her then, sweeping the cap from his head. "My lady, pardon me. I would not have been so bold if I had known it was you."

Deros laughed. "If I had been just another girl, you would not have been so forward? Come, Jeremy, tell me how you came to be here and where you have come from."

Jeremy bowed again and was flustered when Deros slipped her arm through his, leaning close to him.

"I have been frightened out here, and I am glad for your company," she said, looking up at him with her crystal-blue eyes and smiling so that he lost his voice for a moment.

"If there is anything to frighten you here, my lady, it won't remain a threat long, not if there's anything a Line Steward can do to bring justice to bear!"

"It's nothing now. I shall forget all about it. But tell me more about your travels on your way here. How came you to Sweet Rock? Have I seen you before?"

"I ride with Chellin Duchin, my lady, in the Lost Elm Squadron. We were at the river when Famhart engaged Largo the Slayer."

A cloud passed over the face of the sun as he spoke, and it seemed to Deros to grow chilly. She shivered and drew nearer to the young man. "It was a brave thing," she murmured. "We were with Emerald and Kegin and Ephinias. I can still smell those Darien Mounds!"

"You are the one who turned out to be a girl." Jeremy laughed. "That has been a tale that has cheered many a long march. We all wondered how anyone could be fooled by so beautiful a lady as you."

Deros blushed, looking away. "It is easy to do such things when your life depends upon it. I have had much practice. I came from a distant land in the Southern Fetch, in the Silent Sea. The roads are not kind to those who look weak."

"That was then, my lady. These are changed times. It would be safe for you now, for the Stewards have secured all the territories between here and the end of civilized tribes."

"Not my homeland! My father sent me out to find help for him, but I fear even now it is too late. Famhart has promised me aid, but I don't know if anything will be enough to curb the power of the Hulin Vipre. They have risen again, and my father's armies have been hard pressed to keep them at bay."

"Who are these people you speak of, my lady?"

The bustle and buzz of the crowded streets reached their ears then, and a sound of music and light laughter drifted over the warm, early-autumn air. There was the scent of fresh-cut green wood from the many new tables and benches.

"You would not have heard of the Hulin Vipre, Jeremy. You have passed all your years in the Line, and I don't think anyone outside my country knows of them."

"Did Famhart know of them?" asked Jeremy. He could not believe there was anything the man would not know.

"No one knows. I have wondered that the Vipre aren't more widely feared, but I begin to think now that the reason they are so little known is that they never take prisoners or allow survivors. Finally, my father, the Lord of Cairn Weal, sent me for aid. He has been a hand of doom against the Vipre for all these long turnings. Yet he grows old as they grow stronger. They have begun to attack even Eirn Bol, the city that guards our island. That has never happened in the history of my people."

Jeremy's face grew troubled as he struggled with all the strange information the beautiful young woman had given him. "Then there must be something done to stop these ones you speak of! Is there no way to keep them confined?"

"I have yet to tell Famhart all of my story. He has had his own burdens to bear. Linne is growing stronger every day; soon I will tell him the rest." Deros was silent for a moment.

"We have all gone through much these past months,"

agreed Jeremy, shaking his head sadly. "I have lost good comrades too."

Deros put out a gentle hand to comfort the young Steward. "Will you bring Chellin Duchin to the Elders' Hall? I would like to meet him. Perhaps if all the captains of the Line hear me, there may be a plan devised that would save us all from the scourge of the Hulin clans."

"Do you think they are so strong?" asked Jeremy.

"They have spread like a plague in my short lifetime," answered the girl, removing her arm from her escort's as they neared the bakers' quarter.

"What are they like?" pursued Jeremy, trying to imagine some grotesque monster that dwelled among the Waste of Leech.

"Like? Why, you or I—to the eye. Yet they are different inside. They have no hearts."

"How could that be?"

"The Hulin Vipre have only one dream in this life, and that is to become the holders of the ancient scrolls that are kept in the Cairn Weal."

"The what kept where?"

"The Cairn Weal is my father's fortress. The scrolls contain the secrets that have to do with life, and strange powers. My father has kept them all during his lifetime, as his father did before him, and his father's father before him."

They came to Famhart's hut, and Deros held out her hand to Jeremy, who took it for a moment, then dropped it awkwardly.

"I shall expect to see you and your commander soon. Come after the tithing party tomorrow, if you can. I shall be with Famhart and Linne at the Green Tent."

"Chellin Duchin wouldn't miss a chance to gab with Famhart." Jeremy bade her farewell and watched her step through the doorway.

A Wedding Vow

Along the river, great colored canopies were spread as far as the eye could see in all directions, blues and greens and yellows; there were purple stripes with dark red bands, and tall scarlet walls capped with maroon tassels, and near the center of it all was a huge golden domed tent, with lavender-colored roof panels and forest-green edges. This was the wedding tent, and it was here that the bride and groom would exchange their vows.

Emerald had awakened early and begun to dress, finding himself more nervous than before any battle. It took him three tries to lace the front of his shirt, and longer still to tie his boots. He thought of shaving but decided it would wait, and went outside his bedroom into the silent cooks' quarters to see if he could find hot water for tea.

Owen was waiting on the step, and when he saw that Emerald was up, he hurried to the shelter. "I—I wasn't sure you'd be awake this early," he stammered, so nervous himself that he could barely talk without his voice quavering.

"This betrothal and all that's gone with it has set my nerves on edge as badly as if I were lying awake dreading crossing the river into Trew and had to face a dozen of the Rogen."

Owen looked at his friend in astonishment. "I didn't think

this would bother you, Emerald! You've made such sport of me about my difficulty, I had no idea you were so worried."

The minstrel smiled faintly, buttoning the leather frogs that held his cloak in place. "I have been a performer so long that I have a hard time letting anyone see Emerald as he really is. There are friends who have never really seen me, although they have known me from my cradle." He shook his head sadly. "It has long been a minstrel's role always to be the recorder of deeds, and not the doer. There were always songs to be made of all the brave tales of the Stewards, so I was content for a long while to be the mouth that sang the songs. Life passed me by, and I never saw it until we reached the hills of Trew."

"You mean when you met Elita?"

"That, most assuredly, my earnest young swain, but more as well."

Owen paced about, picking at his sleeve nervously.

The minstrel laughed. "You'd think it was you to be wed today, instead of me! Look at you! You calm me down to see you so edgy."

Owen blushed, lowering his head. "I can't unravel what makes them tick," he began, looking for his way through the dark mystery that eluded him.

"Who?"

"Women! Not Elita, of course, or my mother. If only Deros were more like her!"

Emerald reached out and held Owen's arm in a strong grasp. "Deros is fine the way she is. You are dealing with a woman from beyond places we know of. And she has had a bad fright."

"What bad fright?" asked Owen. "You mean the fight in Trew?"

"That, too, but I'm speaking of yesterday."

"What could frighten Deros here in Sweet Rock?"

"A bold rogue from the Gortland Fair. He goes by the name of Ulen Scarlett. Your father and I met him earlier, and then I came across Deros, with him, in the old clearing by the water-ditch. She was shaken and glad to see me. She wouldn't say anything except that she thought he had bad manners."

Owen's face flushed, and his fists were knotted into tight balls, making the knuckles white. "This will be settled before the day is over."

The minstrel shook his head. "Not until after this rigmarole is over. I don't want to disappoint Elita. These things are always important to a woman."

"Can I challenge him afterward?"

"If you feel you must, Owen. Remember, Deros has not asked you."

"I will challenge him. Deros is not some trinket he can play with or insult. This is the Line, and that is not how the law works."

Emerald smiled faintly. "You are beginning to have the same trouble your father has struggled with all these turnings, Owen. You feel the full impact of the Law, and how things should be but aren't. Your mother is that way too."

"Will you point out this Ulen Scarlett to me today?" asked Owen. "I won't do anything to ruin your rituals."

"I know you won't. You are my good and steadfast friend."

Owen grinned. "When we first met, I was afraid you might be one of the enemy, you were so strange."

"No one knows what to make of minstrels. We're like the young hothead with the Gortland Fair, in a way. His likes have no place, either, and is always in one end of the reaches or another, with never anywhere to call home."

"You and Elita will always have a place here, Emerald. My father and mother have already promised that."

"Good Kegin has made my fortunes with Famhart. After hearing him tell the tale of our escape from the Dariens, and our scuffle below the mounds, I'll be kept busy until I'm gray at the edges trying to put it all into song."

"Kegin is an honest man. He only told my father the truth."

"He couldn't explain how we went against your father's word, or how we started out with two young boys who were coming into their own, and came back in the end with one young man and one beautiful young woman from an island in the Sea of Silence. That has eluded Kegin's quick wit, and his penchant is for spilling it all out."

There was a disturbance at the chamber door, and a chorus of voices called, "Once wed, never parted, once loved, never left, twice twenty life stories, all full of gold and wealth, all these wishes we wish you, heaped man-high, filled with summers long shadows, and fall's great walks; the winter will be the waiting for spring's child, and the joining together of Elita and Emerald will come to pass in truth and kindness, and the dawn of a new line."

To the delight of all, music from a mouth harp was joined by a soft lute that followed the music like a small bird in a gentle breeze.

Emerald laughed aloud, hurrying to the door. "Welcome, oh sons and daughters of the Line! I salute you and your friends for now and for all time. Come in and drink a vow with me that I shall swear my life surrendered to my bride, my friend, and my companion, for now and for as long as I shall draw breath in these lower fields we call our home."

An old man led the group, dressed in a lavender cloak, with a dark red shawl spread about his thin shoulders. He was followed next by a middle-aged woman, carrying the blessed wedding bands. Her curly hair shone like burnished gold in the strengthening light.

"Welcome to you, Mother. You bring us glad joy in the omens you have set out for us, and for all times to come." Emerald bowed twice to the woman.

She spread out a blue cloth before the minstrel, where she placed two gold rings side by side. "It is the power and the glory, the ebb and flow of all nuptials, to have such tokens read before the ceremonies. I bring you these tidings, minstrel, from the misty reaches of a land far away. Beware the regions of the infidel, for there a danger lurks for you and yours. Stay away from the Silent Sea, and all will go well for she and thee!"

The woman covered her head with a pearl-colored shawl and retreated, leaving the rings on the cloth before the shaken minstrel.

Owen looked at his friend in surprise. "What ritual is this? That is not part of the bindings!"

"I don't know," muttered Emerald, shaking his head.

The old man reached out to detain the woman, but she

slipped from his grasp and eluded the others who waited behind him to catch a glimpse of the bridegroom.

"Let her go!" ordered Emerald, sensing that the crowd was on the verge of forcibly cornering the fleeing woman. "We have much yet to finish before we can go on the gathering of Elders. Come, let us finish here in good spirits! We will find out more of this later. Come, friends, it is my binding day! Let us be gay and seek to make it one to remember!"

Amid a low rumble of protest, the old man dressed in the robes of the chamberlain stepped forward and picked up the two rings from the blue cloth. "These may be tainted, minstrel. We should take them back for a renewed blessing. There is no profit gained in flinging ill will into the faces of fortune and good luck."

"Will it delay us long, good Chamberlain?" Emerald's face was drawn, although he smiled. Owen saw the faintest flicker of a deep sorrow shadow the minstrel's blue eyes, but it passed quickly.

"It will take no time at all, sir, and you will have gained a freedom from the pall this unlooked-for event has cast over us all."

"Then to it, my good Chamberlain! We still have the rest of the rituals to recite, and I'm getting so nervous, I may have forgotten the vows by the time you return."

The crowd behind the old man hastily gathered themselves together and followed him away to repeat the ceremonies of the rings before the ancient statue that stood in the Temple of the Torch, where the sacred flame of Windameir was kept burning day and night. There were times on the highest holy days that the fire was allowed to burn itself down into smoldering ash, then fanned again into a towering blaze that touched the dark shadow of the night sky with it's fiery tongue.

"What do you make of this, Emerald?" asked Owen.

"I think it all means I have a few minutes respite." The minstrel laughed. "A moment longer to consider my fate and think once more on this great step I'm taking today."

"Let's not forget the old coin you must carry for luck," cautioned Owen. "I have saved you one from the cask of money we unearthed among the Dariens. That was as lucky a time as we're ever likely to see. If we always have the same, we'll be old, wise men by the end of all this."

Emerald's laugh was sincere, but there was a sadness that colored his voice. "We'll be old, Owen, but I don't know how wise. I've begun to see that maybe we are never to master this wilderness here below the Boundaries. I think the Elboreal have been the only race to ever fathom what it's like in these Lower Meadows, and they never speak of it, except to give us their sad songs and sadder stories. Come, help me get into these things! I can't for the life of me figure how anyone ever devised a garment so ill-fitting!" Emerald was struggling to pull a bright yellow tunic over his shirt, but the neck was narrow, so he had to hold his arms above his head while Owen tugged at it.

Suddenly Emerald broke free of his grasp and fell backward, cursing loudly and thrashing wildly about on the floor. "Get it off, Owen! Pull, lad. Pull if you love me!"

The minstrel's voice was so strained and urgent that Owen ripped the yellow cloth with a jerk, and at the same time a squat black spider fell clear of the folds of the tunic and tried to scuttle away toward the dim corner at the back of the room.

Emerald was on it in a flash, stomping fiercely with his boot, until the frightening intruder was dispatched into a large, dark stain on the wooden floor. "Olgnite," he muttered, white and trembling badly. "I have heard of them killing a man in no more than a heartbeat. Praise Windameir it did not bite me."

"What are they?" asked Owen, confused. "I've seen spiders since I was a boy, but I don't think I've ever heard of these."

"The Olgnites are from the depths of the Leech Wastes, Owen. They were never found anywhere else until the invaders began to move back and forth across the mountains."

"Then where could this one have come from? We have had a peaceful time here since our return from Trew."

Emerald had examined his wedding tunic carefully and once again began to don it. "I'm hoping that this is a freak of nature. Maybe a lost spider that has come home with us from the wars."

"And if that is not the way of it, Emerald? What then?" asked Owen.

The minstrel studied the younger man for a time before replying, his face grown weary and crossed with worry lines.

"Then I fear there may be no cause for rejoicing at my wedding this day, my friends, or any rest for us in the Line."

Almost as the minstrel finished speaking, there was another outcry at the chamber door, and the old chamberlain again led a knot of noisy citizens into the center of the room.

Hidden Currents
Flow

As the nervous crowd piled into Emerald's chamber there were other sounds outside: of horses and a clamoring of many voices raised in unison. Somewhere out of the tumult Owen heard the faint call of one of the Line Stewards raising the alarm. Dust, and the heat of the crowd in the overflowing room, made it hard to breathe, and the minstrel was having a difficult time being heard over the roar.

"What is it, Chamberlain? Speak, sir! What news have you?"

"All the sacred statues have been stolen, and your rings taken as well, my boy!" replied the old man, having to shout into Emerald's ear in order to be heard.

"But how could that be? They were with you!"

"I left the rings for only a moment after I blessed them, then went to find your bride to reassure her. Sometime then, whoever it was slipped in and made away with everything."

Emerald shook his head and turned to Owen. "Confound this business! Here I've tried to go along as best I can without creating a row, and before I can say the verse of Naff's Rat, I've got the entire settlement armed and scurrying about like a pack of schoolboys."

"Do you think it could be anything to do with the spider?" questioned Owen.

"I don't know what to think now," he replied, trying to calm the crowd and get them from his room. "Everything will be taken care of!" he shouted. "Outside! We'll form parties and search out whoever's responsible for this!"

"They took the Bear from the place of glory!" shouted a man from the back of the crowd. "That is tenfold ill luck for any who let it be taken!"

"We've not seen the last of that lot from Trew!" cried another. "The Stewards should never have allowed prisoners. It will all end no good, mark my word!"

Owen saw his father at the window near the door then, forcing his horse through the crowd so he could dismount. Jeremy ran from the crowds to take the reins. Linne was behind her husband looking drawn and frail, as if all the noise and motion were making her ill, but her bearing was proud and she made herself sit rigidly upright.

Owen's heart filled with compassion for his mother, who was still not strong from her long ordeal.

"I should see to her," said Owen, struggling for the door.

"See to Deros, lad!" ordered Emerald. "Your mother is in capable hands."

Owen's heart went numb with the thought of Deros being in danger, and he cursed himself for not thinking of her before Emerald had reminded him of her.

"If this is that upstart from the Gortland Fair, I'll garrote him with my own hands," hissed Owen between his teeth. "They've ruined your wedding already!"

"I tell you, it's the lads from beyond the Line that have done this!" Stearborn cried. "Argue with me as you will, I'll see it no other way. If we have a turnout now of those sly dogs, we'll find everything in the wink of an eye."

"You hotheaded old goat, you would have us off hunting a wild will-o'-the-wisp, and it never occurs to you any other way," snapped Famhart, physically restraining his old friend.

"Do you say you doubt the word of one of your chieftains?" shot Stearborn. "Am I to be put out to pasture now that my beard has gone gray? You'd best watch your own house, Famhart Helwin! It's not long until you'll find my boots! I'm gray and wrinkled now, but my eye is steady and my sword and bow arm are as true as they ever were!"

"Hola, Stearborn, you walleyed old war-horse! What are you arguing about now? Too peaceful for you in camp? Weddings and feasts no place for the likes of your restless old bones?"

The graying warrior, his veins bulging, whirled to see his old friend, Chellin.

"I'll—"

"You'll what, you brigand? Stew Chellin Duchin? Come on. We have other matters to attend to than hand Famhart a fistful of grief to deal with. Come on!" He took Stearborn in tow smoothly, followed by a grateful nod from Famhart. Linne dismounted, leaning against the horse. Jeremy quietly offered his arm.

"Here, here, Linne. Are you all right?" asked her husband.

"I'll be fine! Just get me inside! I need to be still for a minute."

Famhart heard the urgency in her voice and taking her other arm, helped her through the milling throngs. Once inside, she sat while Emerald brought her water and presented Jeremy.

"I have the honor of pledging my service to you, Famhart Helwin. I am Jeremy Thistlewood, Line Steward, and I ride with Chellin Duchin and the Lost Elm Squadron."

Famhart returned the younger man's salute absentmindedly, turning all his attention to his wife.

"I'm all right, dear! There's nothing to be alarmed about. It was just so hard to breathe there for a moment in the street. All the people pushing and shoving—and the dust! It was choking me."

"You frightened me, Linne. I thought it all might be beginning again—"

"What beginning again?" asked Owen, interrupting and coming to kneel next to his mother.

"Sometimes when you've been kept captive by one of these dark signs, it's hard to become free of it. There are times and places it finds you again." Famhart spoke softly, holding Linne's hand gently in his own.

"It's nothing, really," insisted Linne. "I was simply out of breath."

"That's a strange complaint to be coming from you, my dear. I've never thought of you as overly delicate."

Linne smiled faintly at her husband. "I'll be fine. Just let me sit here for a bit." She closed her eyes.

While she rested, Famhart turned to Jeremy. "Anyone who serves under Chellin Duchin has my respect. He's a hard one to please."

"Oh, I don't think we please him near enough, sir," replied Jeremy dryly. "We've never yet done anything up to his standards, except in making mistakes. He always says he can rely on us to display inferior judgment, no matter how easy it would be to react sensibly."

The Elder of Sweet Rock laughed, throwing back his head in amusement. "That's the lad! He and Stearborn are fit comrades for each other."

From the doorway a messenger called out to Famhart. "They've found where a nest of the Olgnite had camped, sir, but they were gone before we got there. The men are searching for them now."

"The Olgnites! Oh, Famhart!" cried Linne, a shudder passing through her, leaving a deep chill that made her bones ache.

"They must have been brought back into our borders by all that ruckus in Trew! I daresay that might have aroused their attention, even as far away as the Wastes! I only wonder that they haven't shown themselves before now!"

"Father, I have to find Deros."

"And Elita," added Emerald.

"The chamberlain of Sweet Rock might know where the ladies are," suggested Linne, rising to her feet. "I had just left them together, before all the uproar."

"This is a fine day for a union-making." Emerald snorted. "I charged you, Owen, not to spoil it for Elita, and now it's all fallen out, true to an unlucky minstrel's form."

"Bosh and cubcakes, tar and farnations!" blustered a voice, hovering just above the steady din outside.

Emerald's face lit up, and the worry lines melted away. "Ephinias! Are you back?"

"I wasn't making a mountain of a to-do about it, but I did want to make sure you didn't botch the whole affair, which you've done nicely, by the by!"

"Not my doing," snapped the minstrel.

"Be quiet and listen. Alon has been trying to tell me of a danger that has swept his country from end to end, and I finally agreed to go look. Now I return here to Sweet Rock to find the same thing under way!"

"You mean the Olgnites were there too?" asked Jeremy, still trying to find a form to attach the voice to.

"Olgnites are the tip of a larger problem, young man. If Olgnites were the only ones we had to dice with, there would be much more to celebrate at table tonight than my rash young friend's exchange of vows."

Owen noticed a faint flutter of wings along the rafters of the roof and pointed it out to Jeremy.

"Don't point, you rude jay!" scolded Ephinias.

"Can you tell me where Deros is?" asked Owen, paying no attention to the old man's blast.

"Well, I can tell you where she's not, and that's here," snapped Ephinias, suddenly turning from a small, gray bird into his more familiar form as a man dressed in a dark blue cloak with silver piping along the sleeves.

"Greetings, Famhart, Linne! Your old servant is cranky enough after his long jaunt, and I'm sorry to say I have no good to relate." There was a faint odor of the sea that clung to the old man, and his eyes were a brilliant blue when he spoke.

"It's always good news to see you, Wise One. No matter what ill tidings you bear, we rejoice in the messenger," said Famhart.

"You may not think so when I drag back the dark net of treachery that is being thrown over all the good and decent folk that are left in this play we're parading about in."

"What web of treachery are you speaking of?" asked Emerald, sensing a deep concern in his old tutor.

Ephinias turned to Owen and gave him urgent instructions. "First you should go to Deros! She is in grave danger now. There are strangers among us here, under the guise of guests for the wedding of my staunch young harebrain. That shall not come to pass this day, nor any other, if those who wage their secret war against us have their way."

Famhart leapt angrily to his feet. "If there is an enemy that dares attack the Line at the vow reading of my good minstrel, they shall rue the day they crossed steel with the Elder of Sweet Rock. May Windameir have pity on their poor souls!"

The old master shook his head wearily, waving his hand in front of him. "It won't do, my good fellow. These are not your usual kind of adversaries. These are beings from far beyond anything you've had to deal with here."

Owen, still standing in the door, was afraid to miss anything the old man was saying, yet he was in a knot of apprehension, worrying about Deros.

"Who are you speaking of, Old One? If these enemies are so treacherous and scattered over all our lands, why haven't we heard of them before now?" asked Jeremy.

"They leave no survivors to tell the tale," replied Ephinias. "It is simple. You surprise your prey, devour him, and leave no one the wiser. In my travels I have found countless villages and settlements that had been thriving seaports or fishing harbors suddenly gone."

"Gone? How could that be?" interrupted Famhart. "How does any entire settlement disappear?"

"The Hulin Vipre," answered Ephinias softly, rolling the foul-sounding word off his tongue as though it were barbed.

"Deros said something to me yesterday afternoon about them," said Jeremy.

"Fetch her here, Owen," ordered Famhart. "We may have already wasted too much time. What a fool I've been to think the Line would return to its old, peaceful ways just because the Stewards have won a small skirmish in the battle."

Owen nodded, then left, followed closely by Jeremy.

"She told me about the vipers," explained Jeremy.

"When did you see Deros?" Owen struggled to keep his

voice neutral and eyed Jeremy from under his brow to try to detect if the young Steward was lying to him.

"Yesterday, in the wood outside the settlement. She seemed very upset about something, and I walked back with her," Jeremy said evenly, and looked questioningly at Owen.

"Did she say what she was disturbed about?" pursued Owen, hoping to hear that Deros had mentioned his name.

"She told me of these vipers. She said they live in the country that she comes from and that they are becoming too strong for her father to contain. I gather that her father is a man that would be like a Line Steward commander."

"He is a king," answered Owen curtly. "Deros is the daughter of a king."

Jeremy whistled aloud. "I knew she was someone special! You don't have to be around her long to see that."

The two had come out of the Street of Weavers to the part of the settlement where the soldiers of the Line were quartered, and found their way full of milling crowds, mixed with mounted Stewards trying to keep order. The air was full of dust that choked them and they hurried to find a path less crowded.

"I'm sure Deros will be with Elita. She has lived on the Way of Flowers since our return to Sweet Rock. It should be less hectic than this."

"We would have an easier time of it if we were mounted," suggested Jeremy.

"It would have been easier by far," agreed Owen. "I really didn't set out this morning to run into all this news, though. If I had been prepared, I suppose I would have showed up in battle dress with a full week's rations on the back of Seravan."

"Is that your horse?"

"In a way. He is loaned to me by a friend. Deros rides Gitel."

"She could use a mount now. I don't like the tale the old man told."

"Ephinias has a way of painting a bleak picture. You have to give him his due, though. He does clever fireworks. There were supposed to have been fireworks tonight."

"Just our luck," complained Jeremy. "But what's this? Look to yourself, Owen! Watch your hide!"

The young Steward barely had time to shout out a warning, for a horse and rider were bearing straight down upon them, showing no signs of slacking speed. Owen briefly noted the rider was wearing a dark, blood-red cloak, but he had no time to notice anything further, for the next instant he was diving out of the way of the flashing hooves and feeling the body of the horse, so close to him that the animal's skin brushed his face.

There were others all about them then, cursing and shaking their fists in the direction of the rampaging rider, and another Steward helped Owen and Jeremy to their feet.

"It's the snotty blighter from the horse-riding! Got the fancy girl on the back of his saddle, so he thinks he can ride down whoever he pleases! By the beard of Windameir, I'll have my chance to teach that whelp a thing or two about his manners, I will, or my name ain't the same as my father's!" The Steward was an older man, gone gray in his whiskers, yet by the grip that was used to pull him up, Owen knew the man possessed great strength.

"Did you say he had a girl on the back of his horse?"

"Aye, he did that, lad. The highborn girl who stays with the bride of the minstrel. He plucked her out of a crowd gone ugly, shouting that she had brought a curse on all of Sweet Rock. Snatched her up, he did, and run down half a dozen of those louts in the doing."

Owen was away and running after Ulen before the older Steward finished his sentence, his heart pounding in his throat. He could hear Jeremy calling out to him from behind, but he never let up his pace. He would not rest easy again until the upstart from the Gortland Fair was put in his proper place.

Ephinias
Tells a Tale

Ulen Scarlett rode for the Stewards' Compound, where he knew he'd find Famhart and the other commanders of the Line. The tentative grip the girl had on him tightened every time he spurred Terrier, so he urged the horse on, just to make her hang on the harder.

He had been pleased to see the girl from the Silent Sea being badgered by the angry crowd; she had been confused by the uproar that gripped the camp as the reports of the Olgnites spread, turning sturdy men into frightened children, going back to the fireside tales of their youth, where the oldsters told stories of people like the Olgnites, who had the mysterious powers of being able to change their forms into spiders. She had look frightened and not protested when he pulled her up behind him.

"There's one of the Fair!" screamed a woman, pointing up at Ulen Scarlett. "They're in league with all the filth in Sweet Rock! After him! Pull him down!"

Deros clutched the back of the arrogant young rider. At every jump of the plunging horse she felt the movement of Ulen's powerful legs, spurring on his mount. She stifled her scream, vowing she would not give him the pleasure of begging him to slow down.

"We are almost there, Your High and Mightiness," chided Ulen over his shoulder. "They will find it worth their while to have one of the Gortland Fair in their employ, if he looks to the safety of the precious ladies of the Line."

"I am not of The Line," returned Deros, her anger boiling over in a white-hot torrent.

"But you will be of The Line if you keep on your way! If you're not careful, you'll be marrying the likes of one of these lads and be burdened with squalling brats and a barrel of wash! Mark my word! Come to your senses! If you come away with me, you could lead the life of a queen! I could make a first-class rider of you, with enough time and training."

Deros longed to slap him but only said, "It is not for a daughter of Eirn Bol to be wed without her father's approval. That is a tradition of my country, and one that I shall not be the first to break."

Ulen Scarlett had reined in his proud and prancing steed and leapt to the ground before the shelter of Emerald, where Famhart stood waiting at the door, watching carefully, his hand on the hilt of his longsword.

"Greetings, Steward! I have performed the duty of one of your house guards and plucked this fair fruit from the hands of those who would have tasted her sweetness! It is not a custom where I was born to leave such tasty playthings out for any ruffian to make designs upon!"

Famhart strode slowly from the porch of the shelter as the young man finished speaking, extending his arm to Deros. "You have my thanks, Master Rider, and what reward you will ask. I am relieved to see that Sweet Rock did you no harm."

"It was not the mood in your settlement that allowed me to escape unhurt, sir, but the speed of my animal. This whole affair here smacks of ugly doings, and I'll wager you my life against a jackknife that the fools who hold council with you tonight will accuse my clans of sparking another border war."

A crowd was gathering around Ulen and his horse.

"Have your clans decided to strike a blow against us, Master Rider?" asked Famhart, holding the trembling young girl close to his side but out of the way of his sword arm.

Ulen Scarlett threw back his head and shook his long hair in laughter. "We never broadcast anything that is not on our playbills, sir," he roared, "and going to war against the Line won't be on the list of a show, you can lay to that, stout and fancy! I've come to offer you my mount and body, and you joust with me on issues that even a dim-witted fellow like that lout McKandles could see through before you could pinch out a lamp."

The Elder of Sweet Rock spoke to Deros. "Go on, my dear, Linne is inside. We'll get to the bottom of this whole business soon enough, and then we can see what needs to be done to try to help your father."

To Ulen, Famhart spoke softly, although with great conviction. "If you speak the truth to me, horseman, then you, and any who ride with you, are welcomed as soldiers of the Line. We also thank you for watching over the Lady Deros, who, as you obviously know, has the protection of the Stewards and who is here as our guest from a distant land."

"A pretty prize, I'd say," laughed Ulen as he remounted. "It would be to the advantage of anyone who returned this highborn filly to her family, wherever they might be. I'm sure they are quite concerned with the welfare of their offspring."

"You run ahead of yourself, good horseman. I think it would be wise of you to still your hostile tongue and closet with us as to what shall be our defense against the Olgnites."

"Make ready to find out a more lethal way to deal with your enemies than following that old code of war and warriors, the mistaken notion that he who turns over all his weapons will be spared."

"What more lethal way are you thinking of?" asked Famhart.

"There is a story my father used to tell me of a beautiful bird. It was such a beautiful bird, all the people of the countryside wanted to see it and hear it sing. They came from all quarters, gave up their homes and land, and followed the bird wherever it went. And finally, good Steward, the bird led the people into a wasteland without food or water, where they all perished."

"And the bird?" asked Famhart.

"The bird simply flew away," returned Ulen.

"The bird flew away and left them, good horseman?" An amused smile softened Famhart's face.

"Oh, yes, sir. The bird flew on to the sea, where it found safe haven and lived for many more turnings."

"And the moral, my good fellow?"

Ulen sat straighter in his saddle and patted the prancing animal to calm him. "Never follow a beautiful bird into a land where there is no food or water, good Elder! Even though our eye may see a pretty form, it may often overlook the sure death that lurks behind." The young rider from the Gortland Fair pulled the reins, causing the restless animal to rear, pawing the air, then horse and rider were gone in one fluid motion, leaving Famhart in their wake.

"What was he talking about?" asked Deros, returning with Linne and watching with the Elder as the young man rode swiftly away.

"About pretty faces that lead innocents astray, my girl. By Windameir's Beard, but I think that fellow has some sort of attachment for you!" Famhart shook his head, lost in thought.

Linne gave Deros a reassuring hug.

"These things always pass. The young man has probably been smitten with you somehow. It's not unusual at your age. I had no less than a dozen suitors by the time I was sixteen."

"That is no way to treat your husband, woman," complained Famhart. "Even if it is no longer an issue, it pains me still to think I could have lost you to another."

"Where is Owen?" questioned Deros suddenly, drawing her arm free of Linne's grasp.

"Why, he's gone to look for you! We were taken quite by surprise when the young horseman brought you here."

"There's been reports of sightings of Olgnites, and the good citizens are up in arms against any who are not of the settlement. Owen may be trying to calm them."

"It was your kinsmen who were threatening me," said Deros, looking down. "They said I brought an ill tide with me."

"Oh, I'm so sorry, my dear. You know how quickly these poor people can revert to their old ways. They are bitter, those who have survived these endless border wars; most of the families have lost someone, and that's hard to forget," said Linne.

Far away in the woods behind Sweet Rock, a great commotion flared into a braying of signal horns and shouts, and there was the noise of a crowd of voices, all hoarse and raised as one. "Death to the outlanders! Death to the strangers!"

Famhart whipped his ivory-and-silver signal horn from beneath his cloak and blew a long, strident series of notes, paused, then repeated them. As the last of the echoes died away he drew intensely still, listening for a reply.

It was long in coming, and when the distant, trilling notes were heard, his face lost color, and he ran a hand through his graying hair. "They have slain some of the outsiders. I don't know who, or where they came from. Stearborn and Chellin must ride with me to see what's to be done. It's not that we don't have enough to deal with the Olgnite and their ilk, but now I've fences to mend with all this crew that camp along the borders of the Line. If the people have slain some of the Gortland Fair, or that group of pilgrims who seek the Lame Parson, we shall have more than a few to repair."

"They would have killed me too," said Deros quietly, looking over Linne's head toward the wood.

"Don't think that, dear," soothed the older woman, reaching out to take the girl's hand. "You are known here in Sweet Rock by most of the people. Since you were with Owen and Kegin and Emerald at the river in Trew, almost everyone knows you are one of the Stewards."

Deros shook her head angrily, trying hard not to give way to tears.

"There is nothing for a crowd to respect! They would have dragged me away and stoned me if it had not been for that arrogant Ulen! Where was Owen when I needed him?"

Linne tried to comfort Deros, but the girl pulled away and went into the interior of the shelter, sobbing and holding her arms tightly to her sides.

"I knew I should have listened to my better judgment when I decided to stay here after Trew. I thought I would be able to find help for my father, but I can see there will be no one to spare to go and see to an old man in a strange land. Your precious Line has been attacked, and you'll need all the Stewards to protect yourselves."

Emerald and Ephinias entered the room where the distraught girl cried, and the old teacher immediately made motions for the others to withdraw and leave them alone.

Deros saw the bent figure of Ephinias and drew herself up. "I don't want to be changed into anything, and all I want from you is your help in getting me back to my home!"

Ephinias smiled, putting his hands into the large sleeves of his cloak, looking sheepish, as he always did when he was caught at his tricks. He wiggled his eyebrows up and down a few times, tugged on his beard, then came to sit beside the girl.

"Why did you think I was going to change you into something?" he asked, patting her hand absently.

"That's what you always do, and I'm tired of it. I know you mean well, but I won't have it today! These rustic fools have tried to murder me today, and I know it's been a mistake for me to stay. Just please help me get back to my father!"

The elderly figure beside her suddenly disappeared, and struggling about inside the cloak that was left on the chair was a small, reddish-colored dog with a nubby tail and upright ears.

Deros leapt away. "I knew you'd do that! I hate it when you do that!"

The dog began to speak. She couldn't understand what it said, for it all sounded very unfamiliar and came in short, barking noises. Deros found herself bending over to try to hear, despite her anger at being duped once again by the crafty old master.

"Now you can hear me, my dear," said Ephinias quite

plainly. "It is sometimes tricky when you're trying to listen to a tongue with ears that don't know what to make of what they're hearing."

"Oh, no," cried Deros, aware at that instant that her body was no longer on two legs but now was a short, powerfully built spaniel that was colored a pale golden color. "Put me back at once!"

"I will, my dear, all in good time. We have a few things to discuss now, and you said yourself there are those in the settlement of Sweet Rock who are highly perturbed with all the unfamiliar faces here. These are perfect disguises to keep attention away from ourselves."

Owen burst into the room just then and looked about in confusion, seeing only the two dogs.

"Where are they, Father?" he called. "You said they were here!"

"They are," assured Famhart from the other room. "Our good Ephinias sometimes has his little fun. They are there."

Before the young man could question his father again, he felt his body changing and saw the room seem to grow taller all about him. When he reached out a hand to steady himself, he saw a furry paw instead, and the muzzle of a reddish spaniel pressed up close to his.

"Welcome, Owen. This is as good a time as any to have your attention, as I was just telling Lady Deros. We have much to outline and go over, and you must heed my words well, for there is a great danger to us all coming from the Sea of Silence."

"There has always been a great danger coming from there," replied Deros curtly. "My father had tried to keep the Hulin Vipre in check, before the plague. It was only after that that he fell ill, and began to age and weaken. Now the clans of my father all suffer from that curse."

"What plague?" asked Owen, trying to find out how to move about comfortably in his new four-legged body.

"The Hulin Vipre spread it along our shores when we began to patrol farther out from our islands. It was an ancient secret that has been with our clans for as long as we have been. There were those who thought it was the forgetfulness of the gods, and others who said it was the key to finding the dark sides of the mind. No one paid much attention for a long while, until the coming of Gingus Pashon, the first of the Hulin Vipre kings who made overtures of peace with my father."

"What happened? Didn't your clans know this was a trick?" asked Owen.

"All my father knew was that he had a chance to make a treaty with our archenemies. He dared not let that chance go by."

Ephinias wagged his tail. "We are all given that eternal hope that things can somehow be patched up without too much unpleasantness. Never seems to come to much, I'm afraid, but I'm glad we have it."

"You mean, this traitor sued for peace, then tried to poison your father?"

"In effect, that's exactly what Gingus Pashon did, Owen," replied Ephinias, answering for Deros. "When he released the secret vial into the wells and the sea, everyone began to go through the natural process we call aging."

"We all do that," said Owen.

"Here we've done that for a long time," agreed the old man. "The Elboreal and the dwarfish clans unleashed those keys of the sacred trust when they were given the task of helping to bring all the wanderers out of these Lower Meadows."

"Then why wouldn't that have happened where Deros grew up?" persisted Owen, trying to recognize something familiar in the girl's muzzle.

"Because she and her people lived beneath the sea for a long while. It's only because her islands are now above water that the law affects it in these times. That's because Gingus Pashon put the vial of truth in the wells and sea there. He thought he was spreading a plague and did not know that he was sealing his own fate. Shortly after he had performed his master act, the great Firedome and its sister came to life, and forced the once hidden kingdoms to the surface of the Sea of Silence."

"It's true, Owen. We did dwell beneath the ocean for a

long while. Far back in our history, the clans of my father discovered the two mountains of fire that formed a vast underwater country."

"How could you live under water? Nothing can breathe there without the gills of a fish."

"We didn't live in the water, we lived under it! Our little island was covered by a dome of air."

"Like a boat turned upside down, Owen," explained Ephinias.

"Gingus Pashon put the vials of truth into the wells and the sea there, and it caused an explosion that turned the lava river away from our city. That changed everything. My father says it was then that the end of our people began, but we are not finished yet."

"This was the beginning of the threat to us all," continued Ephinias. "When the Hulin Vipre caused the lava to be let loose, the cycle began again, and the dark times that were before, were again upon the fields of our lower Boundaries."

"What history do you speak of, Ephinias?" asked Owen, thoroughly lost.

"Our history, from one end to the other, my boy. You need a good siege of books before you'll know what's been occurring all this time, before the Line or any of the other events of our own lives here."

"How do you know of my people, Ephinias?" asked Deros.

"I know of all our people," said the old man gently. "We are all of a lot, when it comes to it, one and all, but you'd never know it by our actions here."

"Even the Hulin Vipre?"

Ephinias nodded.

Deros began another question, but the trio froze when they spotted a large, hairy spider. It sidled through a window in the back wall and dropped to the floor with an audible plopping sound.

Owen opened his mouth to speak, but the old man cut him short with a stern look.

Before their unbelieving eyes, the spider's form grew hazy, then was hidden by a greenish mist that blotted out the sun in the room for a moment. When that cleared away, there stood before the three animals a thick, stout man with black hair and eyes, dressed in dull-colored armor that bore the coat of arms of a spider standing beneath a blood-red sun.

A Canceled
Wedding Feast

Outside, the hue and cry of a dozen horns echoed through the air, and the sound of pounding hooves filled the streets.

"The Olgnite! The Olgnite! Take arms, all take arms!"

A hundred separate voices called out the warning, then there was a sea of noise, hardly discernible as voices or even as human, followed by the sounds of steel clashing against steel, and the horrible cries of the wounded or dying, and that awful, unforgettable keen that rose above the noise of battle.

Owen thought of the Darien Mounds and all the trials he had been through, forgetting for a moment that he was in the form of a small dog. The man drew an ugly-looking sword with a long, jagged blade and Owen realized he had only one way to fight. The next instant, he was airborne, arcing straight for the intruder's throat.

The spiderman cursed and slashed viciously at the fleet animal. The blow and the Olgnite overbalanced and fell back heavily, tripping over a table and falling to the floor. Deros was on him then, Ephinias, worked the spell that would return them to human form.

The intruder thrashed wildly on the floor, striking violently at the swift forms that badgered him, and then, just when it seemed that Owen was doomed, Ephinias brought the three of them back into their human form.

"Witches! Bol Haunts! To me, spidermen! We've got the devils of Bragan Bol here!" the Olgnite cried.

While the enemy ranted, Owen and Deros had found weapons on the wall and sought out an opening to attack. "Not so easy, you barbed devils! The clans of the spider have long known how to handle scum like you!"

The man shouted a stream of ugly-sounding words in the Olgnite tongue and whirled about, drawing a short, stabbing knife from the thick leather belt at his waist.

"Watch your back," warned Ephinias, skirting the edge of the room and holding something in his hand that seemed to be glowing faintly, casting odd-colored petals of light on the ceiling.

"*Acccccccch*!" screamed the spiderman. "A Stengil! "Ware, Olgnite! A Stengil! A Stengil!" He slashed and stabbed in a mad frenzy, all the while covering his eyes, with one hand and trying to reach Ephinias.

Owen and Deros both leapt at the same time, and while the spiderman was distracted by the strange object the old teacher held, they closed and finished the intruder swiftly. Their blows were well placed, and the swarthy enemy dropped like a sack of rocks, with a foul gush of blackish-blue blood that smelled slightly of brackish swamp mud.

"Owen! Deros! Here! We have to find where the rest of these louts are coming from!"

"What is that you have?" cried Deros, trying to dislodge her blade from the fallen Olgnite. It was caught in a bony plate, and the girl reached to move it but was stopped short by Ephinias.

"Don't touch the blood of the spider clan! It's foul, and there's a curse that goes with it."

Deros drew back, shuddering.

"What curse?" asked Owen, watching in amazement as the body of the slain enemy began to dissolve into a pool of ugly black liquid, then vanished altogether. In its place was the small form of a dreadful-looking fur-covered spider with large killing fangs that reached forward, even in death, to stab and poison its helpless prey.

"They are as strange and dangerous as anything I've ever crossed," mused the old man. "I've traveled these Lower Meadows from time to time since I was younger than you two, and these creatures are ones I've always remembered."

"What did you have that frightened him so? What was he calling out?" asked Deros.

"This," replied Ephinias. "A simple rock."

"Why would someone like that be afraid of a rock?" asked Deros, shuddering.

"It has a certain meaning to all the tribes of the Olgnite," answered the old man, remembering another time long ago.

"Will it help us drive the others off? We need to clear Sweet Rock of these things. Come on!" ordered Owen, urging the old man toward the door.

Ephinias returned from his reverie and clasped his young friend by the arm. "You must not touch the blood that flows in them! There is a sickness that takes all who do!"

"Then how are we to avoid it? If we do battle, then we have to slay them somehow!"

"Yes, Owen, but we have to try to do it with our bows and lances. In close work we have to be careful of these things, for they can snare you before you have time to escape."

"You have the rock. That was more than enough," Deros said as she rolled her bright festival cloak and slung it at her back, preparing for the fight to come.

"The Stengil," returned Ephinias. "It is an advantage, that's true, but the Olgnites are cunning. They will try to find a way around this little toy."

"And I have the sword of Skye from Gillerman and Wallach. Or at least I have it in my father's house."

"All you have to do is call for it," said Ephinias. "No matter where you are, it will come to you."

"How do I do that?" asked the youth, amazed.

"Simply close your eyes and think of it!"

"That's all there is to it?"

"That's all."

The old teacher was cut short by a loud shriek, followed by a low, moaning wail and the sound of a furious struggle.

A Line war-horn was answered by a harsher reply, one that was unfamiliar to Owen but which curdled the blood in Deros's veins.

The stench of burning flesh reached them at the same time they saw the smoke and realized the house was ablaze. A wild confusion of horses reared and screamed in the street, and a mounted battle took place at the very window Ephinias leapt to, in order to find a way out of the burning dwelling.

"By the Fires of Windameir!" he cried. "The Hulin Vipre!"

Owen pushed his face past the old man's shoulder, staring hard at the unbelievable carnage in the very heart of Sweet Rock. Even when his father and mother told him of the old days of the Dragon Wars, and the Middle Islands, he could not imagine that it was anything so horrible as this.

"I've got to get to Seravan and Gitel!" shouted Owen. "And find my sword!" He leapt down into the narrow yard that bordered the street, filled with rearing horses and riders. In the noise Owen could not hear the reply the old man gave him.

Just as he turned to find a safe way through the raging, surging mob, Deros dropped quickly down beside him. Her face was pale, but she wore a determined look that gave her a fierce appearance. "It's my fight! This plague from my homeland has reached your shores, so it is more than my fight!"

A black bolt struck the window frame and buried itself to the yellow feathers that guided its flight.

"To the stables!" shouted Owen.

Deros nodded, and the two crouched low and ran alongside the fence that separated the shelter from the street. As they entered the lower part of the road, which led away toward the stables, a familiar rider overtook them. Ulen Scarlett quickly dismounted and held out a hand to Deros.

"Come! I'll take you to safety! You won't stand a chance on foot out there!"

"I'm going to find my horse," shot back the girl. "Owen and I are needed!"

Before Ulen could reply, two mounted men leapt the fence in a wild, careening charge, taking Owen and Ulen by surprise. The riders swung heavy swords shaped like clubs and barely missed Ulen's head. Deros had seen the attack sooner and was able to parry the blow with her sword, throwing the man off-balance so that his sword tipped aside, missing his intended victim by the barest of margins.

As the two riders tried to turn their animals, Ulen mounted and was over the fence in a single, fluid motion leaving Deros and Owen to face the two Hulin Vipre alone.

"When they come, strike wherever you can, then get behind the wall here! They won't be able to turn their horses in this narrow alley!" shouted Owen, trying the balance of the unfamiliar sword he had taken from Emerald's room. He imagined it was his own blade, and under his breath he called out to Gillerman and Wallach, just as he had done on more than one occasion when faced with danger in Trew.

Dust choked him, and the noise and confusion of the battle raged all around, but Owen held his ground doggedly, making sure Deros was beside him. Their attackers bore full tilt upon them, ugly swords raised high to strike, the wildly flashing hooves of the horses hammering out in front of them in a deadly rhythm that pounded the senses with a broad sense of icy dread.

A dim blur rocketed past Owen's sight, and he wasn't sure whether he had seen or merely felt the wind of the figure passing close enough beside him to graze his cheek. The accustomed sword was in his hand. In that same instant the Hulin Vipre horsemen came one by one into the alley, and as the nearest of the enemy soldiers came even with Owen, he felt the powerful surge of the sword from the high mountains of Skye pulsing through him, and he swung his weapon with a mighty overhand blow that caught the man square on his chest and sent him toppling backward off his mount, landing, stunned, at the young man's feet.

Deros was there instantly, and with an angry cry she lopped off the man's head in a single stroke. The ghastly object rolled away under the terrified horses' feet.

Ulen, who had ridden so as to come behind the enemy, dispatched the second rider. Terrier reared, and the animal smashed the Hulin Vipre's skull in one swift, deadly blow.

"Well done!" Ulen cried. "We make a good answer to

these ruffians, whoever they are! One thing I know is that they don't sit a horse well."

The girl shook her head.

"They are from her homeland," volunteered Owen, eager to show Ulen that he could answer for her.

Deros managed to speak. "Can you take me to the stables? I have to get my horse."

"Come up," replied Ulen, offering her his hand.

"I'll bring you back Seravan," promised Deros. "If we don't have them soon, it may be too late."

"Let me go with Ulen," replied Owen. "You should bide here. What if these Hulin Vipre find out who you are?"

"They think I'm dead," answered the girl. "My father spread that rumor when I was ready to leave Eirn Bol."

"This may only be an advance guard, but the fact is that they're here, and Ephinias says all of our known world is simply a mirror of our past! We are locked into dealing with these renegades now, as well as with the Olgnites. It's too dangerous for you to go alone!"

Ulen pulled Deros up behind him, and wheeled his horse, pushing Owen aside. He said, "She's not alone, good Helwin. I'll make sure she gets there and back with your horse. It's death to be afoot, even if these raiders do ride like farmers."

Owen's temper flared, but he stood by helplessly as Ulen spurred the horse into motion, leaving him raging furiously amid the fallen Hulin Vipre. He kicked out blindly, then fell back in horror, when he realized he had kicked the grotesquely smiling head that Deros had lopped off the enemy soldier.

"What hurt, lad?" cried a voice next to him. "Are you wounded?"

Owen realized that he was covered with blood, splattered from the beheading of the Hulin Vipre.

"No, I'm all right," he returned, feeling himself to make sure he was whole. "Let's get to the rest of the Stewards. Have you seen my father and mother, Chellin?"

"They were at the square, my buck. Famhart has set the stroke in motion already. The Olgnites have played a black hand, but we shall soon settle their stew!"

"I'm more concerned about these others," said Owen wearily, cleaning the blade of his sword on the tattered uniform of one of the slain soldiers.

"Who are they? Do they come from the Outlands, or down below the Borders?" Chellin asked as Hamlin and Judge joined them. They all exchanged hurried handshakes, relieved to at last be back among friendly faces.

"The Lady Deros can tell us more about them," began Owen, then fell into sullen silence, remembering how she had left so easily with Ulen. But Chellin needed the information, and so, for the safety of Sweet Rock, Owen pressed on, quickly telling all he knew of the Hulin Vipre.

"Have we gathered all our company?" asked Chellin when Owen was done.

"All but Jeremy. I haven't seen him since before the fight began," said Judge.

"He was with me at Emerald's," said Owen. "We were all talking not long ago."

"So he must be someplace close by. Let me hear that horn of yours, Hamlin. See if we get an answer to muster!"

Hamlin took a small signal horn from beneath his cloak and blew two keenly piercing notes, urgent and forceful, which sent chills up Owen's back.

"You can ride with the Chellin if you desire it," offered the gruff old commander. "There are worse companies in the Stewards to throw your lot in with." Beneath the grizzled beard, Chellin smiled briefly.

The sound of a running fight grew closer, and a single deep note came from a horn. The three Stewards broke into a run, weapons brandished.

Owen fell in beside Judge. If Deros brought the horses before he returned to the alley, she would know to wait for him.

"It's Jeremy," Hamlin cried. "It can't be anyone else! I'd know his horn anywhere!"

As they turned the corner they came upon a dozen or more of the Hulin Vipre clan, fiercely attacking a small band. A single Steward stood among them, and Owen recognized Jeremy, fighting desperately beside a rank of civilians armed only with pitchforks and scythes, and getting the worst of the fray. Then Owen's hair stood straight out from the back of his neck. On the ground before the rearing and pawing horse of one of the raiders was a cloak, a beautiful deep crimson cloak that had been a favorite of Deros's, crumpled, torn, and covered with blood and dirt.

The young man raised his sword above his head in a rage, the pain tearing at his heart and his eyes wet with tears of grief and fury. He flew into the knot of enemy soldiers, his longsword afire with the reflected sunlight, and his face a mask of such hatred that even the cold Hulin Vipre fell back before his onslaught.

A Secret
Rendezvous

Ulen lay beneath the cool, musty-smelling shade of the grove of ash trees, trying to stop his reeling thoughts and ease the pain of his injured left arm and leg. It was almost dark, and as he studied the soft, fluffy clouds of the evening sky, he knew it would be a night of shadows, for the moon would set early and he would find easy traveling to try to reach McKandles and the others of the horse-riding. His horse, head low, rested wearily after the long run through the sparse forest. Ulen had walked the animal until he'd cooled down, then dropped from sheer exhaustion and pain. His cocksureness was gone, and his body bore the mark of the prowess of the strangers from the lands beyond the edges of the distant sea.

Ulen rolled painfully over onto his side, trying to reconstruct the ambush that had exploded about them as he carried the girl toward the stables in Sweet Rock, but he remembered little save that Deros had been holding tightly to him.

Then he was falling, knocked from his horse by a blow. It had been a rude jolt, and he narrowly missed a sword stroke, which could have cleaved him, but an overhanging ceiling beam on the corner of a shelter turned the blow slightly, and it only stunned him, instead of splitting his head like a ripe gourd.

When he came to, he sat in the swirling dust kicked up from the battle raging in the street. He found his horse only after a frantic search. Twice he missed his stirrup, but at last, exhausted, he was mounted.

There were sounds of battle in the distance. A fleeting thought of the hapless Owen Helwin, watching in frustration as he rode away with Deros clutching tightly to him, played before his weary eyes. Then the tears of rage and humiliation came, and he knew he must avoid his arch rival at all costs.

Something would be done, he promised himself, once he found McKandles and the others, but he was unable to imagine exactly what. Something to retrieve his lost honor. He did not think of what dangers Deros might face as he worried about saving face for himself and how he would avoid the ridicule of not only his own clan but also of all his admiring followers who had lovingly nicknamed him the Wasp, for his aggressive riding and dauntless style.

There was smoke and dust above Sweet Rock so he dragged himself upright and spurred his exhausted animal. "It's only a bit farther, my brave son, and then we'll rest with our brothers."

Ulen urged the horse forward, on a course that would lead him around Sweet Rock, deeper into the surrounding forest, and closer to the coast. The Gortland Fair had been bound for Swan Haven next, and as always, arranged rendezvous in case any of their party might be lost on the road, or if the Fair had to flee the town. Outsiders were always treated as outcasts, and there was no place now that any of his Fair thought of as home. Once they had felt welcome in the lands of Trew, but all that had changed with the battle at the Fords of Silver, where the Line Stewards banished the friends of Ulen and his Fair. That was what infuriated Ulen about Deros and Owen. He could not understand their attachment to a structure of rock and wood, or talking of their duty to their homeland. And the girl had angered him with her high airs and patronizing ways.

Darkness was falling rapidly as he went on, now parallel

to the settlement, where he could see that most of the fires had been put out and the noise of battle had abated, flowing away to a more distant point, like a noisy tide on a rock shore.

Nearing the rendezvous point, the young horseman's senses became more acutely tuned to all the sounds around, and he tried to see through the dense shadows of the trees in the dusk, searching for a familiar shape or a friendly face. He hadn't gone far when he heard a peculiar sound well known to him. It came again, more distinctly, almost as a challenge for a password.

"You may stop cracking your knuckles, McKandles, and come out at once, before I thrash your ugly hide with my riding crop! Come along with you, and any of the rest of you there may be!" Ulen's voice was full of menace, and he glared about as though he were ready to carry out his threat.

"You has the wag of a silver tongue, you does, sir! If I was to know the creep of my own dam's feet next to my crib as a flea-bitten infant, I would know the sound of the way you rides in my sleep, and on a tar-black night without no fires or stars. I is mighty relieved to sees you, sir, even though you threatens us all with such fool harm as you is always a-carryin' on about!" The man came out of the shadows not far from Ulen, still holding his longsword at the ready and motioning for someone behind him to come forward. "They got Carlig and Rosinda, the blasted sticky gobs they is! I don't know of no others that got loose, but I hasn't been here so long, neither. Has you, Lofen?"

A sturdy man in his later years, with a lined face and a graying mustache, shook his head. "I saw no others leave Sweet Rock. The settlement was again' us, not to say nothin' about all the murderin' beasts that took arms to try to split old Lofen's noggin."

"How did you gets out, sir?" asked McKandles. "We was so hard pressed on all sides, I didn't have no idea of anything but to gets clear of the settlement. When I did, I seen it was no good a-tryin' to save nobody else, and everything had gone plumb to ragged edges, and I thoughts the next best thing for old McKandles was to hightail it to this here meeting spot to see who would show."

Ulen flushed a deep crimson but hid it beneath a show of anger. "They were all over the settlement before anyone knew it. I was gone to see one of the Line Elders, and the next thing I knew, we were hip-deep in screaming women and foreigners who were stoving in skulls. Some were dressed all in dark capes, and there were others who used some sort of sticky glop that jerked the weapons right out of your hand if you tried to strike them."

"We saw some of those," agreed Lofen. "They gave me the cold shivers just a-lookin' in their eyes! It was like seeing the black spots on a snake's belly!" The man shuddered violently.

"I think we'll have to risk staying the night here," said Ulen, patting his animal and giving him the last of the carrot that he carried in a small pouch on the saddle. "Terrier is blown, and there may be more of the riding that will make their way here before dawn."

"Does you think we is all that's left of the fair?" questioned Lofen, his eyes dark and his voice edged with a dullness that flattened his tone.

Ulen looked at the men then, and saw the fear that lurked there. "There is no end to the clan-riding! You know that! Even if there are only the three of us, we still have the makings of the fair! We'll kidnap the most beautiful girls and start the clan from scratch, if we have to, and if that's what it comes down to."

McKandles brightened at the mention of girls. "I was just beginning to take a fancy to one of the Sweeters, and then all this has to blow up! Ain't it always a blessed shame what happens to the poor likes of us lads, lost to the civilized and proper world, where they all sits down to eat with a right proper look on their gobs, and fancy silver gibbets to poke their peas, and here we is, still as single and forlorn as ever we was out on the Plain of Reeds, a-sleepin' with our horses and a-countin' the stars to go to sleep by."

"Stow it up," muttered Lofen. "Don't go on about the wimmen now! Youse'll get something started, and then we is still a-goin' to be out here, lost to our clan, and hunted by them blasted Sweeters. Our right good name and goodwill has been lost too! None of them other settlements will has us anywhere near now. Theyse'll all think we is in shift with these border rats, or whoever they is, and wherever it is they has come from!"

Ulen Scarlett shook his head in disagreement. "We're going to find a way to make sure we are welcomed back to the hearts of the settlement. We shall find a way to endear the name of the Gortland Fair to the settlements everywhere! We're going to find new places to have the horse-riding, and all new shows as well. Stick on, lads! We're bottomed now, but if we play our tricks aligned with the luck, we'll come out of this better than we ever could had dreamed!"

Despite outward appearances, McKandles was a shrewd young man, and he began to wonder what lay behind the passionate display but was careful not to let his thoughts show. "Now there's the way of it," he agreed, nodding his head rapidly. "Wese'll wait here for any of the rest of the lads, and then see what we can make of it all. A fine stew, no matter how we dish it, though, and that's as plain a fact as the nose on old McKandle's face! We is a-goin' to have to be as quiet as swamp skeeters and as cunning as bats!"

Lofen and McKandles gathered what bedding they could from the branches. With simple jerky, the three made the best they could of a cold supper as they watched the twinkling eyes of the stars appear one by one above the dark edge of the forest's roof.

It was past midnight when the first of the late stragglers began slowly making their way to the rendezvous, and Ulen's heart grew calmer.

FIRE
AND
DISASTER

A Waking Nightmare

There was the smell of old swamp mire, crossed with the pungent odor of burned flesh, and in the dusk, a thin, pale fog hung over the eave of the wood like a tattered gray shroud. Deros was bound hand and foot, with a greasy rag stuffed in her mouth. Her head hurt from the pounding against the side of a saddle, and every bone in her body ached. It had occurred to her that she should be frightened.

Deros chose instead to try to remember what had happened, and how she had gotten into such a dangerous circumstance. If only she had listened to Owen, she lamented, her sore wrists chafing against the prickly rope that bound her.

The thought of Owen cheered her. He would come for her. Then her heart fell. She had no idea if anyone at all knew she had been taken, or if Ulen Scarlett had escaped to tell of her plight.

"Here, I'll take this muzzle off. No sense for it anymore now. The Olga are far ahead of the weasel-hearts who make their stagnant holes in the Line." A rough hand pulled the gag away from her mouth. Deros jumped in spite of her resolve not to show her fear.

59

Another group of the band came closer to her tormentor, laughing.

"Feed the shela," taunted one. "She'll need her meat. It's a long ride to the high Flens of Olgarg. Fatten her up on the road, that's it!"

A cruel claw of a hand pinched her arm until she cried out, but it never let go its deathlike hold.

"You'll feel so much more, my lucky one! The test of the Olgnite clans will be sealed in your gore!"

Sudden chanting accompanied this terrifying voice, and the others of the group began to slam their longswords in and out of their scabbards in unison.

> Flesh and bitter, gore and bone,
> mark this tether as your own,
> grounding shela, mortal crone,
> root and cellar, tree and bed,
> croaking toads and devil's-head
> grind us all in washing skies
> full of moons and webs surprise,
> over, over, blind the eyes
> and wander ever in the cries
> of the lost tribe of Olgnite,
> searching for their Mother,
> great shela of ice and death,
> grant us boons, and take
> our breath,
> Olg, Olg, Olg.

Deros felt she was on the verge of passing out, but the iron claw pinched her again, this time at the tender spot on her shoulder.

"Not to escape with faint," the harsh voice laughed. "It would be too easy! You must give us your fear, shela! That is what makes our hearts grow strong!"

With a great effort Deros managed to surpress the scream that lingered in her throat, burning like hot needles against her tongue. There was another viselike grip on her ear, and she did cry out then. This pleased her tormentors, for they relaxed their holds.

"Good shela," crooned one of the spidermen, as though he were comforting an infant who had awakened frightened in the dark. "We have our meal now, and then we go on toward the veltland. They have been anxious for our coming for too long."

A small fire was lit as the Olgnite spoke, and after the flames crept up in strength enough for Deros to see more of the camp, her heart contracted in a spasm that took her breath: There, in the eerie shadows cast by the small fire, danced a dozen or more huge, hairy spiders that had the vague shapes of men, with stiff, bristly tufts of black hair above their eyes and four deadly, dripping fangs where their mouths slashed their faces.

"We don't cook our food, shela." The cruel voice again laughed at her ear. "You are not our meal tonight—no, oh, no! You go with us to the veltland. There is more in store for you than to end up a night feed on the march."

A muted struggle accompanied by muffled cries reached Deros then, but the sounds were so distorted, she could make nothing of them. There were shadowed movements near the fire, and a struggling heap was thrown down near the center of the Olgnites, to the approving nods and grunts of the hideous spidermen. A guttural cheer went up as they slowly untangled the sticky wrapping, and Deros suddenly saw it was a man, and that the bindings were some vast web.

"You might like to watch to see how we feast, shela. We get the most out of our meals. I have never understood how one could get pleasure out of cooked flesh! It spoils the taste."

While the Olgnite spoke, the struggle intensified, followed by a harrowing shriek, as the killing fangs of the spidermen pierced the unfortunate captive's flesh, rending him senseless. In another quick plunge of the deadly fangs all the lifeblood was drawn from the victim, who was then left as a withered corpse, chalky white in the tattered webbing that had been his bonds.

Deros shuddered as another captive was brought forward.

"We have many to feed from tonight, shela! Your nest was a fat one. We have had no fresh meat in days."

Another terrified scream broke the stillness of the night, as the hungry Olgnites drained their next victim of blood.

Deros thought of her knife but couldn't remember if she had left it in her cloak pocket or still had it in the leather pouch at her belt. It was possible it was gone altogether, dropped in the ambush when she was plucked from the back of Ulen's horse and stolen right beneath the very noses of the Hulin Vipre soldiers who fought all about her.

She found herself wishing it had been her old enemies who had captured her, rather than these shape-shifting beings who could take on the form of the ugly, giant spiders, with their terrifying fangs and shiny eyes. At least the Hulin Vipre were familiar to her. As she looked about at the ghoulish forms of the Olgnites, she began to ponder the idea of taking her own life, rather than face being bitten and drained of her blood. Deros moved her bound hands slowly and painfully toward the leather pouch at her waist when she heard the first of the odd noises.

"*Wheweeeeet, whooooo, hoooo,*" came the night-bird call, so ordinary, yet so clearly a signal. The Olgnites were alerted and ready for an attack that did not come, yet they raced about, shouting into the darkness, scuttling on their spider legs, and clacking their venomous fangs together in a warning frenzy.

The birdcalls came from tantalizingly near, which sent the spidermen into a wild hysteria, then far away, where they were almost inaudible.

"Land, you fly scum! Land and give us the feast of your blood!" shrieked the Olgnite who had first spoken to Deros.

From a branch overhead, very near where Deros was tied, a soft, fluttery voice became distinct and clear over the noise of the Olgnites. "You are a tasty loaf for a fellow such as I, you long-legged varmit! We of the sky have long plucked your children from the webs of your deceptive snares and feasted on the females and their eggs."

This speech evoked such a storm of fury among the Olgnites that Deros thought she would be trampled. There was a dreadful gnashing of fangs and screeching, and the clattering of weapons beaten against each other, but the voice did not speak again. Deros felt the speaker sat somewhere behind the curtain of darkness, waiting.

Pursuit

As Deros sat frozen in the terrible darkness, Owen Helwin stood in the aftermath of the battle with the Hulin Vipre, holding her tattered cloak, staring away into the distance. Hamlin and Judge were still searching the enemy bodies while Jeremy and Chellin Duchin kept watch by the distraught young man. Each of them remembered the countless times they had felt as Owen had felt: full of grief, bitter and angry by turns, then finally empty.

"There's no sign of her or the braggart from the Fair, Owen," reported Hamlin, picking his way wearily back through the fallen horses and men.

"That's some good turn, Owen," suggested Jeremy quietly. "There's no cause for mourning before you have proof! They may have been wounded and gotten out of the skirmish. There's a hundred places they could hide here!"

"Then we'll search them all," promised Owen. He needed to *do* something, to act. It did not matter which way he moved, as long as he moved.

A high whinny, followed by a rumbling snort, caught Owen's ear, and he raced to Seravan and Gitel, now waiting with the other horses where the Stewards had left them.

"We have had reports that our charge is missing," began Gitel. "It will not do for us to have been left responsible for a human and to have her lost! We must find her, Owen."

"I—I had hoped you would know of some way to help," stammered the youth. "She was on her way to you when it happened. That Ulen Scarlett from the horse-riding had her with him."

The tall gray animal nodded his head and shook his bridle violently. "That is a name that someone else has mentioned before, Gitel. Think, now! Do you remember where it was?"

Gitel paused, thinking over his long memory. "I have heard it, but I can't put my hoof to it exactly which time it has been, or what meadow we were in. It seems it may have been to do with someone abusing some of our brothers. I can't quite recall it. It will come to us, I'm sure."

"We have no time," blurted Owen. "Deros is gone, and the worst of the worst is loose upon us! Ephinias is probably off piddling with one of his infernal spells, and here we sit like lumps on a log, when we should be on the road! We have to find her!"

"Here, here, my good lad, you're talking to your friends! Of course, we shall be off at once. There's no need to carry on so!"

Seravan waited calmly while Owen mounted, then set off at a brisk pace into the gathering nightfall, followed closely by Gitel. There were startled cries from Judge and Hamlin, and then Jeremy and Chellin, and the rest of the Stewards were in their saddles and hurrying along in their wake, spurring their mounts to catch up to their friend.

"There's no need to try to go any farther in this darkness," called Chellin. "We can do nothing without food and rest. We'll start fresh in the morning."

Owen turned to call over his shoulder without reining in Seravan. "I'm not tired. I'll scout on ahead and leave a trail, if I find anything. You can follow along when it's light!"

Jeremy didn't want to let Owen go on alone and said as much. Hamlin and Judge agreed.

Only Chellin Duchin voted to wait for first light. "I'm an old hand at this sort of game, and I know that waiting till first light won't put off anything. We may miss something in the dark!"

Owen's impatience overcame his respect of the old Steward commander, and he lashed out angrily. "This is an old dog speaking, who doesn't know the way of the new fox! We know nothing of these Olgnites except that they're bloodthirsty and leave no survivors! We don't even know if they travel by night or hole up. Every minute we spend here lessens our chances of finding what's happened to Deros! She may need us, even as we stand here chattering like magpies!"

Jeremy and Hamlin exchanged glances, waiting for the tirade they knew Chellin would deliver.

Instead Chellin nodded, tugging at his beard. "You have every right to think as you do, lad. There is some truth to what you say, but there's a season or two of experience talking when I give you my reasons for waiting until we have light. We can reconnoiter if we please, and I didn't say anything about not keeping our eyes and ears open! If we're to be of any help to the young lady, we shall need to know the land, and what's the dispersal of the people who are holding her."

"We know it's the Olgnite," argued Owen. "Look at the Hulin Vipre troops here! Our Stewards don't leave bodies drained of blood like this!"

Chellin Duchin ignored the interruption. "We can safely say it's these spidermen we have been hearing of, and we have a fair idea of which direction they're going to go, once they clear out of the Line."

The wary old commander paused, looking from face to face. "We know who has the lass, but I, for one, don't want to tangle with that cockeyed lot until I've got proper daylight at my back!"

"I have eyes and ears with me that know how to detect things we might miss," said Owen, dismounting and holding Seravan's muzzle next to his shoulder. "It isn't like I'm going by myself."

"Then we'll all go on," decided Chellin, letting an exasperated sigh slip out in spite of himself. "If you are determined to lock horns with this hairy bunch in the pitch dark, then who be I, as a Steward of the Line, to argue you out of it?"

"Ephinias says to be careful of the Olgnites," cautioned

Owen, remembering what the old teacher had warned him about. "Their blood can give you a fever, so be careful."

"They also have a lethal bite," added Chellin. "Don't be surprised to see them in their other forms, either! They can take on the nature of a great, hairy spider when they want."

"We could change our minds," offered Hamlin. "This sounds more like work for daylight, like Chellin Duchin said!"

"Hear, hear," chimed in Judge, looking about for support. "I never knew anything good to come out of going away half-cocked. There might be something to waiting for first light. We won't lose anything by trying a staid course."

"We might lose Deros by acting like a clutch of darning women," shot Owen hotly. "This has gotten us no nearer to finding her, and we may have lost ground by shamming. I can tell you this: I shall ride, and these two brave steeds will be my eyes and ears in the dark. If there are any among you who consider yourselves to be a friend to me, or to my father or to the Line, I welcome your aid. If it is to be that we part company here, then farewell, and may good fortune always hold you in her warm arms!" He began to remount as he spoke, and swung easily up into the saddle. Seravan moved about eagerly.

Gitel moved closer to him to whisper something to Owen. "Ask them to ride as far with you as the orchard below the Knot! There is good water and grass, and there may be something else there to help you find out what has happened to the girl."

"What do you know of this, you old oat thief? Has something happened to put you in the way of news?"

"News, if you consider that I have heard the White Falcon speak not more than a few moments past."

Seravan blew out his nostrils and stamped a hoof impatiently. "Why haven't you said something before now? We shall go at once! If he is abroad, then we should make all speed to be there!"

"Who is this you speak of?" asked Owen, quite astounded by the sudden seriousness of his two animal friends.

"There is an order of all things, and a time that everything in nature follows, Owen. There are signs that tell you summer is done, just before the first snows of autumn fly, or when the frost appears. In our lives there are signs we look for, or that look for us, but they are much more subtle than the bark of the oak growing thicker to forewarn you of a severe winter."

"What my long-winded companion is trying to say, Owen, is that the White Falcon is the caller that will open the doors to us, and it means that now our next lives will be beginning."

"Who is he? Is he a bird?"

"Oh, that, and much more, lad. Don't be surprised if you don't find him more than a little familiar to you."

Owen was cut off in mid-question by Hamlin and Judge, who had spurred their mounts forward and now took their places behind him.

"Stewards, muster," called Chellin, and the body of horsemen wheeled and turned, each falling into their assigned order and file, and the battle lines were formed. In this skirmisher fashion the group moved out through the darkening forest, led by Owen on Seravan and moving through the evening twilight with a determined gait toward the Orchards, where Gitel had said the White Falcon would be.

Owen was curious and cautious at once, for there was no more specific news of Deros. Seravan and Gitel refused to talk to him of anything other than the unusual weather they'd been having since the strange invaders came across the old Boundaries from the uncharted lands that lay at the edges of the known world of Atlanton.

A Dead Man's Secret

The wind played with the leaves, then a low whistle that could have been human—and a signal. The strain of trying to tell what was real from that which he imagined, caused a thin line of perspiration to trickle down Lofen's forehead into his eyes, stinging them, and making it harder still to pierce the black curtain of the night. Lofen had gone up a nearby ash tree to try to get a fix on what might be nearing their hiding place, but the noise from the wind was greater aloft, and the man listened without a clue as to what was moving below him in the woods. McKandles had to call twice to him before he heard and came down.

"It's a-breezin' up a bit much now," McKandles announced. "We's a-goin' to pull up stakes here with all the bunch we's got and move on. Wese'll leave a mark, so if anyone else squeaks out of this with a full hide, theyse'll be able to tag along after us. With all this mess I's sure it's a-goin' to take us a bit to get untangled."

"I wish you hadn't started about the wimmen," grumbled Lofen. "I was just a-ginin' to puts all that flap-doodle to rest. Now it's a-bangin' right up and down my noggin like a cheesecloth in this here breeze of wind, and I is a-havin' awful thoughts that ain't never a-goin' to do me no good, now or never! I is an old fool that is bound to end up staked to a tree, like as not, and I ain't never even had a chance to be blissful wed!"

"You can count yourself the most lucky of men, my good ragamuffin! Thank your constellar sky stars for a wonderful vision of a man at his ablest and most nobel! Single, Lofen, is them as ain't got the brand or the bridle throwed to them! Single is what keeps us all on the tippy-top rail of the corral, where we can smells freedom and dabble in it like a colt in a fresh spring pasture!"

Out of the windy shadows a distinct voice was heard for a brief instant, and the two men fell silent, straining to hear the sound again.

"Get the chapper," hissed McKandles. "Let's see if he can make sense out of this dish of stirred-up batter!"

Lofen nodded and hurried away to alert Ulen, who stood among a small group gathered about the horses. A heated argument was taking place as Lofen arrived.

"You and them idiots McKandles and Lofen can do as you sees fit, Ulen, but the rest of us ain't going no farther with this! The Fair is finished! We has lost Roz and Deper and Cob, all to them vile pigs from the outerside of the Stretches, and now you sits up like a fancy trick horse and says we is going on to the coast!"

A rumble of agreement with the speaker rippled through the group. Ulen's face was chalky white, and he waited with clenched fists for the small crowd to quieten so he could speak.

Lofen hesitated a moment, unsure of what to do and afraid of his angry compatriots.

"Here, Ulen! McKandles has sent me for you! There's some funny noises or some such, and we needs to has you lend a ear to it."

"See here," shouted one of the dissenters. "Here's the loyal Lofen now, come to fetch the high and proper horse-master!"

"He can have him," roared another. "There's a good match for the new Gortland Fair! Ulen riding a jackass, with his two loyal clowns rolling over and sitting up with their money cups to keep them full of gruel!"

Ulen shoved the old hostler away from the others, barely giving him a chance to talk.

"We keeps a-hearin' some strange signal, but we can't gets no bearing on what it means," explained Lofen, careful to stay clear of Ulen's reach, for the young man was in a white-hot rage.

"Is it one of our clan trying to find us?" asked Ulen through clenched teeth. "I could use more loyal clansmen to help me. All that rabble who survived are the worst of the Fair! They never did anything but cook and feed the stock! I have need of my riders!"

"This don't sound like nothing I's ever heard. First it was sort of a whistle, then it was a moan, or close on like it. With all the wind a-howlin', it's hard to knows up from down, and we still can't find where it's a-comin' from."

The sound of a bird came quite clearly over the noise of the wind buffeting the trees, then fell away into a faint warble that was soon lost to the sounds of the forest being stirred about by the midnight storm.

"That wasn't one of ours," whispered Ulen, slowing his pace to loosen the longsword beneath his cloak. Thoughts of the Olgnite crowded in on his consciousness, and he felt the cold sweat trickle down his back as he looked about him at the deep shadows of the wood.

"It keeps on," replied Lofen. "Listen."

Beneath the dense umbrella of trees the sound was distorted, but it became very much like a human voice, calling out in a strangled rasp.

Ulen's longsword was out in a flash, and he crept forward to where McKandles hid in the bushes.

"It's a-gittin' louder and closer," reported McKandles. "Since Lofen has been gone to fetch you, I thoughts I was had up for sure, but it weren't nothin' but the wind a-blowin' a tree limb up against me back! Near took my whole old age away from me, and like as not would have, if I hadn't had my trusty beggar's-bar here!" McKandles slid his longsword in and out of its scabbard as if to reassure himself again.

"Shhh," hushed Ulen. "We have to make sure what camp we're dealing with here. I don't want any more to do with the settlement of Sweet Rock!"

"Ah, and a shame that is," lamented McKandles. "Ise'll never get a chance to see if I couldn'ta made an honest woman of her."

"Stow it up," grumbled Lofen. "I told you I didn't needs no more talk about wimmen."

The argument was halted abruptly by a clearly audible voice, calling out weakly from somewhere in front of the trio.

"I can't make out what the words is," said Lofen. "It's a man's voice, right enough, but I can't put no sense to what he's after a-sayin'."

"I can't, neither," agreed McKandles. "It's all gobblybunk to me."

Ulen was turned toward the strange voice, his eyes closed, trying to pierce the noise of the wind. It was a human voice, as the two hostlers said, but the words were foreign, which led him to believe it was either an Olgnite or one of the other invaders who had first attacked on the way to the stables where he had lost Deros.

Another cry, followed by what sounded like a moan, made Ulen decide, and he motioned McKandles and Lofen to come to him. "I think this fellow must be wounded, whoever he is. Let's find him if we can, and see if we can't gather some news of who we're dealing with! We might find something that will square us with the settlements here. That would make a nice start for the new Fair."

"There won't be no new Fair if this here is a trap to draw someone out," complained McKandles. "I isn't so sure I wants to get in touch with any of them Outlanders."

"Come on," ordered Ulen, dragging Lofen along behind him. "We need to find out if there is anyplace on the coast left for the Fair to play."

"Now that's different," conceded McKandles. "I isn't again' no news what would have old McKandles back on a tack that might land him next to them fair-smellin' flowers."

Lofen was raising his hand to protest, when from the black shadows there came a man crawling crabwise, in

short, jerky movements. McKandles and Lofen raised their
longswords and leapt, howling, toward the man but soon
lowered their weapons.

"It's just a hacked-up pile of what's left of one of them
Outers," reported McKandles in a relieved voice. "I think
this here dugger is all up! He ain't got no proper arm!"

There was a moan then, as Lofen prodded the wounded
man with his foot. "He still groans loud enough! I thought
there might be a pack of them devils, for all the noise he was
a-makin'."

"Let me see him," ordered Ulen. "We may have missed
our mark by not having found a Sweet Rocker, but this fellow might be of use to us in another quarter."

"Use? I wouldn't think he's got no more use than to swig
up our water and gobble up our victuals," growled Lofen.
"Look at him!"

A weak protest came from the man, who held out his
remaining hand to Ulen and said in halting, stumbling
words, "I speak little . . . of your . . . tongue, napier . . . but I
tell you this . . . I am Athode—of the . . . First Legion. I . . .
come from Jastrin . . . on the . . . Delos Sound. You will force
nothing from me . . . not threats . . . not pain . . ."

Lofen turned to McKandles, scratching his head.

"What's he a-sayin'? Where in the hound's-song is the
Delos Sound?"

His friend shook his head, marveling at the fact that the
man hadn't bled to death with the loss of his arm.

"Go on," said Ulen, kneeling to give the injured man a
drink from the flask he carried at his belt.

"Gradze," mumbled the man, almost choking. Ulen had
to hold the man's head, so he could swallow a small amount
of the liquid.

"You is a-wastin' your time," snorted Lofen. "All we
knows is that we is a-sittin' in a bad wood, full of them that
wants to tan our hides to dry, and now we is a-givin' drink
and comfort to another jackanapes who would just as soon
split our heads as not!"

Ulen silenced his argumentative companion with a cold
glare. "You are not one to know what or who will help our
cause, you shiftless baggage! Now mind your tongue and

help me get this fellow back to where we can have a proper look at him."

For the rest of the night, while the others from the badly disorganized Gortland Fair drifted aimlessly, arguing for and against continuing the horse-riding, Ulen Scarlett bent close to the dying man. He was an officer in the armies of the Hulin Vipre, and as he grew weaker and more confused, Ulen's skillful questions drew information: where threats might have failed, companionship brought results. The man talked on, past the moonrise and starset, and on until the gray-pearl light of dawn began to color the trees of the wood with its distinctive soft hues that marked the coming morning. And he told Ulen of an important mission, a task at which the Hulin Vipre could not fail.

Just before sunrise the man died. Ulen, wrapped in a cloak and leaning wearily over him, straightened, a new-found energy burning in his reddened, sleepless eyes.

An Old Wound Reopened

Pale lanterns and rush lamps lit the chaotic streets of the settlement, each byway a flood of wounded being tended or reinforcements being hurried to one sector or another, with wild-eyed horses herded by riders trying to corral all the loose or hurt animals that ran pell-mell, nostrils flared and terror-driven.

The Street of the Minstrel, which was named in honor of Emerald, was in flames, and many of the crowd there handed buckets in a human chain, trying to douse the fierce blaze that destroyed the row of houses. Others pulled down shelters, trying to make a firebreak.

Emerald stood in his outer room, struggling to remove an ancient harp from its heavy pedestal. "Help me, Famhart! I can't let the fire have this!"

The Elder of Sweet Rock moved quickly to help his friend. "Is this all you've recovered from this day's ill wind?"

Emerald smiled wearily, his face blackened from soot and sweat. "I have my life, and the love of my bride-to-be! She never thought what a send-off I should give her when she agreed to take her vows with an old gentleman of the road."

"Where have she and Linne gone?" asked Famhart, sitting heavily down in the street beside the harp.

Passing friends stopped to give encouragement and seek instructions from their Elder. Many of the crowd lingered on until Famhart sighed and reluctantly put back on his Elder's cloak. "Once we have the fire out here, see to it that the Street of Bakers and the Street of Weavers are cleared of all the enemy dead from the battle. Don't touch the Olgnite with your bare skin. Wear gloves and cover your arms, for they are said to carry a fever!"

"Where are the Stewards, sir?" shouted a tall, thin woman, her face streaked with ashes and tears. "We need them now!"

Famhart motioned for the woman to come forward, but she hesitated, standing above a cloth-covered bundle that lay at her feet.

"It's the wee 'un, sir," whispered a gray-headed old woman who was next to him as she handed another bucket to the line, which still fought to douse the lowering flames.

The Elder of Sweet Rock brushed back his matted hair and looked more closely at the younger woman, standing in shock still, beyond pain for the moment, and looking about her in worried distraction.

"The Stewards should be here by now, and my man is among them. I'm going to have to hurry to get the stew. I always have my man's meal done trim on time. The little one likes to eat at his knee. What a pair the two of them make!"

"Go to her," said Emerald, urging the woman in the fire brigade toward the desolate figure across the road. "Poor thing!"

Famhart sighed, looking at his friend, a strange expression crossing his face. "I don't know how many times I've been through this, yet I think I've finally seen what Linne has been on about all these turnings."

The minstrel scrutinized his old companion's face carefully, noticing the gray at the temples and the drawn, pale color of the handsome features. "We should call the muster, and find Linne and Elita. I'm sure they're tending the wounded at the meeting hall, but let's check."

"Owen is gone too," said Famhart. "I can't imagine where that little vixen Deros is, but I'd wager the two of them won't be far apart."

Famhart braced himself and tried to find his old reservoir of strength to cheer his followers but seemed to stumble about, growing more confused as he did so.

"Let's call back the Stewards," suggested Emerald, a look of real concern crossing his smudged features. "The recall will give us a chance to regroup and find out what's been done, or needs doing."

The older man looked blankly at Emerald for a brief moment. The minstrel leapt forward, just as the Elder of Sweet Rock slid to the street, laying senseless at the feet of a startled woman on the bucket line.

"Quick, woman! Give me the water!" ordered Emerald, on his knees at his friend's side.

"They need it for the fire," she replied, tugging the bucket back from his grasp, which angered him, causing him to curse the woman and yank the wooden container roughly from her hand.

"Your Elder is in need of a drink here!"

The poor woman threw her hands to her head and moaned, pulling at her hair.

"Forgive me, sir! I didn't know who it was a-grabbin' my bucket like they was going to break my arm for it! Sure, and take it, minstrel! Famhart has to blow the call that will bring back the Stewards! Nothing will be able to hurt us then!"

Emerald soaked a kerchief in the bucket and applied the cool bandage to Famhart's fevered brow.

"Rest easy, you old shammer," soothed Emerald.

A mounted Steward happened by, wearing a bloody rag at his head and leading a riderless horse.

"Steward! Here, lad! Famhart is down! Lend a hand!"

The young soldier of the Line turned, a dazed look on his face. "Sir?"

"Help me, lad! Your leader is down! Help me get him on the spare mount you have!"

"That's Dainian's horse, sir."

"Give me the reins" barked Emerald. Then his voice softened. "Here, old fellow, can you mount? We have a horse here for you. We're going to find Linne and Elita and see to your hurts."

"Can't do it," muttered Famhart, now sweating and shaking, his eyes sunken in his head.

"Come along now, I'll help. We don't have far to go." Emerald urged.

"We're forming up on the square, sir! Dainian shall need his mount!"

"You shall have your friend's horse back, lad. Help me get Famhart up!" Without waiting for a reply the minstrel grasped the stricken man and hauled him into a sitting position.

"Get on the other side," instructed Emerald. "We can shove him."

After a few moments of trying to balance the dead weight of the Elder, Emerald succeeded in hoisting him sprawling onto the hard saddle of the Steward's war-horse. "There! I'll take him straight to the square, lad. Ride ahead of us and break a way through the crowd."

Dazed and wounded, the young Steward did as he was told and soon had a way cleared through the teeming crowds in the lanes of Sweet Rock. Where the wedding parties had been, busy in preparation, all was now afire or converted into aid stations for the wounded. The night had brought with it fears of a renewed attack, and the Stewards were gathering in small groups, preparing to make sweeps around the perimeter of the burning settlement and to reconnoiter the surrounding wood to insure that the enemy forces had been destroyed or driven away.

As they neared the meeting hall on the square, Emerald spotted Linne, who was helping to feed a ragged band of small children. Before he could call out to her, she saw her husband reeling in the saddle and ran to him.

"What's happened? Is he badly wounded?" Linne remembered all the days and nights on the long campaign trails, and that horrible feeling she would sometimes get in the very quietest part of the darkness when she lay with her arm around Famhart in a close embrace and allowed herself to think the unthinkable.

"I saw no wounds. He was fine one minute, then he just fell in a heap the next."

Another rider arrived then, and from the commotion and exchange of shouts and orders emerged their old, grizzled commander and friend, Stearborn, covered with blood and soot and looking like the grim face of death itself.

"What dark tidings are these?" he asked, seeing the slumping figure of Famhart. "Say me not that he's taken his end at the hands of these infidels who are among the Line this night!"

"He has gone too far for his strength," said Linne. She stood beside her husband, holding his motionless hand against her cheek, which was wet with tears.

"We all grew too old for our duties long ago," agreed Stearborn. "With the exception of you, my lady! You haven't changed since I knew you as a fresh-faced lass who had captured Famhart's fancy. The rest of us age and rot with old bones and old blood and a thousand old feuds to hasten us along, but you've remained a springtime among the ruins, blessed be that piece of good fortune."

"Go on, you flattering thing! You won't catch me with that tack. I've been among the Stewards long enough to know that pretty talk is a fast way to a hearth-done meal or a bed with clean linens!"

"I could use both right now, but they shall have to hunt me down and run smack at my blind side to catch me! We've formed up my squadron and are taking a run through the Orchard and the Grainyard Wood. I just came back to find out news!"

Emerald was helping Famhart to dismount, and Linne let go of her husband's hand and went to the burly soldier who had dismounted next to her. "See if you can round up Owen," she said, her voice faltering a bit, though she quickly caught herself. "No one has seen him since this morning, and there was a fierce fight going on down the Street of Bakers. I lost sight of him and Deros then, and no one has word of them since!"

The gruff old giant hugged her awkwardly. "You're reaching up a dry creek there, my lady. Owen has taken to his training a size or two beyond good, and I can say from my

end of the pole that I think the lad will be right after his
father's image when it comes to giving as good as he gets."
Seeing that he was upsetting Linne all the more, he blundered on, trying to reassure her. "He's right as a green oak,
no asking about it, and squatting at one of our fires getting
sorted out to come back and find you. That's the worst of all
this skirmishing! First you're here, then you're there, and
the next thing you know, it's past dark and you don't know
where you are, or your mates, or them that want to split your
ears apart."

"I knew one day there would be an accounting. We have
escaped for too long what has been the grief of our friends.
You and I have seen enough times between us to count more
than we can remember, Stearborn."

The gruff old warrior shuffled his boots in the dirt, looking for words. "There is no good in this, Linne. We have to
be strong if we are to come out of it on the other side."

"Get Famhart into the shelter so we can see to him, Emerald. And Stearborn, find Owen and Deros for me."

Stearborn saluted her smartly, relieved and back on familiar territory.

Emerald turned to the young Steward. "My thanks for the
lift! Take your horse now, and find your squadron."

"Aye, sir. I'll follow Stearborn for now. I don't know
where the rest of my lads are. We got apart in the fighting,
and I don't see any of them about."

Emerald stopped the young man. "Have you seen a young
horseman in a red cloak and tall boots? He was a horseman
with the Fair that played here yesterday."

"The bold one? Why, he sat a saddle as good as any I've
ever seen," answered the Steward. "I don't see how he's
steered away from service, the way he rides! I saw him earlier this afternoon, now that you jog my memory. He was
carrying a pretty young thing behind him on his saddle."

"Where was this?" demanded Emerald.

"We were engaged at the time, sir, beyond the Street of
Weavers. Had a gruesome time there with the Olgnites, until
the oldster happened along. He held out a glowing ember of
some sort in his bare hand, and all the devils broke and tried

to get away from us. We had our way clear then. That's when I saw the fellow from the Fair carrying the girl."

"What happened to the old one?"

"After the scuffle died down I looked for him to thank him and to see if I couldn't give him a leg up back here, since he was afoot, but he wasn't anywhere to be seen."

"Good luck, lad! May you strike true and live long!" Emerald waved and slung Famhart's arm across his shoulder to help lift him into the meeting hall, where the settlement healers were gathered. He whispered to Linne the news he had heard from the Steward.

"Where Deros is, Owen will be close behind. I'll take a look down that way and bring you the tidings of our good children."

"Elita wants you," reminded Linne, holding to his sleeve a moment.

"We have had a fine wedding day, have we not? What else would I expect for the betrothal of a minstrel? Fireworks and feasts, with plenty of entertainment and a host of friends to partake of it all."

"Elita," murmured Linne, "just needs to put her eyes on you. Don't you understand that?"

Emerald hugged Linne quickly, then went to find his bride. "I must be getting old," he said to himself, half aloud. "I have been through all this a hundred times, but it stays with me now. I'll have to speak to Ephinias to see what he has to say—if I can find the sly rascal."

Thinking of the old man, a strange, hazy picture of a great white falcon crossed his consciousness, tickling the edges of his vision, and then there was a roaring in his ears, as though a great wind were flowing by and he were high above a field of soldiers locked in deadly combat, wheeling and turning on each other with noisy blows.

There was another vision then, of a lone figure huddled on the ground beneath a dark, shaded grove, but the image faded. He hurried to find Elita. He had talked to her at length of the Elboreal and knew she had the second sight, from being healed by the elves. Ephinias told him she had received that gift when the Elboreal had brought her back from the regions of death. Now his old instructor was trying to reach him with a desperate message.

Elita rose from the side of a wounded Steward when she saw Emerald and hurried to him. "I have just had the strangest thought," she said, looking up from holding his hand tightly between her own. "There is a white bird that is calling you, but I have no idea where it is!"

"I had it too," answered Emerald. "I thought you might know what it meant."

"Only that it is seeking you. I think it may be our friend, Ephinias. He is trying to tell you something."

"Will you be all right here for a while? I have to see if I can find Owen and Deros. Famhart is here as well. If you get a chance, see to Linne. She's not taking this well at all."

"Is Famhart badly hurt?" asked the woman, turning pale.

"I think he's tired and has gone beyond his strength."

"Then go, and I shall be here. Follow the white bird! He will lead you. Oh, Emerald, do take care!"

Emerald kissed her and strode from the teeming hall, full of cries of the wounded and the soft murmur of the voices of those who tried to ease the pain and comfort the fallen. For a moment he considered all the strife and displaced lives, the broken hearts and dashed dreams of wives or lovers or friends, and a great weariness came over him, weighing him down heavily. It must be nearing the end of summer, he thought. I only get these thoughts of warm hearths and home when the autumn is on us.

He dreamed a second or two of a low, warm room, and Elita at the fire, laughing. The picture was rosy and bright for a moment, then darkened with the suddenness of the sun sliding behind a cloud. He could not say what the dark shadow was, but it lingered on and made his skin feel cold beneath his cloak.

A Cowherd's Discovery

Within the low, stifling shelter of the herder Ephinias sat, hunched over the pale rush lamp, tracing the marks on the body of the fallen Hulin Vipre. The red-faced stocky man beside him was silent, his eyes hidden beneath bushy brows.

"Where did you find this fellow?" asked Ephinias, turning to the cowherd.

"He was done in on the rim of the Orchards. Weren't no normal battle, neither, far as I could make out, but I ain't no sojur by a long mark. Don't take one to see this here chuck has done been sucked dry, and by some bite, from the 'pearance of it."

"The Olgnite tribes have that nasty habit, I'm afraid. What interests me is that this fellow seems to have been highborn. Look at the rings and the necklace! You won't see such trinkets on the regular troops of an invader's army."

"I ain't never seen the likes of them baubles, 'cept when the Three Kings is played by the jesters and clowns of The Line."

Ephinias had pried open the dead man's hand and tried to remove a tricolored gold ring from the little finger but without success.

"I could use the price of that for a good three seasons and never have to winter no more with just my stock for company. Old Guzz could court him a pretty wife and move to Sweet Rock."

"This is more than that, my good fellow. I can't quite make out all the signs here, but it looks as though we are looking at one of the high earls of the realm where they come from."

The cowherd uttered a short, stifled laugh. "Seems a jar-full of good that does him now! Look at the pegged-out eyeholes and the stench he's already sending up to turn the stomachs of decent folk who have to earn their keep."

The old teacher went through the pockets and searched the small leather pouch the man had worn slung over his left shoulder. "I want you to go to the settlement and get as many of the Stewards as you can round up and bring them back with you here. Someone will be looking for this one. We need to have a reception party ready for them."

The cowherd went pale, slunk cautiously to the door, and opened it, squinting out into the darkness. "Them folks at the settlement won't listen to me! They never has no time for any of my hard-luck tales, 'cause all they want from me is the sweet milk."

Guzz rolled his eyes up and closed the door softly, his hand trembling. "I think the one that has to go is you! They'll listen to you."

"And you'll stay here with the body?" asked Ephinias.

Not sure of himself, Guzz nodded his assent, but there was a hot steel spring cutting into his gut. "Old Guzz will stay, only I has to have a breaker! I ain't a-stayin' in the shelter with this creepy heap of bones without some piece from you that will see me safe!"

A shuddering of a tree in the wind outside the cowherd's crude shelter jolted Guzz, and he was kneeling at Ephinias's feet.

"Bosh and geldinghams, man! You're a grown human, the same as I, and there's nothing here to harm you, except to know that this proper study in the darker side of the human condition might draw some of his cronies back!"

Guzz would not be put off and hastened on, his voice rising to a high, whining drone. "You is a educated blinker, and one who has all them stories of how things has been for the old times, and for times to come. It wouldn't hurt you none if you was to give old Guzz that there ring you is wearing, just so's I could prove to any who might come here that I has your orders to follow."

"You're a devilish clever fellow for a cowherd, Guzz. I can see you are a hard man to bargain with."

The cowherd smiled a gaping, snaggletoothed smile. "I is known in my elements to be a crafty one! There's more than one about that wasn't able to keep old Guzz in the mud."

"Here! The ring will signify to any and all that you bear my orders! Now heed me when I say that the friends of this fellow will be back looking for him."

"I ain't no sojur," protested the man. "I don't know no fancy ways to fight and doesn't care to pick it up, what with my advanced age and all."

"They won't be asking questions, my good fellow! Look to your steel, man, or take to your heels!"

The cowherd clutched the ring to his bosom and darted out into the darkness. By the time the old teacher reached the door, the man had vanished into the night.

"Well, well," he muttered, "more fuel for this strange fire! Silly fellow has signed his own death warrant running away with all that noise."

He hurried back to the body of the enemy soldier and placed his hand over the face briefly, then mumbled aloud some words that slipped from his tongue in a strange rhythm, and when he was finished, the body seemed to take on a faint glow, then returned again to its cold, lifeless state. "Now, my good man, you will be able to be my ears, so that when your friends come for you, I shall hear what bits of news they shall have to speak of."

From a distance there was the sound of an alarm and a high-pitched scream, followed by the low moan of the wind through the trees. "Poor devil," muttered Ephinias, shaking his head. He went to the door of the cowherd's crude shelter and frowned, looking away in the direction of the cry. "I don't like the looks of this," he said, motioning an arm above his head in a circular fashion and, in another instant, lifted off into graceful flight as a sleek hawk, soaring up the night's stairway in broad, powerful strokes.

As he circled ever higher, his keen eyes spotted the luckless cowherd, left butchered in a ditch. The enemy soldiers rushed to the shelter Ephinias had just left, fanning out on all sides of the trail that led into Sweet Rock. He did not stop to retrieve his ring, lest the enemy return and wonder why a bird was looting the dead.

"Now we shall have some news of their doings when they find my ears." The old teacher chuckled, flying high in his hawk form. "They will need to recover their leader, and I shall be able to see where they have mustered for their attack on Sweet Rock."

The bird veered left and rippled away through the blue-black river of air, until he hung suspended over a dense cluster of well-pruned trees, all lined in long, orderly rows. There was something there that roused his curiosity, so he dipped his wings and hurled downward in the old, wonderful slide he enjoyed so much when he had first mastered the bird form all those turnings ago, as a small boy at his master's knee.

A slight movement and a very faint trace of a pale gleam caught his attention, drawing him ever closer to the earth. As he neared the strengthening light, he saw a majestic white falcon fly up from the forest, a sight that took his breath away and caused him to forget himself for so long, he almost forgot to keep himself airborne. "It's about time we've come to this," cried Ephinias, speaking in the tongue of the hawk. "I was beginning to think I was to be the only one left to try to see to all this!"

"Greetings, brother of the wind," returned the falcon. "It is well we meet this way, for I think we have spies in our camps that would do us an ill turn if they knew of my return."

"Is Wallach with you?" asked Ephinias.

"He's abroad but not with me," returned Gillerman, for it was he who spoke.

"Do you have news?" went on Ephinias.

"All of a nature to turn a decent man's heart to ice, but it's news, none the less. I wish I had something else to report, but that's not the way of it."

"I have an informer," said Ephinias, and he told Gillerman of the corpse.

"Let us go where you can find more," suggested Gillerman. "If we need, we can go in the cover of some other animal or bird kinsmen."

"I think flying suits our need best," replied the old teacher. "Won't be so likely to stumble across these fellows."

"They have proven to be quite second-rate to the spidermen. They haven't the guile or cunning, and they lack that certain coldness of heart. The Olgnites have long been the most deadly of foes, but they never had a purpose to unite them until these last turnings. As they run out of prey in their old haunts, they range farther abroad than they've ever been."

"They are vicious and cruel and do have a certain brutal edge in this battle, but there are the scrolls that are secreted in Eirn Bol, and if they should ever fall into the hands of the Hulin Vipre, the Olgnite tribes will seem as a small trouble when compared to the catastrophe that would follow."

Gillerman fell into a long silence, the white body of the powerful bird glowing against the deep blue-black of the night, then asked, "Does our young lady friend know the whereabouts of the scrolls?"

"I have never asked her, but her father is the last in the line of the Royal House who are responsible for their safety. I'm sure she knows, or knows of how to find out where they are hidden."

"Then we must keep her from falling into the hands of the Hulin Vipre. They are abroad for the one reason, and that is to find the girl."

"She is below us," whispered Gillerman, circling now. "It is highly likely that the spot in question is fully occupied by a large party of ill-tempered brutes who have gone on forever about the hardships of suffering at the hands of cruel

and heartless infidels who have conspired to keep them
without meat or drink all their lives, and who would welcome any incursions with a delighted eagerness."

"What are you speaking of?"

"The Olgnite soldiers!"

An Arrow
in the Dark

The faint hiss of the arrow caused Seravan to alter his course, and the jolt almost unseated Owen. Gitel had neighed a soft warning to Judge and Hamlin, who followed immediately behind, and they in turn alerted the others in the party of the attack. There was no way to determine the direction from which the arrow had come, so the riders dismounted, trying to search out the unseen assailant. Owen stood beside Seravan, breathing hard. "Do you see anything?" he asked the horse, his voice quavering in his excitement.

"Not see, so much," replied Seravan. "*Feel* is more like the word for it. We are near a grave danger here, and I think we shall have to make a stand of it if we are to survive." The cool tone of the exceptional animal made the bland statement even more ominous and threatening.

"Pass the order back," confirmed Gitel. "You want to have all the armed men you can muster at your side."

"Pass the word back," ordered Owen in a hoarse whisper. "Stand to for an ambush."

"I knew it," complained Judge, securing his shield and loosening his sword in its sheath. "We should have heeded good Chellin's advice and waited for first light to be wandering about here in these woods where no one much bears us any goodwill."

"Goodwill comes in small doses, it seems," agreed Hamlin, stringing his bow and taking a quiver of arrows from the back of his saddle.

Chellin Duchin had blown a short signal, and the rest of the Steward squadron had dismounted and now was moving through the wood slowly in a long skirmish line, keeping near enough not to lose their comrades in the dark but far enough apart so as to not present too much of a target.

Another arrow tore the air, striking the shield of one of the Stewards with a dull, metallic noise, making all the party more alert, searching the darkness for any clues as to their hidden enemy. A faint light ahead appeared from behind a cluster of shadowy trees, and the contrasted darkness around the lone lamp made the night even blacker and more foreboding.

Signals from two directions came then, and a volley of shafts hummed through the air, making the particular noise that always reminded Owen of his mother's teapot when it boiled. A cry from one of the Stewards rang out, and Chellin barked an order to the others. "Shaft and bows, lads!"

The skirmishers loosed a volley of their own into the darkness. They shot at random, in enough directions to insure that the fire would keep the invisible enemy down long enough for them to close and engage.

"I hope you're happy," snapped Jeremy to Owen. "If these blackguards turn out to be the Olgnites, I'm holding you to your word about knowing how to handle them."

Owen was silent, intent on notching another arrow to his bow, when Seravan snorted and spoke very closely in his ear. "Your sword, lad! There is one close to us now! The sword!"

Owen's hackles raised, and he quickly put the bow in its sheath on the saddle and drew the sword Gillerman and Wallach had given him. Its sudden brilliance against the blackness blinded him for a moment, and there were cries and shouts of anger from all about, but just at that instant, a shadowed figure leapt from behind a tree at Owen's side, brandishing a two-headed mace and making straight for the young man. Seravan reared, pawing the air, while Gitel backed away, covering his friends on his flank. Before Jeremy or Judge could loose an arrow, the enemy soldier was on top of them, swinging the ugly weapon in broad, vicious circles.

"Swords and shields!" shouted Chellin, moving toward the bright white gleam of light that was coming from where Owen had been before.

A great shout went up from the hidden enemy, and a wave of attackers sprang out all along the Steward's skirmish line. Shouts and screams rent the air as the clamor of battle increased, until at last all was a deadly chaos and confusion in the dark wood.

Owen's longsword was a gleaming, brilliant white pulsing in his hand. He slashed through the guard and shield of two enemy soldiers who had joined the first, who now lay slain at the young man's feet, felled by the slashing hooves of Seravan. Back and forth the three went, looking for an opening and trying to see to keep their footing. The light of the sword was blinding, and even Owen was having a difficult time following the cunning moves of his assailants.

He heard Seravan and Gitel reply, then the two animals were crowding around him, forming a barrier the attackers could not easily breech. Steward horns were calling back and forth now, keeping line and giving encouragement. Another soldier attacked Owen. The sword from Skye cut fiery swaths through the darkness and made bone-jarring contact with a metal breastplate. The man fell back, stunned, and Gitel pressed forward, knocking the other enemy soldier off-balance, which gave Jeremy, who had been fighting beside Owen, a chance to strike a telling blow.

As quickly as the engagement had begun, it was over, leaving the Stewards still in a skirmish line but meeting no resistance. Sweat and dirt mingled in Owen's eyes, and he was slowly recovering his jangled senses, watching the longsword from Skye slowly dimming into a faint, throbbing, pale glow, almost like the fire from a rush lamp that was burning out.

Chellin Duchin blew recall, and the Stewards quickly saw

to their wounded and made a count of any slain or wounded enemy troops. As he walked carefully about the battleground he came across a badly wounded enemy soldier, who reached out and grabbed his riding boot in a tenacious grip. "What have we here?" roared the grizzled Line Steward. "Is he daft in his wound? Does he think he'll deal Chellin Du-chin his death hurt by holding him still till he starves?"

A battle lamp was lit then, followed by others, and soon the dark shadows lightened somewhat, revealing what was left of the enemy ambush party.

Owen turned to Seravan. "Gillerman must be around," he said, placing his longsword back into its scabbard. "The only time my sword gets this way is when he or Ephinias are about."

The horse whinnied, then shook his bridle in agreement. "There will be news of that nature when we reach the Or-chard."

"I'd like to have a little more news now," complained Judge. "All this is taking its toll on my nerves."

"Quite right," agreed Hamlin. "If I weren't so blarmy with all the stylish doings of everything that's gone on in Sweet Rock since we've been about for the wedding feast of the minstrel, I'd think we're engaged in what used to be known in the Line as a border incident with hostiles."

"_Hostiles_ is a likely word to use for these rotters," said Jeremy. "I can't make anything out about them, other than they aren't any local border clans I've ever dealt with."

"Not likely," growled Chellin. "These sarks have the smell of the sea all over them. It won't be any local water, either."

Owen knelt to examine one of the dead enemies. "Deros told me of the Hulin Vipre. I'd say these soldiers are the very ones. She told me of the brass collar pins that they wear on their uniforms."

Chellin squatted beside the wounded man, who still clung to his leg. "There's a cowherd's shelter up ahead. I think that must be the light we're seeing. Let's get him there and see if we can find anything of use from him."

As the other Stewards tended to their wounded and scoured the area for further enemy signs, Jeremy and Hamlin lifted the captive over the saddle in front of Judge and set off toward the dull red flickering light that shone dimly through the wood ahead of them. Owen noticed his sword was glowing once more, a very pale halo of light that flickered from his scabbard. A faint humming began to reach his ears.

Chellin pulled his horse up beside him and asked gruffly if there were other enemy soldiers about.

"I think this is some sort of signal from a friend. It's happened before when Gillerman or Wallach were trying to reach me."

"More elf-wallow," muttered Chellin. "They always drove me to the brinkerside of civility with all their blatherskite about this or that, and not a nub of it made any sense to anyone else."

"My friends aren't elves," returned Owen.

"I know they're not, but I'll wager you my last bowstring that they know some!"

"Hola! Chellin!" cried a voice.

"What passes? Snap it out, lad!"

"Another body. No weapons."

"Bring the lamp. Let's see who we have here."

The light was brought up quickly, and the dim rays shone on the slaughtered body sprawled grotesquely in the ditch, arms thrown out in front of it as if trying to protect itself from the lethal blow that felled it. A pale glimmer of reflected light shone from a ring. Owen's heart stopped, and a finger of cold ice formed in the pit of his stomach. He recognized the familiar signet of his old friend and teacher, Ephinias. A terrible dread weighed him down with a pitiless sadness, and he nudged Seravan aside, moving from the dim glow.

"Is this anyone we know?" asked Chellin. "He doesn't look like a soldier."

Another Steward had dismounted and examined the body. He turned to his commander curtly, dismissing the discovery with a grunt. "It's the cowherd of Sweet Rock! Looks like he got his head bashed by those fellows who fell on us!"

"The cowherd?" echoed Owen. "Are you sure?" He whirled Seravan and turned back to dismount. "Let me see!"

"I can't recall his name, but I think some here might know him."

"Aye, I recall Guzz," replied another.

"Where did he get this ring?" asked Owen. "It belongs to my friend Ephinias!"

"Was the cowherd a thief? What truck did he have with Ephinias?"

"Maybe Ephinias gave it to him," mused Owen. "But for what? And where is he?"

"Let's go on to the shelter. There may be answers there," said Chellin.

"Maybe Ephinias is there," replied Owen hopefully. "He may have some news of Deros." His heart had lightened again and he reached down to retrieve the ring, but when he touched the cold hand, he changed his mind. "I guess the ring has brought bad luck to this poor devil. We'll bury him with it."

"No burial now, my buck," corrected Chellin. "We'll leave that job to the carrion crow and the raven."

The light in the distance glowed dimmer, as though the lamp had been turned down, and the Steward chieftain gathered his men and they struck out once more for the cowherd's crude shelter at the edge of the Orchards. Owen thought he saw a flutter of bright white, moving quickly along over the tops of the dark trees, disappearing into the blue night, which was sprinkled here and there with the first of the late stars.

A History Repeated

High above the patchy fog that drifted above the river and deep green wood, the two powerful hunters of the air roamed, peering ever downward into the darkness, looking for signs of the enemy. Ephinias and Gillerman were both keen of sight, and keener still in the guise of hawk and falcon.

"Too much here for a mere raid," Gillerman was saying. "I've told Wallach time and again that we'd not seen the end of all this business."

"Look! There under that grove!" cried Ephinias. "It's the girl!" The white falcon circled lower, probing into the depths of the dark landscape, until he was greeted with the outcry of a sentry below.

A great deal of activity was stirred up by the alarm, and the two birds circled, watching. The spidermen raced about, slashing and giving cruel blows to trees and bushes, in an effort to detect any intruder in their midst. When Ephinias saw the blind rage of Olgnites, he feared for the captive girl. She was at the mercy of the crazed warriors, and he thought she might be slain in their furious rampage.

"There's Owen," cried Gillerman. "He's bringing the

Stewards. We can help him here a bit if we keep these foul fellows amused. Come on, Ephinias! Let's you and I take up residence in those trees and give them a thing or two to think over while the rescuers get here."

The two birds slowly descended, and Ephinias touched down softly in a tall, stately oak, while Gillerman landed at some distance across the grove.

Ephinias heard the great, booming voice of his friend calling out to the Olgnites, and saw them race about in a frenzy, clacking their killing fangs together in a wild chatter of death and striking futile blows at invisible attackers in the dark. He called out softly but distinctly when there were a dozen or more of the spidermen below him.

" 'Ware, a Stengil! A Stengil!"

The word sent a screaming spiderman leaping about, echoing the word.

"Stengil! 'Ware, Olgnites, a Stengil!"

Great bloodcurdling cries went up all through the wood, and some of the Olgnites were so frenzied, they attacked their companions, slashing and hacking away at anything that moved. Ephinias saw where they had thrown the girl in a heap and was relieved to see no enemy soldiers near her for the moment, occupied as they were with the dreadful presence of their most feared nightmare, a Stengil.

As the first wave of madness died down, Ephinias heard Gillerman call out again, from a different tree, laughing, which caused the spidermen to redouble their furious attack.

A short, ugly bolt from a crossbow buried itself next to the old teacher, and he moved to another tree. The small fire that had illuminated the grisly feast of the Olgnites was now extinguished, throwing the clearing into pitch-black chaos. Arrows and crossbolts flew in all directions, some striking the frantic spidermen, convincing them further that they were under outside attack. Gillerman flew up above the wood now and called to Ephinias.

"Come up! They've gotten too wild for us to stay!"

"Do you see the girl? Is she all right?"

"I can't make anything out plainly now. But I can see that we've done them some mischief that will help the Stewards."

"We should warn Owen," said Ephinias. "I'll go and fetch him."

"No need, old fellow. I've called him. My trusty Seravan is bringing him to us now."

"Then let's go to join them. I'm tiring and need to return to my old form. I'm getting too old for all this rigorous exercise."

"You are only tiring of holding the concentration, my friend," replied Gillerman. "The young hawk you've become would feel no weariness for a long while. Your mind wavers, not the strength in your wings."

Ephinias laughed. "You have struck the right target with that volley! I keep telling myself I should be giving all this over to a young man who can keep up the pace, but here I still am."

"That's what I've argued for as long as I can remember," returned Gillerman. "Now it's all this business of 'great experience,' and 'no one else knows it the way you do.' I've had that given to me so long now, I can't recall the last time I even gave an argument. Wallach says it's because we're the ones most easily lured into a hare-brained scheme to keep coming below the Boundaries, but I'm not so sure. As hard as he tries, it's still hard to conceal good motives."

"That is a treacherous thing to be mistakenly given credit for," agreed Ephinias. "Once they discover good motives in a kindly heart, the end is already in sight, and it's a constant stream of this or that journey, and a list of aid that's needed by someone or other somewhere as long as my wingspan is wide."

A long ripple of laughter escaped the noble white bird. "It sounds as though you've been a good apprentice! The last one I heard complain like that was my good companion Wallach, when he realized that it was going to be a bit more involved than he thought. You hear nothing but biting complaints about everything, except, of course, if it all works out in the final chapter."

As the two powerful birds glided onward, circling, then veering away, they could see the progress the Stewards were making toward the slain cowherd's shelter.

"We have seen the end of the Hulin Vipre who were com-

ing to retrieve the body of their leader. Owen and his Stewards have seen to them—and put an end to my eavesdrop-
ping through the corpse."

"This other bunch is the nastier lot," warned Gillerman.
"They have no driving force beyond the sheer pleasure of
killing! It makes them reckless, and a dangerous enemy."

"They still fear the oldest of ploys, the Stengil," replied
Ephinias. "They have that one weakness, and it's like a
splinter of fear in their black souls."

"I had forgotten that," conceded Gillerman.

"The Stengil lives for the Olgnites. They remember their
old leader, slain by the eruption of the fire mountain, and the
destruction of many of their clansmen."

"Then they still believe that a rock from that mountain can
recall fire and destruction upon them?"

"There have been those of us over the turnings who have
reinforced that peculiar belief." Ephinias chuckled. "When
you have an enemy, it never hurts to let out a few little
stories here and there for them to be aware of before you
finally meet."

"Then your Stengil is not really a weapon at all!"

"A most effective weapon," argued Ephinias. "They believe it can harm them, and so it can. Look at them now, at
the mere drop of a hint of a Stengil!"

"We shall do more than hint at their destruction soon, I
hope. Wallach is at the coast now, trying to gather those
clans to help us prevent the Olgnites from returning to their
homelands. If we can cut them off here, we may be able to
strike a blow that will finish them."

Ephinias sighed wearily. "That's been my hope and dream
all this time, but every battle that seems to draw a curtain
merely sets the stage for a new lot to take over. I had thought
the Middle Islands was the last of it, but here we are still,
circling around in the dark above a battlefield, getting ready
for more."

"You need a rest, my good Ephinias. I can see we've left
you down below the Boundary here for much too long! It all
does grow hopeless, when all you see is the darker side of
it."

Ephinias perked up at the mention of rest, but their attention was drawn back to the Olgnites in the wood below them. "What's this! They're moving away toward the settlement again! More of them coming down through the Orchards. Look! We have to warn Owen! There are far too many now for the Stewards! They shall have to muster the settlement to be able to throw off this horde."

"I shall go back to the settlement. You get to Owen," called Gillerman. "I will tell Seravan, but it would help if you are with them."

"Let's hope the memory of the Stengil is still fresh in their minds."

"We shall be hard pressed if it's not," shot the older man. "Farewell, good Ephinias. Let us meet again in more tranquil times!" With a dip of his wing the magnificent bird wheeled away, moving swiftly, until at last there was only a tiny white fleck of light against the black vest of the night. Ephinias turned then, and plummeted downward with a rushing wind at his ears, ever down, until he neared the earth, then he flared his great wings, braking himself until when he touched, it was like a feather from his plumage lightly kissing the soft earth.

He repeated his spell, and was waiting in the protection of a large elm when the Stewards came moving cautiously through the wood and stepped forth, calling out his name to let them know he was a friend.

DUST
AND
ASH

Unlikely Heroes

From all around them came the ugly drone of the war-horns, harsh and grating on the nerves and sending the horses bolting against their tethers and reins. Ulen worked at quieting Terrier, holding the animal with all his strength, and calling out to McKandles and Lofen. "Round up the ones you can! We've got to get away from here!"

McKandles was being dragged about the small clearing by a wildly rearing horse, eyes rolled back, ears flat against its head. "Warts and damnation on you, you blasted aggravation of my life! Whoa! Cordulat, you blind nag, it's me!"

The animal struggled more wildly, pulling the man behind him. Lofen grabbed the other side of the bridle as the horse passed, and between the two of them they got the animal under control. "I don't think I wants to get up on this contrary beast with his slats up like this!" McKandles grumbled. "It don't seem natural him a-carryin' on this way. He's been through more sorts of blowouts than this without all this extra confabulation. I don't sees why he's picked now to try to dump me on my ears."

Lofen snorted in disgust. "I thinks the animals has more sense than some I knows that goes on two hoofs instead of four. I doesn't knows what all them horns is after, but I knows they ain't a-callin' to collect Lofen Tackman to roust him up for grub. It's them squasher clans, I knows! I feels it in my bones."

"They was raked clean by the Stewards," argued McKandles. "There ain't no tribes out of the Wastes that could be a-conkin' up on all these Stewards!"

"Did you see them hairy things, with them fangs and all? You think the Stewards is a-goin' to be able to stem them up?"

"They always has, and you knows it as well as I. Come on! His Highness is a-tryin' to move us out."

Lofen's face hardened, and he shook his head stubbornly. "The main reason I has kept a-comin' to all these high-falutin' tramps is 'cause I might find me a good woman to take a likin' to me. I ain't never believed so much as half what Ulen Scarlett said. I knows his daddy had big ideas for him, and *he* was as good a man what ever sat a horse in any of the territories I was ever in, but it ain't like it was. These times is a-goin' crosswise of the likes of us, McKandles."

"They is a-goin' more crosswise if we doesn't get on! I knows a time and place will come when we can unhook our wagons and be on our own again, but it ain't yet, you rotten old dog. Not quite yet! We just has to keep our eyes and ears open to what is a-goin' on, and we is a-goin' to come out of this all like a right smart stoat in a full henhouse."

"I wish you wouldn't start on them hens," protested Lofen. "I ain't had nothin' to eat in so long, my gut can't remember what it's for."

"Them Stewards might just have some spare grub," replied McKandles. "If we joins up with them, we is sure to draw rations just like them high-and-mighty flintheads!"

Lofen brightened visibly. "They might be glad to see our ugly gobs, now that them squashers is back! They is a-goin' to need all the sword arms they can wrangle."

Just then, Ulen Scarlett shouted over the blaring horns for them to mount and follow. They fell in behind the young horseman away into the deeper wood, where they were joined by others, until their group had grown in number to fifteen or twenty riders, all that was left of the bustling Gortland Fair. They guided themselves by staying clear of the signal horns, which came first to the right of them, then from the front, then again from the right.

As they neared Sweet Rock the sounds of fierce fighting greeted their ears, and the watch fires along the outer perimeters were blazing high into the night sky, turning the darkness into an ugly orange glow that hammered the sight into their minds with a dull iron fist that numbed the senses.

"We can't get in through that," protested Lofen. "It ain't right that old Lofen dies by them unclean things there!"

"Come on, you rotten bag of wind!" cried Ulen. "Our only hope lies in Sweet Rock!"

"Too many of them," yelled McKandles. "We won't never be able to win through!"

"We're finished if we don't," shouted Ulen, trying to hold back the snorting Terrier. "We're hung and dried if we stay out here!"

Some of the small group turned their mounts, hoping to return to the forest, but soon wheeled around and raced back, their eyes wild with fear.

"There's more of these devils a-comin'," brayed a tall, thin man, who had been the chief hostler at the Fair. His gaunt features took on the ghastly look of a talking skull in the glow of the watch fires.

"That's it! We go on now, or we die where we stand! Everyone who wants to live, follow me! We still have a chance!" Ulen whipped his mount into a wild gallop, and after a split second of hesitation, Lofen and McKandles followed, not really knowing what they were about. And as they went, the rest of the small band followed, all lining themselves as if they were a skirmish line, making straight for the ranks of an Olgnite party that had launched an attack against the sentry posts that stood in the Street of the Fisherman, at the back of the settlement of Sweet Rock.

A large group of armed civilians had been rushed to the defense of the posts, and there were a few Stewards sprinkled through the crowd, but it was painfully obvious that the beleaguered outposts were outnumbered and in danger of falling.

There were shouts and screams of the wounded, and the high, piercing sounds of the horses as mounts collided and

fell. Ulen led his small band directly into the swirling mob
of Olgnites at the sentry gate, hacking his way through in a
charge that took the enemy ranks by surprise, and which
caused them to hesitate the barest of seconds, allowing the
defenders to regroup and repel the attack. Lofen and
McKandles and the rest of the survivors of the Fair broke
through into the safety of Sweet Rock, dismounting to the
cheers of the weary, bloodied defenders.

A young Steward, his left arm in a hastily tied sling,
pulled his horse up beside Ulen. "Good timing, friend! You
have turned it for us here, no mistake. The rest of my squadron will be here soon, and we'll be able to secure this gate."

Ulen dismounted and was checking Terrier for injuries.
"No thanks are necessary, Steward. We are saving our own
hides as well. There are more of these devils coming through
the West Wood in droves!"

"That was the report we've had all night. The other
raiders seem to be done in, but these beggars from the
Wastes are stronger than ever. I hope Famhart has some plan
of action to stop them."

"They ain't a-goin' to stop until every last one of them is
conked," mumbled McKandles. "They ain't no human kind
and don't follow no sensible code."

As the fighting slackened, the defenders turned their attention to their deliverers. "It's them blighters from the
Fair!" cried one man, still clutching a blood-drenched longsword before him. Lofen moved to protect himself, but the
man lowered his weapon and held out a hand.

"Down to it," he said heartily. "I never saw no riding like
that! You sliced them devils up nice, and split the drive they
had against our gate. We would be sucked dry by now if it
wasn't for you lads!"

Ulen Scarlett called out to his followers "Come on, you
Gortland men! These kind folks are thanking us for our arrival! What say you?"

A ragged cheer went up from the riders, along with cries
for help from the wounded and more than one call for food
and drink.

"Come along with you," ordered the Steward. "We have

hot stew at the square, and we can see to getting you more weapons. If you're going to help us against this bunch, you'll have to be armed with more than just longswords."

"I don't want none of them stiff shirts and shields," protested McKandles. "You can't handle a horse proper in all that getup."

"What he means is that he can't cut and run so quick," snapped Ulen. "My brave buckos aren't quite ready for the Stewards, my good fellow. Feed us and give us a place beside you, and we'll be content to do what we're able to do to help you."

"Fairly said," replied the young Steward, who was the same young man who had lent Emerald the horse to carry Famhart. "Come along and we'll see to the mush first. Old Renala has made enough hash to fill us all a dozen times over."

"Renala! Is she the grub rustler? Well, smack me dabsides of my noodle, if that don't tote the boot!" Lofen laughed, slapping his leg in glee.

"What's come unstuck in that pot you use to stick a cap on, you horse tender?" McKandles shook his friend's sleeve roughly.

"Renala is the very one I was a-gettin' slabbed up to," answered Lofen eagerly. "I figured we'd seen the tag end of this bunch for sure, and now I is on my way to a hot grubstake and to see the very one what stoked up my old ticker's fire."

"I hope them that is a-lookin' out for the likes of us poor souls is a-doin' double shifts tonight," growled McKandles. "Lorry be, someone saves us from a man who gets his kit in a muddle over the likes of a skirt!"

"Sour talk don't hurt me none," shot Lofen. "You is dirked 'cause there ain't no softside to tend you up grub."

As the two friends walked beside their horses arguing, Ulen counted the dwindling numbers of defenders in the orange glow of the blazing watch fires and wondered if he had made the correct choice for survival. It grew more noisy in the surrounding woods as the signal horns of the Olgnite brayed and droned against each other, and with every new reply, there seemed to be more numbers in the strength of the enemy troops. A fine shower of soot from the huge fires was layering the air with an unreal light that seemed to dim even as he looked on, and out of that hazy, choking mist rode the minstrel and another band of Stewards, with all the signs of a fierce battle displayed in their faces.

A Desperate Hour

The broken shields and empty quivers told the story. Emerald had a bloody rag wrapped around his sword arm, and there was another black patch of sticky wetness at his knee. His companions were in no better shape, and at the end of the small procession, a boy, no more than sixteen, led six riderless horses.

The minstrel dismounted painfully. A pall had fallen over the celebration and excitement of a moment before. "Hola, minstrel," said Ulen, extending a hand.

Emerald ignored the gesture. "Good fortune, horseman. How have you come back to us? The wood is full of these monsters from hell."

"Are we holding?" asked a reddened, pinch-faced man near Ulen.

The minstrel sat wearily at his horse's feet, pulling off a boot. "That's for the daylight to tell us. If our numbers hold till dawn, we shall probably be able to hold our own. These devils thrive on the darkness."

"We've managed to turn the charge against this post," reported Ulen, turning to his supporters for confirmation.

"Saved our necks, he and his bunch," chimed in a civilian, who had been pressed into service at the last minute.

"We shall all have to stand together through this," said Emerald, pouring blood from his boot and wrapping another strip of his torn cloak around the wound at his knee. "I've left Stearborn to hold the Weaver's Gate. You'll have to hold this post as best you can. We need to rally or we're lost."

"What of Famhart?" asked a woman in the crowd of defenders who had gathered to help the wounded Stewards.

"He's at the square," replied the minstrel, trying to evade the question.

"Is he hurt bad?" asked the pinch-faced man.

"*Spent* is the word. Exhausted. He'll be fit to lead us to battle tomorrow if we hold on through the night."

"And Linne?" shouted a woman brandishing a scythe. "How is the damen?"

"With Famhart," answered Emerald.

"Owen! Where is Owen Helwin?" asked another in the crowd. "Now's the son's turn to repay his debt to his father!"

Emerald replaced the boot and stood gingerly on his injured leg, testing it with a few limping steps around his exhausted horse. "We'll all do well to rally around whoever we're with," he said curtly. "Owen is out with Chellin Duchin, trying to break the Olgnites into smaller groups. If we can do that, we shall be in good stead."

"Then you shall be our leader here! Rally to the minstrel! All come to the minstrel!" The cry was taken up and magnified with additional voices, until the Gate of the Fishermen fairly rang with the call.

After a time Emerald was able to make himself heard over the excited crowd. "Save your energy for the Olgnites! They are driven off for now, but they're all around us and will be coming again. Now is the time to make ready."

The battle fire that had driven their tired bodies began to burn low and die out, and fatigue and fear followed, when the thought of dealing with a renewed attack became a certainty.

The minstrel tried hard to remember that it was but a few short hours since he was to have been wed to Elita, but the unreality of the fighting, and his wounds and exhaustion, left him with no feelings at all, except a desire to eat and sleep. "Ulen, since you've brought more mounted men, we'll use your group as reinforcements for those Stewards who are here. The Olgnites don't sit an animal well, and if we have good riders, we can eliminate as many as we can before they have a chance to really close on us. When they're dismounted and use their spider form, that's when they're the deadliest. A bite from them can be as fatal as their sword or bow. We must try to concentrate our horsemen to the best advantage."

"My group stands ready," shot Ulen, irked that his glory had been overshadowed by the arrival of the minstrel.

"Maybe you is ready, but old McKandles has a powerful lot of say in whether *he* is or not."

"Lofen goes alongside of that," agreed his friend. "And he ain't so sure that anybody else is a-goin' to be for hitchin' up our duffs to these here Stewards. They is paid for sojurs, and it don't make dinkledy whether or not they is split open or skewered! I has a strong like for my hide in one piece, and I is a-thankin' you for not a-handin' it up to nobody elsewise of me!"

Ulen was ready to reprimand his reluctant followers but was interrupted by Emerald. "That's a healthy sign, being concerned about your hide. Dead or wounded, you won't be of any help to us at all, and we'll have to spend good time tending to you, or burying you, one or the other. Just keep yourselves back, and watch the turn of the battle, when it comes. Try to make it costly for the Olgnites."

Ulen slapped his riding crop angrily against his boot top. "I can think of how costly I can make it for these two jacknapes to be here."

A renewed alarm sounded at the outer perimeter of the Gate of the Fishermen, and the minstrel turned to give orders. "Ulen, you and your men stay here and wait upon a need! It may be that your reserve won't be called, but we must count on you if there is to come a blow that falls fast and sure. Listen for the horn here! Three long blasts and a short will be our code."

"Three long blasts and a short," repeated Ulen. "It is my honor to serve so noble a cause. My main regret is that the fair one I would swear my service to is already attached to another."

Emerald reined in his steed, frowning. "I had forgotten the girl for a moment! That's why Owen went out."

"Is the girl gone?" asked Ulen, feigning surprise, flustered in spite of himself, for the minstrel seemed to be able to see straight through him.

"Taken by the Olgnites, I fear."

"Then there may still be an opportunity of rescuing her?"

"We know the Olgnites have no use for captives, save to drink their blood, yet we may hope."

Ulen's heart had quieted as he listened to the minstrel, and he knew his secret humiliation was safe from discovery. The memory of the battle and his loss of face enraged him, but he held his fists tightly clenched and turned away to tend to a loose piece of equipment on his saddle.

"This is likely to be the most costly meal we shall ever eat," he muttered to no one in particular, but Lofen overheard him, and nodded agreement.

A deadly shower of Olgnite arrows rained down upon the street, felling many who stood about. The band of Stewards that Emerald led wheeled their mounts and were gone in a fury of flashing hooves.

"Remember the signal!" shouted Emerald. "We shall all be counting on each other to make it until dawn! Make your blows count!" A wild flurry of horses and riders flashed past, and the minstrel was drawn into the stream of frantic defenders.

"If we was smart, we'd quash all these draw-beams," grumbled Lofen, pointing to the watch fires. "This ain't a-doin' nobody no good but them foul things a-lurkin' around out there in the dark. If I was to have a choice of where to be, that's what I'd do, I would! Let me out there in the woods and have my right proper time to take, and no big fires to lights up my targets bigger than life, and no way to have nobody brings no fight to me!"

"You is a-goin' to get your chance to do that," threatened McKandles. "If you don't shuts that yap, I is a-goin' to sees to it you is throwed out on your ear! Them squashers won't waste no time in pulling your juice, as fat as your mug has been!"

"You may both get to find the woods, and sooner than you think," added Ulen. "We're not going to stay here. You heard what the minstrel said! They're all around us, and the settlement doesn't stand a chance."

Another rain of arrows fell on the street, causing little damage but straining the nerves of the defenders to a fever pitch.

"What about that musician?" asked McKandles, looking away in the direction Emerald had ridden. "They said they was a-countin' on us in a pinch. And if they is all around us out there now, I isn't so hot on just a-throwin' myself into their stew pot!"

"All they has to do is just sit out there and keep up the bow work, and wese'll all be dead or raving lullies by the time morning finally lights up," growled Lofen. "It don't make no diddly-do where we is."

"Pincushions for a lot of them brutes to stick," said McKandles, scowling. "I'd as soon takes my chances alone in them woods, though, instead of just a-sittin' here to wait for them things to flat wash over us like a river at flood!"

Ulen mounted and spurred his horse forward, motioning for his two henchmen to follow. "Come on, you two! The minstrel be damned! I'm going to try your advice for once. It may be better than standing here and waiting for the end."

Ulen Scarlett led his small band up the Street of the Fisherman until he reached a back sentry post that was busy with keeping a wary eye out for invaders. It was easy enough to slip away in the guise of a patrol, into the ominous darkness that ringed Sweet Rock.

Despair

With the numbing darkness that held her mind frozen, Deros struggled trying to regain hope. After the strange voice fell silent, her Olgnite captors bound her in their web, loaded her roughly onto a horse, and led on a bouncing, bumping journey through the pitch-black night. Soon they were joined by what seemed to be an overwhelming number of new enemy troops. They paid little attention to her, although from time to time her guard would take charge of some new prisoner, trussed and thrown over a pack animal like a side of meat. Her guard announced, "We shall have a good breaking of fast, shela! Your nest is full of ripe young saplings for the hungry troops."

The sky had cleared, and a few stars were visible, although there was still no sign of the moon. She could not make out the time but knew it had to be after the middle part of the night, for the sounds were different, and it seemed as though the smell of the trees had taken on an early-morning muskiness that always seemed the heaviest a few hours before dawn.

The Olgnite guard tensed suddenly, and drew the horse she was riding up closer to his own animal. "A lost nibling." He chortled, beginning to dismount. "Oh, reunion of happiness, my stomach and the warm lovely in his lush tubes! Here, my nibling! Come to the feast!"

Deros thought she might escape by spurring her horse on into the woods, hoping that she would come across the Stewards before she could be recaptured, but her guard still held the cord that bound, and the horse's tether, although he was now afoot.

A sound distracted her, one that vaguely reminded her of a bird darting about in the eaves of the trees. It seemed to be coming closer and closer, and there was a louder noise that grew more distinct.

She recognized it as a Steward's signal, disguised to sound like one of the braying of the Olgnite horns, and it was very near. Her guard still suspected nothing and thought he had stumbled on yet another tasty meal in the ill chance of a hapless soldier.

Without warning an arrow crackled through the air, striking the Olgnite squarely between the shoulder blades, and the spiderman toppled forward, dead before he ever touched the ground and without ever uttering a sound.

The body of the enemy soldier landed with a dull thud, and the weight pulled Deros from the saddle, still bound to the corpse. She thrashed wildly about, trying to loosen the sticky webbing but to no avail.

"Oh, a pox on these filthy beasts," she cried, fighting back her tears of frustration, but immediately she fell silent as she heard more Olgnites coming toward the spot where she lay. A cold fist held her heart in a deadly grip, and for a moment she thought she would pass out from fear, but the spidermen rode past, lashing their animals in a frenzy. Arrows flashed about her in the wood, yet there was a deadly calmness in the destruction that lulled Deros to believe that she was lost and that the long road that had led her from her homelands had reached a final end in the dark forests surrounding Sweet Rock, on the River Line.

It was a sad thought, and she began to cry, softly at first, then more audibly, and that gave her some sense of comfort, hearing her own sobs. She was sorry she had been so angry at Owen. Now all that part of her life seemed so distant that it was almost as though she were remembering events from a friend's life, instead of her own.

Out of a dark shadow a dim figure emerged, crouched and

ready to strike with longsword. It was not for another heart-beat that Deros saw the sign of the Line on his shield, glimmering faintly silvery-blue with the reflected fires that burned in Sweet Rock.

"Who goes?" demanded a cold voice as icy as death and as flat as a gray winter's day.

The girl realized he couldn't see her, spun up as she was in the sticky bonds of the spiderman.

"Here," she shouted.

"Lor'be, this is a mess! Don't worry, mate, we'll have you free of all this double quick! I'll have to cut through it, so hold still or I might hurt you."

The Steward had cautiously begun to slash away the outer layer of the Olgnite binding when he suddenly stiffened. As the Steward slowly fell forward onto his knees, the young woman saw the hideous spider form latched tightly to the back of the man, its deadly fangs sunk deep into the soft flesh of his neck.

Deros frantically clawed at her bonds, blinded by fear and a loathing of the Olgnites so deep that she bit her lower lip until she tasted the salty blood in her mouth.

After finishing draining the now lifeless Steward the spiderman pulled taut the sticky webbing that held Deros prisoner. "Here, here, shela! No tasty whelp of The Line will take you away from your new masters! Surely you don't want to leave us so soon, now? We shall have the best of our feast tomorrow, and you shall be there to watch it all!"

The young girl had slipped into a dull, senseless gray space in her mind, and she barely heard the hideous monster, who wound her tighter into the web covering her mouth as he spoke.

There were other sounds then, and a squadron of Stewards slashed their way through the clearing, lopping off her captor's head but not hesitating long enough to see that she was there, concealed beneath all the sticky bonds that held her. Two or three other parties made their way past, then came back, followed closely by reinforcements from the Olgnites, and the two factions waged a fierce fight all around the small clearing, with neither side gaining a clear advantage, until another band of riders appeared, bowling headlong into the fray, which set the spidermen's flank into mindless disarray.

Just when Deros had given up hope of anyone finding her, a rider pulled in his horse just at her side and swung down from his saddle. "Here's a Steward down! I can't tell what squadron he's from, though. I have to move this mess beside him!"

"Come on, Ilian! Leave him for the burial squad. We can't help the poor devil now!"

"I don't see his horse. Did we see any loose animals here?"

"Come on, leave it! We'll sort the losses tomorrow! I don't feel any too snug out here with these things! Come on!"

Deros had made as much of an effort as she could to try to attract the man's attention. She thrashed about as wildly as she was able, and thought she would surely pass out from the effort it took, yet the man had already remounted, and the skirmishers moved away, spurring their horses into a gallop.

Again Deros despaired, but as she lay there, she remembered her father, and the trust he had placed in her, and she struggled against her bonds with a renewed effort. She freed her hands and arms enough to work the web from her mouth, and as she lay there almost exhausted, she heard a small band of horsemen reining in heavily from a hard run.

"Now this has ripped it, I says," muttered a breathless voice. "We is out here among these creepy baskers, and there ain't no way free to the coast that don't fairly shake with their likes all over!"

"We shall see the coast, Lofen, if you'll keep your mouth shut and your thoughts to yourself! All we need from you now is a busy sword arm!"

Deros thought she recognized the voice. The speaker was young, and was angry at whoever he was with.

"There ain't no need for me to keeps my mouth shut now," replied the man's companion hotly. "We is amongst a nest of these vile creatures, and whether I yells or whispers, it ain't much of a tote to anyone!"

"To me," called Deros weakly. "Help!"

"What was that?" shot one of the riders, whirling to see a heap of bodies not far from where they stood.

Deros called again, and this time she was suddenly afraid of being stabbed or shot with a bow before she could reveal herself as a friend.

There was a sound then, of the men hastily dismounting, and Deros felt herself cut free of her bonds. In a matter of a few seconds, she stood dazed and shaken, and face to face with the brash young horseman from the Gortland Fair.

A Terrifying
Vision

The Olgnite hordes had torched the Street of the Bakers and
overrun the outlying posts that marked the beginning of the
Street of the Weavers. Horses and riders alike lay scattered
about, and the stench of death was heavy in that quarter of
Sweet Rock. The battered squadrons of the Line were drawn
thinly in an area that stretched beyond the settlement.
Stragglers from all the units reformed ranks with any who
could still ride and fight. They were growing weaker as the
night dragged on, and the Olgnite army tightened its hold on
the beleaguered settlement.

In the meeting square the fires and clamor increased until
the din was such that in order to be heard, one had to shout
directly into another's ear or make signals to be understood.
Famhart leaned weakly against Linne's supporting shoulder
and shouted loudly enough for his wife to hear. "Where is
Owen! Is Emerald here? Kegin?"

"They are about! I don't know where exactly. Elita will
know of Emerald!"

The bride-to-be was about to answer when a wild shout
went up from the defenders at the end of the Street of
Flowers, and a volley of Olgnite arrows whistled in upon

119

them like an angry swarm of bees, forcing them all to dive quickly for cover. From the woods a great clatter of swords and shields was heard, and the ugly chorus of Olgnite war chants came over the other sounds of battle.

"We must regroup," said Famhart, looking about with alarm at the disarray of the ragged defenders scurrying about aimlessly, falling dangerously near to being panic-stricken and routed.

"There are no Keepers to help us this time," answered Linne almost angrily. "When we grow to depend on strengths other than our own, it is always this way."

"Where is Ephinias?" asked her husband. "He has been able to help us before."

"Gone! Disappeared!"

"They will be together, he and Owen and Chellin," replied Elita. "If we can endure until first light, this tide may be turned. I sense help is very near, but we must not falter now."

Famhart tried to draw himself up and asked Linne to find a horse for him. She was reluctant, for she could see he was in no shape to ride, but she recognized the look in his eyes, from a time in the Middle Islands, and knew it would do no good to try to reason with him now. Linne also knew that it would be of no consequence how or where he died, for the hour was late, and their enemies seemed too strong to repel. She tried to begin to make her own peace with that fact as she set out to find a mount for her husband.

She had not gone far in the confused swarm of defenders when she came across a wounded Steward from the Lost Elm Squadron of Chellin Duchin. He struggled to stand when he saw Linne, but she pushed him back down gently. "Sit still, or you'll open that wound! Here, give me some bandage!"

Linne bound the young man's wound, talking as she worked. "I need a horse for my husband. Do you have spare mounts?"

"We have lost so many, I don't know. My own horse is lame, and I don't think he can stand weight without a rest."

"There's no rest here tonight," replied Linne flatly, looking about her at the line of wounded waiting to be tended, and the rows of the dead who had been brought to the square to save them from the spidermen's army.

"There were horses behind the storehouses on the Street of the Potters." The young Steward rose and struggled to his feet. "If they are still there, I'll go with you to bring them back. I need a new mount to return to Chellin."

"Do you know where he is?" asked Linne, her hopes rising.

"We were hard put to it at the Orchards, and the cowherd's. That's where I left the lads, after they had ridden me clear of the skirmish lines. The dirty blackguards we're up against drink your blood if you're caught!" The young Steward shuddered as he spoke and had difficulty controlling his trembling hands. He calmed them at last by grasping his sword.

"The Orchards, you say?" asked Linne, looking away in the direction the young Steward spoke of.

"Not more than an hour past."

"You have no business on your feet. You must rest while you can."

"I won't let you go alone," he protested. "You need someone to escort you!"

"I shall find someone. You rest now." Linne helped the young Steward to a crude mat laid on the porch of the meeting hall, and after she'd seen him safely tended to, she rushed to the horse he had left at the tethering ring in the great circle before the hall.

Mounting, Linne heard the wild signals of a Steward horn, blowing three long blasts, followed by two short, repeated at intervals for a long time, until they finally died away on the smoke-filled air that grew harder to breathe and which left her feeling light-headed and exhausted. She urged the stumbling animal through the struggling mass of citizens and tried to encourage them with a cheerful word.

Out of a swirl of defenders rushing toward the meeting hall, an old man in a bloodied gray cloak stepped forward and took hold of her arm with a grip that surprised her. As he threw back the hood that concealed his face, Linne let out a little cry. "Ephinias!"

"Yes, yes, one and the same! We don't have much time,

my dear. I've just come from Owen. The lad is holding his own, but I've seen more afoot tonight to alarm my old bones than in any time I can remember. We shall have to leave Sweet Rock if we are to see an end to this nasty business!"

Linne's knees went weak, and her heart stopped as she looked upon the grim features of her old friend as he delivered his news. "But we can't! Famhart isn't able to travel, and there's no way we can move the wounded!"

Ephinias took her hand and patted it awkwardly. "This is a dark day for us all, Linne. I suppose I knew there was something like this somewhere for us, but I always imagined it would be different. We never really prepare ourselves for anything unpleasant. It's always different than you think it's going to be, and it always arrives sooner than you think it will."

"But there's no place left to go, Ephinias! This was the last safe country. Where is left for us?"

"The sea, my dear. Deros has come from where we are to go next."

Linne shook her head. "She came searching for help for her father. The other raiders here this day were from her homeland. It's no good going there! It seems we can no longer protect the Line."

The old teacher looked about them, at the hard-pressed defenders, with their drawn, determined faces, and the burning settlement, which now seemed to be afire in every quarter. "It is hard to see, but there is a reason for this, Linne. Sometimes I can't quite find the energy to be doing something I should be doing, whether it's planting that last patch in my garden or going out and about like this, trying to see my way into what next to do. It always takes a large boot to my backside to get me moving."

Linne was crying quietly and reached out to touch his arm. "I don't need your little lesson, old friend. I can see that it's hopeless here. Help me find a horse for Famhart."

"You go back to Famhart and I'll bring the horses along."

Linne left the old man standing in the middle of the street, his torn and bloodied cloak flapping loosely in the wind created by the fires that had grown in strength until almost every structure in Sweet Rock had been touched by the red sea of leaping flames. He lingered, remembering other sacked towns, other final battles. He was only shaken out of his study of it when a squadron of Stewards almost bowled him over.

"A large boot to the backsides, thank you," he muttered, half smiling. As he hurried away he caught sight of the great white bird overhead, its feathers turning a fiery gold from the reflected fires. Ephinias stopped, trying to see where his friend had gone, but the smoke grew too thick to penetrate, so he hurried on, making his way through the desperate ranks of defenders rushing to and fro in the besieged settlement.

Turning the corner to go to the area of the stables, Ephinias ran almost headlong into Gillerman. "They've taken the wood," he reported, now in his man-form.

"I've told Linne we shall have to leave Sweet Rock."

"How did she take it?" asked Gillerman, who had thrown his cloak back to reveal a longsword very like the one he had given Owen.

"Dazed her, I'd say. Dazed me, to say it!"

"The Hulin Vipre have left their small craft on the river. I'd wager that their sea boats are somewhat closer to the coast, and that we can find them if we backtrack that way."

"There are a lot of people in Sweet Rock. The settlements from all over the Line were here for Emerald's marriage. There may not be boats enough for them all, and it's going to be a tidy task to get the Olgnites to look the other way while we're all creeping out of their lunch basket!"

Gillerman nodded his agreement impatiently. "Yes, yes, I know all that! We shall have our chores laid out for us, no doubt of it. But you and I are going to create a little diversion to keep the spidermen busy long enough to evacuate the settlement. The Olgnites aren't overly fond of water, so once we get our good citizens on the river, we should have most of the worst of it over and done with."

Ephinias laughed, his exhaustion beginning to wear at his judgment. "We shall make a marvelous pair, you and I, old friend. Just the recipe to take on a whole wood full of hungry Olgnites!"

"They'll have their hands full, at that," agreed Gillerman. "It would probably be more sporting if only one of us stayed to do the job, but I don't feel the least bit like being sporting."

"Good! Let's see what we can do to spoil the party for those louts. Meanwhile I've got to get horses to Linne, and we shall have to tell Famhart of our plan."

"Funny thing about places down here below the Boundaries," said Gillerman. "It's odd how caught up you can become with a particular place." His voice had been almost dreamy, and he seemed to be seeing other times as he gazed away into the battle fires that raged through the forest.

"Are you caught up with a particular place down here?" asked Ephinias, surprised at the tone of voice of his old master.

"Fond of, I should say. Nothing I won't grow out of, yet I sometimes wonder."

"Well, I'm fond of Sweet Rock, and the River Line, and some of the folks that go in to make up what my idea of what the place should be."

"Should be empty by dawn tomorrow," responded Gillerman, shaking himself out of his short reverie. "Those that are left after then will be soup for the spidermen's feast."

As if on cue, a rampaging horde of Olgnite soldiers broke through the faltering defenders at the gate on the Street of the Fisherman and now stormed through the chaos of the inner ways of the settlement.

"If there was ever a time for a diversion, this is it," shouted Gillerman, resuming his form of the stately white bird and lifting away into the fiery night.

"What diversion were you thinking of?" called his friend, also changing into his bird-form.

"The Stengil! We shall have to remind these brutes of a little portion of their past." Gillerman wheeled away, with Ephinias at his wing, circling higher and higher over the burning settlement.

It did not take the two long to discover that if their tactics were to fail, all would be lost, for the wood surrounding Sweet Rock was teeming with Olgnite hordes, and the river ran blood-red. They saw Owen Helwin and Chellin vainly struggling beside their comrades to stem the enemy tide at the perimeters of the burning village. The white bird plummeted downward toward the surging Olgnite armies, followed closely by Ephinias.

Old and New

Owen was braced against his horse, fighting next to Chellin Duchin and Jeremy, when the darkness seemed to explode into a golden-colored brilliance that blinded them for an instant. Outlined in that brief flash were vivid impressions of Judge and Hamlin, laying wounded at their feet, and the entire squadron dismounted and fighting a last desperate battle in an attempt to keep from being overrun by the deadly swarms of the Olgnites.

When the fiery, white-hot blast of light came next, and the vision of the flame-belching mountain, the old Steward commander took advantage of the enemies confusion, and blew remount and retreat, all in one breath. Those who couldn't get back aboard their horses were thrown over their saddles by their comrades, and the remnants of the squadron battled their way back toward Sweet Rock, and pressed on through the frantic defenders until they were inside the perimeters. They pulled up in front of the meeting hall in the square, which now was the main aid-station for the healers, who were overwhelmed by the growing line of wounded who made their way from all points of the battered defenses of the crumbling settlement.

"Here's Chellin Duchin," cried an injured man, sitting on the steps of the hall where he was being treated for a wounded arm. "And Owen Helwin!"

"Owen! Owen!" a woman called over the roar of the flames and the growing din of the battle.

He recognized his mother's voice and looked about him.

"Ephinias says we are to desert Sweet Rock," she cried, holding tightly to his stirrup. "He went to find a horse for your father, and hasn't returned."

"Where is Father?" demanded Owen, fearing the worst. "Is he wounded?"

"Not really. But that old scoundrel of a teacher says we have to give up here. All this business now is his work, or my eyes have never seen a closer look at some of his foolery!"

"How are we to leave? We're cut off on all sides by the spidermen! Where is Ephinias when we need him?"

"Where he always is when the going gets really hot," shot Chellin, who dismounted and helped Owen put his mother up into the saddle of Seravan.

The horse pawed the ground rapidly, then danced nervously sideways. "Gillerman says the Hulin Vipre have left their boats on the river. We are to look that way for our escape."

Gitel neighed agreement.

"No one knows exactly where those boats are," protested Owen. "And in the dark, having to deal with the Olgnites, we wouldn't stand a chance!"

"We don't stand a chance here," replied Chellin. The grizzled old commander looked worn and grim. "Even Famhart and the Stewards won't be able to turn this onslaught. We need more men, and daylight, and time to plot out an attack. These devils have a weakness, I'll be blown, or my old noggin has steered me wrong for all these campaigns. We just need to regroup and find where it is we need to strike a blow that will hurt them where they live."

"Ephinias is doing it now," said Seravan. "Gillerman has drawn up a great memory from the Olgnite past, and your friend has a Stengil. This may give us the time we need."

"How will we find the boats?" asked Linne.

"I can try," offered Gitel. "Then I can call Seravan. It may be our only chance, while Gillerman distracts the spidermen."

"I never thought a Steward would have sunk so low as to have to rely on the scout reports of a magician and his horse." Chellin snorted, his brow heavy. "Famhart and the squadrons of the Line have always managed to carry our own crew and tend to the business at hand, whether it was raiders from the Wastes of Leech or the hordes from the Dark One on the way to the Middle Islands."

"You big baboon, you've relied on magicians and their cohorts all along," corrected Linne, reaching out to touch the old Steward. "You and Stearborn always complain the most about help you don't understand."

Chellin Duchin's hackles went up, and he spoke defensively. "Stearborn is a stiff-necked old war-horse who can't be trusted with anything beyond horses and men, and the proper way to fight, whether mounted or afoot! He can't be expected to know anything beyond the duties of a Steward of the Line."

Linne hugged the bristly old commander, laughing in spite of herself. "You couldn't be expected to do something you don't know about. But you do know how to reform a squadron and to reach inside a man for the best he can give."

Shouts of warning erupted about the friends, and for the next few minutes they were locked in a deadly skirmish with a large party of the Olgnite army who had broken through the thinning ranks of the outlying defenses.

"Look to it, lads!" bellowed Chellin. "We shall have to rally the settlement to make a break for the river!"

"Get Famhart," cried Linne. "Elita should be with him."

"Is Emerald here? What a sad wedding feast he's had."

"But not boring, Owen! Not boring by a long pull!" returned Jeremy, who knelt by Hamlin and Judge, binding their wounds. "I thought I was to be in Sweet Rock for a feast and some sashaying of foot, but I missed my mark there."

"You pups get on with it," rumbled Chellin. "I don't want a Steward afoot now! Blow recall down every way here! We have to regroup all our squadrons if we are to win through to the river."

Wild cheering rose as the minstrel arrived, bloodied and

exhausted, followed closely by Stearborn and the brothers, Port and Starboard, who pushed through the crowd.

"Is this the final stand of the Line?" asked Port, looking at the dwindling numbers of defenders in the settlement. "Is this the finish of Port and his good brother?"

"May Trew be well remembered, and a good accounting taken of the scum of the Olgnites!" chimed in Starboard. "Tonight is too dark for even a son of Trew to die! I shall hold out until dawn. No mangy mushpole from the Outlands shall take Starboard or his brother in the darkness!" The two brothers clasped hands then, and drew their longswords, which they exchanged.

"There are no last stands here," corrected Famhart. At last a horse had been found for him. He sat proudly, but all those gathered there could tell he was in a weakened condition, no longer the solid rock of a leader who could instill confidence in his followers, no matter how bleak a situation might face them. Owen then stood up beside his father and, supporting him with one arm, raised the other in an outstretched salute. "Long live Sweet Rock! Long live The Line! A thousand cheers for Famhart the True."

"Long live The Line!" chorused the Stewards. "Long live Famhart the True!"

"Blow recall, damn your eyes!" bellowed Stearborn. "Let's see our way to the river!"

"The river," chorused the growing ranks of defenders who had rallied about the Stewards. "The river!"

"They say there are boats there for us!" shouted a man who had been standing next to Owen and had overheard Seravan and Gitel talking.

"Boats!" was the cry. It circulated around the settlement like wildfire, borne by panic-stricken citizens who could see that their settlement was lost. In every face there dwelled the wild look of the drowning man who is snatched from the flood by the barest chance, just as any hope of rescue has been given up as lost.

There was something in the hopelessness of the situation that bolstered up the spirits then, as always happens when hope is gone, and a thin steel rod of determination takes hold and turns the most mundane fighters into wild and uncontrolled berserkers. Chellin and Stearborn, as well as Famhart, knew this phenomenon, and knew they could put it to good advantage in their flight to the boats they were to search for on the river.

"How do we know that the Hulin Vipre left any of their craft?" asked Judge, readying his battle kit. Hamlin sat unsteadily beside him, doing the same.

"If they got here without anyone knowing of it, they would have had to come by the river," replied Chellin. "And if they came by the river, then it's a dead-bolt cinch they didn't just wade."

"You can lay your eyes to that," growled Stearborn. "And if there's a shred of justice left in this world, the beggars will have left those vessels for us, just when we have the most need."

"They'll be there," affirmed Owen. "Deros said the Hulin Vipre had come all the way from her homelands to try to capture her, so they had need of a seaworthy craft to have ever reached this far."

"She told me many stories of those lands while you were taken by the spells in the Darien Mounds," said Emerald, taking a long drink from the water bags that were being passed around the circle of weary defenders.

"Would you be able to sail one?" asked Famhart. "It has been a long spell since the Middle Islands. I can't remember enough to know whether or not I could manage."

"If we reach the boats, some among us will know well enough to pull like the lads we are to get us out of range of these blackguards from the undersides," grumbled Stearborn. "If needs be, I'll swim with a rope in my teeth and pull the lot of you behind me!"

"Hear, hear," cried Port heartily. "That's a ride we shall relish."

Famhart raised a hand to be heard then. "My good friends and comrades, I have a word or two to give you before we launch ourselves into this venture. You can see that I have worn down to the barest of strength here. I appoint my son, Owen Helwin, to ride in my place, as the true Tanis should. You are all charged to protect and defend him, just as you have so bravely done in all these turnings that you've ridden with me." A shocked silence fell over the gathered crowd, a moment's quiet against the confusion in the surrounding woods.

Emerald broke the moment open by raising his sword and shouting, "Long live Owen Helwin! Long live Famhart!"

Chellin Duchin joined in with a rough chorus, followed by Stearborn, who had slapped Kegin so heartily across his back, it sent him reeling into the horses.

The cries of Emerald and the others were picked up first by the throngs nearby, then the word began to travel throughout the beleaguered settlement. Owen was hoisted onto the shoulders of the two brothers, Port and Starboard. Linne stood beside her husband, with tears glistening on her cheeks in the orange glow of the flames that devoured Sweet Rock, but she smiled, her heart full of pride and sadness.

"You have to bear the torch that will keep the Line free, my son," said Famhart, his voice nearly lost in the noise of the fires, and the great displays of the volcano from the vision of Gillerman and Ephinias.

Owen would have protested, but he saw the exhaustion in his father's face, and the years of war and trials stood out clearly. His mother, too, he noticed, was aged, and there were lines in her face for the first time since her escape from the terrible black hold of the Dark One. He wondered, as he stood there, where it had all changed and when they had gotten old. He turned to Kegin. "Where has the time gone? Are we still who we were?"

His old friend clasped him strongly by the shoulders and gave him a long squeeze. "It wasn't long ago that a certain young buck I know was after old Kegin to dash off and about through the South Channels, he and his little friend, spouting about how this Gillerman was there, and the next thing I know, we're chasing around all over the backside of the basement, up to our elbows in folks who had a sore spot in their black souls for us!"

"I don't stand to be Elder yet," protested Owen. "I'm much too young! One of the older Line commanders should have the cloak."

"The younger, the better," proclaimed Stearborn. "What we need, lad, is steady! A steady line from sire to son, and something the people can sing to, and that will keep our good minstrel here in work for some time to come."

Emerald bowed in agreement. Elita stood with her arm wrapped about his waist, beautiful despite the long hours she had toiled helping the wounded.

"We shall have to find our way clear from here before I can make a story of it," called Emerald. "Look to it, lads! Muster up here for the play and let's set to it! Owen will ride at the side of the oldest squadron leader, and we shall make for the boats of the Hulin Vipre. Gitel will scout for them and tell us the way, then I think it should be for the Stewards to decide among themselves who shall do what!"

"Aye, minstrel, that we'll do!" said Chellin Duchin. "We have the squadrons of Stearborn, Chellin, and the good brothers. With these good citizens here we should be adequate to the job of getting these boats that are supposed to be there to the coast."

"What says Famhart?" asked Owen, looking to his father. He had an arm on his wife's shoulder, and only her support kept him in the saddle.

"I am following the orders of my new Elder. You have your plan laid out for you."

Owen looked out at the faces gathered about in the flickering red light of the flames that burned the youthful memories of the old settlement, before the dark tides of war swept back across the borders of his peaceful world and drew him into the place where he now stood, face-to-face with the father he had always admired and feared. Famhart looked tired and old. Owen nodded.

Seravan whinnied and threw back his head. "My good friend Gitel tells me he has found what you need! We must go now, while we still have this diversion."

A Steward blew remount, and the squadrons all drew up in muster formations and placed themselves on either side of a rank of citizens who lined up, carrying all that they could manage on their backs. There were women crying, and dazed children were quickly herded together, but Chellin and Stearborn gave them no time to dwell on their plight. The procession followed Owen and Seravan, and they went through the Gate of the Fishermen and on into the vast, hostile wood.

Famhart and Linne rode on one mount. Kegin stayed near his longtime friend and Elder, watching over him as he might keep an eye on an infant playing too near a fire on the hearth.

The great explosions of golden clouds, followed by the images of a fiery mountain exploding, lit the darkness once more with such fierceness that it was hard to keep their eyes open to it, but the strong, steady gait of Seravan led them farther into the forest, away from the funeral pyre that blazed behind them.

More than once, after they reached the River Line and turned toward the sea, there were long, backward looks at the death of the settlement, and sad, determined faces turned again to the coast and whatever future there would be beyond the black shroud of the night.

It was the longest watch Owen could remember, moving along in the eerie shadows, listening to Seravan talking to Gitel in a language he could not make out and feeling the weight begin to settle on his shoulders that his father had borne for so long.

The Hulin
Vipre

After the initial shock of seeing Ulen wore away, Deros calmly tried to free herself from the last of the sticky webbing of the Olgnite guard.

"Here you are," began Ulen Scarlett, "all this way beyond Sweet Rock, and I was worried about you. You seem to have changed camps, though, my pretty."

"Thanks to you," she snapped, standing and walking about to get the blood flowing in her legs and arms again. They had been cramped for so long, she was unsteady on her feet and had to stop once or twice because of the flooding pain of her limbs reawakening.

"Well, now, if this don't lift the lid on Granbe's teapot! Look at what we has here, Lofen! A girl sprung right out of that spider muckle-to-do!"

"Fair sight, too, for these old blinkers! Is there any more?"

McKandles thrashed through the stacks of bodies nearby and made fierce faces as he explored, but finally gave up the search, shaking his head in disgust. "Not nothing here but gutted Stewards and them squashers!"

"Are you going to Sweet Rock?" asked Deros, looking

about. She saw the fires in the distance and was shocked to see how widely spread the flames had become.

"We just came from Sweet Rock," replied the young horseman. "They seemed to be having a difficult time repelling these spidermen. My band and I have decided to try our luck at the coast. There is no help or comfort in the settlement now. Any who are left alive will not be far behind us."

"So you've run away again." Deros sneered. "Is that the mark of the men of the Gortland Fair? At the first sign of trouble those brave horsemen find the nearest road away from danger?"

"Here now, lass, that ain't no proper way to be a-thankin' them what has saved her from the gouging jaws of these here squashers! Lofen and I has both rode hard for that worthless settlement tonight, and what thanks has we got to show for it? A busted cinch, an empty gut, and a dozen cuts and gashes from a-poundin' on them creepy baders that is amok in these here woods!"

"Well said, McKandles! That will preserve our manhood nicely, if it was ever doubted. What I see here is a very highborn lady in a wood full of those who wish her no good. That she talks down to those who have saved her is only proof that she is in need of an education as to how things really stand."

Deros became afraid again, looking at the young man. Ulen's long black hair was plastered close to his skull, and his eyes remained cold and emotionless. He reached out to offer her a drink from the flask at his saddle horn, but she recoiled as though he had threatened to strike her. The long ordeal at the hands of the Olgnites had begun to take its toll, and her body began to shake uncontrollably, forcing her to sit down quickly.

Lofen handed her a dirty rag he used to clean his saddle and gear, which she took gratefully, wiping away her tears. He put a piece of his hardtack down next to her.

"Now we is in for it," lamented McKandles. "You can always counts on this here wailing and whining! It most likely is a-goin' to be the cause of all our heads split open a-fore this night is out."

The girl tried to control her sobs, but that only renewed the next outbreak, and no matter how much she willed herself to stop, the tears and cries seemed to come from someone else, and she felt a dark hand hovering over her, although she could not tell if it was real or from a nightmare that had been awakened by her horrifying journey with the Olgnites.

"Stow it up," pleaded Lofen, who had taken a great fancy to the pretty young girl. "There ain't no use in a-ditherin' about them squashers a-findin' us cause of no noise! We is smack in their laps, whether we likes it or not, and ain't nothin a-goin' to change that!"

"Nicely put, good Lofen. What we need to do now, and as quickly as we can, is to move on. I don't know how long this lull will last."

"Where are you going?" managed Deros, able to hold her voice under control by barely whispering.

"Going? It's a hard chance to say we're going anywhere, except maybe straight to the dregs of doom!" replied Ulen, arranging his gear so that Deros could ride behind him. "Our only course is to run for the coast, so that's where our direction lays."

A small hope lit up in Deros's heart then, for she thought of the ship and men who had brought her across the Sea of Silence when she had started on her journey to recruit help for her father. If only they still waited, as had been the plan, and were there! She would have a way to escape all these horrible memories and to rid herself of this arrogant young horseman who seemed to plague her every step. If only Owen could be safe.

"There is someone a-comin'," hissed McKandles. "They is a-ridin' fast too."

Ulen's features darkened. "Up behind me, wench! We shall try to outdistance these riders, whoever they are! Lofen! McKandles! Hang back as far as you dare, and see if you can find out who it is!"

McKandles was already mounting, and scowled in the direction of his leader as he waited for Lofen to mount his horse.

"You isn't after no tricks, is you? I mean, you has the

fluff a-hind you now, so there ain't no need for old McKandles or Lofen. We is wet kindling to your fire."

"I'll give you something you'll wish you had less of, if you don't do as you're told," snapped Ulen, turning his horse to the sea. He was brought up short by a sudden explosion of light that grew in strength until the entire sky above Sweet Rock was flooded with the brilliant glow, and from the midst of that light there came a distinct vision of a whitecapped mountain belching forth a river of molten rock that flowed down its sides in fiery streams and seemed to sweep away all before it.

The horses reared and pawed the air with their hooves, and McKandles lost his seat, tumbling roughly to the ground.

"What is it?" wailed Lofen, dismounting to help his friend. "Is this the last day we was taught to fear as kinders?" His eyes were wide and terror-stricken, his voice very unsteady.

"This whole thing smacks of the magician's trade," said Ulen. "I've seen some of this before."

"You would have done well to have exposed yourself more to their influence," chided Deros, wondering what the chances were that the riders they had heard were Stewards. Her nerves were worn perilously close to the breaking point, and she wasn't sure if she really cared anymore. She knew she would not be taken by the Olgnites again, for she had found her small dagger and knew it would be nothing to take her own life. For a brief moment she contemplated plunging it into the horseman from the Gortland Fair but thought better of it. No matter how offensive he was, he did not warrant death by her hand. Rather he deserved to be humiliated. She thought of him bested by Owen in a public test of strength and skill. She wondered where he was, and as those thoughts ran through her mind she wished she were by his side.

The noise from the colossal snow mountain in the vision rumbled through the night like thunder, and the golden light flared strongly, giving the darkness the look of sunrise, although morning was still hours away. Lofen had his ear to the ground and called to Ulen urgently. "They is upon us!

Old Lofen can't makes nothin' out with all this skathercut a-goin' on, but they is blinkin' well ready to ride us down!"

McKandles had tried to remount, but just as he swung a leg over his saddle, a dozen or more fast-moving riders swept over Ulen's small group, scattering horses and riders in all directions. Deros saw that these horsemen were neither Steward nor Olgnite, and in an odd fashion she was glad that they seemed to be an older, more familiar enemy.

"Who is these dinkin' grabbers?" cried Lofen as his horse danced in circles.

"They ain't no squashers, and that's a fair way towards a-makin' old McKandles feel a deal better!"

"Look to your flank, you blasted oafs," shouted Ulen, giving Lofen a resounding slap with the flat of his blade against his backside.

"They are Hulin Vipre," answered Deros. "They have come for me." Her voice was calm. She had been held in such black terror by the Olgnites, to simply face her old adversaries from her homeland seemed almost like returning to an old, familiar place after a long journey.

McKandles looked at Ulen in disbelief.

"Is that there the cranked on truth of it? Is these here folks after the skirt?"

"Let's see if we can't be a-doin' a bit of old-maid scour work," suggested Lofen. "If we was to give these blighters this here fluff, we might has a chance of a-standin' with our two good hoofs in the sea somewhere down Swan Haven way."

The girl knew from the look that Ulen gave his underling that he would do it if the hooded riders gave him a chance to bargain.

Fiery lava in the image of the volcano flowered majestically over the white dome of the mountain, lighting the scene below with an eerie light.

The rider leading the Hulin Vipre reined in suddenly, throwing back his hood. He was a young man, not much older than Ulen, with long dark hair that curled about his broad brow and startling green eyes. Even in her terror Deros thought the face was handsome, although there was something about it that was cold and unfeeling. With a motion of his arm the young Hulin Vipre halted his group and called out to Ulen in a stiff and correct manner, which showed he was not familiar with the common tongue.

"You are not Steward! Where did you find our prisoner?"

"Who is your prisoner?" returned Ulen, trying to keep his voice level.

"She belong to my father, the grand and illustrious Hulin Vipre, Lacon Rie."

"I know that name," spat Deros. "He is a vile and murderous traitor who lives in the outreaches of my homeland." She said something else in a tongue Ulen did not know. The hooded riders stirred restlessly.

"Shut her yap," barked Lofen. "A-fore she has us all stewed up in a picket!"

"We are not Stewards, nor any tribe that runs these woods, good sir! We are the Gortland Fair, horsemen and fools, to entertain and amuse. We were but on our way to the coastal village of Swan Haven to perform when we came across this hussy in the wood. There are a dangerous pack of fiends loose out here that seem to be on the march against what is left of the settlement yonder. We're making a run for it while we can."

"Give us the girl," said the young Hulin Vipre coldly. "We go to the water now."

"Give me to them," said Deros calmly. "It's your only chance. Otherwise they'll kill you all. There is no reason for them to harm you if you give them what they want."

Ulen's eyes could not meet the girl's. "This is only for now. You can see there is nothing else to do!"

"Give us the girl," repeated the Hulin Vipre, spreading back his riding cloak to reveal a black longsword, decorated with a circle of brilliant stones that sparkled and danced in the golden light of the huge vision of the volcano.

"Don't these characters fear this strange vision?" asked Ulen. "They hardly seem to notice it."

"They come from a land of fire mountains," replied Deros. "They fear them but know you are safe enough if you don't go too close. And they know that if they had the secrets to control them, they would cast my father from Cairn Weal and rule all the islands."

McKandles dismounted again and walked to stand beside Ulen. "If we gives up the fluff to these here bounders, we is a-standin' in a right fair way of seein' the water. I says we does what they says, and no harm." He turned to Deros briefly and tipped the greasy cap he wore on his head. "No offense now, but you can see there ain't no other way beyond this here stack of thorns."

The other hooded riders threw back their cloaks. All were young, and fair to look upon, with clear features and the same startling green eyes as their leader.

"Do you have a name?" asked Ulen, mustering all his brashness.

"I am Tien Cal, the Fourth Collector."

"I am Ulen Scarlett of the Gortland Fair. These woods are full of the Olgnites. Everyone there is fleeing now. You'd best be off if you aren't to be caught here."

"Is that your army?"

"This is only a scouting party," lied Ulen, motioning away toward the woods with a grand gesture. "The others, including a hundred armed men, are on their way now, routing the invaders from the Wastes. You'd be wise to allow us to ride along with you toward the coast, in case you encounter our skirmishers."

The young Hulin Vipre leader studied Ulen and his small band, then eyed the girl suspiciously. "Does this one speak the truth? Tell me, wench! I know a child of the line of Eirn Bol would not lie to me, though she might hate me."

"This is all that's left of the Fair," replied Deros, looking defiantly at her questioner.

The Hulin Vipre circled the small group that rode with Ulen. Taking the girl's horse by its bridle, Tien Cal led it alongside his own and motioned the others to follow. "We have boats on the river," he said. "We go there now. We take you with us so your 'army' will give us safe passage. We see then what to do with you!"

Ulen tried to ride on the other side of Deros, where he could speak to her, but one of the Hulin Vipre guards forced him back, so he had to be content to ride with the remnants of the Fair as they made their way toward the River Line.

Dangerous Paths

The two horses, Seravan and Gitel, spoke in their silent way and thus Seravan told Owen where the boats of the Hulin Vipre were moored by a sandy shore of the River Line, some distance from Sweet Rock. The darkness which had been illuminated by the workings of Gillerman and Ephinias returned once more to the pale-gray, watery light that comes just before dawn. Owen's eyes felt scratchy and dry from fatigue and the smoke from the burning settlement and surrounding wood. Jeremy rode beside him at the moment, nodding off in his saddle. Behind them came the procession of all the surviving citizens, carrying the wounded on litters and in carts. They had been forced to leave their dead. Few of the Stewards who guarded them had escaped injury, and their horses were nearly spent. It did not paint a very hopeful picture to Owen as he rode, deep in thoughts about his father, and the surprising turn of events which had suddenly elevated him to Elder.

In all the years of growing up worshiping his dashing father, Owen never felt that there would come a time when it would all change, like leaves in the wind, blown away into memory.

Jeremy swayed, and Owen roused from his half dream and put out a hand to steady his friend.

"Are we attacked?" spluttered Jeremy, bolting upright and thrashing about for his weapons.

"Only by the lack of sleep," replied Owen. "We still haven't seen anything of the Olgnites. It grinds my nerves to wonder where they are and when they might strike."

Chellin Duchin called "You'll smell 'em, lads! Your nose gets tuned to the scent of an enemy! Never fear about that."

"Do you think he's right?" asked Owen. "I haven't smelled anything in all this but smoke and the stench of death!"

"Chellin is always near the mark. It's been to my eternal aggravation, but it's the truth."

Owen was quiet for a time, then he asked in a lower voice, "Who will replace Chellin as squadron commander?"

Jeremy studied his companion a moment before answering. "I'm not sure. Is it strange having your father turn over the reins to you?"

Owen laughed softly. "You are a perceptive wag. Is it that obvious that I don't have the least inkling as to what I'm about? I wish I knew more about our enemies."

Seravan spoke in his low, mellow voice, soothing to hear. "Gillerman and I have seen the Olgnites in their own lands. Wastes and moors with little mounds of hills. They live in mud houses and raise captive humans like livestock." The big animal snorted in disgust. "No one knows for certain how they got the ability to take on the spider form, although it is commonly told in a tale I heard long ago that the first Elder of their tribes bargained for that power with the Dark One."

Owen shuddered. "I wonder how anyone can go so wrong?"

"Power, my boy. A simple matter. Those tribes were there in that bleak country for so long, barely able to feed themselves. Dirt-poor, as you would say. Nothing to soften the harshness, and it ate into the soul. When you live like that for turning after turning, something warps, just like leaving a sapling to dry after you've cut it."

"It still seems hard to think of anyone going that way." Owen sighed.

"All I want to know about the Olgnites now is where they are," muttered Jeremy. "Hamlin and Judge are the worse for wear after their tangle with the blighters. It gives me the spooks to think about an ambush out here, waiting for them to make the first move!"

"The Olgnites are here," Seravan replied. "They're all around us, but they aren't attacking. Gitel says he has gone through large packs of them, but they've paid no notice. They seem to be holding back to see what we're up to."

"I don't like it! There's something else at work here, and I don't like it."

"Ask Chellin. He'll have a notion as to what it means," offered Jeremy. "Or your father."

Owen felt the weight of a stone slowly crushing down on his shoulders and he wished he could tell his father he was not old enough yet to begin to bear such burdens.

"Here's Kegin, back from scoutings," whispered Jeremy. "He may have the answer to our riddle."

"Hola, Owen! We have company all around us, but these squashers don't seem to be interested in doing anything but following. I can't piece out what they're up to, but I don't think they're holding back because they fear our numbers. We'd be lucky to hold an hour if they massed against us."

"Toying with us." Chellin Duchin snorted. "Cat and mouse. They think they've gotten the upper hand of the Stewards, but by the Hammer of Windameir, we'll give them such a show, they'll wonder that they ever left their mother's side—if the blighters *had* mothers." Chellin's voice grew stronger as he spoke, and his veins stood out on his reddened forehead.

Emerald, who had been riding farther back with Famhart, heard the gruff commander's voice and spurred his horse forward.

"We are all in a row here, no question," he said as he came alongside the newest Elder. "Not at all like Trew or the Darien Mounds."

"Nothing can be like that," replied Owen, remembering

the claustrophobic feeling in the underground tunnels, the vague dread of never being able to find the surface again.

"Your father says these Olgnites are trying to lull us into thinking they're gone, so they can find out what trick we might have under our cloaks. Starboard and Port are all for attacking straight out and trying to clear a path to Swan Haven, instead of trying to find the boats. They think the surprise of that move might just throw the Olgnites off enough for us to win an advantage."

"But these enemies require a bit more than just a headlong attack," said Owen. "The Olgnites seem to have bested the Hulin Vipre, and they've had their own way so far with the squadrons of the Line. No one has been able to break their flanks, and that has cost us dearly. We shall have to try another tack now. We've lost too many of our men to continue wasting them in such pointless fashion."

"Famhart always said that if your cause was just, your sword and bow would make the difference. We're dealing with vermin here, from both borders. I don't believe that they will be allowed to go on unchecked." Chellin growled.

"They're a far piece along with it so far," reminded Jeremy. "They've burned Sweet Rock, we're trying to find a place to regroup, and we've lost Deros, to boot."

Owen's glance grew guarded. "We shall find her," he promised.

Seravan whinnied softly, shaking his mane. "Gitel has seen those Hulin Vipre still alive. He says they are a large party and that they're moving toward the river."

Owen reined in Seravan as the commanders of the Stewards gathered about him. "This news is not welcome. We have two fronts to cover now. What do you think, Chellin?"

The old warrior dismounted and lifted one of his horse's hooves. He was silent for a moment, then straightened up, patting the animal's flank.

"I'd say we're in a right smart squeeze here, but there may be something to our advantage yet. If we can play the two against each other, we might find a place to strike that would hurt them both."

"Hear, hear," agreed Port, holding his leather helmet in the crook of his arm and scratching his head fiercely. "The best road is sometimes the darkest, if no one knows you're on it. I've traveled a few of those in my time, and it was always a quick way to where I wanted to be."

"No news to give your enemy," chimed in Starboard. "That's the heart of the matter, and it'll stand us good use here."

Owen hesitated, looking at his father, pale and weak in his saddle. Linne helped him dismount.

Famhart drew a rough map. The others gathered around to see what he had done, for the watery light was dim, and it was hard to see the line representing the River Line, and the cross, which indicated their present position. "The road to Swan Haven will be here, and this is where the Hulin Vipre have their boats, according to our scout." Famhart paused, looking at Owen. "And a good scout he is, even though I had forgotten that those powers were still at work, thinking that the Keepers had long gone over."

"Don't be so sure," said Seravan softly. "You may be nearer to them than you think."

"We can use them now," replied the weary Elder. "We have lost Deros, and now her enemies hold our fate in the balance with their boats, and the spider scourge from the depths of the Leech are driving us straight into their grasp."

"Chellin Duchin says they may find each other before they find us," reminded Owen.

"They haven't lost us, lad." Chellin growled. "Don't think for a moment they don't know we're here. Whatever else those shifty blackguards are, they are fearless and fierce, and they knew a thing or two about engaging an enemy. Superior numbers are always good to have, for then you don't have to worry about thinking your way through. But their not thinking gives us an advantage, because we've always had to think about campaigns, for we don't have so many lives to play with."

"We could go farther downriver," suggested Jeremy. "Split into two groups. One would draw their attack, while the citizens could load behind the confusion."

"No good," said Famhart flatly. "We're so few now, to divide ourselves further would be fatal."

Emerald had been lost in thought as the others talked, then

leapt up from where he had sat on the ground at Famhart's feet, studying the crude map drawn out on the earth. "The Ellerhorn Fen," he burst out. "There's a way for us! It's the perfect way. The Hulin Vipre and the Olgnites may have us in numbers, but they don't have the knowledge of our home ground. They don't know anything beyond what they've seen, and I doubt any but those of the Line know of the Ellerhorn Fen."

"You may have hit upon our salvation," Famhart said, nodding his approval. "For a man who spends his time making rhymes, you do fair to middling well when it comes to understanding the nature of a battle."

"Someone give old Chellin a tidbit, so he can march along with the rest of you birds! What is this place you speak of? Are there stores and arms there?"

"Better, my good Chellin! Better far than another hundred Stewards! We have dwelled here long enough to know the way of the Ellerhorn, but it is a treacherous place for strangers, for black mud is everywhere, and I've seen it swallow a herd of cattle in no more time than it took for me to dismount my horse. That was when we first came to Sweet Rock and didn't know the nature of the River Line and where it kept all its secrets."

The first faint light of dawn was slowly strengthening, and the weary faces of the exhausted Stewards showed starkly against the pale sunrise. A smell of burned wood hung heavily in the air, and a slight trace of a sharp odor clung to the senses, just beyond the reach of recognition, until Chellin reminded the others about the smell of the Olgnite army.

"You can never mistake an enemy you have fought," he expounded. "Even after years and years I can tell you the way any of the enemies of the Line have smelled, whether it be the barbarous lot from Leech, or the highborn sons of Trew."

Here, Port and Starboard both protested loudly to Chellin, pointing out to him that they were sons of Trew but certainly not enemies of the Line.

"You make jest of my word," rumbled the old commander. "You two infidels know what I speak of! You are sons of Trew, but you are Stewards foremost, and have taken the Steward's vow. I won't have to worry if I have you two at my back, even if you do smell of Trew."

"Tell us more of the Ellerhorn Fen," Owen said, interrupting. "I remember the stories I was told as a child. That sounds to be the most promising way we have open to us."

"Not promising enough for my likes," complained Jeremy. "I was beginning to like life in Sweet Rock, before all this started, and I can't say I take any too lightly to this other side."

Emerald drew a map on the ground next to Famhart's. "Here we are, and here's the river. We are bounded by the Olgnites and Hulin Vipre here and here! We have no way to reach the river except straight ahead, here, so there is no way to win through without a fight. We have no one to spare at this point, so that is to be avoided if we can." He drew another figure between the cross marking their position and the River Line. "Now, this is the Fen. If we can travel this way quickly enough, we could load and be away before either of the other camps are any the wiser."

Signal horns began to sound the braying notes of the Olgnite. Owen lifted his sword from its scabbard to see if it shone with the brilliant light. He did not despair, for it seemed that all of it was a high adventure to be written by a poet as great as Emerald. And as he thought this the minstrel came to stand between Famhart and Chellin Duchin. Kegin was on the other side of the brothers, Port and Starboard. It seemed a vague dream to Owen. His old friend and teacher, Kegin, was at his side, just as it had been when it all started before, only Darek had been there then.

And thinking of his friend, Owen's heart saddened.

Stearborn

Stearborn had led his squadron across the River Line a little while before and now watched the Olgnite war party edging into position. A smell of sulfur, cut by the softer aroma of birch and pine, filled the dawn air, and for a moment the old commander thought of another time, long ago, an early dawn such as this, when he had waited for battle. The memory was a sad one, yet it brought a flood of warm thoughts, too, for a younger Famhart had been with him then, and the Stewards had been strong.

This dawn, the Stewards were outnumbered and on the run, preparing to abandon their home, and he looked about him at his weary troops, faced for the first time with defeat. He shifted position in his saddle, uneasy with his thoughts, and turned his attention back to the enemy across the river.

It was then that he noticed the other riders, moving along stealthily, unaware of the Olgnites waiting farther ahead. Stearborn watched their progress with great interest, for he could not make out who the newcomers were. They were neither Olgnite nor Steward, and their numbers were small. For a moment he thought they might be some stragglers from Sweet Rock, and he was on the verge of signaling them, but then he saw they were dressed and armed as Outlanders, and seemed to be from the ranks of the other enemy

148

troops he had encountered during the previous day and night. A few among them seemed to be prisoners.

The early dawn light slowly filtered through the mists rising off the ground, and pale white clouds swirled about the horses' legs. Stearborn watched as the two groups converged upon each other, trying to detect who the prisoners were. He had noticed that some were from the horse-riding when the fight erupted.

It was short and brutal, and the Outlanders, prisoners and all, were quickly drugged by the bites of the spidermen, wrapped tightly in cocoons of web, and slung unceremoniously over the saddles of their horses, to be carried like sacks of meal. Stearborn saw that one was bound upright in the saddle. He shook his head and turned to Tyan, a young Steward who served as his orderly.

"Ride to Owen, lad, and don't spare yourself. Tell him there are Olgnites here with some prisoners that stand between us and the boats."

"Sir."

"And tell him there's one they are treating with special consideration. I can't be sure in this light, but it looks like a slip of a girl, unless my old eyes are playing me tricks."

Tyan saluted and spurred his horse into a fast gallop.

"Strange times," muttered the old man again, motioning for his sergeants to join him and make a plan of battle.

The Olgnite party had grown with the addition of other groups. It appeared that the enemy plan was to deny the Stewards a route to the boats.

Out of the now brightening shadows at the eave of the wood, Stearborn saw a lone figure approaching. As quickly as he had seen the moving figure, Stearborn lost sight of it and glanced back and forth across the distance.

"The light is making jest of me," he muttered. Loosening his weapon, he walked toward the spot where he'd seen the movement.

Halfway there, the voice, clear and high, almost inhuman, called to him. "Good day, Steward. You have the fairest of days to meet your end. You'll feed my companions with your lovely sap."

"Come out of hiding, you filthy worm! Stand and face

Stearborn if you dare! We'll see whose turn it is to die this day!"

"Acccch," hissed the voice. "Hear me, wretched Steward, for I am Jarbon, trusted by the most high of Olgnite."

"Then stand to, Jarbon! You have reached your end!"

"I come with news, vile one! You can make your death painless and quick if you hear me out."

"What tricks are you after? Your numbers are great! Do you fear the odds?"

"We have no fear of your puny tribe," gurgled Jarbon. "The Olgnite have risen . . ."

The voice trailed off in a clacking of fangs, and an eerie sound that Stearborn finally identified as labored breathing, brought on by great excitement.

"Now hear me out, you Steward swine. I give you a chance to depart this life honorably, with battle, and to be the death of many enemies. Is that not your code?" resumed the spiderman.

There was a heavy smell of sulfur mixed with the pungent aroma of the forest in the early morning, and the silvery mist on the river curled above the water, reflecting back the rising sun. Stearborn's soul was very quiet, as it had been when he was younger, hunting with his father in the mountains. The powderlike snow had squeaked beneath his boots, and the air smelled of ice and pine scents, and the cook fire of the camp. Stearborn always had the same memory just before a battle, and it was the only alarm he needed.

The spiderman crawled slowly down the trunk of the tree, his fangs concealed in a mocking smile, but Stearborn stood his ground. His stomach turned at the hideous sight, but his hand never wavered, and he scanned the melting shadows for any signs of an ambush.

"I have brought no one with me. I have come to deliver this pact. I, Jarbon, am next in line to lead the war bands. We are everywhere now, and have found much livestock. These lands you have lived in will feed us well."

"Your last meal, Olgnite! There is a new tide running." Stearborn was preparing to strike, but the wily spiderman kept carefully out of reach.

"Hear me, impatient giant! Kill me the band across the river there, and I shall allow you a quiet death!"

"Those are your own," spat Stearborn. "Do your own dirty traitor's work!"

"Forlac would be onto us before we could close. There is no love lost between us. He has been the Logul since our Provider appointed him. He steals too much and keeps all the best livestock for himself."

"And you'd eat the prisoners he has now?"

A cunning look spread across the distorted features of the Olgnite. "We wish the prisoners for reasons of our own. That is no concern of yours," replied the spiderman in an oily voice.

"And what would keep me from splitting you from eyeball to kneecap now, my foolhardy tradesman?"

"I fall to your honor! I yield while I am here talking to you. A Steward never harms an enemy who has yielded."

"Crafty blackguard, I'll give you that! I guess, living without law, it is always good policy to know the law of your enemies."

"No matter now, arrogant dog! No matter which way you go, there is only Olga! But I offer you a sweeter fate, and now I begin to regret it. Maybe I shall have to have your sap, to the last drop. I'll let you linger in agony a bit, though, so you can feel it drain from you. You'll see the precious Stewards herded away in bonds and know their ends will be to feed warriors. We shall take the Line!"

"You have miscalculated, my thoughtful friend, and I think that shall be your last mistake."

"Mistake? What mistake?"

"We have nothing to lose now. To make a man desperate, all you need do is take away any hope that might linger in his mind, and you've created a perfect tool for destruction."

The Olgnite laughed a cold, brutal laugh. "You talk to me of destruction! I am Jarbon, son of Jargal the Destroyer! We have bled more of your kind in a month than you Stewards could in a turning!" Jarbon threw back the black leather cape he wore and drew the saw-bladed sword at his hip. "This blade has drunk the life of many, to let me have my fill! It will drink the life of many more!"

A messenger drew up his horse by the group of Stewards. The young Steward dismounted, and noticed the Olgnite talking to his commander. "Sir?" he called in confusion.

"Come along with you, lad, this is Jarbon, a soldier in the Olgnite tribes."

The messenger hurried to Stearborn.

"I have given your colan a way to die that won't be too horrible! He seems to jest with me. If you have any desire to die a swift, painless death, then speak to him and beg him to do my bidding."

"More than jest, good Jarbon, much more than jest! And a Steward is bred with more manners and loyalty than to plead for anything of this life. I've seen the light, and feel the way open to spread my fate among the lost stars behind Pilgrim's Gate!"

Jarbon noticed the odd look in the old Steward's eye and had tensed to move away, but not before Stearborn's hand moved from beneath his cloak, tightly clutching his longsword, which flashed briefly in the red rays of the sunrise and cleaved the Olgnite's head from his shoulders so swiftly that the spiderman never had time to utter a single word. Stearborn stood for what seemed a long moment, the headless body still upright before him, watching the staring eyes of the displaced head roll wide with surprise, the lips trying to form words.

There was movement from the denser part of the wood where the Olgnite had come from. A long, wailing signal split the air. Stearborn wiped his blade with his cloak, being careful to dab away all the dark spots that had gotten onto his sword arm. "Speak up, lad! What message do you bear me?"

"The Ellerhorn Fen!"

"What is it? What do you say?" barked Stearborn, moving to blow his own signal to the men he had stretched out in a skirmish line up and down the river.

"Owen and Famhart have marked the road to go through the Ellerhorn Fen. We are to rejoin the others there immediately."

"I've heard of this place," said Stearborn. "Not pretty stories. No sure thing for us, either." He suddenly laughed, looking at the dead enemy soldier. "But then, there don't seem to be any more sure things, lad! Ask this fellow! He was so certain of himself. Now look at him!"

"Sir."

"Look lively now, and take word back to Owen. My men and I will meet him at the marsh before the Ellerhorn Fen, and we'd best be quick, for there is going to be the devil to pay for my little fit of anger."

Almost in reply to his last words, a great hue and cry went up along the river, and dozens of Olgnite soldiers emerged from the shadows in the early light, making straight for Stearborn's concealed Stewards.

And from the place where the Olgnite leader had emerged, someone else approached. "Look out!" warned the young messenger.

Ephinias, mounted on Gitel, rode out of the thick shrub and underbrush.

Gates of
the Ellerhorn

A gray mist hung over the ground, smelling of old trees and long undisturbed pathways. The sound of the river was all the more noisy over the eerie silence, and it was difficult to breathe. Behind Owen, his father stood, flanked by his wife and the minstrel. Kegin remained mounted next to Jeremy and Chellin Duchin, who were as silent and thoughtful as the brothers from Trew.

A broad, clear morning was growing brighter behind them, but the gray mists only seemed to become more cloudy, and there was a trace of a chill over the Ellerhorn Fen.

"I don't like the feel of this place," muttered Jeremy. "Chellin and I have had dealings with such places in the past, and it was always death and sorrow."

Chellin Duchin, beginning to warm to his task as the odds against them grew greater, dismounted, an almost cheerful look brightening his usually dark features. "We have indeed seen the undersides of a hatful of places, my young cock! Some I never expected to see the outcome of, either, I wager! Good training for the soul!"

Kegin and Famhart, who had managed a few hours of

sleep in the saddle, mapped out the safe way through the maze of quicksand pools and sinkholes for the rest of the remaining survivors of Sweet Rock.

"Look at it," growled Port. "As mean and vile a place as there ever was, even in the darkest heart of Trew, when it was ruled by the Rogen."

"Darker," added Starboard. "Trew at least had a king, crazed as he was. This place belongs to no one, and cares for less!"

Emerald frowned at the brothers. "We have enough on our hands here without all this doomsaying. Famhart and Kegin both know much about the Ellerhorn, and if we pay attention, this will be no more sticky a problem than the thought of having to deal with the Olgnite."

Jeremy had litter bearers bring Judge and Hamlin to the front, and they lay sore and stiff from their wounds but happy to have a diversion and to be included in the planning.

"This is the last clear ground that we'll have to gather," warned Famhart. "From here on in, and until we reach the edge of the Grealing Wood, there aren't enough wide spots in the way to stand more than two abreast."

"And there are things in there that will try to call you aside," went on Kegin, his voice hushed. "When I first was sent to scout these lands, there were old stories from the fireside that haunted me, but the true nature of the Ellerhorn was much more horrible than any of the tales I ever heard."

"They were lost, unhappy souls," said Elita. "The Elboreal told me of many of the old clans from the Golden Years who lost their way and have been imprisoned here for a time."

"Whoever it is, they will try to lure you off the path," added Kegin. "The story is that if they can find one to replace them, they are free to go. So to stray a shaft's length from the path is sure death. Once the black mud has a grip on you, there's no strength that can save you, so pass the word to follow exactly in the footsteps of those in front and don't listen to any voice but someone who is known to you and whom you can see."

In the distance the wood behind them formed a great crescent of green that stretched from the lower river plain, all the way to the beginning of the foothills, rolling gently to the eastward, toward the higher, white peaks of the mountains, twinkling like silver-white signal fires in the far distance. In the center of the wood a billowing gray-black plume of smoke hung ominously in the stillness of the morning, all that remained of the old settlement of Sweet Rock. Owen's heart beat heavily, and he felt a wave of sadness that was new to him, for it had never happened in his life that he had lost a home to return to. Famhart and Linne had both left their childhood havens, and now Sweet Rock was gone as well.

"I hate to see it go," said Emerald, reading Owen's thoughts. "But no place is beyond destruction. I have lost my wedding day, and my shelter, and still haven't made vows to my intended." He smiled at Elita with only a trace of sadness and held her tightly to him. "The Elboreal are probably at the bottom of all this, for they wanted her for themselves."

"Hush, you naughty music peddler! No such thing. They would have come if the fires hadn't started and there hadn't been so much noise. That always scares them away."

Owen's thoughts brightened at the mention of the elves. "Do you think they might still be here?" he asked, hardly daring to believe.

Elita shook her head. "I haven't felt them close for a while now. The time is coming when no one will see them again."

"It is a shame that there will be those who have never seen or heard them," said Emerald.

"A bigger shame if we're all left to these devils," snapped Chellin. "Any help would be welcome now, no matter what quarter it comes from."

Elita's beautiful features darkened, and she gazed in the direction of the sea. "It has always been the way of the Elboreal to help us, and though we will never see them the way they have been, there will always be one or two, now and then, in human form, to counsel or advise."

"We could use less advising and more arms," rumbled Port. "I'd give my right to counsel for a healthy squadron."

"What I wouldn't give for the likes of the old Grand Ash

Squadron, like we once mustered in the wilderness of the Leech. That would be the end of all this, and no questions asked!" Starboard pounded his fist into his palm. "Famhart was there! And Linne! A grand time for the Line!"

"A grander time than we've fallen on now," confessed Famhart, his eyes and mind full of another memory, when he and Linne were much younger. "We have need to remember those deeds, and to be able to teach those stories to all our sons and daughters who will be growing up long after we have passed away."

"That won't be for a long time, Father," protested Owen.

Famhart studied his son, smiling slightly. "We will know when we arrive. At first it's always a surprise to find out how we shall find our way across the Boundary, but in the end it always makes perfect sense."

"You're not getting out of this so easily," roared Chellin Duchin. "You chiseling shyster! If I'm to be forced to haul my carcass back and forth across the Line fighting these spidermen, then I'm stuffed if I won't have you alongside of me."

Famhart laughed, and the brothers joined in, along with Chellin.

"It'll be a grand song to sing if I still breathe," said Emerald. "All the best of stories, of the best of times, when the Light began to fade but did not pass away."

Linne's eyes were shining as she held tightly to her husband's hand. "We have been through all of it, and I sometimes wonder why, but I love you, and I want you to know I've always felt it a great honor to be your wife," she whispered.

He gazed at her loveliness and nodded, unable to speak, for a quaver in his voice made it too unsure for words, so he squeezed her hand tightly in return.

Kegin broke the moment by calling out to the outlying groups, asking that a signal be sent the moment Stearborn's squadron was spotted. "All we wait on now is that gnarled old goat from the Upper Malignes."

"Is that where Stearborn was sired?" asked Jeremy, having only heard wild rumors of the vast highlands that bordered the Mountains of Skye, flanked on two sides by the most savage of deserts. There forests were so thick and over-grown, it was impossible to go on horseback, and difficult enough on foot.

"Born and raised there," answered Famhart, growing anxious about his old friend. "He came to the Stewards after his father and brother were slain by invaders from Lachland."

"How long has he been with you?"

Famhart's face softened, and the worry lines eased as his memories reached back into the long summer in his life when he'd first seen the rough Steward from the highlands of the Malignes. "Since there was a battle to be fought or hard times to win through, I was not long away from my homelands of Boghatia when I encountered Stearborn. He seemed more frightening even then. His horse had a white bolt on its nose, and I remember his beard was a fierce-colored red then."

"You mean the old grizzly was a younger man once? I didn't think anything so rough-edged could have been blessed with having a childhood."

Linne stood and stroked her horse's neck. "Famhart is too shy to tell you of the feats he and Stearborn performed on the day we came to be acquainted with him."

"That was a long time ago, my dear."

"These stories are my realm," reminded Emerald. "I've had no time to do them justice. I shall mark myself a time to spin all those yarns, once we get to calm waters. It would be a good tale to spin on my wedding day."

A faint sound was heard on the slight breeze, almost drowned out by the noise of saddles creaking and horses moving about, grazing on the tall grass that grew near the wetlands of the fen.

Elita's eyes darkened and she paled.

"What is it?" breathed Emerald, reaching out to touch her hand.

"Voices," she murmured in reply. "Voices from the fen."

"What are they saying?" asked Famhart, stepping beside her and trying to listen more closely.

"They say they are the Elboreal," returned the woman, her breast heaving. "They say they are come to help us."

Owen's spirits soared, and he rushed to mount Seravan excitedly. "Then we shall make it to the boats!"

The lad tried to turn the big animal's head toward the path and into the ominous gray mists of the Ellerhorn Fen, but Seravan held his ground sternly. "You are deceived by the first of the Lost Ones," he replied evenly. "They can see your thoughts and use them against you."

Emerald held Elita's hand tightly, gazing away into the mists that hung a few dozen paces in front of them, although the rest of the surrounding wood and countryside were becoming bathed in the warm morning light.

"I'm beginning to wish I'd forgotten the Ellerhorn," he said. "I'd forgotten all this other dark business."

Linne looked anxiously over her shoulder, gazing at the woods behind them. "I wish Stearborn would hurry!"

She had moved to be beside Elita, and her voice was tight with worry. "Are you still hearing the voices?"

"Yes. They sound so real. I know it can't be my old friends, for they won't answer me, but they sound so very real. I guess my heart wants to believe, so I'm easily tricked."

"They sound like the voice of Trew," comforted Port. "It does ring a certain bell inside me. Starboard hears it too."

The other brother nodded vigorously. "It is almost the pure sound that a son of Trew would hear," he agreed.

"More dangerous than any voice you could think of," said Chellin Duchin. "I hear the end of us all in these soft tones. Promises of help, and calls to come to them, all leading to an end that Famhart spoke of."

"But what if it is the Elboreal?" argued Owen. "If they only come in times of great need, then they are certainly right in being here now! The Olgnite have us outnumbered ten to one!"

Elita shook her head sadly, with a faint trail of tears down her pale cheeks. "These are but our own hopes calling to us."

Another sound had begun to find its way into their attention then, more urgent and not quite so subtle. The horses began to grow restless, Seravan's ears perked up, and he whinnied loudly in excitement.

"What is it?" asked Owen, reaching out to put his hand on the big animal's bridle.

"Gitel! He's with Ephinias and the others."

"Stearborn?"

"He's on his way."

Kegin paced from Famhart to Chellin Duchin to Emerald. "Will this draw the Olgnite into an attack before we get into the Ellerhorn? It isn't a place to be caught out here, with no cover and no room to maneuver!"

"The Olgnite are very near," replied Seravan. "They are holding back, but I can't say why."

"Maybe Ephinias has weaved a spell," said Owen.

"We'll need more than spells when you come down to it." Port snorted.

"Don't forget to stay in the tracks of those in front of you," reminded Famhart, organizing the first group to enter the threatening gray wall of mist that marked the beginning of the Ellerhorn Fen.

"Pass that word back again," echoed Kegin. "And don't listen to anyone you can't see! These things that dwell here are dangerous."

"Well, now, that's the kind of morning I like," boomed Starboard. "A powerful great horde of squashers behind us, and something like the worst of Trew before us. That whets my appetite right hearty!"

"No time to eat it if we had food," grumbled his brother.

"And no time for you two ruffians to be talking about grub when we don't have it," chided Chellin Duchin. "I'd send this young pup of a lieutenant back to have them set up the kitchens, but I don't think we have the makings of more than one more meal, and we'd best hang on to that."

"Cheerful lot, you bunch," shot Kegin. "I always knew it wasn't much of a promising affair to have too many dealings with men who spoke in jest about their breakfasts."

"We'll break our fast on gore this morn, if my old wits aren't all turned to lead! Look at the woods there behind Stearborn's lot!" Famhart's voice was steady, although there was a chilling edge that sent goose bumps down Owen's back. When he turned to look, a leaden gray stone settled over his heart and threatened to stop his breath. Behind Stearborn's squadron was a solid wall of the Olgnite troops, jogging along slowly in the wake of the Stewards, beating their swords against their shields in a dull, relentless rhythm, and calling out in a deep, guttural chorus for the blood of their prey.

FOOTPRINTS
IN
THE
SAND

Ambushed

Once on the other side of the river, Ulen Scarlett had seen the signs of an Olgnite ambush but said nothing. Lofen and McKandles rode at his side, and the three of them watched as Tien Cal held tightly to the reins of Deros's horse. The rest of the Gortland Fair rode behind nervously, casting fearful looks at the ominous eaves of the wood, their hands ready at their weapons.

From somewhere ahead, the sound of the river reached them again, for they had left the water and now were approaching it once more. Ulen's mind was racing, torn between relief that the enemy force had not killed them all at once and a desire to devise some plan that would enable him to escape with the young girl who had looked at him so pityingly when Tien Cal came. That thought drove him to madness, knowing that she had seen the darker side of his nature. He rode on, glowering, and waiting for the Olgnite attack.

When the spidermen flowed over their small party like a storm battering a lee shore, Tien Cal fought fiercely, still holding the bridle of Deros's horse. There were slain Olgnites in a heap around the Hulin Vipre prince, but the odds were too great to overcome, and one by one his band fell. Ulen lost sight of Lofen and McKandles for a terrifying moment but struggled clear again, and the three of them formed a wall to keep the crafty enemy off their backs.

Deros broke free of her captor and spurred her horse, vainly trying to clear the skirmish lines of the Olgnites, but the animal stumbled and fell, throwing her senseless to the ground. The fighting raged over her.

Ulen lost sight of the girl, for he had two Olgnite soldiers to contend with. "Look to it, Lofen! Behind me!" cried Ulen, his voice muffled by the screams of wounded horses and the cries and shouts of the bitterly struggling foes.

"I's here," called Lofen hoarsely. "Kandles is with me!"

Another wrangler pulled even with them for a moment, wide-eyed in his excitement, but a charging Olgnite threw the man from his saddle and was on him in a flash, sinking his poisoned fangs into the screaming man's throat and sucking him dry of blood almost before the man's plea for help had died away.

McKandles drove his longsword through the Olgnite and recoiled when all the fresh blood of the spiderman's victim gushed out in a powerful red stream, then turned to a more putrid black as the Olgnite's life slipped steadily away.

"Go careful with them swats," growled Lofen. "I was near drowned then in that blackguard's blood! I doesn't want no part in no squasher's juice, neither!"

Before McKandles could answer, another wave of attackers were on them, and a deadly struggle began, raging back and forth through the small glade that bordered the river.

Ulen and his two underlings managed to stay together, although they were cut off from Tien Cal and his dwindling following. Deros still lay in the maelstrom of flashing hooves and fallen bodies. The Hulin Vipre's commander was still mounted and had left a terrible wake of maimed and dying Olgnites behind him, and it looked as though he might win through to the water, but a new wave of spidermen rolled over them from the left flank and overpowered them. The last glance Ulen had of the scene was the Hulin Vipre soldiers being trussed tightly up in the sticky webbing the spidermen used to bind their victims.

Lofen called out frantically then, and was rendered senseless by two powerful bites from an Olgnite who had dragged him down from behind. Before Ulen could move to aid him,

McKandles disappeared into a heap of swarming enemy soldiers. There was a sharp stinging pain in the back of his neck, and as the Olgnite warrior roughly dragged him toward where his two companions lay, Ulen dimly realized that he had been bitten by one of the spidermen.

A great burst of rage exploded inside him, but he was rudely tossed into a heap of other senseless victims, awaiting their turn with the web makers, who spun out the sticky, foul-smelling bonds, clacking their fangs together as they worked and rolling their small, bloodshot eyes in wild anticipation. Ulen didn't black out but hovered in a state of sickening semiconsciousness, watching in horror as the webs were bound tightly about him, until all that was left undone was a small space around his face. His breath came in short pants, and he tried to clear his thinking, but to no avail. Just as his captors bundled him aboard a horse, he caught sight of Deros again, remounted now, and being led toward a large Olgnite, with a bright-blue sash about his waist, who appeared to be a high-ranking leader. Before Ulen could look further, he was thrown roughly over the saddle.

"Here's a fat one," laughed an Olgnite. "He'll keep me warm when we make camp tonight."

"There's more of these across the river! We'll have a feast that we haven't seen the likes of since that juicy settlement up above the big lakes."

"And lookie there, what the Tarlgan has taken! She will please the Obelmal, or my jaw ain't wagging!"

The voices droned on. Ulen felt the movement of the animal beneath him, and tried to tell which direction they were going, but could not. His stomach grew weaker, until he had to vomit at last. There was no place for the bitter tasting bile to escape the webbing. Soon he was choking and gasping for air, and he finally blacked out, only to come to again a short time later. There was enough of a passage in the confining binding to allow him to gasp short, sweet gulps of air into his bursting lungs. He made himself control the panicked temptation to call out, which would have choked him again. He concentrated on calming his thoughts enough to try to devise a plan of escape. He recalled seeing the thick, sticky webbing being wrapped about Lofen and McKandles, and a sinking, hopeless knot of fear gripped him. He fought against it, knowing he would be doomed if he gave up hope. As long as Deros was unbound, there was a chance for all of them, but he would have to be ready, and not give in to the dark voices that called out to him from inside the black shadows that lurked in the deeper parts of his mind.

He was aware of the strangest sensations. It was an unbelievably sweet aroma at first, of a rare blossom in full bloom, that made his mind go back to when he was a child, laying in a field of clover, watching his father round up the spring foals. Then there was the awful stench of stagnant, brackish swamp mire, heavily tainted with sulfur. He drifted in and out of consciousness, sometimes painfully battered about on the hard saddle, and sometimes floating above it all, feeling nothing. When he caught himself in those moments, he knew it was a dangerous bite he had received, for he could not move his arms or legs, and his breathing was heavy and painful. Ulen tried to reason as well as his drugged mind would work, but he could not imagine why the poison of the spidermen only affected him at times, then at other times, he seemed all right. Lofen and McKandles had made no move since they were captured and wrapped tightly in webbing, and Ulen began to fear that they had already been slain. He spent much of his time angry at the two bungling underlings, but they had been with the horse-riding so long he thought of them as family, and their loss was not something that he could allow himself to think of at the moment.

His thoughts were interrupted again, by the halting of the horses. There was a great stir among all the riders, and many signal horns sounded, with odd notes like the cries of dying things, tortured beyond endurance. A great sense of excitement prevailed among the Olgnite forces. There was rough laughter, and the terrible sounds of fangs clacking.

A passing pair of Olgnite warriors walked by close enough to him so that he could hear them plainly, down to the eerie way their throats clicked as they breathed. "We have the roads all shut down to the river. The pinkers couldn't get to the water when we burned their holes, so they're trying to reach the place where we saw the boats, and the ones from the sea."

A rough laugh followed, and another voice spoke. "Those boatmen didn't have enough sap to keep anyone alive long! I hope their countrymen are fatter."

"No need. We'll have a good farm started, once we round up the rest of the nest we burned. They breed well, these pigs from The Line. We should have enough stock from them to start a strong farm, where we won't have to do so much raiding as now."

"That would be a good poke, heh? Old Root and Gruel, folks of leisure, staked out on their farm, running a few head of these lowlanders for juice! I like that idea!" The spiderman clacked his fangs together rapidly, a strange little melody that sent shudders down Ulen's back, and made him squirm beneath the sticky webbing that held him relentlessly.

Their conversation was stopped by the grating blast of a signal horn, followed by the loud bray of an answer.

"They're across the river! They have slain Jarbon! Death to the weasel-hearts! Death to the pink pigs!"

A horrendous hue and cry went up, deafening Ulen, and the spidermen all about him clanged their swords against their shields, and uttering their foul oaths of vengeance on the heads of every human inside the borders of The Line. He heard Deros cry out then, in the lull of the harsh voices of the spidermen, and he tried to twist his cramped body so he could see her through the sticky bonds of the web.

Deros screamed again, then fell silent.

"Good shela! Now you have made me happy! I will savor the whip now, since it gives you so much pleasure."

Ulen could not see, but knew it was the Olgnite leader with the blue sash, who spoke.

There was a hissing crack then, and the girl cried out once more, although she fought to control it.

"The Olga has found what the shela likes! That will please our Protector! You can dance and sing for him when we reach the veltlands. He will be pleased with his little ones! We have many lives for him to drink, and a shela that will sing for him at the tune of the strap!"

Ulen was on the verge of trying to roll over again, when a sudden pressure against his neck shut off all his air, and he felt himself gliding back into a brilliant darkness, full of stars, and a blood-red haze that hung like a moist curtain before his eyes.

Deliverance

Gillerman flew high in the blue ridge of sky above the edge of the Ellerhorn Fen. He could see the sweeping panorama below, and the battle that was slowly moving toward unfolding. The skirmish lines of the Olgnite were three deep as they advanced across the last clear space before the edges of the fen. A few Stewards hurried along before the enemy army, looking like small leaves blown on before a harsh wind. There were volleys of arrows crossing back and forth in high arcs above the battlefield; the bright blue feathers of the Stewards, then yellow and black from the Olgnites, as the lines grew closer and closer together.

Gillerman watched carefully. He spotted Ephinias on Gitel, and as they had arranged, all the birds of the woods around Sweet Rock, thousands of them, in all shapes and colors and sizes, formed into huge fans of color spread out against the blue of the sky and grew so thick that the ground below began to darken, as though huge clouds had come to drown out the sun. Each of the winged creatures carried in its beak a small pebble, which glimmered and shone in the sunlight, turning from early-dawn pearl to a fiery red. As the swarms circled near the ground, Ephinias rose up in the saddle of Gitel and stirred the wind with his hand. Blazing sparks shot forth in a whirlwind of fire that gathered strength and moved to cut off the enemy hordes that moved to attack.

Gillerman spread his great wings and spun out a trail of kites from his passing, each in the form of a giant bird, so huge in size that they frightened the smaller wrens and finches. They also threw a dark terror into the hearts of the Olgnites, who in their spider forms had a certain primal fear of their natural enemies. The kites lumbered slowly about, gliding gradually downward in long, lazy circles, undaunted by the showers of arrows that erupted from the Olgnite ranks.

The Steward war-horns sounded, urgent and brave on the crackling air, and a chorus of squadron chants were heard against the chaos that was flaring over the field of battle. The Fir and Ash squadrons sang their hymns lustily, and the Lost Elm joined in, although it had lost many of its strongest voices. Chellin Duchin's bass could be heard leading his men, followed by Port and Starboard, and Stearborn, last of all, reckless in his wildness of heart.

On the ground, Owen and Seravan led with the first of the parties into the gray mists that guarded the entrance to the Ellerhorn, and immediately felt the cold chill grip their bones. The bright light of day behind them turned into a muddy brown. Kegin was directly in front of him, but Owen was having difficulty keeping his dim figure in plain sight and called out to ask his friend to slow down.

"We can't slack our pace now," returned Kegin, studying each step carefully, for the snares of the Ellerhorn were always fatal. "We have to get far enough in to leave the Olgnites without a clear trail, or at least far enough so our archers can cut down their number. Their troops won't count for anything once we reach the pass called the Elbow. That's where we shall have our chance to get our own back at them!"

From behind Owen the sounds of a furious battle raged, but he could see nothing of what was going on. The mists had thickened, and the air grew even more chilled. Many smells beset Owen and they all reminded him of the old crypts below ground in the Darien Mounds of Trew. Kegin never faltered and kept calling back to him every few feet as he carefully picked his way along the treacherous path.

Linne led the next group. A long procession of the survivors of Sweet Rock passed into the swirling gray mists. There was confusion at first, for the Olgnite army had thrown the perimeters of the Stewards dangerously near the edge of the Ellerhorn at places where entry would mean certain death. The Line warriors held, and after Gillerman began his spells they were able to hold their own and keep a way clear for an orderly retreat.

Emerald sent Elita with Linne and stayed behind with the remnants of the Steward squadrons, to keep the spidermen at bay until all got away into the safety of the gray mists of the fen. Stearborn's squadron was engaged on the right flank, with heavy attacks driving through his lines in places, and he signaled the minstrel to rally a small group to repel the solid ranks of enemy soldiers who poured over his position.

Gillerman's giant birds did the trick in the next breath, even as Emerald and Port led a relief force to beat back the Olgnites who had broken through the Steward lines.

"What in thunder?" roared Port, seeing the great black birds that wheeled and dived on the surprised Olgnites. "It's the prophecy of Trew himself!" The big man spurred his horse into a cluster of confused spidermen and, with all the fury of a crazed animal, killed or frightened away all of them, following along with his longsword, which ran with thick, foul-smelling black blood. Starboard was not far behind, and the two of them came dangerously close to being cut off from their lines when a renewed attack came from the left, where Chellin Duchin held his ground at the head of his own squadron. Jeremy wheeled about and brought a quick feint against the leading enemy charge, which allowed the brothers to retreat to safety.

"My thanks, pup!" bellowed Port, his face wild with the fire of the battle.

"And mine," echoed Starboard. "This will be a good day for Trew!"

Chellin reined in his horse next to the brothers. "We won't be able to hold them much longer! Get your squadrons ready to go into the fen. We'll keep the buggers back until you're in!"

"We can't leave you out here without some of us aboard to keep you braced against a flank sweep! They still have us cut short, coming on us like they are!" shot Starboard, looking to Port for agreement.

His brother was covered in blood and dirt, and his face was a mask of grim determination. "No son of Trew ever left a comrade in need, when it comes down to stand and deliver! I won't be the first to sully that good name!"

"Confound your eyes, you two will be the death of me quicker than one of these squashers! The path into the fen is so narrow, they can't mount a full attack, so there's no good holding back with me! Make for the fen now, so we can all get in before we're meat for this bunch!"

Starboard and Port drew to the side and conversed hurriedly, holding their restless mounts in check with some difficulty. The battle had intensified, then abated somewhat, and many of the Stewards nearest the entrance to the gray, misty gate of the fen had disappeared into the mysterious shroud.

"Come along, lads!" shouted Port, emerging from the discussion with his brother. "To the fen! Ride like the hounds of Trew are on you, and don't stop till you've gotten in!" He put the battered silver-and-gold horn to his lips and blew a short call, which was answered immediately. "We're off, then, you ill-tempered old goat! Look for us just inside the fen. We'll cover you from there!"

"No need," returned Chellin. "If what Famhart says is true, we won't need to bother with the Olgnites if they follow us. The bog is deep and never gives up its secrets!" Something in the enemy lines caught his attention, and he diverted his full concentration to the advancing horde of Olgnite warriors. There was one in particular that caught and held his eye. "Look at that devil, the one with the blue sash! What do you make of him?"

The brothers from Trew scoured the battle lines until they found the spiderman Chellin Duchin had spoken of. "Tall beggar to be one of them!" observed Port.

"He's got someone riding with him," continued Chellin. "I can't tell for all the dust being kicked up if it's a lieutenant of his or a prisoner! Not bound, as I can see."

As the Steward commander spoke, one of the huge birds of Gillerman swooped low over the heads of the Olgnites, drawing a shower of their black arrows that arced up through the air menacingly but seemed to pass through the elusive form without harming it. The smaller birds of the forests came, showering the spidermen's ranks with a hailstorm of the tiny pebbles they carried.

A groan escaped the Olgnite lines, and from somewhere in the depths of the drawn battle formations came a cry that was magnified and repeated, slowly swelling in strength until it fairly rang throughout the front, from one end to the other. "Stengils! 'Ware, spidermen! Stengils! The filthy beasts have dropped Stengils among us!"

Emerald drew up his horse near the gateway to the fen to wait for Stearborn and Chellin Duchin to lead their squadrons in, and for the brothers from Trew, who hung back dangerously close to the Olgnite front, continuing to strike with lethal accuracy even as they withdrew. There was something in the sight of the Olgnite leader and the rider that was next to him that held the minstrel's attention. A gust of wind cleared away the swirling dust kicked up by the pounding hooves, and he plainly saw Deros, held by a rope about her neck and led about by a giant spiderman with the blue sash. His mouth went dry for a moment, then a terrible anger boiled over inside him, making him clinch his fists until he drove his nails into his palm.

"They've got Deros," he announced in a deadly calm voice. "Send for Ephinias! I have to speak to Ephinias!"

A young Steward at his side saluted and trotted away, looking for the old master in all the confusion of the chaotic field, dodging the enemy shafts that constantly whirred and crackled through the air. The black arrows with yellow feathers stuck in the ground in such numbers that they began to look like a new plant that had sprung from the earth.

"I have to get this news to Owen," Emerald thought aloud. "We have to find a way to save the girl, or we won't be able to reach her old homelands." His heart pounded heavily beneath his tunic as he thought of Elita and how it would feel if it had been her captured by the Olgnites. A terrible fire began to consume him then, and his anger became white-hot.

Chellin Duchin reined in his horse next to the minstrel and

dismounted quickly to tighten his saddle girth. "This break will give us time to get into the fen," he grunted, looking back over his shoulder at the way the battle was progressing. "If the brothers will hurry the withdrawal, we could be out of here before those squashers have a chance to regroup."

"They have the girl," said Emerald, still looking at the distant figure held tightly by the side of the Olgnite leader.

"What? What girl? What's this you say?"

The minstrel pointed out the spiderman with the blue sash. "Look beside him. It's Deros!"

Chellin Duchin reached into his cloak and pulled out a small leather bag, carefully taking out a silver-colored tube and wiping both ends.

"The Elboreal always had a handy way with their hands, and I've cherished this little gift of theirs as the years have gone on." He extended the tube another inch and put it to his eye, rotating it back and forth to draw the scene he saw into clearer focus.

There in the midst of the Olgnite army was Deros, her face streaked with dirt and tears, an ugly length of black rope tied roughly about her throat. She seemed unharmed otherwise and was kept on a close tether, next to the large Olgnite who wore the blue sash across his battle dress and urged his followers on with a great deal of howling and clacking of fangs, taking obvious glee in jerking the unfortunate girl who was almost out of her saddle.

"It won't be easy to get her back," pronounced the old commander. "She's smack in the middle of the nest there. I don't know if we have anything left in reserve to try to rescue her."

"We have to," said Emerald wearily, feeling a sense of loss and frustration that grew within him. "There's no need going on without her."

Chellin looked at his friend and clapped him gently on the arm. "Today is as good as any to quit this life! I have always hoped my end would be something very like this! No chance of victory, but old Chellin Duchin put in his sword for the right side and fought his way to glory with one last run on the scourge from the Boundaries!"

"No need of that yet," replied Emerald. "Gillerman and

Ephinias are both with us. We may have recourse to something other than a main attack."

Port and Starboard arrived at that moment, winded and bloody. "We've given 'em something to remember us by," shot Port. "Old colors of Trew were always blood-red, and we've done well by that today!"

Starboard nodded, his exhausted arm hanging by his side, still clutching the longsword covered in the thick black blood of the slain Olgnite soldiers.

"We'll need more," returned Chellin. "Now we find out they hold the Lady Deros!"

"What?" echoed the brothers together.

"That's exactly who they hold," went on the minstrel. "I've sent for Ephinias or Gillerman to see if they can come up with a plan to help us get her back."

Starboard looked back. "Another four fresh squadrons would do it," he mumbled. "Or if your good master trickman could conjure up a plague that would finish the Olgnites' hash once and for all!"

Emerald's eyes lit up then, and he shook Starboard vigorously by the shoulder. "You're a wonder, my friend! I was lost here thinking of how we could never overpower them, when all the time it's a lesson of another color! Come on, Chellin! We have to find Ephinias!"

Emerald led the startled Steward commander away then, racing for the gate to the Ellerhorn, looking for his old teacher. Somewhere in the depths of the old man's mind the minstrel knew was the key to the girl's deliverance. He found Ephinias bent over the body of a small freckled wren, gently picking up the lifeless body, and taking from the tiny beak a small, glowing pebble that seemed to flare into life as it touched the old man's palm.

Into the
Enemy's Camp

Strange lights and noises had been seen and heard by the survivors from Sweet Rock as they wound their way deeper and deeper into the Ellerhorn Fen. The gray mists gave way to a muddy brown haze that distorted everything into grotesque forms and shapes and seemed to deaden sound. Owen had been shaken more than once by what appeared to be a four-armed shadow in front of him, with a horned head, only to find it was Kegin, riding a few paces before him.

There was the smell of old, rotting trees, and water that had been dead for turnings on end, mixed with the pungent aroma of some flowering plant that lent a sweet perfume to the other heavy, malodorous things that grew, then died, then crumbled away into decay.

Lights flickered briefly just beyond the fringe of the brown haze. They were dull reds or greens, and they came only a few times before the sounds started, and the sounds lasted still longer. Sometimes he heard the distinct sound of the sea, with waves washing against the shore, and the light-hearted cries of gulls, and at other times the wind through the tall, stout trees of some mountain valley. It seemed to Owen twice or thrice, that he actually heard snow slide off a fir branch and drop softly into the drifts below, but it was so subtle, he couldn't be sure.

Over all this he heard someone calling out his name from somewhere behind him. "Owen! Owen Helwin! Speak out, lad!"

Remembering the warning about the deceptive voices in the fen, Owen tried to make out who it was that called out so urgently.

It came again, much clearer and much closer to him. Seravan snorted and shook his mane. "It's Gitel and Ephinias," he said, pulling up of his own accord.

"It may be one of those lost souls in the fen," cautioned Owen. "We can't be too careful!"

"One of the lost souls in the fen wouldn't call to me as Gitel does! They can't see the thoughts of our race."

"Owen! Seravan!" called the voice again, closer still.

"Let them show themselves before we answer," warned Owen, throwing back his cape and loosening his longsword. As he did so, he saw the pale, golden-white glow softly coming from the scabbard, and when he removed it a few inches, the soft humming began.

"It must be them," He sighed, relief flooding through him. "Can you see Kegin ahead of us? I was worrying about who was behind us, I've slowed down."

"He is just ahead," answered Seravan.

"And those behind us? How has Ephinias gotten by them?"

The big animal chuckled a sound that resembled laughter. "His feet are not always confined to the path others must take. They are behind us, too, but they will have thought the voices were from the fen."

A looming shape, outlined in gray against the brown haze, moved forward toward them then, gliding so smoothly that it didn't appear to touch the soft, clammy earth of the fen.

"Ephinias," said Owen, "it *is* you!"

"Of course, my boy. I am always me—mostly—although I seem to remember some times I may have fooled myself."

The two horses stood side by side, engaged in their own discourse, while Owen and the old teacher dismounted.

"We have to go back, lad! It seems as though the spawn

from the wastelands have captured our young friend. It won't do to leave her!"

Owen's heart fell, and a leaden taste in his mouth made his tongue thick.

Seravan's voice grew more grave as he addressed the old man. "Have you seen her?"

"Stearborn sent word to Famhart not an hour past, and I have seen her myself, tied to one of those things. I came directly here once I found Gitel."

"Gillerman will be needed," agreed his mount. "The spidermen are crafty foes, and they have too many for us to fight."

"Where is Wallach? Is he anywhere about?" asked Ephinias. "There can't be too much help where the girl is concerned. We shall have the devil to pay if anything happens to her now."

"You speak as though you know some news," burst out Owen. "Are you up to more of your old tricks? You never tell us anything until after it happens!"

Ephinias frowned, growing thoughtful. "I guess it may seem that way sometimes. I think it's more likely that I've forgotten or just go on thinking that everyone is able to know my mind."

"What shall we do for Deros? How shall we rescue her from these beasts?"

"Easy does it, my young buck! Easy does it. I'm sure they are using her for bait, or else they wouldn't have bothered leaving her free for Stearborn to see! If I know anything at all of this lot, it's that they are brutal and savage and not too bright. Easy to read, I should say."

"They don't need to be anything else," broke in Kegin, returning to find his friends stopped on the dim trail through the fen and ready to berate them for slowing down their progress. He fell silent, seeing the stricken look on Owen's face.

"They have Deros," replied the lad, a numbness stealing over him that felt colder than the chill of the dark bog. "And we don't have the numbers to save her."

Owen stood beside Seravan, playing with the saddle straps and rearranging gear with a single-minded purpose until

Ephinias came to look at him evenly over the tall animal's back.

"There is a way, but it will be dangerous," he said.

"Everything is dangerous," shot the youth.

"It is a job for one," replied the old teacher. "I have just left Emerald. I told him of the idea I've had, and he says he will go along to make sure you reach the Olgnite lines."

Owen turned his face away from the old man's. "You know I would go," he said hotly. "But what good will my death do for Deros?"

"Not as you are, my boy," went on Ephinias. "I have a way in mind that won't stir up the spidermen until it's too late."

"Changing me with another one of your spells? What good would that be? Those devils devour the life of anything!"

"Not of their own," countered the old man, a wry smile crossing his worried features. In the dim light of the fen he looked much older and very tired. "We have a back door to use here. I would like to take Famhart in on our plan, if I could find him."

"He is to help guide the last of the group through," replied Kegin. "He and I know the fen the best, so we split up."

"A good thought. There are still many dangers, and it's never too wise to have all your arrows in one quiver."

"What mischief do you have up your sleeve, Ephinias? I begin to dread your answer when you get so closemouthed." Owen's thoughts were scattered, but he could only bear to let himself think momentarily of Deros in the hands of the hideous spidermen from below the Leech Wastes.

"Do you remember when the first Olgnite came on us in the room at Emerald's?" asked the old man. "When you were in the form of the dog?"

"How could I forget it?" snapped Owen.

"You recall I warned you about the blood of the spiderman and asked if you felt strange?"

Owen grew short in his impatience. "I remember something to that effect! Do I have to answer riddles while Deros is lost?"

"Not at all, my boy. I am merely pointing out to you something that I feared at the time, for in your guise of the dog you bit the spiderman's throat. There is a curse on them that affects any who are infected by touching their blood. It makes them dangerous, not only for who they are but also because they can cause you great illness or death in the very act of slaying them."

"I told you I didn't feel strange then! I don't now! It didn't affect me at all."

Kegin's interest was aroused by the discussion, and he wanted to hear the rest of it, but he knew they would have to move on, for the masses of the exodus of Sweet Rock were beginning to catch up to the leaders. "We shall have to go on now, sir. The path is a narrow one, and if we're not quick about it, the last ones into the fen won't have room to get in ahead of the spidermen!"

The old teacher nodded hurriedly. "By all means, go on. Owen and I shall stand clear here so the others can pass. Perhaps Famhart will find his way to us."

Kegin quickly mounted and turned his mount toward the murky brown light that hung over the trail ahead. "I'll try to get these folks on. If you have a need to signal me, I'll wait for our old code! You remember it from the Darien Mounds?"

"In my sleep, my friend," replied Owen. "The tune from Emerald's hornpipe dance. But it doesn't seem to go so well for us here above ground."

"Go on, lad! See the others through," ordered Ephinias, mounting Gitel.

Kegin rode on, leading Owen's party. "Take care of yourself, lad. I don't want to have to do any explaining to your father," he called.

"You look to yourself," returned Owen. "We'll see you in the Grealing Wood."

Ephinias watched the people silently as they filed past, their faces drawn and pallid in the eerie light.

"It's not a pleasant thought to be here after dark," said the old teacher. "I hear many strange things—"

"What do you have for me to do?" interrupted Owen brusquely. "Am I to go as a bird or as a dog?"

Ephinias saw the young man's difficulty and did not reprimand him for his rudeness.

"It is a difficult thing I ask, my boy, and a dangerous proposition as well."

"The Olgnite army is danger enough," snapped Owen. "We don't count anything after that."

"There are dangerous things that are beyond the mere threat of death, lad. What I am asking of you is one of those."

"What could be more dangerous?"

"Not dying," replied the old man, "and being unable to die, caught in a curse that would drag on and on over many turnings."

"Speak plainly! Ephinias, I can't understand all your shadowed speech."

"The beings who are in this fen are here because they could not learn a better way. They will eventually be freed from here, but until they are, every minute is a day, and every day an eternity, with nothing to do but boil in their own bitterness and revenge."

"Who are they?" asked Owen, his impatience waning as he studied the old man's intense features.

"They were from many clans who used to dwell here when this was a fair valley, and not this treacherous hole you see now. They pay for their misdeeds in a way that they shall remember."

A clammy wave of fear stole down Owen's back, and it seemed that the very ground they stood upon was alive with evil intent. "What curse are you talking about, Ephinias? Are you going to try to change me into an animal, so Seravan and Gitel and I can reach Deros?"

"An Olgnite, that's what I'm going to change you into," replied the old teacher, watching Owen's face intently. "You have touched the spiderman's blood, so I can do that. Otherwise nothing I could do would enable you to take that form, no matter what spell I used."

"You will turn me into one of them!" shouted Owen, his eyes widening.

"It's the only way to reach Deros. Once you and Deros are on Seravan and Gitel, the rest is fairly simple."

"An Olgnite," repeated Owen, making a sour face. "What if she doesn't know me?"

"She will know Gitel and Seravan." Ephinias paused, reaching out a hand. "The dangerous thing I spoke of, Owen, is that once I've enabled you to take on the spiderman's form, the curse may be so strong that I won't be able to call you back. That is something which is beyond me."

"What about Gillerman or Wallach? Surely they could make the switch."

"They can't overpower one's will. If the curse is strong, you will want to stay in the spiderman's form, and nothing we can do can make your will alter."

"You've never had trouble with changing us before," went on the young man, torn by thoughts of rescuing Deros and his fear of the spell Ephinias spoke of.

"You wanted your own form back. That's what I mean. There is a chance you will be chained like the rest of the Olgnite. They have a dreadful fate. I can't make you risk it, of course, and I'll understand if you refuse to try."

"Will I feel differently?"

"I don't know, Owen. I have never taken the form, so I can't say what you'll feel like. It might be nothing, or it might be a great temptation to have the power they wield."

Owen stood between the two tall animals, stroking both of them as he watched the ongoing procession of the survivors of Sweet Rock winding their way along in the wake of Kegin.

"We'll be with you," assured Seravan.

"And we'll try to keep you from going too far under the Olgnite spell," added Gitel.

"It may be our only chance to get our good friend back, lad. She will surely be lost if we don't try something, no matter how desperate."

"What would my father do now?" asked Owen. "Or Emerald?"

"Every man can only answer for himself, Owen. We all must face these things somewhere along the line. No one knows until it is time."

Owen drew himself up with a sigh and gritted his teeth. "Then let's start," he said, trying to center his thoughts on Deros, and his father, and the soft, throbbing light that once again had begun to hum through the longsword at his side.

A Splinter
of Evil

Inside the black mirror of night, a heavy river of breathing crept about Owen's awareness, buzzing softly at him like an unseen insect. Behind his eyes, visions of a blood-red sun rose up out of a greenish mist, and he could hear the awful roar of thundering voices, calling out in a dreadful tongue he could not understand but which grated on his ears and frightened him. As he reeled about the spiraling tunnel he had fallen into, the murmuring drone of Ephinias barely reached him. He could only faintly make out the words, and there were hideous images of great spiders with their killing fangs extended, and bloodshot eyes wide in excitement as they closed in on hapless prey.

Owen reached out to protect himself from the cruel monsters and was stunned to find his own arm covered with a coarse black fur. As he held his hand up closer to his face he saw the rough skin and the clawlike nails. A strange taste was in his mouth, salty and hot, and he realized he had bitten his lip. The taste gave him a strange, overpowering feeling of elation, and he wanted to experience it more. He struggled with a very dim part of himself that rebelled at the new intruder in his thoughts, but that other part was weakening, and the lust for more of the exciting feeling was growing more solid in his being.

A movement near him attracted his attention, and he craftily moved sideways to see what it was, and discovered an old man, dressed in well-worn riding clothes, looking anxiously at him. Dull and pounding, his blood began to hammer at his temples, and a great, overwhelming desire gnawed at his stomach, propelling him forward toward the helpless man, his newly discovered killing fangs dripping venom and clackingtogether in time to his heartbeat. Thoughts of sinking his fangs into the soft throat of his victim filled him with a thundering excitement and made him creep eagerly nearer, circling around his prey in a sideways walk, half crouched to spring.

Just as he prepared to move in for the kill, a tall horse came into his line of sight, stepping between him and his victim. Some voice from a dim hallway in his mind was speaking, but it was overpowered by the strong desire to slay the man and drink his blood.

"Hear me, Owen! This is Seravan! You have to hold to the sword Gillerman gave you or you'll be lost like all those other poor souls. Hold to the sword!"

It was a puzzling thing, hearing the animal speak, and his mind, covered as it was with the dim red haze, could not understand what it meant, but he obeyed the horse's words and sought out the hilt of the longsword at his side.

As Owen touched the cool handle of the sword of Skye, a slow awakening came over him, almost as though he were coming up from a deep lake of troubled dreams. A feeling of white heat ran through his arm and flashed in waves over his senses. Gillerman spoke hazily to him in a strange tongue. He swam in and out of focus, then there was a soft white glow surrounding him.

Owen heard Ephinias speaking to him very plainly. "Don't lose touch of the sword, lad! It's your only hope of staying clear of the spiderman's curse. They are very strong, and you can fall under their sway too deeply if you don't keep connected to something that will pull you back."

"I don't like this, Ephinias! Change me back! It's too horrible!"

"You will need this form, Owen. Our only hope of getting Deros back safely is for you to go in this guise."

A wild pain tore through the youth, but he heard himself say he didn't care. The ache around his heart grew so intense, he thought he would drop from it, but the dull roaring in his head called for gore, and his red eyes grew focused on the old man again, until the heat coming through his body from his hold on the sword calmed him once more.

Ephinias took out a small pebble from a hidden pocket in his riding cloak and held it out to touch his young friend.

A wild look of horror spread over the hideous mask that was Owen's face, and the spider form cringed and tried to get away from the dreadful thing that was thrust at it.

"Take it, Owen! Keep it in your cloak! It's a secret you can have as a last resort! You may need something to play a little extra surprise on our good Olgnites."

Owen recoiled farther from the small glowing stone, but Ephinias put it in the inside pocket of the cloak the young man wore.

"We shall have to go now," said Seravan. "It is a long way to where we must wait, and we shall have to go carefully, so our troops won't mistake Owen for the enemy."

"He certainly could be that," offered Gitel. "I feel spooked just having him here."

"If all goes well, it'll be over soon enough. We need only a little luck, and we shall be out and away before the spidermen know what's happened." Seravan replied.

Ephinias patted Owen's arm, in spite of the grotesque disguise, and managed a small chuckle. "I never thought I'd have to revert to these base tricks, but then I guess we're living in strange times. In my childhood there were rules for everything, and I always thought the rest of the worlds below the Boundaries were especially beautiful and offered much to learn."

Gitel neighed impatiently. "You should hear Wallach talk about all this! According to him, there never has been a good thing occur across any of the Lower Meadows, except the fact that you eventually are able to leave."

"Look where that got him." Seravan snorted. "Here we are still, off on another jaunt into one more dangerous place, hoping for the best and depending on a half-baked spiderman here to help us through! I swear by the Mare of Mareath, if I finish up this business with all my hide intact, I'm never going to come out of that beautiful back pasture up near Caldance Lake."

"Well said," agreed Gitel. "Now get this handsome fellow on your back, and be off for the eaves of the Belin Grove. That looks to be as good a place as any to wait. The Olgnites will be all over the area by nightfall."

"Come up, Owen," ordered Seravan gently, standing still to wait for the young man to mount.

Owen's eyes had grown more bloodshot, and he stared about balefully at his friends. "I want out of this form," he said, glowering. "You have to take me back!"

Ephinias shook his head firmly. "It's no use arguing with me! There is one way, and one way only that we shall be able to help Deros, and that's if you stay in this form, and succeed in reaching her. You are feeling strangely now, I dare say, but you'd hate yourself if anything happened to the girl, and you had stood by without doing something to help her."

The truth of that flickered briefly in Owen's heart, which was dangerously drawn to the blood-red misty visions of the spiderman's consciousness. He renewed his pledge to try to help Deros, but by the time he was astride Seravan, the other, colder part of him returned, and he had ony thoughts of killing and drinking blood to stop the awful emptiness he felt in the pit of his stomach.

"Take him now, and keep a weather eye out for him," cautioned the old teacher quietly. "Gillerman and I will be with you shortly, but here is our best chance of getting the girl through the camp and out to where you might be able to carry her on to safety."

"Wherever that might be," said Gitel mockingly. "I haven't seen anyplace I would describe that way since I was a colt."

Ephinias smiled sadly. "That seems to be the way of it below the Boundaries. I've been about down here for a few turnings, and I always come back to that place that reminds me I am still in the Lower Meadows."

Slowly a clumsy idea wound through Owen's consciousness, below the rage and bloodlust of the Olgnite form. The feeling was awkward and powerful, and consisted of a lovely young girl, such as he remembered Deros when she yet wore the disguise of a boy. There was music, sung by a familiar voice, and after a brief search for a name to put to it, the face of the minstrel appeared to him, seeming to speak, looking anxious and earnest. "Emerald," muttered Owen, having trouble mouthing the word and finding his speech thick and slurred.

"That's the slipper to wear, lad! Keep your mind open to your friends, and we shall see this through yet!"

"Windameir forever!" said Seravan, and he began to move lightly away, hardly disturbing a blade of grass in his passing.

"Windameir," repeated Gitel. "We'll see you in the Grealing Wood, Ephinias. Luck ride with you!"

"And you three," answered the old man, watching as the two horses moved away into the brownish mists of the fen. They had not gone more than a dozen paces before all trace of them had disappeared, and the sound of their passing was muted and swallowed by the dank air of the bog.

Ephinias waited a moment more, then took to the air in his hawk form to find Gillerman and to direct the two animals toward the leader of the Olgnites, who held Deros captive.

"I'm getting much too old for all this," he mumbled to himself as he lifted up on his wings and climbed slowly up into the patchy sunlight above the mists that shrouded the Ellerhorn Fen.

Below him he could see the winding procession of the survivors of Sweet Rock and, in the distance, the Grealing Wood. As he banked away toward the Olgnite lines, he saw the dark hordes through the woods, and the three small figures of Owen and the two horses working their way steadily through the treacherous footing of the bog toward the enemy positions. The young man was still astride Seravan, which relieved Ephinias, for he was gravely concerned that Owen might not resist the curse of the spidermen. He hadn't expected it to be so powerful, nor that Owen would undergo all the strong emotions he had witnessed. The main hope for the success of the rescue mission rested now with the two horses and the sword from Skye. Perhaps Owen could be kept under control long enough to grab Deros from her captors and get back to safety where Ephinias could quickly undo the spell.

Ephinias shook his wings in a graceful, gliding motion and rode down the back of the wind for one more close look at his young charge. Far in the distance he caught a brief glimpse of a silvery reflection all across the horizon and smelled the strong, salty presence of the sea, waiting patiently.

Distant Thunder

As the long afternoon wore on, the Steward squadrons held the Olgnite hordes at bay, until the last of the stragglers from the ruined settlement was safely into the gates of the Ellerhorn Fen. Stearborn brought up the rear and sat wearily in his saddle, talking quickly to a messenger he was sending ahead to Chellin Duchin, telling him he was preparing to withdraw and leave the entrance to the fen open for the spidermen. Between the two of them, they had devised a retreat that would hold many surprises for anyone following close upon them, and Chellin had gone ahead with the preparations and had his men set about the business of rigging the traps and snares along the path.

Another young orderly drew up beside Stearborn, who was still occupied with his messenger. "There's a lone Olgnite coming along the front of the lines, sir! It looks like he's come from the fen."

Stearborn turned to the new arrival, a look of surprise on his grizzled features. He'd had no sleep, so his eyes were red, and his voice came in the odd, rasping sounds he made in his throat from the old wounds. "How has a spiderman come to be leaving the fen? Are they in behind us, lad? Are there reports of that nature?"

"One rider, two horses," reported the young man. "He

bore away straight after he left the fen and set off north, making toward Sweet Rock."

"What the devil could that mean?" growled Stearborn. "They are a shifty lot, and there's no telling what mischief they've cooked up now."

"We could trail the one rider, to see where he's bound," offered the young Steward.

"He's bound for more of his friends, by any hook," snapped Stearborn. "I'd give a month's grog ration to know what he's been up to inside the fen, though! That tickles my fancy, that does, and old Stearborn never can pass up a mystery." The old commander knotted his brows into a dark mask that frightened his companion. "How would you think of a quick sortie, lad? You and me! The rest of the bucks can get the civilians on into this forsaken damp hole that's the Ellerhorn, and you and me can go back a bit for a good prowl around to see what this squasher is up to."

"Sir?"

"You can lay to it that there was something up when he found his way in and out of our lines and he didn't get drowned by that infernal mess of a bog."

"Do you think it would be wise to venture out there now, sir? We're surrounded on all fronts by the Olgnites."

"It wouldn't be wise, but then old Stearborn has never taken a fancy to anything above the practical. Beans and briny-bread, swords and shields, that's always been my tune, ever since I was a knee-whacker of a lad, getting my lessons at my old mater's lap, holed up in the high mountains where I was brought into this travail we call the life of a Steward."

Stearborn didn't give the young man time to reply and instead spurred his horse forward in the direction the lone Olgnite had been reported traveling. "Come along with you! This is a good time to stretch these old hides out! They've not had a good gallop in a day or two, and it's no good spoiling them with too much walking."

The young Steward hastily moved his mount after the old commander, checking his weapons on the fly. He had heard wild rumors about Stearborn but had not previously experienced the gruff commander's volatile habits or hasty decisions.

They had gone but a short distance when Stearborn picked up the heavy scent of the Olgnites. "They're all around here, lad! Keep a weather eye out and mark the trail back, so we don't get separated from our bolt-hole."

"This is where I saw him turn into the wood," reported the young man. "He went straight up this cut."

Stearborn reined in his horse and studied the faint trail that led into the denser part of the forest, which smelled heavily of the enemy troops. Bright sunshine lingered on the deep green of the leaves. There were no animal sounds, which spoke of the danger, and only a faint rustle of a breeze that barely moved the boughs of the trees and stirred up small dust motes in the golden light at the very bottom of the clearing where the two riders had drawn up.

"This is a poser, if ever I saw one, and I've seen a few," said Stearborn, speaking in a low voice. "I smell the Olgnites, but there's also something else here that I can't quite put my sword hand to."

"I don't smell anything," reported the young Steward, testing the air in great sniffing movements.

"Try for the easiest smell of all here."

"What's that?"

"The Olgnites! Smell it! It's heavy enough to choke you. If you were never to know another scent, you'd be able to find this one as easily as you would your sweetheart in the dark."

The young man sniffed cautiously back and forth, trying to detect the strong scent Stearborn described.

"It's not as easy as you say," he protested, then began to try again.

"Here! You'll never get the hang of it like that, my buck! You look like a teapot blowing in a quilting bee! Just turn your sniffer to it and heed what it has to say!"

Stearborn gazed intently away into the near distance where the edges of the deep forest began and pointed. "There's where our crafty snake has gone in! He's riding at a fair trot, but not like he was being chased. The horses aren't sweating that hard."

"You mean you can smell the horses?" asked the incredulous youth. "How could that be?"

Stearborn clucked his odd laugh, the air leaking through the old wound. "You keep your lot thrown in with me, my buck! We'll have you made into a passable scout before it's all said and shot." He threw a leg over his saddle horn and sat sideways for a moment, looking at the ground below. "The horses aren't from the Leech or anywhere else below the borders. They must have been captured from some of our lads."

"How can you tell that? It's all grassy here."

"The hoof print! That's easy enough to spot, even in this tall cover. They weren't by here long before us, and we Stewards use a regular shoe that's easy to spot. These aren't Steward stock, but they aren't enemy, either."

"It might be the other raiders we saw," suggested the young man.

"They're easy to peg, lad. They have a pattern that fairly shouts out that they're from a distance and of another country."

A change in the wind caused Stearborn to pause momentarily, staring away into the darker patches of the wood, where the shadows seemed to move and sway to the breeze in a way that caught and held the old commander's eye. "What handle do you go by, lad?" he asked, changing the subject.

"Morlin," replied the youth, saluting. "The Fourth Ash, but they've been badly hurt, and I don't know what's become of most of us."

"Picked up by the rest of the squadrons, like as not. The Fourth Ash was a good company. I'm sorry to hear you've had it so tight!"

Morlin's eyes began to well with tears but he caught himself, wiping them away with the back of his hand.

"We'll see who else we can find when we're safely in the Grealing Wood," said Stearborn. "There may be others of the Fourth who have come through just like you and had to hitch up with whoever was handy. That's the way of this business sometime. You think you'll get used to it one day, but that day never comes."

Morlin looked at the gruff old commander, surprised by the softness of his tones.

Stearborn cleared hs throat and went on in a more severe manner. "Let's ride just a bit farther and see where this queer bird has landed. I sense he's very close!"

A rustling in the air above caused the two Steward warriors to look up quickly, for neither of the two had heard the wing beat until it was almost upon them. The younger man was struggling to free his longsword when Stearborn reached across his horse and stayed his hand.

"Pull up, lad! This is an old friend if I'm not mistaken!" The powerful hawk descended gracefully and alit on the outstretched arm Stearborn held out. "Greetings, good hawk! Do you have news of a nature that might tickle the scruff of an old soldier? Or maybe help him keep his hide intact for a day or two longer?"

Clutching Stearborn's arm with his strong talons, Ephinias rocked back and forth once or twice to steady himself, then turned his sharp, piercing yellow eyes upon the man.

"We have set in motion a plan to retrieve the Lady Deros," he said in a thin, scratchy voice. "But we've had to use a gruesome ploy that I fear has more far-reaching consequences than I had mind of."

Morlin, struck dumb in amazement at the sight of the bird perched on Stearborn's arm, and amazed at its speech, made a slight motion to clear his throat but was drawn up short when the bright yellow eyes turned on him.

"You two have seen Owen?" Ephinias asked.

"Not passed by us, he hasn't," answered Stearborn. "Have you seen the lad, Morlin?"

After a short, deep breath the young man was able to reply in the negative by shaking his head, since he still could not find his voice.

"Then you may not have known you've seen him," continued Ephinias, chuckling with a raspy bird noise.

"We were following an Olgnite who has just come from the fen," explained Stearborn. "We would have seen Owen if he were about! My old eyes aren't gone so bad as that!"

"Your eyes are keen as pins, old friend, no doubt! But sometimes there's more to a sword than its sheath! You have to look inside to find the blade."

"Always the riddles, you old trick master! One of these days we shall see the time when you speak bib side out, and no froth to confuse us!"

"I'm not making riddles here. The spiderman you saw was leading another horse?"

"Aye, that he was."

"Then it was Owen, with Seravan and Gitel."

Stearborn's eyes narrowed, and a terrible scowl darkened his face. "Have they taken Owen? Curse their bloody souls!"

The hawk was almost upset from his perch as Stearborn swung around in his saddle. "He is safe enough for the moment, but I have had to give him the Olgnite form so he could get into their midst. There was no other way to get to the girl."

"Was he willing?" asked the old Steward. "There is a grave danger there. I have heard tales at the fires that a man can be drawn under that curse that is the Olgnite bane."

"He was reluctant, but he has pride where the girl is concerned. But after I gave him the form, he asked to be brought back."

"And you refused?"

"Seravan and Gitel are with him. And he has the sword of Skye."

"He's very young, Ephinias. This may be a sore test."

"He is the new Elder! That will count for something, and he was the only one who I know, other than the girl, who has touched the blood of an Olgnite and not sickened! Back in Sweet Rock, he was exposed to it. I could give him the form because of that."

"I've touched their blood enough this day," growled Stearborn. "The wood and fen run with the foul, black stuff!"

"Is there a sickness that goes with it?" asked Morlin, studying his hands closely. "I have slain two of the spidermen today."

"Only if you touch it to your lips, lad, or if it has been spilled near your stores or water."

The young Steward dismounted, examining his water and saddlebags.

"So Owen is dressed out now as a squasher," mused Stearborn. "All the more reason I should stay out here to keep an eye out, so he doesn't run afoul of any of the other squadrons. You can't tell one of those blackguards from another!"

"I was following along for the same reason and will return him to his old form as soon as the errand is through. There's no need leaving him in that tormented prison any longer than need be."

"Shall we wait out here to help Owen and Deros?" asked Morlin.

"There are enemy troops all about you here," warned Ephinias. "There is a clearing just ahead, under the eave of the wood! It's clear for the moment, and it's not far from where Owen and his horses are."

"Will they come back this way?" questioned Stearborn, checking his weapons."

"I will lead you. Keep an eye out for me, or for the white falcon. We will show you where to look and tell you where the enemy is."

"Shouldn't we have reinforcements? The two of us will be no good in a pinch!" said Morlin.

"We aren't out to do battle, my buck, just to lead Owen and the girl back safely once they're free of the Olgnite lines."

As they talked hurriedly, a small patrol of the enemy soldiers rode out of the shadow of the wood a good distance from where they sat and set off at a gallop along the edge of the fen in the opposite direction.

"Looking for a way in, I suspect," said Ephinias. "This is one problem I don't think our good spidermen were looking for. It's their sort of place, though. I'm surprised they hadn't discovered it long ago."

"There's more!" whispered Morlin urgently. "Just there! Coming this way!"

"Look to it, my good friend! Keep your eyes to me and I'll try to steer you away from these louts. Good hunting!"

Without another word the powerful bird lifted away from Stearborn's arm with a vibrating wing beat that sounded like claps of distant thunder. As he rose higher still, the two Stewards heard him call "Good hunting," once more, then he turned gracefully in the air.

Hawk and
Falcon

Deep inside the Ellerhorn Fen, neither Famhart, nor Linne, nor any of the others saw the sleek hawk as he circled about the rafters of the long, blue afternoon sky, watching a grotesque Olgnite warrior waiting silently in a thicket beside a clearing. There were two horses there that stood motionless as statues. The long, golden sunlight buzzed alive with the drone of the bluebottle and bee, and there was a faint trace of burned sulfur, or the smell of dead water from mires long gone sour. The hawk kept a wary eye out for the two Stewards who stole carefully along, out of sight or hearing of the Olgnite patrols that ranged throughout the thicker parts of the woods.

A great commotion had been stirred up where the Olgnite leaders' held their council. A great many messengers came and went in a drumbeat of hooves and dust. Deros was led about the inner camp by her captor, who cruelly lashed her across her back with the hard leather riding crop he carried. All the enemy troops nearby boomed in unison to her cries, with resounding shouts of "Olga, Olga," and dark war chants that filled the wood until it reached the ears of the fleeing Steward party, winding their way ever deeper into the unforgiving fen.

Ephinias circled high above, watching the enemy encampment, marking every detail in his head, and trying to discover a weakness which would allow Owen and the two horses to reach the repulsive Olgnite chieftain who wore the distinctive blue sash. Subordinates scurried back and forth with maps, or cases filled with bottles and glasses so the officers could drink gruesome toasts in the blood of their unfortunate captives. The old teacher could see the makeshift compound where the prisoners were held, constructed very like a cattle pen from the settlements of The Line. Unmoving bodies lay there, spun tightly into the foul black coils of the spidermen's webs.

Ephinias lifted his eyes toward the horizon, where he could see a pale glint of the reflected sun from the sea, and spotted the tiny figures far down the river, making their way slowly in the direction of the Olgnites. "What's this?" he called aloud. "More carrots for the stew?"

A tiny white dot in the distance grew larger, slowly coming toward him, and he recognized the graceful white falcon as it neared, gliding down the blue sky's back in an effortless motion. "Greetings, windwalker! Who are our visitors from the river?"

"My service, skyrider! We are seeing more of the ones from the Silent Sea. Hulin Vipre?"

"Come to reinforce their brothers," replied Gillerman.

"They'll need more than those few to undo the Olgnites."

"They don't appear to be in that line of work," said Gillerman, hovering near the hawk. "They are after the girl. She has told enough of her tale to convince me of that."

"Just when we think we have a clear path to sail, something stirs the water until it's muddy," answered his friend.

"Wallach has been after a lightning bug in the dark for some time now."

"What lightning bug? What's Wallach been up to?" asked Ephinias in exasperation, not used to his own medicine.

"He's been traveling in the territory of the Silent Sea, and on a certain few islands there in particular. I don't think the

Hulin Emperor thought there would be such a force to reckon with in these parts."

"Neither did we," countered Ephinias curtly. "I can't imagine what I was doing that I overlooked the magnitude of this bloodthirsty lot of Olgnites."

"The same as always, my friend. We see only what we are given to see. No one could have been alerted to the trouble along the borders of the Leech before it was too late."

"It's well beyond that now. I doubt there is anywhere in these lower parts that is free from the threat of the spidermen, if even the Line Stewards haven't been able to contain them."

The great falcon veered slightly and rose higher to get a better look at the approaching Hulin Vipre.

"The Line Stewards will have help from another source. It won't be the extra bow arms, or swords that do the deed, but a rather more simple answer, as always."

Ephinias winged his way higher, to be beside his old friend and mentor. "It will have to be something quick as well. If Owen takes Deros from the Olgnites, then there will be no holding back the lash of their fury!"

"That is the one thing we can count on," countered Gillerman. "We must always take into account the most obvious parts of the riddles we seek to solve."

"That doesn't take a thinker to decipher. Look at the woods below us! It fairly crawls with the spidermen!"

"A rule of thumb is that everything always balances," returned the falcon. "Even when we don't readily see it."

"I see a serious problem in balance here," cried Ephinias, spotting a roving patrol of the Olgnites, which was moving perilously close to the two Stewards who followed behind Owen.

He plunged downward until he was a blur of speed, then pulled up short of the treetops just above the spidermen's patrol, letting out a high-pitched screech that caused them to rein in their horses, and send a volley of misdirected arrows upward at him. Ephinias lit in a tall fir that concealed him and began to recount aloud all the ways an Olgnite could be slain. "Blood of the black bottlefly and grime from the fireside of a farmer," he called. "Leaves from the Holy Trees of the Lone Sound and music of a reed flute after dark."

"Curse this mite!" roared out the Olgnite leader. "Bring me his eyes! Don't let him escape!"

Arrows flew near Ephinias. He easily evaded them with his quick bird movements. "Blood! Blood!" roared a chorus of the Olgnites, drumming swords against shields. Thundering hoofbeats pounded in the thicket below him, and the noise and signal horns were so loud and strident that the old teacher was sure his friend Stearborn would hear and find a safe way around the enemy soldiers.

High above, Ephinias saw the tiny white form of Gillerman turn into a cloud, which resembled a fortress with a tall watchtower. Ephinias was so engaged trying to decipher the meaning of the cloud shape, he was almost tumbled from his perch. The Olgnites had taken great double-headed axes to the trunk of the tree he sat in.

He flew cautiously, keeping to the shadowy depths of the treetops until he was sure he was out of range of the enemy arrows. The Olgnites were still raging about where he'd left them, cursing and shouting, and a savage cry went up at the sound of a great tree crashing to the ground below him.

Ahead, and nearer the river, Ephinias saw the first of the strange boats the Hulin Vipre had used to travel upriver from the sea. If they had been discovered by the Olgnites, they had been left unharmed to lure the fleeing settlers and Stewards. These boats were useless now, for the only escape was through the Ellerhorn Fen, and that would bring them out in the Grealing Wood, close to the River Line, but far beyond these boats.

"I wonder if these new reinforcements will stop nearer the wood," thought the old teacher aloud, nearing the spot in the clouds where Gillerman had disappeared.

Ephinias almost bumped beaks with his friend as he flew into the mist. The two birds veered to avoid a collision.

"More men, more boats," reported Gillerman. "This may prove to be a blessing yet. I've been so caught up in these times, I can hardly remember from one day to the next all the lands we're supposed to keep watch on, and all the tribes and clans that need a bit of counsel now and then."

"And, of course, we come to the Olgnites, who have no need of our counsel and want nothing more than to have a warm victim to feed on."

"Nasty lot, but they've kept the borders of Leech free from any other marauders! Very like those fishes with all the teeth that keep the seas swept clean of the lame or dying."

"No lectures on the overall rightness of things, please," begged Ephinias. From this height he could see that Stearborn was safely beyond the enemy patrol and very near Owen's position, where the young man had stopped to await sunset, when he could try to slip into the Olgnite camp unchallenged. "Keep an eye to these new brigands on the river! I have to go down now to see if I can guide my young spiderman into this nest of vipers. If there are any fireworks, I hope you'll see to it we aren't disturbed too much?"

"You have my oath, old fellow, if I have to hold the lot of them back with my beak."

"Thank you," called Ephinias, already descending silently on the wind, dropping out of the late-afternoon sunlight onto a tree limb above the heads of Stearborn and Morlin, who at the moment were dismounted, and were talking over what should be done next. They were discussing the Lame Parson, a legendary figure who roamed at will throughout the Lower Meadows collecting a following of stragglers and outcasts of all the settlements and who was credited with knowing the whereabouts of the Sacred Grove, where the Three Trees grew. He was not lame, although he went about with the aid of a vicious-looking staff, carved with the likeness of a bear. Ephinias had come across the man once in a small glen, and had taken tea with him.

"They say he might have taken up with the Dark One," Morlin was saying, pouring out a small amount of water into his hand and splashing it onto his face.

"Aye, that's been said both softly and harshly, by them with grudges and them who fear him! I can't say of any of it, for I've not come upon the man, for good or ill, in all my turnings carrying the banner of the Line Stewards."

"Then he might be dead, for all we know."

"Might be, but I wouldn't count any too much on that. Most of the stories these last few years say he's gone for a sailor and has been biding his time out on the salt sea, searching for the way past the Elven Roads to the Havens."

Morlin studied the old commander earnestly. "Do you put any store in any of those tales of the elves, sir?"

Stearborn laughed his short, wheezing, staccato bark. "Damn my old bones, but I do, lad! I've seen things that would set your eyes straight out of your head." The gruff old chieftain's smile softened, and he nodded his head twice in rapid succession. "Made you feel all good inside to be around 'em, it did, though it weren't too comfortable. Never knew which way the wind would blow with them and it took a fair time to get over it when they packed up their kit one night and hightailed it out of all our lives, going without a word to anyone."

"Gone?"

Stearborn nodded. "The day they left, it rained all the way through till the stroke of mid-watch, just like the sky was crying over their passing."

Morlin couldn't be sure, but there was something very like tears brimming in the old Steward's eyes for a moment, but it was only for the barest moment, and then Stearborn busied himself tamping down a piece of sod at his boot tip.

"It was a sad day," added Ephinias from his high perch above the two men. "And the Parson has been gone from sight almost as long as the Elboreal, although no one could say for sure if that boded good or ill for most of the settlements."

Looking up, Stearborn gave a little salute to the hawk.

"Owen's just beyond here," reported Ephinias, "and the Olgnites have their main camp not more than a few good bow shots farther on. We'll wait for dark, then the lad will be free to move."

"I don't like this waiting," complained Morlin. "The sun will be down in an hour, and then here we'll be stuck out here with the Olgnites all around us, waiting for someone who looks just like the rest of them!"

"He'll have the girl, with any luck," replied Ephinias. "And they'll be on Seravan and Gitel."

"Horses all look alike in the dark," muttered the young Steward.

"These won't. Keep your eyes tuned for the kind of light that looks like a lantern glow, only brighter. It will mark our man and let us know one from another."

"Is he going to be carrying a lantern out here?" asked Morlin in an exasperated tone. "The last thing we need is to be spotted."

"The lad is a bit loose in his logic," apologized Stearborn. "I haven't had time yet to tell him any of the better stories of all the goings-on that happen when you're hooked up with interesting folks like yourself."

"He shall be surprised in more than a few ways, then," replied Ephinias, laughing lightly but always keeping one eye on the sky, watching for Gillerman.

A scattering of clouds had begun to drift over the wood, covering the sun for a moment and creating deeper shadows in the thicket where the two Stewards stood talking to the figure of the hawk perched in the tree. The breeze that sprung up had a chill to it, as though it were remembering winter, and Morlin wrapped his cloak more tightly about him. "Blast this wood," he complained. "It has all the dampness of a bog."

"Not so much as we'll have a chance to see before this is all over," returned Stearborn, his eyes and ears straining to read any new threat on the wind. "Once we get our spider-man and the girl safely back, we still have the Ellerhorn."

The young Steward's spirits were thoroughly quashed by that news.

"It's the only way open to us now," confirmed Ephinias, readying himself for a quick flight to see how the lay of the land was, and to find news of Owen.

Olgnite signals from both sides of them erupted at once, and the hawk strained upward to find a high corner of sky from which he might watch, calling back over his wing to stay low and not give away their positions. Owen had heard the signals, too, and had turned to Seravan for an explanation when the two spidermen came crashing through his hiding place, riding hard. A dim part of Owen reacted out of fear, and he began to draw his longsword, but the other part of him stayed the weapon, and he held up a gaunt claw in greeting.

"Quick, Olga, ride for the fen! Ride like a blade of doom for Olag! We have to round up our troops now! We strike tonight!"

Owen's hackles bristled, but he managed a grunt in reply and mounted Seravan.

"We have news for the Olag that will please him." One of the spidermen cackled, his laughter making his killing fangs clack, a deadly rhythm that sounded like dry bones rattling in the wind.

"No way out but one," roared the second warrior. "It all goes only to one place, and there we wait!"

"No way out, so little pinkers get out of one corral into another! I hope they don't walk too much juice off!"

Owen's mind grew clouded with the red haze again, and he heard his fangs clacking together in reply to the Olgnites. The three of them galloped through the wood, deeper into the heart of the sprawling Olgnite war camp, until just at sunset, they drew up in the inner circle, where the blood-red tents of the Olag lay, surrounded by hundreds of spidermen and lit by the dirty orange glow of dozens of watch fires that had been built in preparing for the coming night.

The Archaels

As the last dim rays of the muddy light faded into a black shroud, Kegin lit a torch and watched as the wavering, pale flares behind him grew in number, until there was a snake-like procession of lights, running on until they were swallowed in the distance.

"It will be easier by night," said Kegin to the point man who moved steadily along his side. "Now I can tell how far ahead of the others we are."

"I don't want to get too far in this hole," answered the man, who was a young conscript from the school of bakers. "There are eyes watching us!"

All along the path, to both the right and left, Kegin could feel the eyes, rather than actually see them. "There's nothing to fear from them if we don't listen to them or miss our path."

"It's getting darker and harder to see. Maybe we should pull up for the night!"

Kegin shook his head resolutely. "Can't stop here. Famhart is behind us, and he expects us to go on until we clear this bog. The Grealing Wood is our way out!"

"If we reach it!"

"We'll reach it if we go slowly. I've been through this fen before. It can be traversed, but you have to keep your wits about you."

"My wits are plucked tight as bowstrings already!"

"So are everyone's. It's no good thinking about it."

The young conscript moved on in a sullen silence for a few paces and drew up so suddenly that it caused Kegin to bump headlong into him. "What's gotten into you? Why have you stopped?"

"L-look," stammered the young man, pointing in front of them to a pale, shimmering light that moved slowly about in a circular motion a few feet above ground, not more than a stone's throw away.

Kegin already had his signal horn ready to sound a warning, and his sword at the ready. "Slip back until you meet whoever is coming next behind us! Tell them to pass back the word to ready their weapons!"

"Who can this be? I thought we were the only ones who knew the way in here!"

"Now somebody else knows," snapped Kegin, his thoughts racing through all the grim possibilities. When he had first made an attempt to chart the path through the dangerous bogs, he had met no other travelers, and knew of no one who would venture into the mire. The dreadful stories of the curse reminded him that the ghostly lights were nothing they wanted to meet in the darkness that grew ever deeper as the sun's rays were absorbed by the cold, dank heart of the Ellerhorn Fen.

The lights went out, just as quickly as they had appeared.

"Are we seeing things? Weren't they there just then?"

"Keep your weapons ready," admonished Kegin, calling a halt until those behind could come up. "This is no place for a fight, but it won't be to their liking either, whoever it is."

"Or whatever," added the young man. "It may be the Olgnites. Maybe they're gone around the fen!"

"Not enough time," shot Kegin, trying to convince himself. As he turned his jumbled ideas around in his mind, Linne arrived.

"Why have we stopped, Kegin?"

"You and Elita should be behind us. We've seen lights ahead."

"Lights? How could that be? Is it Ephinias?"

"No, my lady, I don't think so. He always likes his fun, but he would have made himself known to us by now."

"There are no lights now. It may be nothing more than a trick of the bog. I've heard of things like that."

"These were lights, right enough, my lady. Bright as you please and moving around," reported Kegin, still trying to pierce the pitch darkness in front of them, listening intently. "Let's call a halt, to see if there is any noise ahead. Pass the word back."

The young man hurried along the procession, making its way behind Kegin, and soon disappeared into the hazy mist that blurred the lights, making everything very dreamlike. Very gradually the muffled sounds from the line behind grew still, with only the occasional jingle of a pack harness or the creak from a saddle breaking the growing stillness.

Linne moved unexpectedly beside Kegin, startling him.

"I'm sorry, Kegin. I guess we're all too tense."

"Shhhhhhh! Listen, my lady! Ahead of us! It sounds like bells!" Linne tried to calm her racing thoughts, and to stand still long enough to try to hear what Kegin described as bells. At first there were other noises from the movement of the settlers from Sweet Rock, or the Stewards who guarded them, but soon she began to perceive, very faintly and right at the outer realm of her hearing, what seemed to be tiny chapel chimes, dusting the air with their fine, tiny peal. "I think we had best see to this," said Linne, straightening and turning her drawn face to Kegin.

"Shall we wait for Famhart?"

"He should stay with the rear guard. No one else is as familiar with the fen, and he should stay there to guide them."

"Then we should send scouts! I don't like this dead-water hole any too much, and I certainly don't like it now, when we can't see beyond our rush lamps."

"If they had intended us harm, they wouldn't have lit the lamps to warn us. That would make no sense."

"You may have something, Linne. I hadn't thought of it that way."

"It may also be some other of our allies who have sought refuge in the fen."

Kegin held his guttering torch out before him, peering so intently into the darkness that he failed to see the round figure of a face right before him. It was shrouded in a hood and wore a dark beard, but the eyes were clear blue and had a friendly sparkle.

When the man spoke, Kegin jumped back so suddenly, he almost upset Linne.

"A fair wind to ye, travelers! What fine business brings you into the Grimpen Mire this night?"

Kegin took so long to answer, the man turned to Linne, who seemed less shocked at the sudden appearance of the odd apparition than her companion.

"We are fleeing the Olgnites, sir, and have found this to be the only place we have a chance to elude them."

"Olgnites, eh! *Blackhearts* is the word for them, and a hand to your crossbolt to drive 'em back where they crept out from!"

"Good adwice to anyone," agreed another voice, and a second man appeared beside the first, looking much the same in feature and dress.

"What colors do you fly?" asked the first man. "Dalman or Glenin?"

"I don't know the ones you speak of," said Linne. "We are of the Line and are under Steward banners."

"I knew they weren't Dalman," affirmed the second figure. "You can always spot their kind by the tattoos and hair! Wery hard to miss."

"Wery," confirmed the first. "You don't wear the skin pictures, by any length, do you? Charming custom but hard to come by."

"You've always hankered for that fancy brightwork, Findlin, even though you know it's the dreads to endure while they do it!"

"Rightly so, rightly so, Lorimen! Does a body good to see it through! Clears up the smoke in the chimney, if you get my drift."

"I do, but I don't think our good cousins here mind the course we'we set! Pay no heed to us, good wanderers, we're folk of another nature, sometimes contrary by trade or whim, but we mean well to all who mean well to us!"

Kegin recovered himself enough to speak to the strangers, although he was still shaken by their appearance in the depths of the Ellerhorn Fen. "How come you to be in the Ellerhorn?" he asked. "This is no place for anyone to be without the direst of reasons."

"Dire? Reason? The Grimpen Mire is but a backyard to us, and we harbor here from time to time to tend to a few simple duties that require some place priwate."

"Findlin is the Chamberlain of Fionten, and as such must carry out the postures of manhood whenewer it's required."

"We have come to introduce our good lad Enlid to the mysteries and workings of the Book of Dreams. It's done ewery time we exchange an old man for a younger leader."

"Dead, you know," said Findlin. "The old ones keep doing that to us, and we're forewer aggrawated by this perplexing state of affairs. Young Enlid seems to be of a more permanent sort, though."

Lorimen agreed, nodding vigorously. "Topping bloke, just turned his twentieth quartet. Should outlast all of us."

The rush lamps had appeared again as the small party talked, and in twos and threes the settlers from Sweet Rock began to gather where their guide had come to a halt, speaking to the strangers. There was a murmured rush of speech that passed back and forth among those who couldn't see what was happening, who didn't know the cause of the delay.

"I'll go speak to the others," offered Linne. "They'll work themselves into a fright if I don't calm them now."

"Who shall, good lady? The Archaels pose no threat to any who wander this bog, unless they be of black blood or intend harm to those who can't arm themselwes!"

"Thank you, good sir," answered Linne. "We of the Stewards hold to that same code."

"Can we pass on through?" asked Kegin. "We may need to have a clear way to the coast soon, if the Olgnites break into this dead water here!"

"The coast? That's where we're going, as soon as we finish our errand here."

Linne returned from her task of sending messengers to explain the unexpected delay to the others and directed a question at Findlin. "Have you come through from your side of the fen this night?"

"Aye, my ladyship, and the night before as well. We hawe a camp clear of this bog, so that we can sleep easy while we await the boy."

"What boy? Is there a boy with you?" asked Kegin. "We're looking for one of our own now. He is trying to rescue a friend from the spidermen."

Findlin shook his head slowly. "Such a dangerous task to place on the shoulders of a young man! But the lad we await is Enlid, our newly grown Carinbar. His rituals hawe already been half done, and all that remains is that he come through this bit of the Grimpen Mire."

"It sounds as dangerous as what Owen has to do," replied Linne. "I would never have let my son go with Ephinias if I'd known what the old fox were up to!"

Kegin flushed, looking at his boots. "I had no say, Linne! Ephinias told me I was needed to lead the others, because I've been through the Ellerhorn from the North Wood all the way to the Grealing."

"It's not your fault, Kegin. I'll have a word or two with Ephinias when next I cross his trail. He knows to watch out for my tongue."

"You say your son is trying to steal a prisoner from the Webling? What a dreadful danger he faces! They are the worst of our banes, and we seem to hawe so many these last years."

"Do you quarter near Swan Haven?" queried Kegin. "We have allies there."

"We know Swan Hawen, but our hunting grounds are farther east, in a place named Fionten," answered Lorimen.

"Those are places beyond my ken," said Kegin. "But I know that the Southern Fetch runs on eastward for a time."

"On and on," returned Findlin. "You could sail around until you met yourself again, trying to find the end of that stretch of water."

Linne returned to the subject of the boy the two strangers spoke of, leveling a stern glance at Kegin. "What is the task you've set for the young man of your party? What has he to do in this dreadful place?"

"To touch the heart of it and unite with us tomorrow in this place."

"Has he light? And arms?" asked Kegin. "If not, he'll be at poor odds to be moving about freely in the dark."

"He has only his wits to protect and guide him," said Lorimen. "That is the ritual that all the Carinbar must fulfill in order to take the duties of leading our scattered clans."

Kegin looked gravely at the two strangers. "I hope that won't prove his undoing," he said. "These are not times to be unarmed and without friends."

"Oh, the lad has his friends, and more, to watch over him. We hawen't let him get too far beyond our reach."

"I don't think you understand the nature of the threat, good strangers," explained Linne. "All our settlements in the Line have been burned, and all our people are now on the road through the Ellerhorn, looking for a new start at the sea. The Olgnites have massed all their numbers into a gruesome army that's marching behind us, destroying everything in its path."

Lorimen and Findlin looked at each other blankly.

"The Webling hawe done all that?" asked Lorimen.

"And more. We've barely eluded them this far, and even now they are at our gate to the Ellerhorn, trying to find a way in to capture all that's left of our company to feed on!"

The two strangers held a hurried conference, then drew up their hoods to take their leave. "We hawe to find Enlid now, but we'll wait at the growe that ends this mire. We may be able to join our bands until we reach the coast."

"The Grealing Wood," said Kegin. "That's where we're bound. Can we help you with your search?"

"Findlin has probably told you more than he should," scolded Lorimen. "Our most sacred rituals have newer been known to anyone outside the Archaels."

"Your secrets are safe enough with us," comforted Linne. "We are all at risk of death here, and there may be no more rituals from any side that will survive, other than the Olgnites." Linne offered her hand to the two strangers, who seemed anxious to be on their way. "You have the poor help we can offer you, now or at the Grealing Wood. We shall have need of all the numbers we can muster, if we must fight the Olgnites on the other side of the fen."

"We hawe a party waiting at the growe, and more down riwer at the coast," said Findlin. "We can muster two hundred men."

"Better than none at all, but we could use ten times that number." Kegin saluted and turned back to his own troop. "We may as well get on with it. I think we've jammed up the road here long enough."

"Farewell, my lady! May luck ride with you!" said Findlin, and he returned Kegin's salute.

Lorimen's face was pale beneath his hood, as he, too, saluted and turned to proceed on into the darkness of the fen ahead. A sudden flash of light caught his eye, and he grabbed his companion, dragging the surprised man away before he could say another word, and the two of them disappeared from sight only a few feet beyond Linne. There was the distinct peal of small bells then, barely dusting the air with their faint sounds. Kegin turned to speak but was cut off by the unearthly shriek that tore through the dank air, setting all their hair on edge. It came again, and their party moved forward once more, weapons at the ready.

Secrets of
the Fen

The giant lurched forward out of darkness, trailing a great ax behind him. His face was a hideous green, with a dangling jaw that reached almost to his chest and eyes that shone a dull red from sunken sockets. He made the unearthly sound again, which echoed in his throat like a grating reply and which sent chills down the backs of all who saw the horrendous figure.

Lorimen and Findlin came tumbling back, their eyes wide in terror. "Bogmots!" they whispered hoarsely. "The worst of them all!"

Kegin had notched an arrow to his bowstring and released the shaft straight at the giant's heart, but it simply vanished through the huge figure, dispelling the image of the giant into a billowy wisp of greenish-gray mists.

"Bogmots!" confirmed Lorimen. "They always trick you like this to protect themselwes."

"You can tell the real ones by their eyes," added Findlin. "The real Bogmots have no color to their eyes. It's eerie to look upon, but you can tell the real ones that way."

Linne had undone the packet at her saddle and strung the small, strong bow that was there, wrapped safely in the sealing cloth she had received as a gift from the Elboreal. "I have elven darts here, Kegin. They are forged and fashioned in the Havens and carry enough of that magic to perhaps waylay anything from this bog."

"The bells work as well," said Lorimen. "We hawe the elven bells that are used to rest weary bones and to let the small ones know they are among friends."

"You know of the Elboreal? Have you ever seen them?" asked Kegin.

"Their roads cross our lands in a place or two. An elf can't get back to his proper place without going past the Archael's front porch. Many's the time I'we watched those fair ships ply those waters beyond the Horinfal Straits, outbound for the holy waters where the Elboreal hold their most sacred of rituals."

"Have you ever crossed paths with my friend Ephinias? He's the one to know whether or not an arrow will hurt whatever these things are." Kegin's brow was furrowed, and a thin trickle of perspiration made his eyes burn.

"Rings no note for me," replied Findlin. "Is he a powerful man?"

"Very." Kegin nodded. "But always somewhere else when you need him most."

"It does seem that way sometimes, I swear," said Linne. "I'm sure he's watching over Owen now, though, and I would rather him be there."

A howl of fear swept through the procession behind the small group as they talked, and as they turned, they could see the pale, greenish wraith moving about among the lamps and hear the screams of women mixed with the more strident calls of the men.

"What are these things?" Kegin gasped, trying to find a clear shot with his bow.

"Bogmots, friend! Bogmots are the worst, most wicious sort. We'we only seen them a few times, but they always signal disaster." Lorimen had pulled back his ankle-length cloak to reveal a sword almost as long as his own body, sheathed in a dull copper scabbard.

"Bogmots aren't kind," added Findlin. "They're sometimes harmless, but we can't count on that to be the case.

Your arrow won't hurt it, unless it's the real one, but the iron in the point will cause it to disappear for a time."

"Then it won't be wasted," said Kegin. "I don't want to hit anyone else, though."

"I hear Emerald's signal!" cried Linne. "That means the others are all inside the Gates of the Ellerhorn!"

"Without the spidermen, I hope. We seem to have an abundance of enemies who wish us no good!"

"The Archaels are in the same boat," said Lorimen. "We'we done what we can on the borders and helped the Parson when we'we been able, but every day more clans turn away from the old laws."

"We don't have to worry that," returned Kegin, running to where the giant figure roamed about, sending waves of fear through the survivors of Sweet Rock. "Can you give me some idea as to how you might contain something like we're seeing?"

"You can call the names of the Lords of the Malichran," suggested Findlin.

"I would gladly do it," shot Kegin, "except that I don't know any such names."

"Repeat them for him," ordered Lorimen. "If that doesn't work, we can always use the dust from the tombs we found near the Crooked Spire."

Findlin gathered his cloak about him and hurried forward with Kegin, muttering in a low voice an odd-sounding rumble of noises that might have passed for speech. As they neared the huge greenish figure the Bogmot whirled toward them, its face contorted in rage. A Steward beside him loosed an arrow at the dreadful apparition, just as Kegin released his own, and once again the giant simply vanished into thin air, leaving behind only a strange, rotten smell of damp earth and dead water.

"Good work," shouted Lorimen. "The names worked!"

"And two good Steward shafts," reminded Kegin breathlessly. "Names are fine things when they've got the backing of cold steel."

Lorimen hurried to where Findlin stood amid the group of stunned settlers and Stewards. "Did you see the eyes?" he asked. "Were they red?"

"Yes," replied his friend. "It is still not the true Bogmot."

"Then he'll be back. You may as well prepare your band for that. He'll keep coming back."

"If they're only anshees, there's nothing to fear from them," said the young Steward who now stood beside Kegin, his bow poised with another shaft already notched.

"Anshees or not, it frightens people and runs off horses, and if you make a false step here in the Grimpen . . ." Lorimen paused and made a slashing motion across his throat. "Finished!"

Kegin nodded grimly. "You've got that proper! I didn't see this thing when I was through here, and I'm glad enough for that."

"They don't always show themselwes. I think the size of your party is what's drawn him. As long as we'we come here for the trial ceremonies, we'we only seen them two other times. Our old chamberlain discowered them first, when he was here with the older brother of our last Carinbar."

"Are there other surprises you haven't told us of?" asked Linne, stringing another arrow to her elven bow.

"We'we newer mined all the secrets of the Grimpen, my lady, although it has often been our backyard. I can't say if the old dwellers were all ewil or not, but from our commerce here, I would be prone to say they didn't hawe keen respect for other liwing things, especially if it happened to be a stranger." Lorimen opened his cloak and drew out a weathered parchment map, wrapped carefully in a leather cover. "This has been carried by all of the attendants of the Court since there was a Court to rule, and you can see here that this bog wasn't quite as mean when this waymarker was drawn up."

"The older guides we'we used said this only got so bad after the last of the Wars of the Great Flying Snakes," said Findlin. "Before our time, but we hawe the record of our forefathers." He laughed a small, tight laugh. "I can't recall too many of the incidents they talked of that would hawe reassured us on any account."

"I think I shall find Famhart," said Linne evenly. "This

whole business grows uglier, and I would like to hear what he might have to say about this."

Kegin nodded quickly, relieved that she was going back to a safer place in the line. "See if he has any words for his old lieutenant! We could use all we could get here."

He had just finished speaking when the horrible shrieks began again, this time farther back in the procession, and shortly they were followed by the death cries of a horse trapped in the remorseless grasp of the treacherous bog. Screams and the sounds of horses bolting tore the heavy cover of the darkness as Kegin and the two strangers raced toward the spot where the greenish glow of the wraith moved back and forth among the terror-stricken settlers.

"The elven arrow, Linne! Shoot!" cried Kegin over his shoulder. "The thing is driving all of them into the bog!"

He heard the soft twang of her bow, and saw the golden-colored shaft, deadly and true, sink straight into the heart of the monster, but as before, the greenish mists dissolved into thin air, leaving nothing behind but the stench of its passing.

"We've lost two horses and a poor baker from the settlement," reported the young Steward. "That thing came right out of nowhere, and before the blighter could dismount, he and his two horses were into the mire there!"

The faces that ringed the spot were gaunt and drawn by the soft rush lamps, each one locked into his own thoughts, all at once grateful and guilty that it hadn't been them that now lay dead at the bottom of the terrible muck pit.

"Have everyone dismount," ordered Kegin. "We don't know where this thing will strike next, and there's no way to keep a horse from bolting. Better to lose an animal, if it has to come to it."

Over the confusion of the milling settlers a long, thin call came from the direction to the rear of the procession, and Kegin tried to quiet everyone so he could hear. It was a Steward signal plainly enough, but so faint that it was difficult to decipher.

"It sounds like Famhart," cried Linne.

"Can you go back and see what he has to report, my lady? I can't leave here now, with this thing running loose."

"I'll go with her," offered the young Steward.

"Go on, then! Find what Famhart has, and then send this lad back to me! You stay there with your husband. You don't need to be here in this!"

Linne smiled at her old companion. "I do believe you get to be more like an old mother hen every day."

"It's true, my lady! There's no sense in you being out this far to our front!"

"That's where I've been used to being for as long as I've known you, Kegin Thornby, and you know it."

"Times are changed, my lady. We aren't as young as we once were!"

A sadness crossed Linne's face then, her eyes took on the deep mysteries of the Elboreal, and she nodded. "We always end where we began," she said. "All the places we've been and seen, and now it's another start, just like when I came from my old home to Sweet Rock."

"That's the way of it," added Lorimen. "For all the turnings I've been and seen, it always has a beginning right at the spot where it should end."

"I have always had a secret hope that one day the whole play will stop, and we'll all have a laugh and go back wherever it is we came from."

Lorimen turned to glower at his friend. "That's heresy, Findlin! If any of the Alders should hear you say anything of that nature, you'd be exiled as quickly as the Parson!"

Kegin's ears perked up at the mention of the name of the legendary figure. "What Parson do you speak of?" he asked quietly. "Is he someone from your part of the world?"

"The Parson?" Findlin laughed. "Oh, no, he's from everywhere and nowhere, as far as anyone can tell. He is heard of now and again throughout our warrens, but it's always no good news to the Alders. Drives them all fairly blinking, he does, with his stories and odd beliefs about the here and hereafter."

"Hush, you old goat," warned Lorimen, blowing out his cheeks. "That kind of loose talk is ill advised, even if we're out of earshot of the others. It never does to be too fast with a tongue, especially where it concerns *him*!"

"Bosh," rejoined Findlin. "He's a friend to any who needs one, and his ideas don't sound so farfetched to me. Makes as

much sense as a lot of the driwel from the Hall of Alders,
most times."

Lorimen glowered at his friend but said nothing more;
instead he turned his attention to the more pressing problem
of the Bogmot. "Do you hawe any wanity glasses among
you?" he asked, looking at Linne, who had yet to leave.

"Vanity glasses? I haven't thought of those since the
raiders came. I can ask about it on my way to my husband,
but we left Sweet Rock in such a hurry, I doubt that any of
the women would have had time to carry away such a thing.
Shall I send you one, if I find it?"

"I assure you, my lady, it would go a great deal of the way
toward clearing up this nasty business. I'we just remembered an old biddy's tale from long ago, which told how to
trap one of these beasts. I newer had a way to do it before,
so this will be a perfect test, if you can find a glass among
your followers."

"Hurry, Linne," urged Kegin. "We don't know when this
thing will be back."

"And it will be back," promised Findlin. "If it can capture
someone, it will be freed from the prison it's kept in, and
whoever is caught will be forced to take its place."

Linne mounted and rode at a gallop toward the rear of the
procession, keeping her bow at the ready across her saddle
horn. All along her line of travel, the lamps cast dim
shadows over the faces of the weary travelers and set the
edges of the bog in the near distance alive in an eerie dance
that stretched the nerves to a breaking point. As she rounded
a slight bend in the path and passed from sight, the dreadful,
shrieking cry of the Bogmot rose again, this time near the
middle of the long string of settlers who huddled closely
about Famhart.

A
TEST
OF
TIME

An Enemy
War Camp

In the great Olgnite encampment the war drums rolled and thundered into the darkness, while the grotesque forms of the spidermen leapt and danced in the fiery orange shadows of the watch fires. Deros was dragged onto a horse and led about the camp by the Olgnite in the blue sash.

"Olga, Olga," boomed the voices to the drums. "Blood! Give us blood! Give us the sweet sap of our victims!"

The troops were worked into a killing frenzy, and the girl watched in horror as some of the prisoners were brought forth and slaughtered in front of their leader, who drank blood from each victim before he turned the rest of the feast back to his followers. She was beyond all hope. All that mattered to her now was the manner of her death, and she clung to the small knife Stearborn had given her when she had first come to Sweet Rock, a time that now seemed so remote and faraway to her, she could hardly recall her foolish dreams of recruiting an army to help her father.

Deros gripped the handle of the knife so hard, she thought she would surely crush it beneath her cloak, but the pain in her hand helped her build her courage to do what she knew she must. Feeling the sharp edge of the small dagger press against her heart, she began to try to recite all the old hymns and chants she had been taught as a child, and it seemed her vision blurred from the tears of rage and fear she felt, and another voice, that of her long-departed mother, whispered to her, coaxing her to persevere for just a while longer. The voice was so real that she blinked open her eyes, expecting to see the soft smile of so long ago and to hear all the old, deep secrets her mother used to sing to her at night after the rest of Cairn Weal was fast asleep.

A horrible face loomed next to hers out of the chaos, filled with killing fangs, and the terrible red eyes that burned with bloodlust, but a voice she knew spoke reassuringly in her mind. "We are here, my lady! Don't fear us. Your loyal servant Owen is on my back."

"Seravan!" cried Deros, shocked, then bursting into tears. "Is it really you?"

"Gitel is with me. We are come to fetch you."

Seravan was bumped rudely aside by the Olgnite chieftain in the blue sash, and he lashed out viciously to drive Owen away from his captive.

"Keep your distance, webless swine! This shela is only for Olag Grieshon!" He lashed out again with the thin whip, which bit deeply into Owen's arm, causing a black, snake-like welt from his elbow to his wrist.

Deros called out, trying to find Seravan again.

"We're here, my lady. We have to keep Owen near you until the attack. We have worked out a plan to try to free you from these devils."

"I was ready to kill myself," sobbed the girl. "There was no other way."

Seravan snorted, ruffling up his mane and tail and looking hard at the weeping captive. "There's never an end to it! We have to hang on, to escape these foul things who hold love for no living thing. Think of your home and your kinsmen! Hold on!"

"Where is Owen?" asked Deros, suddenly giddy, then frightened at once, for fear Owen would be taken captive as well.

"Here I am," growled the young man, his horrible features drawn into a mask of fierceness that terrified the girl.

"Your own true heart—your sweet, lovable Owen. Look at me now, Deros! Do you see your old friend from the Darien Mounds. I have Ephinias to thank for this!"

The girl screamed, tugging at her tether hard enough to pull her captor back in his saddle. When he saw the same Olgnite soldier near his prisoner again, he raised his whip to flail him once more. "By the Mountain of Thunder, you shall taste the leather until your hide is gone! No blood for you this night!" The cruel whip lashed out, flaying more skin from Owen's exposed arms, and he pulled hard on Seravan's rein to try to wheel away from the Olgnite chieftain.

Seravan's voice rang out then, cold and hard, calling out to the Olgnite in their own tongue. "I have found a way into the enemy's bolt hole, oh, Olag! I went there this afternoon and can show you a back door that will leave all the pinkers helpless for us to pluck like ripe meat!"

Grieshon's red eyes darkened, and he yanked back on his reins, making his horse stumble and almost causing Deros to lose her seat. He pulled at the flaps of his copper battle helm and jerked it off his head, showing the two terrible scars that ran from his cheek to his eyebrow and across his gnarled left ear. "Speak up, you puke of an eggless mother! What are you saying? Do you know a way into this nest of mice?"

"If you want the pinkers up in a pretty hash, I know the back door to their little hideaway. They think they can escape us through that dead water, but I know the road. There's no way out for them."

Grieshon raised a fist and called out in a menacing tone. "Slag! Murdam! To me! Who is this groveling wretch that he has scout reports before me?"

The two Olgnites who had been called wheeled their horses hard about and pulled up next to their leader. "No one knows more than you, oh, Olag Grieshon! He lies to court your favor," reported the one called Slag. "There is only one way after the pinkers, and they have blocked it to us so far! Tonight we shall sweep them away into our pens and feast well. They have no escape."

"There is a way in that I know," repeated Seravan. "It will save you a hundred riders or more. The pinkers will never look for us to come by the back way."

The big Olgnite clacked his fangs together hurriedly, looking steadily at the rider before him. "Where have you earned the right to advise Olag Grieshon as to how he shall slay his enemies? Are you Rhylander bred or Lachmede? You are lucky I let you draw another breath!"

"I give way to Your Lordship," answered Seravan, keeping his rider faced in such a way that Owen's helmet concealed him somewhat, so the Olgnite could not see who was speaking. "I have served you long and well and wanted to give you a gift of these settlers, without striking a blow or losing any more of our own."

"You know the rule! He should have his tongue cut and leave him to die on his own."

"With a nest of ants to help him pass the time more slowly while they chew his brains," added Murdam.

"A wager," shouted Seravan, having to butt the animals the two Olgnites rode to keep anyone from getting too close to Owen. "A wager for blood!"

Olag Grieshon laughed a wild, snarling laugh. "We have a blood wager! All hear, we have a blood wager! Slag, Murdam, stand to, and we shall hear the terms!" The cruel face of the enemy leader glared fiercely about in the flickering firelight, and all through the ranks of the Olgnite encampment, crude pitch torches were handed out, in readiness for the impending attack.

Seravan danced lightly sideways, forcing Owen to cling tightly to him to avoid being thrown, and called out in the same cold voice, "My life is forfeit if I can't lead you to the pinkers without a loss and without the Steward scum finding us out!"

"Your life is forfeit now, you bag of worms! Make it worth our while to wager! Throw in your mount and the one you lead! They are fine beasts, and my own string is ridden down chasing these sweetmeats from the Line."

"Done," shot Seravan, looking sideways at Gitel.

"We shall have the fire then, and the burning! As soon as we have all the torches lit, we move! If you fail and are not slain by the pinkers, then I myself shall feed you to the flames, but only a piece at a time!"

Slag and Murdam cackled with glee, clacking their fangs

together in a chattering symphony that was echoed by all the spidermen around the leader. Olag Grieshon raised his sword high above his head and shouted an order that sounded like a long, hissing breath. In every direction the Olgnite army lifted their swords and answered their leader, until the wood was drowned in the sound and the trees shook. The call was ended with a roll of thunder as the soldiers pounded their shields.

Tinder brush was dragged behind every horse, and soon a bonfire grew and was fed, until a tower of flames leapt and danced higher than the surrounding eaves of the wood, while the Olgnite army heaped more fuel onto it, chanting and calling their blood songs and repeating tales of massacre and plunder. Owen sat stiffly on Seravan's back, his fangs silent but his mind racing. "What have you gotten us into?" he finally growled under his breath. "You were supposed to see to it that we got back safely!"

The big animal snorted, rattling his bridle. "Sometimes you have to walk over the coals to escape the fire."

"Ephinias never told me how bad this was to be. I'm here now, but the things in my mind won't leave me alone! It frightens me, Seravan. Sometimes I seem to vanish and this other thing takes over!" Owen's face was a contorted picture of agony, with the hideous mouth and fangs twisted into a grotesque echo of a smile.

"Hold to the sword, Owen! It will only be a little while more, if they take our bait!"

"It won't matter if they take it or not," replied Owen curtly. "We shall either be killed by them or by drowning in the fen!"

"Look at Deros, lad! See how she holds up to this! You're not yourself," said Gitel coaxingly.

"Let's try to speak to Deros again," suggested Seravan, and the two horses, with their fevered rider, milled about until they came close to Deros without being singled out among the Olgnite troops.

"You've done well so far!" said Gitel. "You might as well offer me up to our Olgnite leader as a gift. He's already says he fancies us."

"Good sense in horseflesh. A good idea, old fellow. Let's see if we can arrange that."

The girl was next to them then. Gitel calmed the animal she was riding and spoke in her mind. "Can you hear me, Deros?"

She nodded her head, although she stared straight ahead, watching for any movement from Olag Grieshon's hand which held the thin whip.

"We are going to see if we can't get you onto Gitel before we move. That way we'll have half our work already done."

"What happened to Owen? Who has done this?"

"We had no choice. There was no other way to reach you."

"He's awful!"

"Ephinias can put him back to rights as soon as we're done here."

"Oh, Gitel, there are others here! Ulen found me in the woods, but we were overtaken by Hulin Vipre, then the Olgnites caught us all! I would die rather than stay here longer with these filthy beasts!"

"Who's captured? Ulen?" questioned Owen, his eyes grown redder and a savage smile spreading across his distorted, swollen features.

"None of that," reprimanded Seravan. "You are to keep still and let me do the talking!"

Owen's heavy form began to sway in the saddle to the thunder of the Olgnite war chants, and he reached to draw his sword along with the rest of the enemy warriors but encountered the same strong surge of light and sounds he always did when he grasped the handle. It shocked the strange intruder that now occupied half his mind, causing Owen to cry out in pain and fear.

"Now he's done it," whinnied Gitel. "If he keeps this up, we'll be discovered!"

"They'll pass that off as bloodlust," soothed Seravan. "These beasts are as unpredictable as a March foal. You never know what they will have next."

"All the more reason to be away as soon as possible."

Olag Grieshon noticed Owen near his captive again. "Here, you spindly web-robber, have a little of my special message to those who would become bigger than their betters!" The thin whip cracked out with a loud report, and the harsh tongue of the leather tore at Owen's throat. The Olgnite leader snapped the long coil suddenly, pulling Owen from his saddle, and sent him sprawling amid the churning hooves of the horses.

Seravan reacted quickly, protecting the young man from being trampled by the horse Deros rode, and allowed him space amid the crush of the animals to remount.

"Oh, great Olag, stay your hand! I meant no harm here! I was trying to reach you to offer you this fine mount that I have taken from the Steward scum. Your prize rides a horse that is beneath her status as your prisoner, and I need only my own. I would be honored if you would take him, as a gift of allegiance from me."

Owen remounted as Seravan spoke. The Olgnite chieftain coiled his whip. He had replaced his helmet, which gave his smile a more sinister look.

"You are wise, my squirmling! I am pleased when loyal troops bestow gifts of gratitude. Slag and Murdam have been lax of late, it seems." He turned suddenly on his two scouts, lashing out violently with the whip. "Haven't you, wormhearts?"

"He's trying to soften you toward him, if he should lose the wager," warned Murdam.

"Should he lose, I'll have both horses."

"Take my gift, oh, Olag, and let us ride on."

The huge Olgnite leader glared about once more, his red eyes afire with a killing madness, and he raised his sword again to renew the frenzy of his troops. "We want blood!" he shouted. "Blood of the infidels to fill our hungry veins and to drive our race on to the grandness that was promised to us when we swore the oath!"

A great shout deafened Owen then, as every soldier in the Olgnite army took up the chant that rang in his head like dull, leaden bells, slowly weakening his hold on the sword and bringing back the empty hunger deep in his Olgnite heart, making him thirst for the blood of the pretty prisoner on the horse beside him. He was at the point of reaching for her when Seravan foresaw the move and shied.

Olag Grieshon took the reins of Gitel and pulled the un-
protesting horse to him, admiring his fine head and abruptly
dismounting to unsaddle his own steed. "Quickly, Slag! I
shall have a new beast to carry me to our victory feast tonight! Help me change my gear!" Before Seravan could act
to stop him, the Olgnite chieftain with the thick blue sash
was mounted upon the back of Gitel.

The Crooked
Spire

In the darkness the stifling smell of the Ellerhorn Fen grew
more rank, filled with the sharp, pungent odor of torches. A
low, evil-looking mist shrouded the ground, slowing their
progress to a snail's crawl, while Kegin and another scout
inched forward cautiously. Every nerve was strained to the
breaking point as the procession kept their weapons ready,
looking for the next appearance of the ghastly monster with
the horrifying face. Peering anxiously about, the young
Steward next to Kegin whispered to Findlin, who walked
quietly along, his eyes and ears alert for any movement
beyond the torchlit trail.

"Is there any way you can spook these things?" he asked,
his voice pinched tight.

The Archaelian turned, and spoke softly. "A thing like
that is always spooked. Their existence is a horror to them,
as well as to all who have the ill chance of meeting them.
They are to be awoided."

"I would gladly agree to that! But how to do it?"

Findlin shook his head gravely. "Stay away from the
places they haunt."

Word was passed up through the line that all the squadrons

231

were safely into the fen, leaving the way open to draw in the Olgnite hordes, which were in close pursuit. "With any luck these devils we've got behind us will draw away the Bogmot with all their noise and numbers! Good match, by my way of thought!" said Kegin.

"We are wery near the Crooked Spire," said Lorimen. "That's where we left Enlid. We could draw up there a bit, for there's good ground to be had."

"Is that on this path?" questioned Kegin, for he had found no such place on his one trip through the bog years before.

"The path we take runs right to the front door," answered Findlin. "It was from the days before I was counted chamberlain, and I reckon it was there for a time before that. There are carwings in the hearthstones that date it all the way back to the War of the Flying Snakes."

"I never came across it. You mean to say there are two ways through this bog?" Kegin's face was drawn into a worried frown. "I hope the Olgnites don't stumble onto another trail!"

"There are a dozen or more, my boy!"

Another messenger arrived, out of breath and white-eyed. His horse stamped and fidgeted nervously as he dismounted calling, "Famhart says Stearborn is gone! The squadrons are all in, but no one has an account of Stearborn. Chellin Duchin is taking his men back to wait at the gate, so Famhart wants you to find a way to pull up until we have news."

Kegin's voice was hard and even. "Has anyone seen him? Surely one of his lieutenants must know something."

"The last they knew, they were hard pressed in a withdrawal and were at rearguard action holding the Olgnites at bay. He was there then, but no one's seen him since."

"Damn the black luck if this turns out true," spat Kegin, jerking his head backward toward the entrance to the fen. "Off with you! Tell Famhart we're holding up at an old church our new friends have told us of. It's off the path he knows, but I'll send a man who can guide him through." Kegin looked questioningly at Lorimen. "Would you be willing to go back to bring the others on?"

Lorimen pulled his hood back, nodding. "It's not much to ask. There are two ways to the Crooked Spire from here, and it wouldn't do to take a wrong turn onto the dozen other trails that end up at the bottom of the Grimpen."

"Be careful, lad," cautioned Findlin. "I don't want to hawe to explain your absence to any of those who wait for the return of your worthless hide!"

"Keep your eye peeled for the youngster," reminded his friend. "Enlid may be in the grawest danger."

Findlin's brow knotted, and he peered away into the gray-shrouded bog before them. "I hope he's kept to our plan. He's a good lad."

Somewhere in the near distance ahead of them, the faint green glow of the Bogmot turned the darkness beyond the torchlight into eerie-colored shadows that wavered and leapt beneath the roof of the trees in a crazy dance that stirred the horses into nervous activity.

"Find a glass," added Findlin. "We won't be shed of this ugly slugworm until we can trap him solid."

Lorimen clasped hands with his friend, and their eyes met for a brief moment, then he was gone, riding behind the Steward messenger who had come from Famhart.

"Which way do we take to find this old kirk?" asked Kegin.

"The Crooked Spire? We go west at the next fork."

"I never saw those branches as anything that would take me through," replied Kegin. "I kept the sun in sight as best I could, when it was daylight, and traveled with it. I spent a bad night, I can tell you, while I waited for dawn. That's when I started to hear the voices of the dwellers." He paused. "Do you think we'll find your lost one?" he asked, looking down at his hands as he spoke.

"Enlid? I hope the lad has lasted through this. I would like to think we'll come on him somewhere along the way."

"Our new Elder is out among the Olgnites, as far as we have heard. It's hard to keep my mind off that. He's a good lad, too, but very unseasoned. This is a lot to thrust on his shoulders at his age."

Findlin grunted agreement, smiling faintly. "Seems as though I'we heard those words spoken about ewery single youngster I'we ever known. They most surely spoke it about us as well, when we were still in short leggings and hanging about near the old soldier's fires, waiting to be grown."

Kegin thought briefly about a summer long ago, with the gold and red of fall slowly crowning the woods around his home, and his shy questions to his own father, asking for permission to ride with the Stewards of The Line. "I'm sure they had words for us," he agreed. "Maybe some not so kind."

"I will regret it if Enlid is lost. I hawe grown to like the boy and hawe known his family now for many turnings. Fionten is a sea town, and his father, and his father's father, were shipwrights there, and kept almost all our captains with good wessels under them."

"Do you have boats at the coast now?" asked Kegin, recalling their own problem of craft to carry them away from the advancing Olgnite hordes.

"Enough for our party. We didn't look to take passengers from these parts. But there are wessels to be had in these ports all up and down the slackwater bays, and with any luck at all we can find you transport."

Famhart's lieutenant had grown to trust the stout man who walked beside him in the knee-deep mist, churned a rusty, reddish brown from the dull flames of the torches. "We shall need to have ships that can carry us into the Silent Sea."

Findlin whistled. "Those are far waters! What driwes your thoughts to those places?"

"Chance and ill luck," replied Kegin softly. "It seems the old ways have been chased back into the darkness again. All the vilest of beings from every Boundary have sprung up in force, and even the strength of the Stewards is not enough to keep them down."

The Archaelian shook his head sadly. "It is an old tale, cousin. I hawe one or two of those stories to relate, as do we all, no matter where we hail from."

A rising curtain of mist was smoking higher in front of them, forming a pool that swallowed the torchlight almost completely and caused the winding procession to draw to a halt to study the new obstacle. It felt colder than the surrounding air and smelled faintly of musty caves.

"This is the turning," reported Findlin. "We hawe to take this path to reach our stopping place."

"The kirk? Can we get through this? It looks too thick."

"It will slacken off once we're through a bit. There should be a split trunk here somewhere, if we keep a weather eye for it. Marks the trail dead center. Makes a dash right across what looks to be a deep pool, but it's good ground."

Kegin groped blindly about in the heavy mist, feeling it in his hair and beading up on the folds of his cloak. "Are you sure of the way? I can't see anything."

"Poke with a stick! It'll be the rocks that give you the way you want. Tap along out there! You can't miss it," Findlin said encouragingly. "No sense in wasting any more time here waiting for the Bogmot to come back, if we can get to his burial mound. They were all buried around the old church, so they have no desire to be about the place where they escaped, unless it is to scare anyone else off who might find out their secret."

"They escaped?"

"The Bogmots! Yes, escaped. Ewery one of them is buried there by the Crooked Spire, and ewery one of them steers clear of the place because of the chance they might get pulled back into their tombs."

"Sounds like a story for the cubs around a fire. Surely you don't believe in all these stories?"

Findlin looked earnestly at his new friend. "I beliewe whatewer is true," he said in a cool tone.

"I meant no disrespect," apologized Kegin.

A large, gray shape loomed ahead of Kegin, wavering in the torchlit mists. Drops of moisture caught the torchlight and reflected it back, until the damp wall before them looked solid with dull flames that caught at the hem of the darkness and caused gaunt shadows to whirl and dance dangerously close to the advancing party.

Kegin drew his longsword with a quick, rasping sound, looking to Findlin. "Is this another surprise you know about?"

The man nodded, his hands away from his weapons. "One that we are looking for."

"What is it?" asked Kegin, his breath coming short and measured.

"The old Crooked Spire. It was a hawen at one time, with monks from the old religions."

"In this ungodly place?"

"It was different then, and there were gods here once, of one heawen or another." Findlin paced forward quickly, hardly stopping to check his way. "Come on. There's solid ground here! Room enough for eweryone, if we pull in tight enough."

Kegin stood a moment longer, studying the mist-covered spire rising up out of the depths of the bog, tilting at an odd angle upward until the top of the old tower was above the grayish curtain. "It still has a bell there," he said doubtfully.

Findlin looked up, following the hand that Kegin was pointing with. "So it does! I doubt anyone would have made their way in here to sack it. Not much call for a bell that size." He shook his wrist, and the elven bells sounded ever so lightly, faintly tickling the edges of the hearing, almost on the verge of a dream.

From somewhere beyond the gray, misty trail behind, a faint reply to the bells came once, then twice more.

"It's Lorimen! He's on his way back."

"Then there must be news!" Kegin's brow darkened as he squinted into the shadows, anxious for any word of Stearborn and Owen.

Linne appeared from the mist, followed by the stocky Archaelian, who triumphantly raised an object for Findlin to see.

"A glass, by Ghadsly's Beard, a wery hard object to come by in these times, but we hawe it now!" Lorimen broke into a little jig, holding the treasured object aloft.

"Careful," warned his friend. "Don't break it before we'we got the Bogmot! No sense cackling yet, you loose-witted old cob!"

"A bride carried it away from her new home," explained Linne. "It was a gift from her groom, and she had only had it a day before Sweet Rock was burned."

Kegin shook his head. "Poor Emerald. He didn't have much of a chance for a wedding feast, either."

"They shall have it yet," promised Linne. "Elita is not going to be done out of her due by that ragtag lot of spider-men."

"What news of Stearborn? Was there any word yet?"

"Chellin Duchin and his squadron have gone back to the gate to wait. Someone saw Stearborn and an aide ride out just at the last, heading toward Sweet Rock. Famhart said Stearborn does things like that to worry him."

"Then there must be something afoot that he would risk such a thing. Perhaps Ephinias was there."

"Perhaps. Famhart says we must hold for a bit, to give everyone a chance to rejoin us."

"This is the perfect ground to do so, my lady," said Find-lin. "Halfway to the growe, and there's enough good solid dirt to stand the lot of us on. We can hawe a rest here, as well, and maybe it wouldn't turn to naught if we did try to signal Enlid, Lorimen. With all the noise we're making here, it might draw the lad back for a look."

"Not after our warning," argued the other. "This will only frighten him more."

Kegin and another Steward shouted a warning as the upper half of the abandoned church suddenly was bathed in a pale halo of light that appeared in the bell tower. Another sharp call came from farther back down the line, and the greenish, wavering shadow of the Bogmot danced wildly about on the mist curtain that seemed to have grown denser. A soundless wind crept over the companions, reeking of time forgotten and carrying a chill that dampened every heart.

A Legend
Speaks

Kegin was vaguely aware of trying to shield Linne between himself and his horse while blowing a short note on his horn, to let those behind know they had come under attack. Lorimen and Findlin sounded strident notes on the stag horns they carried at their belts. A shaft, a full yard long and fletched in brilliant blue and yellow feathers, buried itself at Kegin's boot tip, followed by another signal horn, deep and melancholy, that was answered by what seemed a dozen more of the same. The surrounding mist was alive with reflected flames, making it hard to distinguish forms that moved between light and shadow.

A horse screamed nearby, and it was followed by another. Men called for help in getting the animals out of the bog. As Kegin struggled with his rearing horse he stumbled against Findlin, who had drawn his sword and had the blade before him, watching for an enemy to appear from either quarter, the bog, or from within the confines of the old ruined church.

"That's no Bogmot," shouted Findlin. "Whoever shot that is flesh and blood like us!"

"I'm glad for that information," called Kegin notching an

arrow. "I didn't think it had a hollow look to it. That's cold iron at the tip, and a fine turned feather on the top. Good workmanship."

"I don't watch so closely for the workmanship of an arrow when someone tries to skewer me," said Lorimen, drawing out his sword, a shorter, two-edged blade with a row of inlay around the guard and down its entire length.

"It was a warning, it seems," replied Kegin. "But it hasn't scared off the Bogmot!"

Another horse screamed from the pitiless grasp of the bog. Arrows whizzed by their heads in the thickening mist, until Kegin shouted orders to hold the bow shots.

"I'we got the mirror," called Lorimen. "All we need do is get close enough to the thing to catch its image and we'll hawe it."

"You may get your chance sooner than you want," cried Kegin, pointing at the growing greenish figure moving steadily toward them.

Linne carefully notched one of the elven arrows, waiting calmly to shoot. She moved away from Kegin so she should have a clear shot.

"The tower! There's someone in the tower!" shouted the young Steward at Kegin's side.

As they turned their eyes upward they saw a rapid movement in the bell tower of the ruined church, which was now lighted by the faint golden glow of what looked to be an ordinary rush lamp.

"Who could that be," asked Kegin, turning to Findlin. "Could that be your lad come back here?"

"Not likely," returned the stout Archaelian. "He wouldn't show himself. We'we taught him better than that."

"Send someone to cover the church," ordered Kegin. "Make sure whoever's there stays put until we've dealt with this thing out here."

There was a hurried tramp of booted feet as a platoon of Stewards raced to secure the ruins of the ancient church. Close upon their passing, there came the growing cold wind that seemed to blow in front of the Bogmot's passage, as it rolled forward in the smoking mist, straight for the place where Linne and Findlin stood.

"Bring the glass, Lorimen! Steady as you go!"

Lorimen fumbled with the object momentarily, then hurried to his friend's side. "Wait until we hawe it in the glass, my lady," he said, his voice dry and urgent. "We hawe only the one chance to do it, for they know about these things and won't get close enough again to be caught."

The greenish cloud grew, blown on by the freezing wind, until Kegin felt that his bow arm weighed too much to hold, and the grip on his arrow began to loosen. "Where is the hellish thing?" he snapped, every nerve taut. "Why doesn't it come?"

"It's here," whispered Findlin. "It senses something!"

"I'we got the glass under my cloak," said Lorimen. "Do you think it saw it?"

A faint sound began then, whistling low, then rising to a staccato finish. It came twice more, then stopped. Findlin cocked his head, a dark frown knotting his brows. "That's a signal, or I'll be wide of the mark."

"Is it your lad?" asked Kegin.

"No."

"There it is again! Look! It's stopped the Bogmot!"

The companions looked toward the greenish shadow and saw that it had stopped a dozen paces in front of them and seemed to hang undecidedly, pulsing faintly.

"There's someone moving in the tower again," cried Kegin. "Guards!"

"The door is barred," answered a Steward. "We can't force it."

"Break it," shot Kegin.

"Aye, sir," came the reply, and then the solid sound of bodies crashing against hard wood.

"Let's rush it," said Findlin, speaking closely in Lorimen's ear. "That way we'll hawe a chance to trap it in the glass before it can escape us!"

Lorimen looked sideways at his friend. "I'm not gone that soft in my nob! Let's see what it's up to first—"

"I'll take the glass," interrupted Kegin. "We can't let this thing stay loose or it'll drive every horse we have into the bog! Come on, Linne! You shoot, and I'll try to get the blackguard in the glass."

"You don't know what you're doing!" protested Findlin. "It takes a trick to lure it in."

"Then tell it to me quickly," replied Kegin, "before it's gone and we miss our chance!"

Above them, in a deep, resonant, somber tone, a great bell began to toll, slowly and with a long, sonorous rhythm, making the mists vibrate and shaking the very ground beneath the startled party.

"Break the door!" shouted Kegin angrily, racing to help the men at the church entrance.

"It's too thick! They've blocked and barred it."

"A window, then! Hurry, lads!" Kegin looked over his shoulder and saw the greenish form of the Bogmot wavering, almost as though it were dissipating. "I've got to get the mirror! Keep trying to find a way in!"

Findlin and Lorimen were beside Linne, and the three of them advanced cautiously toward the monstrous form, which had not moved to avoid them. Lorimen held the mirror in his cloak tightly, waiting for the moment to raise it.

"We have to see its face and eyes," reminded Findlin. "It won't work unless we do."

"I know that," snapped his friend. "Now keep your bow hand ready. You, too, my lady!"

Linne felt the thin, icy edge of fear knot in her stomach as she moved forward, and she clutched the elven bow tightly, drawing strength from the feel of it and remembering all the times long past when she had found herself in other moments of danger. Kegin was running to catch up to her when the greenish shadow was blown away by the wind, leaving the horrendous form of the monster gaping at them, its lower jaw revealing the drooling, tearing fangs and the terrible claws that were its hands, reaching out to grab and hold them.

"The glass!" cried Findlin as he and Linne drew their bows together. Lorimen ran forward, fumbling with the small mirror beneath the tangled folds of his cloak. He fell, tripping over a gnarled tree root. The vanity glass flew from his grip as he stretched out his hands to break his fall, and landed almost at the feet of the advancing Bogmot. Its slitted eyes blazed a dull reddish fire that leapt higher when it saw the object at its feet.

"Grab the glass!" roared Findlin. "It will know what we're up to!"

Kegin scrambled forward, grazing the monster's side as he strained to reach the mirror. A freezing wall of mist enveloped his arm as he pushed his hand forward to grasp the mirror, and he had no feelings in his frozen fingers. No matter how hard he tried to will his hand shut, he could not pick up the small object. "Shoot!" he yelled, overcome by a dizziness and a shortness of breath, almost as though some huge hand had crushed him to the ground.

Kegin saw the yellow and blue feathered shaft strike through the center of the Bogmot, burying itself in the soft earth behind.

Where the nightmarish figure of the ghostly beast had stood, there was nothing but the mists of the bog, and the three arrows, all lined in a row. He crawled forward quickly and snatched up the mirror from where it had fallen into the damp earth. He could see the odd-shaped prints of where the Bogmot had stood in the damp ground and felt the freezing cold hand again that had threatened to crush the breath from him.

"Who loosed this shaft?" he asked, plucking it from the ground and turning to the still stunned Findlin and Lorimen. Linne had notched another arrow and stood scanning the mists for any sign of where the dreadful creature had gone.

"It came from behind me," managed Findlin.

"From the tower," added Lorimen. "It came from the tower."

When Kegin glanced over his shoulder, it seemed to him that a large shadow spread over the base of the ruined spire, caught between the torchlight and the rush lamp that burned in the upper part of the old church. "My thanks, then," he uttered softly under his breath. "Whoever you are."

"Are you all right?" cried Linne, hurrying to his side. "Do you have the mirror?"

"It won't do us a lead arrow's worth of good now," broke in Findlin. "The Bogmot has seen it, and he'll awoid us now."

"That would be as good as we could have it," returned Kegin. "At least we'll be rid of him!"

"Not rid of him at all," corrected Lorimen, dusting himself off and straightening his cloak. "He'll simply go back to attack the others who have no protection."

"Then why isn't it leaving?" asked Kegin, who, in turning toward the ruined spire, saw the green shadow flickering through the mists, near a stunted grove of gnarled trees that looked as though they had never seen a summer sun.

The two Archaelians looked at each other in surprise but simply shrugged their shoulders in reply.

"It's moving behind the church," said Linne. "Look!"

A powerful light began to show from the broken spire, blazing down directly onto the madly writhing Bogmot as it struggled wildly to remove itself from the brilliant golden-colored light. A ragged scream of agony rent the murky air, and a sound like great rocks scraping together reached the companions, and they watched in stricken wonder as the light from the old church grew even more intense, followed by the low and measured tolling of the ancient bell that hung in the tower.

"There's someone coming down!" yelled one of the Stewards at the door. "I hear his footsteps!"

"Stand away," ordered Kegin. "Be ready with your bow."

"Whoever it is, they shot at the creature," reminded Linne. "They may not be enemies."

"They wouldn't want a monster about, either," returned her friend. "Just because they shot at the thing doesn't make them our ally."

Without warning the stout wooden door that had kept the Stewards at bay swung open with a scraping, creaking noise, and there before them was a giant of a man, with dark curls of hair that lay about his shoulders and a grim face covered with a black beard streaked with gray. In one hand he carried a stout staff, and in the other was a great longbow, taller than Kegin. At the man's back was a full quiver of the yard-long arrows with the distinctive blue and yellow feathers.

Findlin had recovered enough to start to speak but was brought up short by the appearance of a small man, dressed in russet and green, who swung himself smartly about on his

muscular arms, for there were no legs showing in his
trousers, which he had knotted jauntily up at the knees. The
man's face was that of the very young, although his eyes
showed a cornflower blue that was older than the sea and
somehow sad. Linne recognized the mark of the elves immediately.

"Who stands pounding on the holy door with a sword?"
boomed the voice. "Don't you recognize sanctuary where
you hail from?"

"No sanctuary do they know," chimed in the crippled one,
dragging himself into a sitting position on the last step of the
church. "They are ruffians from The Line and know nothing
but war and bad weather."

Kegin's temper was short, and he bordered on flaring up
until Lorimen whispered to him under his breath.

"I think the drag-leg is daft. I'we heard tales that they
hawe the eye of the Old Ones and are treasured as prophets
by some."

"He may or may not be. Do you know him?"

"Never laid eyes on him before, yet I'll lay a week's rations that this is our Parson we'we been seeking."

"The Lame Parson," breathed Kegin.

"The same! Fits all the bills, including the fact that I
spoke to a boatman earlier, along the shore before we came
inland. He talked of him as if he had seen him sometime in
the prewious day."

"Looks to me like our boatman spoke the truth," said Lorimen. "I don't see how it could be anyone else."

"Ruffian Stewards all! They take their pleasure in the
harsh woods and live far from friends, they do."

"Enough, Twig! There are Archaels here, too, or I'll have
lost sight of the way they carry themselves."

"Fionten is kind to Twig! He has seen more than one
Midsummer's Eve in the good company of happy Archaelians."

"Fionten it is, my good man, and Archaelians we are,
Findlin and Lorimen to be exact, and we hawe the good
grace to say we hail from our homeland with a true heart and
a generous spirit and beliewe in treating all like friends, until
they've prowen otherwise."

"Twig's recommendation is enough for me," boomed the big stranger. "He is shy a few of his wits, but he pleases me, makes me laugh, knows every animal by its first name, and can speak to the wind."

"There are other things I can do, too, but it tires me. Twig is old now and can't go on the way he used to."

"Do we hawe the honor of addressing one called the Lame Parson?" asked Lorimen. "Meaning no offense, sir."

"I don't go by that name, nor do I take easily to it, citizen. You could just as well call me anything, and I would answer. I have been keeping my eye out for all of you, creeping back and forth on the slipperiest foundation I've seen since the last holocaust that swept us away into the Middle Islands to wrangle things down to manageable size."

"Then what shall we call you, sir?" asked Kegin.

The big, burly figure looked down at his badly crippled companion and smiled. "You could start by calling me Twig's friend. Then you might shorten that a bit to friend, or brother, however you are more accustomed."

Kegin straightened his shoulders and faced the tall figure in the church door. "We meant no disrespect, friend, but we were fighting a Bogmot. We had it cornered until we dropped our mirror. Now I don't know where it'll come at us next."

"It's at peace," replied the Parson simply. "They have stirred above this forsaken ground long enough. There are seasons given to everything, and they have served their season out."

"You mean the thing is gone?" asked Findlin, incredulous.

"*Gone* is not quite the word, but they won't be back here again."

"Bogmots are bad creatures, hurt Twig if they could. Gone, gone, like the green smoke over the grass. Won't be back!"

Findlin cleared his throat and moved closer to the large figure who still loomed in the doorway, leaning on his bow. "Do you hawe news of a lad out here? We left him off yesterday and were to meet him at the old growe with the twin trees."

"Twig has seen all in the wet bog! No place for a young

man to be alone, even if he has strong legs. Bog is deep and
hungry all the time."

"You say he's fallen into the Grimpen?" asked Lorimen,
his face draining of color.

"Twig not say."

"My friend here knows where everyone and everything is
in the Ellerhorn," said the Parson. "It will take some coaxing
to get him to tell. You must be ready to move on from here
soon, for there are many dangers now, all around the fen.
My scouts tell me we are surrounded by those tribes from
the Wastes of Leech."

"The Olgnites," confirmed Kegin. "They have such
numbers now, even the Line Stewards can't hold them in
check."

The Parson shook his cloak back from his body, withdrew
a leather chart case, and handed it to his companion. "Find
the road to the grove, Twig, and help these good pilgrims to
it. We will have work to do before this night's through."

"Twig knows," he replied, pausing to laugh a short ripple
of laughter that sounded like a small child pleased with a
toy. "You two with long legs! Come tread carefully behind
short Twig, poor Twig, who lost his pins to a lion in the cold
mountains of the Maligne."

Linne had remained silent beside Kegin, but now she
spoke, addressing the giant of a man who went under the
name of the Lame Parson.

"My name is Linne, sir, and my husband's name is Famhart. We were at the Middle Islands, in the last great war,
and had the honor of knowing a good number of heroes who
fought bravely for Windameir and who are known to us,
although we be but poor souls lost on the road now, trying to
find a haven where we may last out our days in peace."

The man's dark eyes seemed to take on a twinkle then,
and it seemed to all who saw that he actually laughed. "So
you were some of that rowdy crew," he said, chuckling. "I
thought I sensed among you some that were of another time.
The Keepers and the Elboreal are in short supply now. The
dwarfish clans have long gone over, and there aren't many
left here to count who witnessed the terrible beauty of the
dragon. Welcome, little sister, to the fold of my poor follow-

ing, if you'd wish it. You and all your clan. It is but a poor showing, but perhaps we might be the better for it in time."

"I only see your friend Twig," said Findlin. "Is he your following?"

The Parson tilted back his dark head, and the black curls, tinged with gray, shook as he roared out laughing. "Aye! That's the set of it! Twig and I, alone and homeless, wandering about this cruel land to rally together any who still hold a love for the Light."

"You hawe our serwice, then," said Lorimen. "The Archaels will be counted on that day of reckoning among those who breathed their final breath with the High King's name still on their lips. And I wish you'd say if you know anything of our missing lad!"

"Good," boomed the Parson. "We shall have need of all who ride to that banner! Twig!"

"Twig not see the Archael go in the bog. He is safe enough, hiding now! But Twig is gone, all gone! He'll find the way for those who are his friends!"

"Could we wait a moment more?" asked Linne. "Famhart is coming behind with Emerald and the others, and my son is still among the enemy trying to rescue one of our own."

The Parson came down the two steps of the ruined church and stood next to Linne. She saw a finely wrought golden chain at his neck, with the likeness of a bear hanging as a talisman on the broad chest, and could smell the deep-woods smell of the man, as if he had just that moment come out of an ancient glade.

"Then we shall see what can be done to find the lost ones. You may wait here at this travelers' shrine. There is no danger here now. My trusted companion and I shall do a bit of snooping and see what's to be seen."

"We shall send a troop of Stewards, sir, if you like," offered Kegin.

"Thank you, my friend, but Twig and I need no more than each other. We've traveled this way for more than a few turnings now, and have always been safe enough."

"There are Olgnites out there," warned Kegin.

"Weblings of the worst sort," added Findlin.

"They are not difficult to deceive," replied the mysterious

Parson. "Twig can hold them at bay with his fool's play. And if the worst comes to it, I have my men look after their old leader."

"Twig is a fool," the cripple echoed. "Good fool. Knows all the dreams."

"What's he saying?" asked Lorimen. "And were your men the ones signaling just before the Bogmot came?"

"They were."

"I thought as much," said Findlin. "I knew my ears hadn't led me up a wrong turning."

"Twig said he knows all the dreams. What does he mean?" asked Kegin.

"He has the Old One's eyes," answered the Parson. "A handy thing to have in times like these."

"Then we can wait here for you?" questioned Linne.

"Not for me, little sister. You may wait for your husband and son, but Twig and I have errands that are far from here, and we have not time enough to stay on."

"But we'll see you again?" asked Kegin, feeling a sudden pang of sadness that the strange giant was leaving.

There was an odd smile on the bearded face then, and for a moment the torchlight played tricks on the onlooker's eyes, for it seemed the large figure transformed into a shape that faintly resembled a bear, standing on his hind legs, looking out at them with kind, intelligent eyes that saw through a man's heart, or beyond clouds, or mountains, or time.

"Oh, you shall certainly see me from time to time," he said. "Twig shall dance for us then, and turn fancy somersaults in the air with his wit, and we'll have more time to sit and hear the end of this tale."

The Parson stepped into the gathered circle of Stewards and settlers, took the small man on his back like a rucksack, and strode straight through the crowd, on into the darkness that waited beyond the guttering and streaming torches and rush lamps, vanishing there as quietly and suddenly as the moon swallowed by a cloud.

By the Back Door

The booming war cry of the Olgnite hordes was overwhelming, driving the warriors into a frantic rage, whirling and smashing their swords against their shields and clacking their killing fangs in a staccato, chilling death song. Deros watched, petrified, as Olag Grieshon lashed his whip until it almost touched her, then let it curl slowly back to his boot, smiling his wicked, malformed smile. "There, there, shela! The whip is not gone! It wouldn't leave you without its caress! Not at the moment of our greatest victory, when we are on the edge of defeating and drinking the sap of our most hated enemies!"

The whip cracked again, close to her arm, but did not touch her flesh. Deros tried to draw away from her tormentor but could go no farther than the end of the foul-smelling tether that held her close to the spiderman.

Gitel, who carried the enemy chieftain, moved slightly away, so that the lash wouldn't reach the girl, but he paid for his movement with a harsh dig of spurs into his ribs. It took all the animal's control to refrain from pitching the Olgnite off and smashing the ugly spider form, but he chaffed at his bit, tolerated the hideous, foul-smelling weight of the rider, and kept on with the plan he and Seravan had decided upon.

Owen rode still at Olag Grieshon's side, looking more and more like an Olgnite warrior as the spell drew him deeper into its hard embrace. Seravan was having a difficult time with the lad and could hardly keep him under even a faint sense of control. "You have to hold the sword, Owen! Grasp the sword! Now!"

Owen's eyes rolled back in his head, and he heard nothing but war cries and the drumming of hot blood in his ears. He was dimly aware of the horse's voice, but he could not hold to his old senses long enough to concentrate and kept slipping away into the dull fires of the torches and the deep chanting of the Olgnite warriors as they sang their blood song, working themselves into a killing frenzy.

Gitel tried to keep close to Seravan, but the gouging spurs of the spiderman kept driving him farther away, and soon they were surrounded by the Olgnite captains crowding around their chieftain. The darkness settled over the wood with a suddenness, and the torchlight threw wild and ragged shadows over the moving army of the Olgnites, making it seem like a great snake, slithering through the forest with a dull glint off naked swords and dully polished shields, and cast back more randomly from the metal caps and helmets the enemy soldiers wore. Deros was kept on a close tether by Olag Grieshon, and the girl was in tears as she felt the lash of the harsh whip once more and saw the badly misshapen form of Owen reveling with his head thrown back, roaring for blood with the rest of the Olgnite soldiers.

"Slag! Murdam! To me! We shall see how the set of this sortie will go! If our good scout here can do what he says and get us into the pinker's camp without them knowing, then all is well. If he can't . . ." The enemy leader paused, looking at Owen, smiling a crafty smile. "Then we'we leave him to the bog! That will settle that."

"We should leave an ambush at the river where we saw the outlander's boats," warned Murdam. "These pinkers are as hard to run to earth as a weasel. Just when we have them, something comes up to snatch them from our grasp!"

"They won't be snatched this time," assured the Olgnite

chieftain, looping another coil of the smelly black webbing over Deros's hands, binding them roughly to her saddle horn. She fought vainly against the rough claws that tied her, but to no avail, and her heart sank, for she could no longer reach the hidden knife.

"Oh, Ephinias, if you are anywhere near, please help us!" she whispered through gritted teeth, her tears stinging her eyes and leaving a salty taste in her mouth.

A voice reached her mind then, not the old teacher's but as familiar. "Your job is to hold on to your horse no matter what happens," Gitel said. The horse had managed to move closer to the girl's mount without Olag Grieshon being aware of it.

"That's all I *can* do," wailed Deros bitterly. "He's tied me to my saddle!"

"All the better, little one! When the moment comes to act, it will be lightning fast, and there will be no time for mistakes."

"What can you do now?" wept the girl. "You are a prisoner too!"

Gitel's ears went back, and he bolted forward with such suddenness, it almost toppled the startled Olgnite leader, dragging the girl's horse with him when he took flight.

"Curse this filthy screw!" screeched Olag Grieshon. "Pull up, you worthless hack, or I'll have your hide for my buckler! Hold up!" He jerked the sharp bit so hard, it tore Gitel's mouth.

Seravan's voice in his mind calmed him, and Gitel allowed his hated enemy rider to control him with the spurs. He blew out a loud snort, raised his ears, and danced nervously sideways, as though he had been spooked. His companion's voice came again, this time aloud. "You must forgive him, Olag! He was a Steward mount and is ignorant of the great warrior Grieshon!"

"He won't be long," spat the Olgnite. "I'll have the steel and whip to him until he'll breathe no breath without waiting to see if I mean him to have it! I've ridden nags better than this to death in the campaigns, and by the Red Mountain of Leech, I'll use his hide for my tent before I'm through with him!"

"A sorry tent," returned Seravan, unable to stop himself. "He would leak like a sieve and stretch dry on a frame."

Gitel shot a piercing look at his companion but was wrenched around by his rider.

"Then we'll have to teach him better manners," fumed the spiderman. "By the gore in my heart, I'll have this puny beast wishing it had been slain with its wretched Steward master before this night is out!"

A shrill, grating signal horn bleated over the great, thundering noise of the moving Olgnite horde, and Olag Grieshon spurred Gitel even more savagely to catch up to his banner carrier, who held the blood-red cloth that portrayed the sword piercing the sun, which Owen had seen on the shield of the Olgnite in Emerald's room in Sweet Rock. "They've caught scent!" shrieked Olag Grieshon. "The scouts have caught scent of the pinkers! Form up your lines and be ready for the attack!"

"Olag! Olag!" came the booming cry, and the noise of swords and shields clashed again, adding to the deafening rumble of the horses' hooves.

The Olgnite chieftain jerked Gitel's head up brutally and held back, leaning across his saddle to speak to Owen. "Now, my fat webber, you shall have your chance to please Olag Grieshon. My scout says the Steward scum are waiting in ambush for us, so we can give them our own surprise if you haven't lied to me!"

Owen's mind clouded with hazy red thoughts, and he clacked his fangs rapidly. Seravan answered quickly for his rider. "I have not lied, Mighty One. My road lies out of sight, and we can catch them all from behind in their lair! They'll never know where we came from. Lots of pinkers, then!"

Owen uttered a guttural sound, his eyes rolling back, and he reeled dangerously in the saddle. A dark shadow, edged in green, covered his vision, and he struggled to see beyond the dim curtain, then screamed in terror as it parted, and there was his old face, hideously distorted, pressed close against his vision, with the terrible killing fangs sunk deeply into Deros's throat. The waking dream was so horrible and so real, it shook him from the grip of the Olgnite spell, and the human part of him scrambled to recover control. He gripped Gillerman's sword tightly, feeling as though he would squeeze it until he crushed it, and he called out weakly to Seravan. "Help me! I can't fight this much longer. I'm losing my hold!"

"What say? Speak up, you worm! Olag Grieshon can't hear!"

There was a general uproar then, as the Olgnite troops broke out of the denser wood, and the horses ran more freely as they approached the long meadow that bordered the Ellerhorn Fen. In the more open, unbroken ground they formed a skirmish line that spread in both directions for a great distance. The streaming torches flared behind the riders, making ugly red blazing sparks in the sleek black coat of night. For as far as Owen could see, the lights ran on, giving an unearthly reddish-orange shadow to the Olgnite chieftain and keeping Deros's face in shadow, as she was jerked roughly along beside her captor.

The fen was marked clearly by the deeper shadows behind the wall of mist that hung more ominously in the night hours, and the fires from the enemy torchlight reflected like a solid sheet of burnished copper. As they approached, Olag Grieshon reached over and snatched the reins from Owen's hands. "I will keep you beside me, in case your shortcut is guarded by the pinkers! I don't want to have to search to find you when I want your heart!"

"They won't know we're there," replied Seravan, in a cold, steely voice. "It will be a clear and costless victory, oh, Olag."

"Murdam! Slag! Call up the creepers! We'll put them at the front of the line!"

As his order was carried out, Olag Grieshon rode slowly forward with the captive girl on one side, leading Owen on Seravan. The Olgnite warriors called creepers began to pour toward the front of the battle formation, wild eyes glinting in the torchlight. Their armor was nothing more than soft leather jerkins, and they were armed only with short, wicked-looking daggers and choking cords, and as they passed their leader, they all rose in their saddles and gave a silent salute, then were gone, taking their places in the front ranks of the advance.

"How far are we from your secret hole?" asked Olag Grieshon.

"The way in is just beyond the three rocks ahead," returned Seravan. "It is narrow, so only two or three at a time can pass the trail!"

"We'll have a quick look with the creepers," said the big spiderman. "They have a nose for these things." The Olgnite leader and his two lieutenants reined in, holding tightly to Deros's horse and keeping Owen between them.

Slag reached across Murdam and grabbed the front of the young man's tunic. "You is soon enough going to feel the quirt-string of the creepers, you is." Slag snarled. "If they don't find no pinker hole, we is all going to have a sport with you before we drains you out!"

A slashing hiss cut through the air, and the wicked whip of Olag bit into Slag's wrist, causing him to flinch and to drop Owen back into his saddle. "Enough! We ride now! The creepers are in!" Olag Grieshon pointed to the beginning of the fen. All along the front lines the enemy troops waved streaming torches and hammered their shields with their drawn swords, a savage excitement burning in their eyes as they felt the nearness of a coming massacre.

Deros tried to pull away from the close rein the spiderman had her on and was rewarded with another blow from the whip. He slashed at her again just as Gitel pranced away sideways, so his second blow missed the girl but landed harshly on the horse's flank.

"You scattered brute! You may have had that bad habit from the Steward scum, but I'll beat it out of you here!" He cut Gitel again with the whip, drawing blood on the big animal's rump.

"Steady, lad," cautioned Seravan in his friend's thoughts. "Just a little more."

Owen had fallen into a nightmare again. Drawn under by the Olgnite curse, he drifted in and out of a red, fiery hell, his heart drumming with the shouts and cries for blood, and the hollow hunger that rose inside him like a growing pain in his gut, turning his vision to a red haze and forcing all thoughts from his mind but the need to kill and drink the blood of a victim.

Seravan comforted him. "Be ready, lad! We won't have much time once we reach the fen! It shall be soon now!"

Owen leaned forward over the horse's neck, close to Seravan's ear. "Help me! I can't fight these feelings much longer. Call Ephinias!"

"It won't be much longer now! Hold fast, lad! The Olgnite is on Gitel, which is not what we'd planned, but it will work nicely enough when the time comes."

Deros was weeping at his side then for a moment, as the crush of attackers racing for the entrance to the fen forced the horses closer together. Owen watched dully as the girl looked at him, then cringed, her face a mask of horror and revulsion. "Even Deros finds me hateful," he spat, torn by a wave of self-pity that swiftly turned into a killing rage and washed over him with such strength, it was all Seravan could do to contain the hunched, grotesque form astride him until they crossed over through the mists of the fen and into the pandemonium that had broken out there on the heels of the creepers. A long, dark line of squat trees marked the entrance of the bog, and the Olgnites had gone through a small cut in these, safely for some several hundred paces, until the leader with the blue sash kicked Gitel brutally and dragged the girl and Owen in beside him. Murdam and Slag followed closely behind, with a dozen more hard upon their heels.

Out of the corner of his eye Owen caught the barest hint of motion, a small movement distorted by the torchlight and flickering shadows, but the next instant he recognized the colors of a Steward shield and saw the burly form of Stearborn barreling into the Olgnite leader, flanked by another younger man he didn't recognize, slashing at the foul, black rope web that held the girl. A horn went off with short, urgent notes, then the cries of startled Olgnites were heard as Murdam and Slag rode to aid their chieftain. Seravan drove hard sideways, hurtling himself against the chest of Slag's horse with such force, it unseated the man and almost threw Owen off as well. Then there was the cruel noise of the bog sucking down the senseless Olgnite, before he had had a chance to utter a single cry.

Murdam slashed at Owen, catching his shield and the back of his arrow quiver, and was preparing to direct another blow at his head when the youth grabbed the handle of his own sword out of reflex and felt the pulsing, painful stab of energy that flowed into him from the blazing hot sword of Skye.

"Use it!" Seravan snorted, wheeling aside to pull away from the Olgnite. "Use the sword!"

Owen's wrist was bleeding from a nick the enemy warrior had given him with the first blow, and the sight of his blood set off such a raging tide within him that he parried the next blow with his own blade and drove the spiderman backward from the combined force of his sword and the momentum of Seravan blocking the other animal.

There was a scream from behind, and when Owen whirled to see, the Olgnite chieftain and Stearborn were gone, vanished from sight, and the girl's horse was struggling wildly in the grasp of the bog, shrieking in terror, its eyes rolling up until nothing but stark white showed dimly in the swirling flames of the torches. Signals were coming from everywhere behind now, and in the next breath Owen felt Seravan jump the distance between the girl and solid ground, landing close enough to await Gitel, who had emerged from the thickening gray fog.

"Throw me the rope," called Gitel.

"I can't," cried Deros. "I'm tied to my saddle horn!"

"Jump, Owen! Throw her my reins!"

He leapt from Seravan's back and threw the leather reins before Murdam overtook him, cutting viciously at him as his charge carried him past the youth. Deros grabbed at the small leather straps and quickly wrapped them about her hands as the dying animal beneath her was sucked farther into the dreadful maw of the Ellerhorn.

As Owen dodged, the small pebble that Ephinias had placed in his cloak fell free and began to glow dimly.

Murdam, catching sight of the hateful object, shrieked loudly, his horse retreating a step backward. "'Ware, Olgnite! A Stengil!"

Owen's own pulse raced, his muddled brain flashed warnings of danger, and then he saw the grotesque hulk looming out of the mist behind Murdam and recognized Olag Grieshon instantly, his misshapen body covered with a shiny slime and raging toward them with fangs spread wide, a howl of unutterable fury coming from his throat.

Owen threw the Stengil into the Olgnite's face just in time to avoid being cleaved in two by the wickedly curved black sword. Deros, who was barely pulled free of the bog by Seravan, hurled the small dagger Stearborn had given her at the same time.

"Up, lad!" cried Seravan. "Up, lad! The girl!"

Owen was stumbling about blindly, his vision suddenly dim, then gone, from the flashing glare of the sword and the Stengil, but he somehow managed to find Seravan's stirrup. Someone mounted before him, clawing at him to help him into the saddle. Gitel neighed a warning then, and the reeling darkness began to sway dizzily under him. A brilliant patch of stars and a pale, trine moon hung low over the long, black landscape below, traced only by a splinter of silver where the River Line ran, and Owen fell, spinning slowly into a vast softness that smelled of heather. There was a flash and a stab of pain so intense he knew he was dying, burning like a white-hot fire, then there was nothing but the throbbing wing beat of a great white presence that hovered near him, until he could not tell if it was a wing beat without, or his own heart pounding slowly in his aching chest.

The Brothers
Shine

In the distance Famhart and Emerald heard the great commotion of the Olgnite army, and the low clouds overhead reflected the thousands of torches of the enemy hordes as they gathered for their attack on the Ellerhorn. Chellin Duchin sat quietly astride his horse, watching the shifting dark visions in the sky and playing idly with a short dagger that was carried at his belt.

"What do you make of it?" asked Famhart, looking to his old commander.

"Maybe they've found that old war-horse Stearborn," answered Chellin, squinting at the dark sky where just a hint of stars were beginning to break through. He spat and wiped his mouth with the back of his hand. "That old buck will have a hand in this business somewhere."

"But he had no squadron behind him," argued Emerald. "Surely he wouldn't be so foolhardy!"

Famhart laughed and clapped the minstrel on the back. "Stearborn is from the Malignes! There is no such thing as being outnumbered or defeated! There is no word for *surrender* in those high mountain clans, and there's no more honorable death than to fall in a hopeless cause."

Chellin Duchin nodded, a wry, sad smile creeping across his weathered features. "Aye, that's why he joined with the Stewards when he did!"

A dozen or more Olgnites came into view then, riding hard toward the distant flames and noise and were shocked at the presence of Chellin's squadron, which fell on the patrol, quickly dispatching them after a short, brutal fight.

"We shall have need to see what's drawn these brutes into the open," said Famhart, still looking worn and frail but driven by the desperate need for news of his son and Stearborn, and to know the reason for the sudden appearance of the entire Olgnite horde at a point away from the well-laid snare they had baited at the entrance of the Ellerhorn.

The ground was disappearing once more in the fog. The Steward rush lamps reflected pale gold against the mist, showing all the anxious faces as they waited for the attack of the spidermen.

Elita, who had been tending to Famhart, pointed to a silvery-white shape that seemed to be coming toward them over the stunted trees and thorn-brakes. "Look! It must be news!"

Emerald at first thought it was Ephinias, but saw as the bird drew nearer, that it was a great white falcon with piercing yellow-gold eyes that were at once fierce and kind.

The bird flared out his powerful wings to their full length and landed on the ground next to Famhart, walking about with the odd, awkward gait of a bird of prey. "Greetings, Famhart! My service, minstrel! I have news from the distance yonder, where my old friend Ephinias is at work tending to our young apprentice Olgnite. They have fallen out with the enemy and are free of the Olgnite lines, making for the grove in the Grealing Wood."

Emerald made a noise to interrupt the falcon but was cut off with a stern look. "There were a number of the spidermen drawn into the bog there, and they've lost their leader, so this may be as good a time as any to make your retreat."

"My service, windwalker!" returned Famhart. "Who are you?"

"Gillerman," answered the bird softly. "You might recognize me if I were in my other forms, but you may recall my name."

"Owen Helwin speaks of you constantly," said Emerald. "All I've heard from the first time I met him was Gillerman and Wallach this or that."

"Spoke of us, did he?" asked Gillerman, obviously pleased, motioning on the air with his wings while hopping about to stand next to the minstrel.

"Have you news of any Stewards there in the fight now? Were there any stragglers that you saw?" asked Famhart. "There should be some Steward troops there who were separated from their squadrons."

"I saw no squadrons or stragglers," replied the bird. "There were a great many spidermen, although their numbers have been reduced by the hungry mire of the Ellerhorn."

"Can we lure those louts this way?" questioned Famhart, disappointed by the news and trying to see more clearly into the curling black smoke that hung as a dark shadow against the night sky. The smell of the heavy flames of the torchlight reached them then, and the booming war cries faintly fluttered at the edge of their hearing.

"If we can convince them this is the way to freedom! And blood! They are hungry now and need to kill before they weaken too much. The unfortunate prisoners they hold won't feed them all for long."

Port, who had listened quietly, suddenly stood, adjusting his sword and buckler as he did so. His brother, who had been facing him across one of the battle lamps, rose with him, and they approached Famhart in a deliberate manner, their spurs making small jingling noises as they moved.

"We have something to say," Port announced.

"Say on," urged Famhart.

"Let's sashay back down that way to get them after us again," suggested Port. "If we can get them coming this way, there's a good chance we can lure them in or pick them off at our convenience as they try to tame the bog!"

Starboard nodded vigorously as his brother spoke. "The ground here is hard enough to fool almost anyone, until it's too late. Then *splut*—" The brother from Trew made a motion with his hands indicating something being dragged under by the unforgiving fen.

"It might be just the time we need to secure our own position and to find our way on to the coast," said Famhart. "If they're busy there, they might not have time to play about with us."

"Best not to miss the chance," argued Chellin. "If we don't know where our good louts are, we're in deep trouble. I'm with Port. I think we should strike a blow here, to lead them back to our good snare. But we'll need reports. Can you give us that?" he asked Gillerman, who had been carefully studying the men as they talked among themselves in the soft glow of the battle lamps.

"That and more," replied Gillerman. "If there are no longer settlements here and these spidermen overrun all the old countries, it will be hard to be among these Lower Boundaries." A slow, measured beat began then, as the snow-white falcon lifted to rise from the cold, gray, shrouded earth of the fen. "I'll set them off this way if I can. Ready yourselves! There's no second place in this fight. They are strong and outnumber you, but a different wind blows now, I think. The heat from the old mountain is starting to come our way if I'm not mistaken!"

There was a smell then of burning torches and sweat, and the low murmuring of the men as they set about preparing for a fight. They watched the graceful falcon ride higher on the wind, circling higher into the dark blue cave of heaven, until he was at last out of sight. Chellin Duchin turned to the others then, and barked out his curt commands, bringing them back to the tasks at hand. Jeremy was at his side, and Judge and Hamlin painfully outfitted themselves in their battle gear, despite their wounds.

"There's always this," groaned Judge, wriggling into his leather coat. "No matter how much in need of rest we are, good Chellin always manages to find us some frolic that'll keep us out of our warm, dry beds and away from the feast!"

"Don't forget the fair ones who would be waiting on us," added Hamlin. "If we had listened to our Elders, we would have shunned this life of a Steward like a black pestilence and become merchants or weavers."

"You'd have lasted a week and been driven from settlements from here to the borders," chided Chellin. "No one could have taken as good care of you as old Chellin Duchin! You wastrels will be hard put to it to keep up with the rest of the squadron this night, so you'd better look to it and put yourselves somewhere we can keep an eye on you!" The old commander's tone was gruff, but he helped Judge into his battle garb.

"Do you think the falcon can draw the Olgnites into our trap?" asked Jeremy.

"If we move the squadrons in a way that makes them think we've run into a dead end and are trying to backtrack, they may fall for that ruse." Famhart's eyes were narrowed in deep thought as he tried to see what plan might lure the Olgnites into their snare.

"It looks as though it won't take much to get their attention," added the minstrel. "Whatever has gotten them that far, we won't have much to do but show ourselves."

"And there's no reason we shall have to hold back, now that we know Owen and Deros are clear," said Famhart. "Nothing for it now but to slay as many of them as we can and make our way to the coast."

"I shall go to Linne and tell her Owen is free of the Olgnites," offered Elita. "She will want this news badly."

"Stay with her," said Emerald, grasping her hand tightly. "We shall be back this way soon enough, and it may be dangerous here, with the Olgnites following us in!"

"You can put your spur straps on it," growled Port. "If I have to ride right in and spit in their eye, they'll be hot after old Port's sap, right enough. But he's a sly dog and has a nasty bite!"

Starboard laughed grimly. "Two brothers from Trew are up to no good this night! We may evoke the old king's curse if need be, to blight these devils with!"

"We'll need everything we can get," replied Famhart. "So blight away! Chellin! You and your squadron take the flank and cover our open side there along the woods! Port, you and Starboard set some of your men here at the entrance, so that when we come back, you can close the pincers on them."

"Like an iron vise," muttered Starboard, crumbling an imaginary victim with his gloved hand.

"Emerald, you and my lads will do the honors of being the slap in the face for our brutish friends out yonder. No unnecessary risks, just enough to get them after us. We don't want a fight in the open ground, and it's getting hard to find our cut into the fen here, so we'll leave it marked with torches. Remember to steer straight between them or it's all up!"

"We'll make sure the torches are kept," said Port. "Keep a weather eye for 'em when you come back. It's darker than the dungeon at Rogen Keep beyond the rush lamps, and that accursed fog is thickening again."

"Sound the muster," Famhart said quietly over his shoulder to the Steward who stood there. "We ride now!"

Emerald had uncovered his bow and quiver and arranged the elven mail shirt Elita had given him beneath his tunic, talking in a low, hushed tone to the girl who waited beside him. She hurriedly kissed him. She walked quickly toward the front of the procession and did not look back.

"Look at that!" cried Jeremy as he mounted. "They're trying to torch the bog!"

In the distance the flames and noise of a great multitude of voices raised into a growl of rage, and the shields were pounded into a frenzy of sounds then, growing slowly stronger, like a great wave in the darkness, rolling toward the shore.

"Something's really riled them now," said Chellin Duchin, adjusting his stirrups for the coming battle. "It will be left for us to give them something to remember the Stewards by."

"Aye, damn their black souls," spat Port. "The sons of Trew will call up all the demons of the old homelands to help them find their way to the cellars of hell where they belong!"

"We'll have the blackguards' colors this night to carry away, or my bones won't budge from this infernal mire!" added Starboard.

"The colors, it is," roared Chellin Duchin. "I'll stand the

round for the man who gets the colors! That'll send 'em packing after us."

"Have a care," cautioned Famhart. "All we need is for them to follow us back here! We have no troops to waste in a prolonged fight!"

Chellin looked levelly at his old friend and commander. "We have never wasted a life to my knowing," he said softly. "And if we don't get the colors of these devils, Stearborn's loss will be too much to take."

A look of understanding passed between them then, and they finished their preparations in a silence broken only by the thin jingle of cinch or bridle, the rasping sound of steel being drawn and checked, and the heavy, excited breathing of the animals.

"Light the battle torches," ordered Famhart.

The word was passed back down the line, and in twos and threes the crude pitch torches flared up angrily, until the cold, gray mists of the fen were afire with the red reflections, and at a short note from his horn to advance, Famhart led the first of the squadrons out into the blue, moonlit green between the wood and the fen, which formed a broad alleyway that ran all the way toward the flames in the distance and which seemed to have grown and spread farther out on both sides, filling the darkness with a guttural roar of chanting and the dreadful drumming of sword against shield.

"Skirmishers out," called Famhart, and the squadron spread out into its fighting formation, spaced a few feet apart, and began a slow trot forward. Chellin Duchin's followed suit after Famhart's, and dispersed into their battle formations. Port and Starboard were the last out, and the two brothers recklessly drove their troop forward, to be at the spearhead of the feint, both of them calling out in hoarse voices to encourage their men and shouting back and forth to each other in the old tongue of Trew.

Emerald rode at Famhart's side, watching his friend closely, although it seemed the exhaustion had melted away with the terrible promise of the coming fight. There was a definite light in his eyes, but the minstrel was unable to tell if it was from a fever or from the excitement of the battle fire that had put it there.

"Elita will thank me to put you back in a safer spot," said Famhart, glancing over his shoulder. "For a man who escaped the wedding feast with a whole hide, you are living at the ragged edge and pushing your luck a bit in this."

"Better here than in that putrid mire," replied Emerald. "The air is so heavy there, you can't get a breath that's free of decay and damp!"

"We may be glad for it, once we've put this nest of hornets up!"

The pace had increased steadily, and in order to keep up with Port and Starboard, Famhart had to signal a faster pace still. The brothers from Trew raced headlong toward the enemy, swords gleaming in the streaming torchlight and calling wildly to the Olgnites that their deaths were on the wind.

"I hope we can reel them back in time," said Famhart, urging his horse to a gallop. "Those two can reach battle fire more quickly than any but Stearborn and Chellin Duchin, and they're the last to cool!" As he spoke, the first of the enemy outriders was encountered and quickly slain. They had mistaken the brothers for a patrol of Olgnites and not seen their mistake until the last moment, when they recognized that the howling men were human and not their own.

A wild volley of arrows descended upon them out of the darkness, some from near the woods on one side, the rest from a place at the bog's edge on the other. They spurred their mounts harder and outdistanced the archers who had also been surprised to see the full contingent of embattled Stewards charging even though they were hopelessly outnumbered by the Olgnite horde.

Famhart and Emerald heard the terrible crash of colliding armies as Port and Starboard breeched the enemies' lines, for Emerald the battle din dropped almost to silence, the odd, deadly quiet that he always experienced in the heated pitch of the fight. Almost at once he, and Famhart beside him, were engaged by a dozen spidermen, caught off their guard but quickly recovering. Chellin Duchin's squadron went in to their left and was lost in the turmoil of horses and men, plunged instantly in mortal combat with the enraged Olgnites.

The spidermen directly following their Olag had come upon the quick confrontation when the two Stewards had attacked inside the fen, and they had seen the fall of their leader and the death of Murdam and Slag. Reeling from the ambush, they alerted the others, who roared their bloodlust and began to rage about, destroying everything they touched and torching the rest. They had tried without success to set the fen afire, to burn out their prisoners and any Stewards who might be there, but the rotten wood in the bog was too wet to burn. So intent were they upon destruction that the spidermen had not seen nor heard the approach of Famhart and the other Steward squadrons until the last moment.

The force of their charge carried the Stewards deep into the enemy formations, and they soon found themselves caught up in a vicious fight that was too heavy in numbers at the onset and grew more so as they stayed on. Famhart blew a long, steady note to signal retreat and spun his horse around, but the animal stumbled, sending him sprawling headlong under the horses of the Olgnite soldiers on both sides of him. Emerald saw his friend go down and was beside him in a flash so that Famhart was able to throw himself weakly behind the minstrel.

"Here's a horse!" cried Emerald. "We have to ride for the fen now! We're in too deep!"

"Ride! I'm behind you!" cried Famhart, slipping from one horse to the other and gathering the reins in one flowing, practiced motion. The memory of the horseman from the Gortland Fair flickered through his mind then, and he smiled in spite of himself as he spurred the horse forward. He realized with a start that there were other animals tethered to his own, and he quickly cut the rope, watching the terrified beasts disappear into the dark behind him. They were pack animals, heavily laden with strange bundles. He saw Emerald ahead, cutting through a line of Olgnites, dodging their blows, and followed closely behind.

Arrows sang their buzzing note over his head, but he was free of the enemy lines, and looking quickly to both sides, he saw all the squadrons flying back for the entrance to the Ellerhorn, save as usual, the brothers from Trew. They rode ahead of the pursuing army, holding aloft the blood-red banner of the Olgnites flapping wildly in the wind.

Far ahead, seeming like two small pins of light in the dark shadows of the fen, Famhart saw the two lines of rush lamps that marked safety. He spurred his exhausted horse onward, following closely behind the pounding hooves of the big gray the minstrel rode.

Shadow
Riders

Near the tower of the old church, Kegin squatted beside his horse, longsword and bow ready to hand. Lorimen and Findlin had gone ahead on the faint trace of path that led through the ruined churchyard, to muster the other Archaelians and to see if they could find a sign of Enlid. Linne sat in the soft earth next to her old companion with the elven bow across her lap, looking away at the fiery reflections in the sky above the fen.

"It looks like they've burned half the wood," she said half aloud, but her thoughts were elsewhere, with her son and Famhart.

"They won't be able to fire this damp hole," Kegin snorted. "That's one thing we can be grateful to this bog for."

"Do you think Findlin and Lorimen will find the lad they brought? They seem so sure of themselves."

Kegin started to answer, then saw the look on Linne's face and changed his reply. "The Olgnites aren't into the bog, and the Parson has stopped that thing that attacked us. There's a good chance he may have already made it to the Grealing Wood and is waiting."

Linne smiled faintly. "Thank you, good Kegin. Your kindness helps me keep heart."

"Owen will be all right, my lady. He has Ephinias looking after him."

"That's what worries me," replied Linne. "Sometimes his 'looking after' is the next worst thing to have happen."

"We have no news to the contrary, so we must stay on the tack that all is going well. It will only rob our spirit if we think anything else."

She reached out and touched his sleeve. "You are ever the one to see the light side, old friend."

"There is only one side to see when you think of it," he replied. "I have ridden to the Steward colors so long, that is all I know. To do otherwise would be disloyal."

A voice reached them then, hailing Linne from a distance back among the procession and nearer the entrance to the fen. "My lady Linne! Here is news!"

"Here!" cried Linne, springing up and running toward the voice.

There was a stir of excitement that buzzed through the waiting ranks, and Elita hurried to her from the crowd, tears glistening on her cheeks; on her face was a smile of relief that melted Linne's reserve. The older woman, too, burst into tears as the two embraced. "Owen is free of the Olgnite lines, and they have the girl. Gillerman came to us and told us that. Famhart and Emerald have led an attack out of the fen to draw the rest of the spidermen back to the trap we've laid at the entrance. They left just as I came to you, so I have no news of that."

"There's news enough there," replied Kegin, his face turned to the boiling, fiery sky in the direction of the Olgnite encampment. "With luck we shall have them drawn in here where their numbers will be a hindrance."

"All the squadrons went," continued Elita. "They wished to avenge Stearborn."

Kegin's voice was unsteady when he spoke, and he looked away from the two women. "There is no further word of him?"

Elita's silence answered his question, and he paced nervously back to his horse, adjusting his weapons and fiddling with his saddle and gear.

"If Gillerman was there, it may bode well for our friend," soothed Linne. "He's too crafty and tough to be waylaid by the Olgnites."

"He's crafty and he's tough," returned Kegin quietly, "but bad luck is still bad luck. It can happen to anyone."

"Our luck may be turning," said Elita. "Before he left, Gillerman said something about a burning mountain changing the tide of this attack."

"I'd prefer another ten squadrons of Stewards to a burning mountain," snapped Kegin, looking toward the flaming sky.

"Findlin said they could raise another two hundred men," said Linne.

"It'll take more than those bungling oafs from Fionten," shot Kegin angrily. "They couldn't even handle the Bogmot without losing the one advantage we held. If it hadn't been for the Parson, there's no telling what would have happened."

"You are too harsh in your judgment," said Linne. "They are harmless enough, and I like them. You smart from your loss of a comrade, my friend. We all feel Stearborn's absence."

"I won't believe he's gone until I hear word from someone who saw it." Kegin's eyes were dark and troubled in the glow of the rush lamps, and he picked his bow up, notched an arrow to the string, and let fly the shaft, in the direction of the battle—noise that dimly reached their ears.

"Famhart may bring back news," said Elita hopefully. "They will have seen the whole field afresh."

"We should ready ourselves in case the Olgnites come this far in," said Linne, looking for a ploy to pull them all out of the deepening gloom over the disappearance of the salty old Steward commander, who had known them all through the years of struggle for The Line. She remembered his eternal stories of border uprising, or rebellion, and the floors he had ruined by his insistence on wearing his spurs indoors.

"There are signals now," called out a Steward sentry, left to guard Linne. "They've reached the Olgnites' lines and are coming back! I've heard the retreat sounded!"

"Let's make ready, then," cried Kegin, eager to turn his thoughts away from his sadness and loss. "Hop to it, now! Let's see if we can't load this path with a few surprises for the spidermen! They are good with webs to snare their victims, so we shall copy their style and see if we can't feed these bog wraiths a few of the Olgnites to sour their stomachs a bit!"

All along the line of citizens from Sweet Rock, the call went out to prepare to flee, once the last of the Steward squadrons were into the Ellerhorn once more and those of the patrol left with Kegin set about rigging man-traps strung from the rocks and stunted trees, and old-fashioned trip springs, which shot a bolt from a crossbow into a man or horse from concealment and was meant to maim, rather than kill. They were old tricks, gathered over the years from the bloody border skirmishes that the Stewards had for so long been drawn into, and lethal, shadowy fights with the invaders from the far regions of the Wastes of Leech or the Plain of Reeds. Over a period of time, Kegin realized that the brutal tactics of their enemies had become standard warfare for all the armies, until now it was simply a matter of practical means, a simple device with but one use: to kill or cripple an enemy. He thought about that briefly, then jerked himself back to business. "None of that, lad! Not now! Maybe when we're safe on the coast and away from this god-forsaken bog!" He half muttered his thoughts.

"Are you all right, Kegin?" asked Linne.

"All right, my lady? I should wonder at it, but if you mean now, then yes, I'm well enough."

Linne shot a slanting glance at him but was occupied with the women of the caravan as they organized an aid station for their men. She had them split into groups, some tearing cloth for bandages, others preparing litters for the horses to move wounded with, and yet others arranging arms and stores to be divided among the squadrons when they came in to regroup and restock. Before long, a horn sounded a series of urgent calls, signaling that the Stewards were racing for the fen and that they had wounded with them.

"Hop to it!" shouted Kegin, readying everything for a

plunge onward and striding forward into the rising mists in the direction in which the two Archaelians had gone.

"I should have kept one of them with me," he said aloud to no one in particular. "This road may split again, and they've left no word as to how to get out of this maze." He was almost jarred out of his senses when he saw a dark form rising out of the gloom ahead, making straight for him. His hand had lifted his longsword halfway from its scabbard when a familiar voice put him at ease.

"Put up, citizen! It's only Lorimen, come to see you safely to the growe. Findlin thought I should come back, since it looked to be an all-night job to reach the others and find Enlid."

"Hola, friend! You're a welcome sight! I was just thinking of you."

"And not with many good words, either," interrupted Linne, who had followed him into the shadows beyond the rush lamp to ask him about provisions.

Kegin flushed, remembering his harsh words earlier about the two Archaelians. "I was worried about Stearborn," he apologized lamely. "I haven't been myself since we've come into this miserable, wet hole."

"No one escapes the nature of the bog," said Lorimen cheerily. "I once spent three days and nights running here, and it took me a week of sunshine to shake it out of my pipes! It's not a natural place for those used to liwing in the light."

"It seemed to suit the Parson well enough," returned Kegin. "Doesn't seem to throw him any more out of sorts than he already was."

"I wouldn't be so quick to say, one way or another," answered Lorimen. "Some say it's better not to dwell too long on those things you don't know about."

"I'd like to know a lot more of him! And after all the danger he knows we're in, he just loads up that cripple and leaves us to ourselves!"

"He did get rid of the Bogmot," reminded Lorimen.

"I liked him," said Linne. "There's more to him than meets the eye. I can't put my finger on exactly what, but his eyes put me in mind of someone from long ago, when we were in the Middle Islands."

Lorimen pointed excitedly at the Steward sentry waiting by Linne's horse. "Look!"

The young man was frantically waving an arm to catch Kegin's attention, and the long line of rush lamps slowly began to wink out one by one, like stars in a smoky heaven.

"The others are coming! Come on! Lorimen, you stay with me to show me the track! Linne, hold closely to my horse, so we don't get lost in all this. I don't want to have to explain to Famhart that I lost you as well."

"He knows I can well enough take care of myself if need be. He would never hold you responsible."

"He might if he finds out I let Ephinias take Owen, and then without an argument to save my soul. I told Ephinias I'd go in the lad's place, but he said it had to be someone who has touched the blood of the spidermen."

"Owen was the one to go," said Linne, brushing back a loose hair from her forehead. She had noticed in the past few days that she had gone decidedly gray and began to wonder to herself how long she would have to wander about homeless this time, or if she would ever have a safe haven where she and Famhart could grow old in peace. She had often spent sleepless nights in the past, wondering how it was she had come to do all the things she had hated so much, and been involved for so long with wars and the sadness that went with it, and the long, lonely feelings that sometimes found her. "Owen was the one to go," she repeated. "And Elita has said that Gillerman told her Owen was free."

"That relieves me, my lady, more than I can say."

"We have to hold to Windameir's guidance in these things."

"That leaves me cold sometimes. I hardly know what to trust, beyond the Steward's code and steel!"

Linne laughed gently, touching her old friend on the arm. "You are as stubborn as the rest of your lot! You profess one thing to the world and hold another in your heart. But you don't fool me, Kegin Thornby. I've known you too long now to be put off by your stories and growls."

He blushed again, stammering.

"No use arguing with me. A woman knows in a way a man can never fathom. Call it the Sight if you will, or magic, or a witch's spell. If you were married, you'd know more about this."

"I was almost married once," replied Kegin, a faint trace of sadness edging into his voice.

Linne was one the verge of teasing him but stopped herself. When he did not continue, she asked quietly, "What happened?"

Kegin shook his head. "I don't know. Never did know. She said something about her father not wanting her betrothed to the empty life of a Steward."

A faint smile crossed Linne's face. "Does this look like an empty life to you?"

He laughed in spite of himself. "I wouldn't describe it as such."

More horns sounded then, and the muffled noise of hoofbeats reached them. "They've reached the fen! Quickly, Lorimen! We shall have little time to be ready."

"One of those signals was Findlin," reported the stout Archaelian. "They are gathered not far from here. Shall I hawe them hold where they are?"

"Aye. Hold and wait for us!"

Lorimen pulled the small signal horn from his cloak and blew a series of notes, then waited, listening to make sure he had been heard. "There are other signals there than Findlin!" cried the man.

"They may be Stewards," returned Kegin. "We have some stragglers loose."

"These are not yours. I can't make much out, but they're calling among our own horns plainly enough."

Elita had joined them and noticed the small bracelet of bells worn by Lorimen. "Those are very like the Dreamers," she said. "They sometimes wore those."

"I know," said Lorimen.

"They were fond of things like that. They sounded horns very like the ones you're hearing too."

"Could that be?" breathed Kegin, hardly daring to let his hopes rise.

"Could that be?" repeated Linne, looking evenly at her

beautiful friend. "They promised they would be back for your betrothal."

Elita lowered her head, and what appeared to be tears reflected off her cheeks in the light from the rush lamps. "I had hoped they would. This bog plays with sounds. I can't tell for certain if it's not a trick."

"The Parson called the Bogmot home! Wouldn't all the rest of the bog wraiths be called back with it?"

"I don't know, Kegin. I don't feel that everything about the fen is evil, but I don't know if all the dark things are gone," replied Linne.

"Sound your horn again," suggested Elita. "Let me hear once more. It may have been echoes."

Lorimen hastened to comply and blew another series of notes, then waited for his friend to reply, which came a few seconds later.

"There are two separate horns, right enough," said Lorimen, peering intently into the darkness in the direction of the sounds. "I can't make the other out, though."

"We'll find out who they are soon enough," shot Kegin, turning back to try to detect the riders coming behind them. "Let's be ready to move as soon as Famhart comes into sight. I'll signal to have word passed the minute the Stewards are spotted!" He blew another short call and was answered immediately. The other horns were heard from that direction as well.

"Could it be the Olgnites?" asked Lorimen, perplexed.

"No," answered Kegin, shaking his head.

They watched and waited then, smelling the heavy, oily fires of the riding torches and the sweeter aroma of the rush lamps, mingled with the damp air of the fen, which reeked of decay and rotten wood and the faint, sickly odor of swamp lilies, which bloomed throughout the bog.

"Damned funeral weeds," growled Kegin. "That smell is enough to turn your stomach."

"Listen!" cautioned Elita. "That's Emerald's signal."

"Ready up, then! Let's get to it," cried Kegin, calling back to the Steward who was his second in command. "Call them up, lad! Let's get to it! Pass the word back to watch out for the snares we've laid!"

Little by little the line of settlers and Stewards began their slow movement forward, following along closely behind Kegin and Lorimen, who led the way into the dense fog that covered the trail.

"How can you see where to go?" asked Kegin. "I've lost the path!"

"Here! Look at the trees, good citizen. Up near the height of your saddle. I marked it coming back, so I wouldn't lose it if the ground fog got too thick."

"You're very thorough," remarked Linne. "That's a small eye for detail that I appreciate."

"Like I said, we hawe been about here in the Grimpen on more than one occasion, so we'we learned the small tricks."

"It's one I hope we never have to use again," shot Kegin.

"We may not need it further," added Lorimen, not responding to the sarcastic tone his companion had used. "The fog seems to be lessening there ahead. It's clearer ground, and it spreads outward on both sides of the trail into solid ground for a bit."

Kegin turned to speak to Linne and saw the first of the riders out of the corner of his eye, standing at the very fringe of the misty curtain that slowly receded as the long procession wound into the clearing Lorimen had pointed out. The Archaelian had halted in the center of the trail and stood stock-still, staring. "They're motioning us to follow," he said at last, as one of the hooded riders rode into the clearing and beckoned.

"Who are they?" questioned Kegin.

"I don't know. I hawen't seen the dress before."

Elita spoke then, coming to stand beside Kegin. "They're friends. I don't know who they are, but they're friends."

"They're going in the right direction," said Lorimen. "As long as their way goes alongside ours, I guess there's no harm."

"Can you hail them?" asked the Steward.

Lorimen walked forward, as though he would approach the rider, but as the Archaelian neared, the rider in the path, and those on both sides, vanished into the mists.

"Hola, friend! My name is Lorimen, from Fionten. I carry

no ill will for any and am a friend of those who side with the Light!"

There was only silence for an answer, and the sounds of the advancing caravan behind them.

"What do you make of it?" asked Kegin, appealing to Elita.

"They are old, and they are friends. They may not speak, but they mean us no harm."

"Linne?"

"Lorimen has said it. They are on our trail, so it will cause no difficulty."

As soon as Lorimen had returned to his companions, the riders returned, beckoning to them again. Beneath the hoods, their eyes seemed to flash, and their long cloaks trailed over the saddles and down to their boots, entirely covering each rider. They turned as a troop, and the fidgeting horses stood stamping and pawing at the ground, eager to be off.

"At least they're real enough," said Kegin lightly but a little too loudly. "Their horses are blowing just like our own."

"Don't be too sure," answered Lorimen. "We'll see what we'll see when the sun is up, and we have something better than rushlight to see by."

The hooded men rode away then, although as their companions followed, they heard the jingle and creak of harnesses ahead of them and saw an occasional glimpse of one of the horsemen. They had gone on for sometime when Lorimen drew up a hand to halt the group, a perplexed frown darkening his flushed features.

The Changeling

"What is it?" hissed Kegin under his breath.

Lorimen shook his head slowly from side to side, a puzzled look on his flushed face. "This isn't the path to the growe! At least not by any chart I carry."

"What?"

"They hawe turned aside somewhere! This crossroad was newer one I took. As far as I know, the way they're going leads farther into the mire."

The winding string of rush lamps and torches behind drew to a halt, like dim, blazing sparks of light collected into an eddy that swirled at a dam.

Linne called Elita and waited, turning the problem over in her head. If the wrong way was taken now, then they would all be lost in the Ellerhorn, even though they had successfully evaded the Olgnite swarms and seemed on the verge of being able to reach the coast and safety, where they could regroup and begin a campaign to drive out the enemy hordes. That thought suddenly exhausted her, and she felt a weariness that made her shoulders slump, and speech seemed an impossible task.

"What is it, my lady? Are you ill?" asked Elita, alarmed at the pale features of her friend.

Linne reached out and steadied herself on Elita's arm. "No, just tired. We have reached a crossroad here, and our new ally has said the path the riders are leading us on goes on farther into the fen. I wondered if you had any feeling about this? I know you sometimes have the Dreamers' eyes and can see things that others can't."

"The eye of the Dreamers is closed, my lady, but I have no fear of the riders. They are from another time and are friends."

"How can you be so sure?" questioned Kegin, who had been standing beside Linne, trying to decide which way to take. "No one can get close enough to ask them!"

"You don't have to ask them, as we know it. They have a light about them that is plain to see."

"All I've seen is that if you try to approach them, they cower away like rats skulking in a cellar!" Kegin shot a slanting glance at Elita.

"They may be friends," muttered Lorimen, "but I hawe no knowledge of them. What shall we do?"

"I say go on the old way," replied Kegin. "It's where help will be waiting and where your men are to meet you!"

Almost in answer to the questions asked of them, the riders appeared again through the mists, pulling up their mounts and waiting impatiently just beyond the caravan. The same hooded rider who had approached before rode out from the rest.

Linne's horse whinnied, pawed the soft earth, and was answered by what seemed to be an echo of the silent rider's animal.

"The horse appears real enough," said Kegin.

"He's trying to speak! What's he saying?" Lorimen had taken a step toward the man.

As he neared the rider, the horse began to back away, until he was once again among the others who formed a line in the smoking mist, which slowly swirled around the horses' hooves and cast eerie shadows about the cloaked figures upon their backs.

"They want us to follow them," said Elita quietly. "They are helping us so they can rest. They have been in this fen for a long time, waiting."

"Who are they? Can you tell that?" asked Kegin, looking at the beautiful woman who was to wed the minstrel. He had always been half afraid of her, since she was once saved by the Elboreal and could sometimes see things mortals couldn't, and heard music from the air. "Can you hear them?"

"They speak like the Dreamers speak," she replied. "They have only the voice of air and earth."

"Their animals are real," insisted Kegin.

"They are the steeds of the Lost Ones. They are not flesh and blood as you think."

"I heard the horse," argued Kegin.

"We heard something that might be an echo," answered Elita. "Yet they are determined that we should follow them. They know something."

"What do they know?" asked Linne. "Can you hear?"

"They know something and want us to follow. That's all I can understand."

"Linne?" questioned Kegin, looking to her for orders.

She hesitated, then took Elita's hand and held it tightly for a moment. "We'll go with them."

"Even if it's farther into this bog?" asked Kegin.

Lorimen nodded. "I'd like to find out the answer to this business. It seems that they were the ones who turned out Bogmots, and these riders are another lot, from the other side. It would only make sense that there should be a balance to it!"

"Balance! You call these things a balance?"

"There are stories about the old days, before we first came to the Grimpen Mire. The maps showed two settlements, although they were long gone by the time we began to trawel here. One of the settlements must hawe been where the Crooked Spire stands, but I don't know where the other stood."

"Do you think that's where they're leading us?" asked Linne.

Lorimen frowned, lost in thought, stroking his chin. "I know not, my lady."

"Look!" interrupted Linne. "There ahead! Lights!"

"Is that your troop?" asked Kegin. "Maybe they're coming to meet you."

"Not from that direction."

"They're gone now," reported the Archaelian. "They'we wanished."

"The riders are going that way. They want us to follow," said Elita.

"We may as well go on. We're this far, we may as well see the end of this."

"Come on, then! Let's hop to it! Findlin will be surprised if we come on him at the growe, and we don't pass him on the trail there! That'll be worth it, to shake his old salt up!"

Elita waited beside Linne while Kegin and Lorimen began moving again, and the long string of rush lamps behind started flowing forward slowly, snaking away into the mists toward the rear. Farther back, there were sounds of fighting still, and the faint calls of the Steward war-horns, as they piled back into the fen, and fought to hold the Olgnites at bay.

"I hope this isn't one of our worst ideas," muttered Kegin. "This reminds me overmuch of a hole in the ground in the Darien Mounds. I hate to have to rely on the good instincts of a magician or a woman."

"They do seem to let one in for trouble," agreed Lorimen heartily. "Fionten is full of the spell workers ewery summer at the Mid Ewe celebrations. It is always mischief and strange behawior! It was one of those nights during a Mid Ewe festival that I was forced into a marriage when I was still no more than a stripling."

Kegin stopped and looked questioningly at the man. "You mean you had too much wine and took advantage of a maiden?"

Lorimen laughed a sudden, explosive laugh. "Oh, no! The father of a young lady I knew got himself full of a malted barley drink that was quite popular there and offered me a tidy situation in his merchant's guild. I was a wery poor young man and had no prospects."

"And you did it?"

"The young lady was wery handsome. I don't suppose I would have secured my future without thinking of that. It was a good arrangement for a number of turnings."

"All from a Mid Eve Fair with magicians!"

"They are a wery closemouthed lot. I'm not sure they're

so easy to deal with. I'd rather palawer with a seaman or a soldier. You know where they stand."

"What happened to your wife?"

Lorimen paused, pulling a small silver chain from beneath his tunic. "She was lost to the great storm in the Year of the Ram. Most of Fionten was adrift with the tides, and a great many perished. I newer found the heart to try again."

"Perhaps there is another Mid Eve Fair still in your cards," replied Kegin quietly.

Lorimen put the fine chain back under his tunic and sighed. "I don't know if I'd be ready for that. It took a long time to grow used to each other, and ewen then she hated my journeys. My happiest moments were when we had gone and come back, and the fire would be stacked high with logs, and a cold wind would be hunting in the streets. I'd undo the chest then, and show my treasures to her one by one, like a great king sharing his jewels with his queen. She lowed that game."

"Did you sire a family?" asked Kegin, talking to ease the tension. He tried to keep the ghostly figures of the riders in sight, but the fog grew denser as they retreated farther into the heart of the great fen, and it became more difficult to discern the dim figures from the shadowy darkness that loomed ever blacker as the night neared the stroke of mid-watch.

"No. There were no little ones. I have sometimes regretted that in my old age."

"You can't be all that old."

"I'm older than you might think, citizen. We come from a hearty stock along the coast."

Lorimen paused, touching Kegin's arm lightly. "The Lady Linne is calling you. See what she wants. It looks as though they are bearing straight on through. If I had my charts here, I'd say we're nearing the inner part of the Grimpen. There used to be a wall that ran through it, put up after the bad years."

"I won't be long," said Kegin, handing the Archaelian the reins to his horse and striding back to walk beside Linne.

A strange smell had slowly begun to spread, very subtly at first, mixed with the oily fires of the torches, the sweeter smell of the rush lamps, and the decay and rot from the bog. A very slight change in the color of the sky had also brought out the first of the early-morning stars, blazing whitely in the lower horizon of the east.

"Elita says it is a sign. Look, Kegin."

"I see it, my lady. It is the Magician."

"Ephinias and Gillerman must be successful in their work."

"I hope so. We are in short shrift of good luck these last days."

"It's coming on light," said Elita. "Soon we shall be able to see what we're about."

"So will the Olgnites," replied Kegin, his frown of concentration knotting his brow. "I hope Famhart and the others have led the blackguards in a hot hurry, or they'll be able to see our handiwork."

Horns traded calls behind them in a shrill, high tone, and the wild blaring of the enemy horns followed closely behind.

"It sounds as if you have your wish," said Elita. "They aren't so far behind."

Kegin listened intently, then smiled tiredly. "Those you hear so close won't be with us for long! They are coming through a part of the fen that has no bottom."

As his voice fell away, there came the sounds of chaos and destruction over the other early-morning sounds, with the screams of horses and spidermen being sucked into the open maw of the Ellerhorn and the frantic signal horns calling to guide the survivors back out onto solid ground.

"What we are smelling is the sea," announced Linne. "I couldn't quite tell what it was before, but it's the sea."

"How could that be, my lady?" asked Lorimen.

"I don't know. You're a seaman! Smell for yourself. Let your mind release the idea that we're locked into the Ellerhorn."

The Archaelian took a few cautious sniffs before rumpling his face into a scowl. "It's the rottenness of this mire that I get."

"I feel it, my lady," said Elita. "There are seabirds too. Their calls lift the heart."

Kegin stood resolutely beside Linne, testing the air with

his nose and trying to listen as intently as he was able. "It's beyond me, my lady, but I take you at your word. If you sense the sea, then I shall tell the others to be ready."

"The only thing I can see that would put us anywhere would be if this trail our speechless guides have brought us on is near the coast," muttered Lorimen. "But I hardly understand that, for we'we been here often, and know the Grimpen as well as anyone, and newer found such a place."

"No one could know this place truly, except those that died here, and maybe the Parson and his friend Twig," said Kegin. "They looked to be a pair that might have time to plot out a dark hole like this."

Lorimen shot the Steward a look intended to silence him. "You should newer speak harshly of him, friend. He may well know all the troubled souls and places that fill up our charts with danger marks, but that does not make him a part of it."

"Are you saying he's not dangerous?" asked Kegin.

"More dangerous than you might beliewe, but not because he is ewil or from the Darkness."

"Do your people have ships waiting?" asked Linne, addressing the Archaelian.

"We have three wessels, and sturdy crews, my lady. There were two landing parties as well. One was to stay with the ships, and the other to escort us here and wait until Enlid completed the rituals."

"How far is it to Fionten?" asked Kegin, calculating in his mind how many craft would be needed to transport the Steward squadrons and their horses, and all the surviving citizens from Sweet Rock.

"A two-week sail if we have a fair wind. A month if we don't and have to beat back up the coast."

"Would it be possible to find ships enough there to carry us on into the Silent Sea?"

"That's a woyage that's long and dangerous, my friend. You wouldn't want to strike out that direction without stout ships and crews that were seasoned salts of the Horinfal."

"But could we find ships in your home?" persisted Kegin.

"You could. It would take time. They could be built, or bought from some of the other ports along the coast."

"Have you seen any of the other Outland boats in your travels?" asked Linne, turning the subject for a moment. She had been thinking of her son, and the young woman from the distant country.

"Outland boats, my lady? There are many standards that ride the wawes, and I know a good number of them and hawe seen more which I could neither hail nor identify. The sea is full of those, both friend and foe."

"These were in the attack on our old settlement. They came to capture a girl, a princess, who came seeking help for her father in Eirn Bol."

"Do you know their colors?" asked Lorimen.

"Only that they're Hulin Vipre."

At the speaking of the name, Lorimen bowed his head and made a quick little gesture with his hand across his heart. "The Scourge," he hissed vehemently. "The Black Tide."

"They have boats left that we shall try to find and use," said Linne. "Those who came for the raid on Sweet Rock were killed, between the Stewards and the Olgnites."

"A nasty business," grumbled Lorimen. "Fits them well, right enough. They'we done their share of making widows and leaving fatherless children."

"Could we get crews to sail their vessels?" asked Kegin, following Linne's line of thought.

"Perhaps. We'd have to smoke out the craft and air her. I don't think a seaman from our coast would board a ship till she was swept clean of the bad deeds done by her old masters."

"Then we may find enough ships to hold us, and that would be able to help us reach the Silent Sea?"

"With time and luck," replied Lorimen.

"We shall certainly be in for our share of that," said Linne. "After all this it will be only our due."

"My thoughts, too, my lady," said Kegin, going back to the head of the procession and staring after the departed riders. "Are they still there, do you think?"

"They're there," answered Linne. "There's something else there as well. I can't quite make it out. It looks to be some sort of stonework."

Lorimen paced nervously forward and crept on until he

was almost lost from sight. "It looks like the old walls," he exclaimed excitedly. "We hawe reached the old boundaries of the mire!"

Kegin reached the spot and looked at the new find, gazing at the crumbling stones that still stood chest-high and ran off in a line, straight as an arrow both east and west.

"As the Grimpen slowly fell to the Darkness, those who were left for the Light tried to fence off the ewil that was growing there. In the old days, according to the books, this ran on both sides and was guarded to keep any innocent trawelers from falling wictim to the ones there who had turned to the Dark One."

"So there were some left who didn't fall?" asked Kegin. "All was not lost."

"It wery seldom goes that way," agreed Lorimen. "There were those then, and I think our guides now are from the good side of the issue. If we are at the wall, then we may be nearer the coast than I thought."

"And the Grealing Wood? We were to meet Owen in the Grealing."

"The growe! By the Helm of Galt, I forgot that! That's where we were to meet Enlid, too, and the others."

"Are we far?"

"I don't know anymore. I've gotten turned around here in all this, and I can't figure where we are until we're out."

"There's no need fretting now," called Linne. "Let us go on to the edge. We'll find our way then." She turned to listen over her shoulder, looking back at Kegin apprehensively. "It sounds as though there are a lot of the spidermen still in the fen! I hear their horns!"

"It may take some time to lose them, my lady. Never fear! Their numbers can't turn to their advantage here."

"They can turn against us if they follow us through and learn where we're going," she replied.

"Then we shall lose them or make a stand," replied Kegin unconvincingly.

"They hawen't gotten through yet," reminded Lorimen. "We don't know ourselwes how the outcome will be, but I doubt wery much that our guides are going to show our enemies where we'we gone."

"That's assuming our guides are friendly," replied Kegin dryly.

"They are! Come on. Let's get to the bottom of this so we can put your doubts to rest. You are as tart as my old Aunt Imoline, and twice as ugly. But come! We have some wessels to find for you." Lorimen pumped his sturdy legs into a fast trot, and he followed away after the hooded riders, calling the others to hurry. They had gone forward no more than a quarter league when the racket behind began to subside and the Olgnite horns grew fewer and farther between.

A messenger arrived from the rearmost Steward squadron, commanded by Port and Starboard, to deliver the enemy colors to Linne with the brothers' compliments. There was also word from Famhart and Emerald, who sent their love and to say they were safe.

"All that's left is to find Owen, Deros, and a packet of ships, and we'll sail away free." Kegin laughed. Linne's look silenced him for a moment, then he went on. "Not quite free, perhaps, but happy and with a new start."

"You would be welcome to Fionten," offered Lorimen. "We hawe a friendly face toward all who respect us. It's an open port, and we hawe much commerce, even in these troubled times."

"Thank you, good Lorimen," replied Linne. "Your hospitality is most welcome. I'm sure we shall have need of it to gather our strength and see what next is to be done." She still rode, and Elita walked at her side. In the shadows ahead, another mounted figure loomed, outlined by the dark gloom behind and the rush lamps in front. It lingered there a moment more, then moved forward slowly.

Kegin thought at first it was the hooded riders again, then saw that this figure was smaller and bent forward over the horse's neck, as though holding on to the mane. He had just stepped forward to grab the animal's bridle when Gitel's voice rang out bell-clear. "Come with us now. We've been waiting for hours!"

"Gitel?" cried Linne. "Where is Owen?"

"He's with us, my lady," replied Deros, pulling back her hood to reveal her long hair and fair features. "He is still suffering from the spider curse. Ephinias thinks he's through the worst of it, but he still looks horrible."

Linne kicked her heels into her horse's flanks. "Tell Famhart where I'm gone," she called over her shoulder, then was gone into the thickening mists. Deros caught her up and went ahead on Gitel, who surefootedly led the rest of the way to the hasty encampment, where a small fire burned and the old teacher was in deep discussion with Seravan, watching the fever-burned tossing of the grotesque figure before them.

Twig Dances

Owen could hear the voices calling to him from beyond the harsh red haze that trapped him. Some were familiar, and others vaguely reminded him of something that had happened somewhere, but the strange intruder in his awareness blocked it out before he could understand it or try to remember more. The red curtain closed him in again, and the terrible emptiness inside his gut made him twist in pain and tear at the leather ties that held him strapped to the crude wooden frame.

Another voice, close to his ear, seemed to explode into his brain, making him struggle all the more violently. "This is the worst I've ever seen it," said Ephinias, his voice tight with anxiety.

Gillerman, who sat beside him, agreed. "Even our combined efforts seem to leave him unchanged."

"I doubt myself at every turn now. I was the one who insisted on him staying in Olgnite form."

Seravan, who had been grazing nearby, neighed softly. "It is something other than your work that has him trapped. I sense another presence here, beyond you."

"It seems to be so. But who?"

A dark wind came up from nowhere, scattering the flames of the small fire and setting off an explosion of sparks that popped and snapped dangerously near Ephinias's cloak.

"Do you think as I do on this?" asked Gillerman.

"The Dark One? Who else could it be, unless she has awakened and is strong once more?"

"The Middle Islands held her for a time. We knew she couldn't be banished for good, for these Lower Meadows indeed are hers by right. No one ever denied her that. But her treachery at trying to keep all who were sent here for their lessons has disturbed the scheme of things. Windameir has been dealing with this since the Beginning, and it doesn't look as though it shall have an end anytime soon."

"If it is the Dark One, then we shall need help in getting him back safely."

"We shall all need help to strengthen our resolve. The timing is always a blow upon the heels of another blow. For too long have we left our good sense in check, my friend. Wallach and I have traveled a good deal these past turnings, and it would have been evident to anyone but a pair of blind old goats like us."

Ephinias shook his head slowly, knotting his brows in heavy thought.

"I don't think it's anything we've done or not done down here on the Boundaries. It seems this is the way it all resolves itself here, in the end. We're much too hard on ourselves. We'd be able to remember how it all ends if we set ourselves to it and didn't get so distracted by all the goings on here."

Owen struggled more wildly against his bonds, and Ephinias placed the sword of Skye on his feverish body, hoping the touch would pull his tormented mind back to them.

There was the sound of approaching hoofbeats then, and Seravan whinnied in greeting, then called out aloud to his old friend. "Come, Gitel! We need your help."

Linne dismounted. Deros remained in her saddle, exhausted.

"Linne may be able to reach him. There is no tie stronger than a mother and child."

"That is a hopeful thought," replied Gillerman. "Yet

sometimes these things follow no law or rule. I haven't seen one so lost in a binding in a great many lifetimes."

"There's a part of him that is struggling to stay," went on Ephinias. "It's all my fault. I knew how powerful the workings of the Olgnites were, yet I could see no other way to reach you, young lady. Owen seemed our only hope."

"We will get him back," vowed Linne. Her face betrayed no emotion as she went to stand beside her son, who struggled in vain to free himself from the leather bonds. She reached out to touch him and was greeted with his bared spider fangs, which still were dangerous, and the black matted hair had not fully disappeared.

"Be careful, my lady! He has threatened us all with death if we don't release him. He is still strong enough to break through most bonds. I've left the sword on top of him there to hold him at bay."

Linne's eyes welled up with tears then, and she dropped to her knees beside her son. "Can you hear me, Owen? I'm here to help you."

The distorted features of the young man seemed to soften for a moment, then the hideous snarl returned, which bared the killing fangs and turned his eyes a blood-red.

"Watch out, my lady. Deros was nearly bitten that way. He still has venom enough to kill."

"What can we do, Ephinias? There must be some way to call him back."

"We are doing all we can, my lady. He has improved, but some part of him is holding back."

"That couldn't be! No one would want to stay in that spell!"

"It is a strong binding, my lady. It wears on you little by little, and it will creep in upon you unawares, especially if you have no experience."

Linne tried again to touch her son's brow, which was covered in a thin sheen of sweat. "He has a fever."

"This power is burning him up from the inside," said Ephinias. "It is a struggle for him to cast off the curse."

Owen's face took on a more grotesque form, yet beneath the ghoulish features of the spiderman his mother could recognize the handsome, innocent face of her son. "Owen! Can you hear me?"

"Blood," muttered the lad in a garbled voice, his clawlike hands reaching to grasp the woman's arm.

"What can we do?" asked Deros, trying to hold her tears back. "He's getting worse."

Gillerman's face darkened, and he touched Owen's forehead. "The lad's burning up! The Olgnite fire is consuming him. If we don't do something, and quickly, I'm afraid we'll lose him for good."

"No!" cried Linne, falling on the writhing figure of her son, who fought savagely at his bonds. She escaped his fangs and tried to hold him close to her, but the blood-red light in his eyes only burned more intensely as he sensed a victim so close at hand.

"Leave him, my lady," urged Ephinias. "It would do him no good to know he's harmed his mother."

Linne still knelt beside the fever-tossed form, holding tightly to his thrashing arms.

"Can you call Wallach?" asked Ephinias. "Perhaps all of us might be enough to call him back."

Gillerman looked away toward the distant sea. "I'm not sure I can reach him now. He's far from us, and on a dangerous mission himself."

"At least try," urged Linne. "We can't just let Owen slip from us!" She sobbed silently into her hands, burying her face. Deros tried to comfort her but felt helpless in the presence of such grief.

"We have to try something. If I only had some of the water from the wells of the Darien Mounds left, that might help."

Ephinias brightened. "That might do it," he agreed.

"It is too far for us to travel, and the time is too short," replied Gillerman.

"I could try," offered Seravan.

"We need you here, old friend. There is no need to split our party now. Whatever is to be done shall have to be done with all of us present."

A slight stir of the forest breeze alerted Gitel, and he pawed restlessly beside Seravan. "Someone's coming!"

"Douse the fire," hissed Ephinias, and the flames turned a dull golden color, flared once, and were gone, leaving the small encampment plunged into a tense darkness.

Noises of approaching hoofbeats were heard then, and a gruff voice that rang familiarly over the muted distance called their names aloud.

"I know you're hiding somewhere about. By the spurs of Windameir, I'll have you all hided if you don't stand up and let your old friend clap his eyes on you!"

"Stearborn?" cried Linne. "Is that you?"

"Not one person else, and don't let 'em cloud your mind with all that ruckus about the old dog finally laying along-side of dying without so much as a whimper! By crack and crown, I'll wager any around that this old goat will be to the funeral pyres of all of them before it's said and done!"

As Linne stumbled forward to embrace the old warrior her eyes caught another movement next to him. In the wink of an eye the Lame Parson's huge form filled the space, his small friend Twig astride his back.

"Greetings, sister. I found this scoundrel and a friend wading in the bog a while back. It seemed there might be more required of him than that, so I set him loose, hoping you could find some use for him."

Linne fought to hold back her tears. "Indeed we can, sir. This is a terrible time, though. My son is burning up with a fever and is in the grip of the Olgnite curse. We can't seem to pull him back."

Stearborn strode to where Ephinias and Gillerman waited beside the strapped-down lad. "This is a blessed waste of the young pup. Why are his arms lashed down?"

"You can see why! You have but to look at him," replied the old teacher. "He has the blood madness of the spider-men."

"Then let's see if we can't break him of it," bellowed Stearborn, and began unloosening the bonds that held Owen's arms.

"Wait!" commanded the Parson, coming to stand beside

the Line commander. "We might harm him if we allow him to go free. If he once gets the taste of blood, we'll lose him, for he'll slip further under that curse that has been the bane of the Olgnites since their fire mountain blew and they have been left to their fate."

"Then what shall we do?" asked Linne. "Even Gillerman and Ephinias haven't been able to bring him around."

The Parson nodded. "That's true. What I think we need here is some small magic. Maybe Twig has something that might help." The big man eased his friend off his back and swung him down beside Owen.

"Twig knows the spider clans—oh, yes! Twig knows where they hunt and how they kill. Many of Twig's friends have died by the ugly black squashers." The small, legless creature danced an odd dance, suspended on his arms, and turned a back flip to land on the other side of the stricken youth. "Twig has seen this fire before! Burned two days in his old friend Frog!"

"What did you do?" asked Ephinias.

"Twig did nothing." A slight smile curled his ancient, young features into a bittersweet portrait. "But Twig knew how to call the others to help."

"Who did you call?" pressed Gillerman.

"He called up the Elurin," answered the Parson. "Something that we should do as well."

"The Elurin?" questioned Linne. "I've never heard of any clans by that name."

"It is no clan," corrected Gillerman, "but spirits of the forest. It is an old form of workings that have pretty much been overlooked by the modern school of thought."

"Twig will call them," said the Parson, sitting down next to Owen and motioning for his small friend to begin.

Stearborn eased his sword in and out of his scabbard a few times. He and Morlin, who had arrived with him, battered and bloodied, and covered in the sticky black mud of the fen, squatted down on the other side of Linne to wait.

Twig spun and whirled about, until no one could believe he had no legs, and a slight change come over the gathering. The fire had flared up again and swayed to and fro in rhythm to the dwarf's movements. New colors appeared there, in blazing blue sparks and fiery golden pools that rippled back and forth in the air above the wood. A wind whipped the fire into a dancing flow of hot embers, which glowed brighter still as the legless figure twirled wildly about.

Deros watched as Owen grew more agitated in the light of the dancing fire. His tormented body was racked by several violent convulsions as the colors changed before him, and the small figure went on with his dance. She could see Owen's eyes focus on the fire and the fear there.

Ephinias felt older and more tired than he had felt in a very great while. "I didn't think it would be so much trouble to bring him back."

"We forget the great power of the Dark One," said the Parson. "She does not always get her way by force alone. Sometimes she attacks from behind, with temptations we are not prepared to reject."

"No one is beyond her reach," agreed Ephinias. "Even I have felt her call on occasion."

"That part of the Law is strict and unbending," said Gillerman. "There is no going on until the weakness to give in to her has been overpowered."

"He's only a boy," protested Linne, suddenly seeing Owen as he was as a small youngster, holding on to her skirts in the kitchen in Sweet Rock, waiting for her to set the table for their evening meal.

"He's a young man now. He has seen some of the many faces the Dark One can use already."

"Can we help?" asked Deros, staring at the tossing figure of Owen and the wild gyrations of Twig. The fire had leapt higher and seemed to take on the form of what appeared to be a giant face, its blazing eyes boring straight into all there.

"Twig can see you, great ones! Twig sees you! Can you help your poor servant Twig?"

A voice, or what could be called a voice, crackled out with a roar of blazing sparks. "What do you wish of us, small dancer? We are here."

Twig did a backward somersault, landing agilely on a log before the fiery form.

"We have one with us who is held by the spider curse. Twig can feel him here, caught by the black demons. They twist his soul."

A faint whooshing sound from the fire came then, and the colors melted into blue and green, wavering around the still struggling lad strapped down before it. The hues changed again, into a brilliant white with golden blue edges that began to gather in a whirling motion, flowing faster and faster around Owen, until the heat was so great, it drove Linne back, leaning against Stearborn, who tried to shield her from the blistering blast.

Twig disappeared into the white-hot maw of the blazing furnace, dancing wildly, making grotesque shadows on the stunted trees around them. Great lights and dark clouds shot upward, filling the sky with a boiling cauldron of colors.

Deros heard Owen shriek out a name, and then a cry of pain, but she was unable to reach him, for the fire storm blew violently around him, rising upward like a cyclone of white-hot flames, lifting away toward the high stars that hung in a small black patch above the wood.

"This is going to be a fat beacon for the squashers," grumbled Stearborn, watching as the fires blazed higher. "I can only hope it frees the lad soon, for we'll be needing to move on quickly now."

The Parson spoke to Linne in a kind tone. "Your son will be freed, little sister. This is a small way to repay you for your help to my own son, once."

Linne's eyes brimmed with tears.

"Your son?" she managed at last.

"It was the Middle Islands. You knew him there as Borim Bruinthor."

Her heart stopped, and a long flood of memories swept her away into another time long before, on the bitter fields of war that ran on across the beaches and hills of those distant islands.

"Now, my friends, you must quickly see to your friends and make your way from here. The Olgnites have lost their strength to the hungry bog, and I have seen to it the end of the Bogmots has come to pass. The coast is waiting for you. Good Ephinias and Gillerman will carry on from here."

The Parson joined the great, fiery cyclone and was gone in a moment of fire and smoke, leaving behind the smoke-shrouded form of Owen, now quiet and unmoving, in a deathlike stillness that struck a chord of bottomless anguish in his mother, who fell weeping on her motionless son.

THE
SAILING

Sunrise in
the Ellerhorn

The slow greens and blues of sunrise crept over a faint, rose-colored sky, driving away the last of the pockets of dark shadows in the hidden recesses of the Ellerhorn Fen. With the passing of the night there were animal and bird sounds where there had been none before, and the stagnant smells that had been were replaced with newer, fresher scents of green and growing things.

Owen's fever-racked body lay as still as stone through the night, and only Gillerman's reassurance convinced Linne that her son yet lived, so cold and still he lay. As the dawn began to creep over the fen the first rays of the sun washed over the lad, and though still groggy with her sleepless vigil, Linne saw a faint flutter of his eyelashes and heard a small, weakened cry.

"Ephinias! Gillerman! Come here quickly! He's moving!" cried Linne, reaching to untie his bound wrists.

"No, my lady," warned Kegin, who had spent the long night waiting next to her, placing his hand gently over her own. "He may still be under the curse."

Linne broke free of his hold and went on untying the bonds. "If he's not freed after the Parson's work, then he may as well be dead. I have seen work like that in the Middle Islands. Whoever you may think he is, he is one of the Old Ones."

Voices and movement announced more arrivals, and as Linne struggled to undo the last of the bonds, she saw her husband and Emerald pull their horses up near them and dismount.

Famhart strode to Stearborn and held his old comrade in a mighty bear hug that made even the great Stearborn gasp for breath.

"Hold, Famhart! You've stove in the old ribs with your tickling!"

"Emerald, come here and help me thrash this rogue for throwing such a scare at us!"

"Hola, Stearborn! The word was out that the squashers had you up for stew!"

"My bile would have fouled their workings," laughed the old commander. "Morlin and I had no trouble with the spidermen, but this bog was near the end of us, had it not been for the good Parson and Twig."

"Where were you? No one had reports, except that you were still out beyond the lines."

"Aye, minstrel, beyond the lines, and beyond the Olgnite lines as well. Young Morlin and I were trying to keep an eye out on the youngster there and were doing a right smart job of it, too, until all the hustings were broken off and our plan went by the boards in a hurry."

"The Olgnites found Owen before we were ready," said Morlin. "We were hiding, watching him, when these scouts rode through, and he had no choice but to go on. We rode along behind, but we had to hold up when they went right into the main camp."

"That gave this old dog a start, I can tell you." Stearborn snorted. "Two of us outmanned a thousand to one. Good odds for Chellin Duchin but a splinter too rich for my old bones."

"Their camp stretched all the way to the woods to the east and back north, almost to Sweet Rock."

"It was a dark moment," conceded Stearborn. "Ephinias

was guiding us, but we lost him when their war camp got boiling over and they were ready to attack."

"I thought we were done for," added Morlin excitedly. "There were spidermen all over us, but Stearborn killed two of them with a piece of sword work I've never seen the likes of, and we stole their cloaks and helmets."

"A regular piece of goods we were," continued Stearborn. "Had ourselves nested in with that bunch of bloodsuckers slick as you please. In the dark I guess we looked as fierce as the rest of them."

"There was a close brush or two, but we just bluffed it out, hoping for a point when we could see our way free and maybe try to find Owen and the girl."

Deros took up the tale. "When our move finally came, Gitel threw Olag Grieshon into the bog, and we all managed to escape. Owen was left in the Olgnite form too long, and we've feared it may have been too late, except for the Parson and Twig."

"There's where we were, by the Rod of Esulus, and no good left coming to plead for mercy up to our throats in the heartless black craw of this foul place. Morlin and I were finished by all rights, and I'd already told the lad farewell when up bolts the Parson, bigger than life, and that amazing monkey of a man he calls Twig," Stearborn continued.

"I didn't think there was anything anyone could do, but he just reached down to the edge of the mire we were in and touched it. The next thing I knew, Stearborn was hauling me out by my ear," finished Morlin.

"At least they're good for something." Stearborn growled good-naturedly. "You never use them for listening, so it's just as well they're big enough for handles!"

Linne was still kneeling by Owen's crude bed of boughs and soft pine needles and turned a tearstained face to her husband. "I think he's breathing," she said, trying to hold back her sobs.

Famhart quickly knelt beside his wife, holding her close to him. "He will pull through this. He is a strong lad."

"Strong enough to have withstood the worst of the Olgnite bane," confirmed Ephinias. "The worst is past now, thanks to our friend."

"I haven't seen nor heard real news of him since before the last of the Flying Snakes," said Gillerman.

"I wonder where he has gotten to now," mused Famhart, lost in his own memories then, and his eyes clouded as he thought of those dangerous, desperate days along the beaches and mountains of the last fortress of the Dark One.

Owen moaned and opened his eyes, blinking in the bright light of the new morning.

"Quickly, Linne! Some water. His mouth is parched." Famhart tried to make his son more comfortable while a drink was brought.

Deros was at Owen's other side, wiping his matted brow. "I think he's waking up," she said, holding her breath anxiously.

The first of the long procession began to arrive then, led by the gruff Chellin Duchin, who sat stiffly in his saddle, followed by Jeremy and Judge. Hamlin rode farther back, helping another wounded comrade.

"Hola, Famhart! Linne! I see we have our stout new Elder patched and ready for duty again. That's a good sign. These old bones of mine are getting too brittle for all this horse work. I want to find a place where I can sit of a morning with my boots propped on the table and watch my breakfast brought."

"Hah!" exclaimed Famhart, looking over his shoulder. "When we see that day, we'll all be too old to care for food or comfort! Come down and sit. We shall have the supper now that we didn't have a chance for last night."

"Those squasher devils gave us a start, I'll grant," grumbled Chellin, dismounting painfully. Emerald saw the blood on the riding cloak then, and hurried to help the old commander down.

"It's the same old pin! Bloody devils are always fond of sticking me there."

The minstrel saw the leg was slashed badly above the knee and called for a healer to attend to him.

"Let me have a look," said Ephinias. "Sometimes I have better luck along this line of work." He sat Chellin down beside his horse and drew back the torn breeches to examine the wound. He shook his head, muttering softly, "Another gnat's wing deeper, and we'd be looking for a suitable resting place for the great Chellin Duchin."

"This one won't be my end." Chellin laughed dryly. "The wound that holds my death still dwells in the sword."

While the healers were called and Ephinias tended to dressing Chellin's wound, the crowd grew, as the long line of settlers and Stewards continued to come in. Owen was tossing fitfully, half conscious, and Linne and Deros bathed his head with cool rags while his father offered water every time the lad seemed to call out for a drink.

Emerald leapt to his feet when he saw his betrothed arrive, and rushed to embrace her. Elita was exhausted and covered with blood from caring for the Line's wounded, but her tired features brightened when she saw the minstrel. "How fares Owen?" she asked, watching Linne sitting beside her son.

"The Parson came. I don't know much more, except that the crippled one who was with him called up a fire storm and we thought it had taken Owen, but when it was over, the Parson and Twig were gone, and here's Owen, just as you see him, still unconscious but free of the Olgnite spell."

"That will be grist for your mill." Stearborn laughed and wandered about, greeting his old comrades and searching out members of his own squadron. There was much noisy greeting of friends, and loud, teasing calls bantered back and forth as friends were reunited or had news of missing friends.

A pair of pathetic men dressed in tattered rags made their way forward to try to speak to Emerald. "Begging pardon, sir, but could Lofen and McKandles has a word with you?"

Emerald looked at the two blankly, not recognizing them at first. "Speak on, friend. You have the minstrel's ear."

"We is sore pressed to has a word with your leader too," continued Lofen, knotting the smelly rag of a hat he wore tightly in his hands. "We is cut off from all them who is a-kin to us, and we was a-thinkin' we could hitch our gear up with you."

"We ain't no dandy sojurs, but we does know them worthless brutes you ride as good as any that is about on two good pins, and we works cheap! Two squares and a place to flop our heads come night, and you has two of the best hostlers that ever come out of the Gortland Fair."

Emerald laughed, then hurriedly assured the two he was not laughing at them. "I only just now recognized you," he explained. "You're from the Fair! Where is Ulen? Is he with you?"

McKandles's face fell into a worried frown. "I can't says what has rightly happened to Master Ulen. We was overtook by a solid wall of them squashers, and the next thing I knows, they has us all trussed up tighter'n a wild-eyed bronc at breakin' time. Ulen was there then, but I doesn't know what's happened since then."

"We was a-fightin' as best we was able," said Lofen. "Wasn't no way we was a-goin' to get loose, but we come close to it a time or two. Ulen wasn't no sweet maid to be with, but we was his own kind, and we has stuck with him all these turnings, 'cause we is horse folks and we has to bind together."

"He was fetched up alongside this Hoolin fellow, a prince or some such as that. Told Ulen we was a-goin' to go back with them to wherever it was they come from. That young lady there was what them Hoolins was after, and we didn't have no loose rope nowheres to turn, so we was a-goin' along, a-hopin' to find out what we could and to keeps our hides all of a piece." McKandles hung his head, unable to meet Deros's eyes. "We never meant no harm. There wasn't no other way to deal with them high-handed Hoolins, a-bein' outmanned like we was."

"I bear you no ill will," assured Deros. "Your leader is a spoiled brat, but I wouldn't wish him dead at the hands of the spidermen or the bog."

"Oh, Ulen Scarlett is no lost whelp when it comes to a-slippin' by, my lady. If there was any wee crack to escape through at all, our Ulen would be there in the flick of a whip." Lofen looked to his companion for confirmation.

"He's most likely freed by a Steward squadron by now," said Deros. "They've been finding others held by the spidermen, tied up in that foul webbing they use. Reports have been coming in since the battle last night of people found and saved."

"We'll see to it you get clothes and arms," said Emerald. "You'll need horses, too, I take it?"

"Aye. Our beasts were snipped from us when we was dumped in the squasher camp. I was half balmy from that poisoned bite, but I did see them things a-roundin' up all the animals."

"Terrier was Ulen's mount," added Lofen. "He's a-thinkin' more of that horse than he does anyone, if we is a-talkin' about the truth of it! Ain't no lady be a-standin' for them tricks. If he is still a-breathin', the odds is in favor of his a-lookin' all over Scrim and back down Scrum to tries to find him." He paused, rubbing his stomach. "I doesn't think the first sight of food is a-goin' to fill up my belly, neither. I has had some rough times, when I was glad enough to have a animal under me and to be part of the Fair. We has seen a bit of country since those days. I wasn't no fond heel-dog of Ulen's, but I doesn't find it sits easy with me, a-thinkin' of him gone."

"I think we shall find a good use for you both, once we've got you armed and clothed. You'll feel better when you've had something to eat." Emerald called out to a Steward nearby and gave orders to take care of the two downcast Gortland men.

McKandles stopped briefly as he was passing Deros and spoke without raising his head. "I is powerful shameful of what we done, a-turnin' you over to them Hoolins, and I just hopes you doesn't go to your grave a-hatin' old McKandles for his yellow backbone."

Deros recoiled from the man's abject demeanor but caught herself and reached out to touch his ragged sleeve. "You didn't behave any differently than any of us would have. You were outnumbered badly, so it's no mark against you."

"It would be a mark again' any man to just belly up without no scrap, but since you has been after a-givin' us a new start in this here outfit, us'll both do our busted best to try to do you proud."

Deros was distracted by the sudden call of her name behind her. Owen had spoken from his delerium and was thrashing about wildly in the firm grip of his father and his old friend Kegin.

"He seems to be coming out of it," Famhart said. "I think he can hear us now."

Ephinias and Gillerman bent over the lad and conferred briefly.

"It looks as though we have our young man back," confirmed the old teacher after studying Owen's eyes a moment. "The spidermen have lost him."

Linne sobbed, clinging to her son's hand. Famhart held her then, and urged her to rest after her long vigil. "We shall all need food and rest. None of us would be able to go on now without it."

"They're setting up the kitchens. There will be a meal soon," said Elita.

"This will be a feast not many of us thought we'd see." Stearborn growled, and stood beside his old comrade, Chellin Duchin. The healer had split the bloody trouser leg and was busy with his salves.

"We haven't heard the last of these devils," warned Chellin. "They may have lost their edge, but mark my words, they won't leave us alone for long."

"We should be able to regroup at the coast," said Stearborn. "From what Morlin and I saw of the Olgnites, their hordes are cut down to size and I think they'll take the short way home to their borders."

Deros reached into her cloak and held the small knife that Stearborn had given her when she had first come to Sweet Rock in the guise of the young boy, Derek. "Their Olag is dead," she said, quietly shuddering inside as she remembered the terrible dark time she had spent as his captive.

"Aye, and well he should be." Stearborn growled. "The Parson and I came out of the bog on you all in an ambush. Morlin's shaft split another squasher dead in the center of his ugly mug, so I think we may have a breather before they return to the Leech to find another chieftain."

"I thought I was dreaming when I saw you there," replied Deros. "It all happened so fast."

"The Parson had just fished us out of that sinkhole we'd slipped into. It took our horses and would have had us, as well, if it hadn't been for his quickness."

Famhart called to his old friend, and Stearborn answered gruffly, going over to stand at the side of the stricken youth.

"Has he come 'round?"

"Not yet. He's taking water, though."

"He could be this way for an hour, or a day, maybe more," explained Ephinias. "I've seen this kind of infection once or twice before, but never this bad."

"Should we try to move him?" asked Linne. "Would that be dangerous?"

"No more dangerous than running the risk of staying here," answered the old teacher, turning to Gillerman. "What do you think?"

"I would fall toward moving. There is a chance to reach White Bird without more interference from the Olgnites, and I think there will be an opportunity there to assemble whatever we need to rebuild our defenses."

A hearty voice interrupted Gillerman then, and Findlin and Lorimen joined the others, walking up with their peculiar seaman's gait.

"You're wery wise in speaking of White Bird," offered Lorimen. "They have good wessels there now, and with any sort of good fortune at all, my friend Findlin and I can engage one of them to take young Enlid here to Fionten, then return with a proper fleet to take your people anyplace you might have a mind to go."

"White Bird is well known to us," added Findlin. "The Olgnites have taken our crew and sunk our wessel, but the men of White Bird are a hearty lot, and they will be well pleased to come to the aid of any who threaten their neighbors."

"It sounds as workable as any plan we've got," said Gillerman. "There won't be anything more for us at present, Ephinias. I think we shall have to look in on Wallach. It worries me that he has not reported back of late."

"Are you going to leave us without knowing Owen is all right?" questioned Linne, overhearing the two talking. She was holding a cool, wet rag to Owen's forehead, trying to bring the lad around.

"He shall be all right, my lady. The Parson has seen to that, or rather Twig, and his call to the Elurin."

"And he's gone too!"

"But not beyond reach, my lady," soothed Gillerman. "We shall not be beyond reach, either."

"And you have your work cut out for you now, and this regrouping of the Line will take you some time to accomplish. In the meanwhile these good Archaels have offered assistance from Fionten."

Elita was with Emerald, holding tightly to his hand and blushing slightly. "Do you think there is a chaplain in White Bird who could finish our vows?"

It was Emerald's turn to laugh and blush, and he embraced her in a sudden hug that lifted her off her feet. "They will most certainly have one. If they don't, we shall call upon Ephinias to do the honors, since we he was late to our first try."

"Good gracious, children! I had forgotten all about your marriage!" He clasped Emerald's hand vigorously, then took Elita's. "I shall be delighted to help you read your vows and mark the bindings."

"It will be a saddened feast," said Elita. "The first happy event turned tragic when the spidermen came."

"And the Hulin Vipre," reminded Deros. "The most despicable enemies from both borders. But it should not tarnish your vows, my lady. This will be a time of great rejoicing now."

"We shall need new rings, Ephinias," said Emerald. "Our others were stolen from Sweet Rock before the attack."

"Or at the first of it. The holy relics were taken as well."

"The bear statue?" asked Ephinias.

"Yes, and other things too. The rings were the mystery, though. It made no sense why anyone would have wanted those. They were of no import to anyone besides us."

"There was that old woman," remembered Emerald. "She made such an odd thing of it, I remember it very well."

"What old woman?" asked Elita.

"One of the soothsayers who came to join in the feast. No one knew anything about her, except that she came from the north and drew good pictures from casting the ashes in a fire."

Ephinias had grown thoughtful, stroking his beard. "We

shall have to examine this. It is strange that the relics would be taken, and stranger that your rings were gone as well. Were they in the chapel?"

"Why, yes," replied the minstrel. "And this old woman had spoken out, but no one paid any mind to her, or if they did, they thought she was a madwoman."

"Those oracles often are," agreed Ephinias. "They can be dangerous as well."

Movement and noise caught Emerald's eye then, and he was drawn into wondering who the newest arrivals were, who caused so great a commotion.

He didn't have to wonder long, for within a moment's time the two brothers, Port and Starboard swaggered through the crowd. Upon spying the minstrel, Port removed his silver horn and blew a long, thrilling note that caused all their hearts to leap within their breasts. "Stand down, by thunder, and feel the roll and tide of the Line Stewards come across your grave, all in formation, and riding as though there is no tomorrow or yesterday!" Port bellowed out the words, at the end of which Starboard blew another long call.

They were both blood-spattered, and their eyes betrayed the fact that they hadn't slept, but their energy was raw and powerful, and as they closed to hug Famhart and his other Line commanders, the crowd broke into spontaneous cheers.

Chellin Duchin struggled to his feet, although obviously in pain, to embrace the two stalwart brothers. "Well, buckle my grave cloth, if it isn't the two ugliest louts this side of Trew!"

"Trew," repeated Emerald. "That's where I've seen that old woman." He clasped his hands tightly to his head, trying hard to recall something further.

"What old woman?" asked Starboard, sitting down wearily beside Chellin and starting to peel off his battle garb.

"There was an old woman, a soothsayer, who was at my betrothal vows," explained Emerald. "She gave me a warning, but I had forgotten it until we spoke of the relics being stolen from the chapel."

"Was she toothless with eyes of a different color?" asked Port.

"And maybe a long scar that looked like a scald on her face?" went on Starboard.

The minstrel's face showed his concentration as he tried to recall the physical features of the soothsayer. "I can't remember. It was all such a muddle."

"A man on his wedding day hasn't got room for thoughts of anything but his bride," said Kegin, laughing.

"She was old, I do recall that," confirmed Emerald. "And she wore a silver crescent in her ear."

The brothers looked at each other. "Was the piece a moon?"

"Yes! I think that's what attracted my eye. It was fine workmanship, and I wondered how she had come by it."

Port reached out a hand toward his brother, shaking his head. "I hate to hear news of this nature when I'm tired. I had hoped you and I wouldn't have to deal more with her, or her mad brood. Now it seems our duties aren't done yet."

Starboard nodded gravely, turning a worried face to the others. "The unfortunate stars present at our birth gave my brother and I harsh chores of tending to a family left without a father. There were troubles abroad then, too, and he rode with the king of Trew to war and never returned."

"Left us, Starboard and me, and a baby sister, to the hands of a somewhat reluctant mother."

"Did her best at it, but she wasn't ever meant to be a wife or mother. Left us for the animals to raise, as it were, and later the Unling tribes who wandered Trew in those days, playing with the air and woods as babes in a nursery might."

"Our sister took up with those people and lost all touch with the world. Children of Trew have always been known for that."

"I never knew you had a sister, you old goats! Were you afraid of telling Chellin?"

"You'd find no chance of a sweet skirt there, you ape, mark me! She was a test of patience when she was small, and it sounds as though she's followed her designs all the way to now."

"You mean this woman with the silver earring is your sister?" asked Emerald incredulously.

"Aye! It matches the one Starboard and I wear." Port

pulled back the long salt-and-pepper hair that fell to his shoulders and revealed a small, crescent-shaped earring.

"What would she be doing in Sweet Rock?" asked Starboard.

"Searching for you, perhaps," offered Ephinias.

"She'd want no part of us." Starboard growled. "We came to a parting of ways long ago, and I doubt she's found a way to forgive my brother and I for leaving Trew to join the Line Stewards."

"Her warning was very real," said Emerald. "She seemed to believe what she told me."

"She would be very good at that kind of business," agreed Port. "Too bad we could never train her to be our eyes and ears. What a scout that power would make!"

The kitchens had been set up, and the preparations for the meal interrupted all further conversations for the moment, filling the air with wonderful smells for a hungry crowd. The cooks began their rounds, and a small, makeshift tent was set up over Owen, where Linne, Famhart, and Deros took their food to wait for a sign of his recovery.

All through the ranks of the camp, weary soldiers ate readily after watering and caring for their mounts. Soon a warm glow of well-being led them to think of sleep, after the long night and the exhaustion of the battle.

Chellin Duchin, along with Stearborn, Kegin, and the brothers, were at the flap of the tent where Owen lay when he began calling out to them, as though in a dream. Linne and Deros tried to calm him, but his voice grew louder still, and it was as though he saw a great battle in his fevered mind, for he called out warnings again and again to them, until finally the force of his cries startled him awake and he sat bolt upright on the crude pallet, his eyes wide with fear, and looked around in a daze, trying to comprehend where he was.

A look of bewilderment was replaced with joy as his eyes fell on Deros, and he smiled weakly and held out a hand.

"Hello, Mother. You look well," he said to Linne, still holding Deros's hand.

"We have been worried about you," replied Linne. "You've given us a scare."

"I'm better now. I can't remember all of it, but there was something very dangerous going on. I couldn't quite put my hand to it, but it was as though I was being overpowered and dragged away into a place I didn't want to be."

"It's all right now. Rest," said Linne.

"And just now I thought I saw all our friends in great danger! Chellin, Stearborn, and the brothers! They were being led into a trap, and I couldn't get to them in time to warn them."

"They're right outside," assured Famhart. "I'll bring them in."

Before Famhart could move, Stearborn poked his head into the tent, a gruff smile on his weathered face. "You'd best be getting your strength up, lad! We've got a dozen errands to keep us at it. No laying abed letting us old ones do it!"

"No," murmured Owen. "We can't let you do it. You have all done your share already. It's time for us to bear the load now." His voice was weak, but his eyes were clear and gazed on something beyond Deros's shoulder. Yet every time she looked to see what he was staring at, all that was there was the rising sun over the Ellerhorn Fen, growing higher in the sky.

Stearborn and Famhart both were on the verge of speaking further, but the young man's eyes closed, and he fell back on his rough pillow. In his dream, or dream of a dream, he saw once more the horned ships on a vast, clear blue sea and heard the sounds of the seabirds calling to him, speaking a name over and over. He could not quite make out the sound, but he clearly saw the arrogant face that had been turned to him as the brash young man from the Gortland Fair rode away with Deros behind him, mocking him and leading him on toward a place he could not quite see. Then, by the horizon of this ocean, he could make out land, rising up from the blue waters, and behind it were blazing fires that signaled to him, warning of danger and difficult times.

Just before he lapsed into sleep, the vision of his friends being led into an enemy ambush appeared again. This time at the moment he was trying to raise his voice to shout out a warning to them, a great white bird appeared, scooped them up in its powerful talons, and carried them away into a cool, cloudless heaven, where only one brilliant white star blazed and a silver crescent moon hung low over the horizon, pulsing softly in time with his breath.

The Ring
of Tien Cal

Although Ulen was waiting for the attack, it surprised him by its suddenness. It was swift and deadly, sweeping through the Olgnite ranks like a wildfire through dry kindling. Horns blared desperately from every direction, and Ulen Scarlett, bound and wrapped in the thick, foul-smelling webbing, strained and struggled to see who the attackers were as he lay limply over the saddle where he'd been thrown.

He had lost track of Lofen and McKandles and could no longer see or hear the Olgnite chieftain who held Deros, but he could sense by the bitter fighting that the spidermen were in a bad way and trying to make the cover of the surrounding wood. Swirling and wheeling about, the smell of blood and sweat became so powerful, it choked him. The horse he was tied to broke free from the rest of the pack animals and began to gallop away, its ears laid back in terror, straight toward the ominous eave of the Ellerhorn Fen. There were runaway horses behind him, although he could not tell if they bore the grisly cargo that was to feed the Olgnite war party.

Arrows flew as thick as hailstones, and Ulen had a brief glance of a huge Olgnite warrior reaching down to grab the bridle of the horse he was tied to, then a long black shaft shot straight through the spiderman's throat, which covered him in the vile black blood that spouted out in a sudden gush, frightening the horse more and sending the crazed animal straight on into the beginning of the fen.

The wide glade that ran between the edge of the woods and the Ellerhorn gave way to thick, low, stunted trees, and the smell of dead water and decay. The wild struggles of the animal almost threw him headfirst into a gurgling black pit, which seemed to be sucking both the animal and its cargo down into an evil-smelling mud that burbled hungrily, as though it were a live thing devouring its prey.

Torchlight, dim and uneven at first, began to move jerkily toward Ulen, who at last had realized where he was and that he was in mortal danger. He tried to call out for help but found his bonds so tight about his arms and shoulders, it blocked the wind from his throat, and all he could manage was a low moan. A noise beside him caused him to twist painfully to his right, where he saw another victim tied to a horse, which screamed its terror and struggled madly against the unrelenting black mud of the sinkhole.

A sharp jerk threw Ulen's body onto the hard horn of the saddle. A coil of webbing was pulled from his chest and around his neck. The horse was sunk to its chest in the mire and crazed with fear, but Ulen managed to roll forward onto the animal's neck. He struggled to free his hands and arms as the gulping quicksand burbled over the animal's back. By the light of the weak and flickering torches that roiled and swirled about in the near distance, the young horseman of the Gortland Fair could see clearly the fate that awaited him. Before him, another horse and rider, an Olgnite, were dragged down into the foul mud, leaving not a trace behind, although he heard the choked cry of the enemy warrior as the black mud closed over his head.

Ulen's mouth was opened to utter his last prayer up to the Hostler of Gwanith, the only god he had ever been told of, when two Line Stewards appeared abruptly at the bog's edge and tossed him a coiled rope that struck him painfully across the shoulders.

"Wrap it around you, citizen! Our only chance to pull you

free is to tie you on to my horn and drag you out before that
vile muck gets hold of you!"

Ulen barely had time to get the rope over his head and
under his arms before the Steward urged his horse to a trot,
jerking Ulen suddenly backward, knocking the breath from
him. As he was dragged rapidly past the horse behind him, a
hand reached out to grab hold of his, and for a moment Ulen
thought his arm would be pulled from its socket. A cry
escaped his lips, and he grasped the hand. The man's hold
broke, but Ulen felt a small piece of cold metal clutched in
his grasp, and he clinched his fist tightly to hold on to it,
even as he watched the horse and the bound man sucked
below the surface of the bog.

In another instant Ulen was free of the quagmire and on
dry land, battered and sick to his stomach, but still in one
piece, holding tightly to the object in his hand. He opened
his fist to look at what he held just as the Steward who had
pulled him to safety rode back to him, coiling his rope.

"You're a lucky sod, my man! Another breath and you'd
be bones at the bottom of that pit, along with those other
devils from the Leech! You're on your own, though. We've
got others to reach. Keep an eye peeled. There'll be a free
animal for you here somewhere."

"Where are you bound?" asked Ulen, looking about him
at the flaring torches and listening to the sounds of a full-
pitched battle at no great distance from where he stood.

"Bear toward the fires and Steward horns! They're blowing now. You can't steer wrong."

Ulen was ready to question the man further, but the two
Stewards spurred their mounts and were gone into the dim,
torchlit shadows before he could speak.

A great clamor of men and horses came from his left,
where the Steward had pointed. The noise and confusion of
the battle grew even louder, and the flames leapt and blazed
in the deeper parts of the heavier woods there, illuminating
the dark blue of the sky with crazy figures in the fires, and
showers of sparks roared high above the tops of the trees,
looking like flaming stars gone mad in a frightened dance.
Ulen slowly began to make his way in that direction, pausing only briefly to look at the cool metal object in his hand.

As he opened his palm his eye caught the dull fire of red gemstone, set in a golden band, winking against the wavering, fiery light. Ulen held the ring up so he could examine it against the light better and was startled when the winking red stone came slowly to life, throwing strong reflections about him, followed by a cold voice from the very air itself, calling out a strange name it took him another moment to comprehend and remember. "Tien Cal," repeated Ulen. "The Hulin Vipre prince! It was him in the bog! I've got his ring!"

A short, guttural sound emanated from the ring then, and it grew hot to his touch, but he never let go of the small gold band, clutching it tightly to his chest.

"This may be my salvation yet," he muttered to himself, dragging his stiff, aching body along toward the fighting. "If I could only find those worthless louts, I'd almost be happy to see them again. I've got to find them if they're alive," he vowed to himself, and his ears perked up, for he heard the sound of a horse coming along at a fast pace somewhere out of the dark very near him, and from the animal's gait it seemed to be riderless. He put the ring on his second finger of his left hand and prepared to stop the animal. There was another following, and it seemed to be two lost horses, wandering about in confusion after losing their masters. A big bay came up out of the darkness first and shied upon seeing Ulen, but a chestnut following along behind him came directly up, obviously calmed by the reassurance of a human. Ulen caught his bridle and held the horse's mane tightly in his hand, talking soothingly to him and patting him gently.

"You're not the Terrier, but you're a fine beast. You'll be able to get me safely away from here, at any hitch, and I think the farther from this bog, the better. Your friend ahead there is going to end up in the belly of this foul place if he keeps on like he's going." Ulen patted the animal again and put the reins over the horse's neck, making ready to mount.

The fires away toward the deeper woods had grown higher, and the noise of the war-horns was a steady roar now, drawing him onward. The horse was skittish in the darkness and the wind and twice tried to buck, but Ulen's expert riding skills kept him firmly seated, and he went on talking in a calm, steady voice to quiet the animal.

"Easy, my son! You don't want to lose another rider today. We need to reach friends before that, and we may have to save your strength in case we have to take to our heels."

The horse blew noisily, tossed his mane, but kept on at a steady pace, seeming to take Ulen's words to heart. There were many slain men and horses strewn about now, and Ulen had to urge the spooked animal on past a vast heap of dead Olgnites, who were slowly beginning to transform back into their spider forms, then vanishing altogether, with only the firelight reflecting in the pale green slime left behind to mark their passing.

A troop of horsemen carrying torches appeared out of the wood ahead, riding hard, and on a course that would cross his own long before he reached the place where the Stewards had indicated their perimeters to be. He could make nothing of them at first but soon realized, with a sinking heart, that the men he saw now were of the same band as the lost Hulin Vipre prince, Tien Cal, and they had seen him already and were making directly for him, coming across the last open space at a hot pace, lashing their horses.

Ulen realized at once that he could not outrun the riders on the tired horse he rode, so his mind frantically reached for something that might save him. He cursed the Stewards for leaving him and put the ring back inside his cloak pocket, trying to form a plan.

As the riders closed upon him, Ulen Scarlett spurred his horse boldly forward and raised a hand to signal them to stop. He reined his heavily breathing animal in when he pulled even with the first of the Hulin Vipre patrol and began spouting out a tale full of deceit and treachery, of how he had come from Tien Cal with a message to his Emperor.

A square-faced man in his middle forties, who wore an insignia of rank at his shoulder, thrust out his torch and looked Ulen over coldly before he spoke. "You are a man of the Inland realms! What would you have in the way of commerce with Tien Cal?"

"He's lying to save his skin," blurted the rider next to the leader. "His horse will be of use to us. We need all the mounts we can get to see us safely back to the boats!"

"You are riding an animal that belongs to us," said the first man. "You may step down quietly, or we can serve you another way."

Behind him, Ulen heard a crossbow being latched back and knew it was time to play his only trump card. If the Hulin Vipre soldiers did not recognize the ring, all was lost. His palms were wet as he reached into his pocket for the ring, and he panicked for a moment when it became tangled in the cloth, but he produced it and held it out to the enemy leader. The red gemstone caught the flare of the torches and burst into a deep crimson fire.

"Tien Cal will hear of this! Is this the way his followers treat an envoy of their prince?" The young man forced all the anger he could muster into his shaky voice and tried to look disdainfully at the man beside him, who was already dismounting to prepare to ransack his possessions and gear.

"Let me see that," ordered the man, holding up a hand to halt the others. "Where have you come by this?"

Ulen held the ring out close enough to the man's face so that he could see with no doubt that the ring was truly the same one worn by the high prince, Tien Cal. "Tien Cal charged this to me as a safe passage to his Emperor. I have news to give him of his quest here, and a ransom to demand for Tien Cal's freedom."

Another man, sitting his saddle beside the leader, leaned forward and held his naked sword next to Ulen's throat. "This is how we'll ransom Tien Cal, you Inland swine! We have ways to find out all you know, and where you hold him! You've made a sad miscalculation about the resolve of the Black Hood! We never leave our own behind, alive or dead!"

"Stand to, Darlich! I have my own piece to speak here!"

"Then speak it," growled Darlich. He returned the sword to its scabbard. "It irks me to draw my sword without it drinking blood, Astrob! It goes against the seam of all that's natural!"

"We'll see what's natural soon enough," replied the leader, Astrob. "This Inlander has the royal signet, and I shall be interested to hear his full story. Tien Cal may have indeed given this man a message. Let us hear it!"

"It is for your Emperor," Ulen went on, bluffing. He sat taller in his saddle and tried to hide his shaking hands from his enemies as calmly as he was able.

"The Emperor is safely in the Blor Alhal. He does not deign to leave the realms of his kingdom on such missions as we are on. Speak if you have a message! We shall deem whether it is worthy of our Emperor's ear."

The torches whipped wildly in the wind, and the smoke from them trailed away past Ulen, making him suddenly need to sneeze. "It concerns the scrolls," said Ulen, his voice lowered dramatically. "And it is for his ear only. Tien Cal has made me give my most sacred word that I would speak to no one else."

Astrob forced his horse forward and halted, the torch barely a pace from Ulen. The two animals bumped each other and sidestepped nervously, blowing and snorting. "How do you propose to speak to His Worthiness when he is a full month's sea journey away? Do you have wings to fly, my man? Or feet to walk across the sea, as though it were but sand?"

"Let me tickle him with the binder," called out a trooper from the rear ranks. "That will have him singing soon enough."

"Aye, the binder!" another called. The man pressed forward, holding out a grim, black device that glinted in the torchlight, with two metal straps across a plate and a large screw attached to its top.

Ulen's insides went to water and he felt a cold knot in his stomach, but he reached out his hand with the ring and spoke in a clear voice, with only a ragged trace of shakiness. "Your prince has men who have rocks for brains," he said disdainfully. "You will forfeit his life and lose the message he sent for his king if you harm me."

"We'll take both the ring and the message," replied Astrob coolly. "Darlich!" He barked out the name, and just as the man moved to take hold of Ulen's horse, the young rider from the Gortland Fair fell into a quick dismount, ran his horse forward, and lifted himself back into the saddle at a dead run. The advantage was small, but enough to give him a head start on the Hulin Vipre patrol, which now savagely spurred their animals in pursuit.

Some torches were dropped and angry cries broke out, but the darkness covered him and the man with the crossbow aimed his shot wide and to Ulen's left. He knew his horse had not enough speed or stamina for a long run, so he directed his path straight into the fire and noise of the battle ahead, where he might lose his pursuers in the confusion. He cast a quick glance over his shoulder just in time to see Darlich drawing ever nearer to him, a long, blazing torch held out before him, aimed squarely at Ulen like a lance.

Another twenty paces and the man was almost on him, and Ulen crouched on his steed's neck, acting as though he were terrified and unable to defend himself. The others of the enemy party called out wildly to their comrade, urging him on, but they were farther back, mounted on slower animals. Ulen could hear the drumming hooves and the heavy breathing of the sturdy black, and just at the last minute, right at the moment Darlich tensed to strike his blow, Ulen shot straight up in the saddle and stood to kick the man's head. Darlich dropped the torch and Ulen dismounted at the run and swung himself under his horse's belly, coming up between the two plunging horses, where he finished the job he had begun by pulling away the stirrup from the off-balance man. As he heaved himself back into his own saddle he tipped the Hulin Vipre rider backward over the horse's rump, then leapt from his own mount to the swift black of his unseated adversary and quickly drew away from the pursuing troop. He heard their curses and shouts of anger but kept giving the big animal his head, and they raced on, now with almost the speed of his beloved Terrier.

Ulen gritted his teeth and thought of his narrow escape, but he hadn't long to wonder at his next move, for there, directly before him, was the single white-and-gold banner, fluttering in the darkness, lit by the pale fires from the woods and the battle torches carried by the Steward troops. Ulen ran in among them at full speed, crying out a warning of the pursuing Hulin Vipre.

"Stand to, Stewards! I've brought you new enemies to slay! Behind me!"

The two enemies collided headlong in the wildly swaying torchlight. Badly outnumbered, the Hulin Vipre who were not killed in the initial contact took to their heels and fled away into the darkness, flinging away their torches so they couldn't be followed.

"Let them go!" ordered a Steward captain, marshaling his troop around the banner. "We'll wait for daylight for that work."

Ulen had reined in and now trotted his heaving mount back toward the man, dismounting and walking the last few paces to rest the spent animal.

"What squadron, trooper?" asked the Steward captain.

"My name is Ulen Scarlett. I'm of no squadron but from the Gortland Fair. We were playing Sweet Rock when all this business broke loose."

"The horse-riding," repeated the captain. "I did not know if any of your lot had survived."

"I was held by the Olgnites until two of your men dragged me out of the bog back there."

"Well, good fortune to you, friend. If you have a wish to, you can join us. Our losses have been great these past few days. If not, the rest of the settlement of Sweet Rock is bivouacked somewhere close by. I haven't had a full accounting, but if you let your eyes be your scouts, you'll find your way in." The torches smoked and flared, and the Steward captain ordered new ones to be lit. "We can't see even with these, but it's better than hunting in the dark," he said grimly. "These blasted squashers have broken off into small groups, and now we have these others to deal with as well." He sighed. "It shall be a long night in hell, by the look of it."

Ulen thanked the man and eased back into the saddle of the tall black horse. He walked the animal slowly toward the next island of torches, which moved and flared in the darkness ahead, and the dim orange glow outlined the beginnings of the stunted trees, which marked the entrance to the bog he had just escaped. There seemed to be much activity in one particular spot, which he made for, and as he neared it, he saw that there were a great many Stewards going and coming, and that some of the squadrons were disappearing on into the inner parts of the fen, riding to and fro without apprehension. He hailed a nearby rider as he approached and asked the way to the survivors from Sweet Rock.

A lanky youth in the colors of the Lost Elm Squadron pointed toward the procession of men and horses making their way into the deeper recesses of the bog. "You'll find a collection point just beyond the next turn in there. Any who have lost their squadrons can regroup, or go on as they wish. I have word that some of the others are in the vanguard, with Kegin Thornby and Linne Helwin."

Ulen started to think of ways he might ingratiate himself with the wife of the Elder of Sweet Rock. He was deep in his own schemes when a warning shout went up behind him, and when he turned to look, a hundred or more black-clad riders were sweeping down on him, bound for the safe entryway into the fen. Even as he kicked the big black into a run he knew he would not be able to outdistance them and would be caught in a crush between the Hulin Vipre and the Stewards, so he jerked his horse hard to the left and made a desperate run down the very border of the fen, saying a silent prayer to his only god that the ground would hold up for another hundred yards, which is all that stood between him and freedom.

He spurred the horse again and crouched low on the animal's neck, keeping his eyes to the grove of trees outlined in smoky shadows by the torchlight from the scores of riders that whirled and turned as they locked in combat or disengaged. If he could make it there, he knew he would have a chance, although the single safe entry back to the refugees from Sweet Rock might be cut off to him.

In the daylight, he thought he would be able to gain his bearings and, if nothing else, try to direct his path toward the coast and the settlement of White Bird. The Gortland Fair had played there once, some time before, and he felt sure he might meet up with other stragglers from the horse-riding. It might be, he thought brightly, that even McKandles and Lofen would be upon the same road.

In another three strides Ulen was safely in the cover of the grove and out of harm's way for the moment. He clutched the ring and pressed on, sure in his heart that the information he had gotten from the dying Hulin Vipre, and the tiny trinket he had accidentally taken from the powerful Tien Cal, would be the key to his fortunes, wherever his destiny might lead him.

Talk of
a Journey

After his first awakening, Owen slept for a day and a night. When he awoke again on the morning after, small sentry fires trailed white plumes of smoke into the crisp air, and the days were beginning to feel more like autumn. A light sheen of dew crowned the helmets of the Stewards and made the fen feel damp, until a fire could drive off the chill. Noises that had not been heard since before the destruction of Sweet Rock greeted Owen's ears, and he lay with his eyes shut for a long while, remembering, and yet in another part of his mind hoping that it would somehow be his old room again, with his mother busy in her kitchen, preparing the morning meal.

He peeked then, and his heart beat faster when he saw Linne sitting next to him, asleep with her back against the tent. Deros was standing beside the flap, looking out at the pale sunshine that shone beyond. There were regular sounds outside, of men talking, and somewhere a woman's laughter reached him. Pots and pans clanged and clattered, and he heard the sounds of animals moving about, with the squeak of leather harness and the jingle of spurs and weaponry.

Someone stopped to talk to Deros, and Owen listened carefully, trying to place the other voices, but couldn't.

Deros spoke in a strong voice, as she argued a point. "I should go on with you to Fionten," she was saying. "You said you have ships there that could make the passage into the Sea of Silence."

"Yes, we do have wessels capable of that trip, my lady, but I can't say we would find crews willing to go! It's wery dangerous in those latitudes, and I don't know if there are any allies to be had there."

"You can count my father an ally! He would reward you with whatever you desired if you bring me home."

"Goods they could bury us with," piped another voice. "It is not a wise thing to be weighed down with too much rewards in these times."

Deros grew agitated at the obstinacy of the two speakers. "There may be no time left for my father," pleaded the girl angrily. "If there is no assistance coming to him, it means an end to Eirn Bol and all the other islands there. That may not sound like much to you, but it means the loss of the sacred scrolls, and that would signal the end of us all!"

Deros had told Owen stories of her homeland, and of Cairn Weal, her father's castle and estate. He remembered something about sacred scrolls, but he could not recall exactly what it was. He tried to listen harder to the voices outside where he lay.

"Please, my lady, calm yourself. Archaelians have no desire to leawe neighbors in peril, no matter where they may be, or how distant they are. We hawe always been a people to stand against a common enemy."

"You missed these scurvy rotters," growled Port, holding up an Olgnite war helm.

"There won't be much danger from the Olgnites," said Ephinias. "Not in these parts for quite some time."

"They've done enough damage already! Sweet Rock is burned, and the Line is in shambles. Look at our squadrons here! Everyone has taken losses, and it's going to take time to put it to rights!" Owen could hear Stearborn pound his knee with his fist. "And the new Elder is still a green lad yet."

"A changing of the guard is in the air, you ragged heap of worn-out bones," said Chellin Duchin, rubbing his injured leg. "We have a few turnings left, but I wager our use now will be to try to ready these young upstarts we've raised from pups. It shall be their turn now to try to put order back in the Line."

"You talk like an old woman knitting at the fire," rumbled Starboard. "I never thought I'd hear the great Chellin Duchin speak like this. Him with the name of the Bloody Hatchet!"

"Like it or not, it's time to reckon with the truth," Chellin continued. "I may be reckless in some areas, but my brain hasn't been addled so badly that I can't find my good sense when it's staring me in the face."

Owen found that by concentrating all his strength he was able to roll over and lift himself to an elbow. With what seemed an extraordinary effort, he sat up in his crude bedding, feeling dizzy and sick.

Deros was speaking again by the time he had managed to calm his heaving stomach and try to crawl on his hands and knees to the tent flap so he could see more of the unusual conference that was taking place there. His mother stirred once uneasily in her sleep but did not wake.

"If you let me go with you and find a boat to take me home, I shall be able to aid your cause," argued the girl. "We have no troops to offer, for we have been besieged for as long as there has been a history to the Silent Sea, but the aid I offer is held in the scrolls of the Alberion Nova. My father has told me of their power and that so long as they remain in safe hands, we shall never perish at the hands of the enemies of the Bright Star."

Ephinias and Gillerman sat together on the far side of the fire, taking their tea in small silver stirrup cups. At the mention of Bright Star the old teacher blinked and took his cup away from his mouth. "It has been a long winter or two since I've heard that name." His features cleared, and the years seemed to drop away from his face.

Stearborn frowned, twisting with his fingers the hairs of one side of his beard. "Who is it you speak of? I don't recall any Bright Star."

"She was the maiden who won the East," answered Gillerman. "Stories differ as to where she came from, but it's generally accepted she was born in the islands somewhere in the Sea of Silence."

"She was from Isle Ahorte," said Deros. "I learned that as a little girl. All my people have always honored her. The sailors say their prayers to her, and every home on Eirn Bol has an icon of her."

"Who was she?" asked Port.

"According to the most ancient sources, she was an elven princess who fell in love with a human in the golden era of Atlanton, before the coming of the Dark One." Ephinias smiled slightly. "Those were very pleasant days. I remember the long afternoons on the river when I was hardly more than a boy, watching the water birds chase bugs."

"Was there ever a time before the Dark One?" muttered Stearborn. "It would be news to me. . . . But what about this Bright Star, girl? You were saying something about the scrolls being able to help us with rebuilding."

"Ever the one to come to the point, Stearborn." Chellin laughed. "That's more to my way of thinking. I'm one to chase a line of history down, but I'm also curious to know any bit of information that might help keep my hide whole another day!"

Deros continued, pulling out a small icon on a ribbon she wore around her neck. "I have carried this since I was small. My father has a matching piece. The one I have was my mother's. She passed it to me when she died. Together the two make a key to fit a lock in the very heart of Cairn Weal. The scrolls of Alberion Nova are kept there."

Gillerman stood suddenly and paced about restlessly, walking behind the others that were seated in a circle around the fire.

"I've heard stories that these scrolls are in one place or another—proven false, so far," said Ephinias. "When the Council of Light began their task of keeping these Lower Meadows long ago, the scrolls were given into the care of appointed stewards across the lands, as a set of rules to govern by. If they are indeed the scrolls of life, the Alberion Nova, then the danger of their being lost to enemies is beyond reckoning. It might not mean the end right away, but without the truth of the Law being preserved and taught to seekers, then litle by little it would be forgotten, and there would be no way out.

"These Boundaries would be at an end," he continued. "People would forget their beginnings, and after a time what Owen went through with the curse of the Olgnite would be common to all. Without a guide it would be evident how it would all end up."

"As squashers?" asked Starboard, incredulous.

"Or worse."

"The Hulin Vipre are the cruelest," said Deros. "They have no deformities, but that makes them the more hideous. They are a handsome race but with the same dark side as the spidermen. They are full of hate and vengefulness and will stop at nothing to achieve their goals."

"They were stopped smartly enough by the Olgnites," reminded Starboard. "We saw how that went, when the two of them were thrown against the other."

"The paradox of it all," replied Gillerman. "If a fire runs wild, the very thing that kills it is that it has no fuel, for it's consumed by that which gives it life."

"So you will help me get home?" persisted Deros, addressing the two Archaelians. "You can see how important it is!"

"We newer said we wouldn't," answered Findlin.

"If you can conwince the crews to man our wessels, we'll take you off the edge of Atlanton and back, my lady," said Lorimen.

"Where is the minstrel?" asked Chellin. "I've never heard a more silver tongue than his! He'd do the convincing, all right."

"He and Elita are together somewhere." Ephinias smiled. "We are to complete their betrothal vows as soon as we reach the coast and have a chaplain."

"Do we have a way to the coast marked clear? Is the course free of the spidermen?" asked Starboard.

"We have our best scouts out," replied Chellin Duchin. "Famhart has asked for all our reports tonight, so we can decide when, and in which way, to move."

Ephinias rose and looked at the sky, streaked with high, scudding white clouds. Away in the direction of the previous night's fighting there were hundreds of ravens, circling above the enemy dead from the battle. "It looks as though we may have a change in the weather before long. I think we should have a look while we can."

Gillerman nodded. "We will have to go quickly if we are to find Wallach. I grow more concerned as time goes on."

"Are you coming back?" asked Deros. "You always do this right when we need you the most."

"Yes, my dear, we're coming back," assured Ephinias.

"And no form changes? I don't want to face any more of your animal tricks."

The old teacher laughed. "I promise. But they have always served us well."

"I know something bad is about to happen every time you start out with one of your lessons and make a point by giving us another form. The last time it was dogs, and look where that has gotten us!"

Ephinias nodded, remembering the room in Emerald's shelter, when the first of the Olgnites had appeared. "We shall certainly have to see about all this in the future," he said, chuckling to himself. "I can see your point."

Linne awakened then, and panicked when she saw Owen's bed empty. She started up, still half asleep, and bumped heavily into her son, sitting on his haunches at the tent opening, where he had been following the conversations of his friends with great interest. She smothered him with a hug. "Look at you! You're up!"

"I feel like I've been trampled by a horse," he replied. "I tried to stand up, but I get dizzy."

"You'll be fine. You've been very ill. Can you eat something?" Linne began to fuss about the small brazier in the tent, looking for water for tea and for travel cake.

"I can try." Owen's thoughts were racing after he had listened to Deros pleading to be taken home, and he had a difficult time explaining to himself why he was so depressed and listless. She had not mentioned him once and seemed on fire to leave.

"Your father left you these things," said Linne, pointing

to a mail shirt and a brocade purple vest to be worn over it, denoting the rank of Elder. Her eyes glistened as she watched her son.

Owen's heart stopped a moment, and the cold reality of it all filtered back into his senses. He remembered his father passing along the responsibility of Elder and his fear, and all the blood left his face. "I can't do this, Mother. I am going with Deros." His words startled him, and it was as though someone else had spoken.

"What? You can't, Owen! You're not strong enough."

"I'm going with her," he repeated doggedly.

"We'll talk about it when you're better." His flustered mother poured his tea.

"I will be fine, Mother. Deros says she's leaving with someone when we get to the coast, and I'm going with her."

Linne looked around the small tent, searching for an argument to give, but found only a mother's sadness. She took a deep breath and remained silent.

"I heard Deros talking. There is someone with boats who said they would take her home."

"It is Findlin and Lorimen, two Archaelians from Fionten. They found us in the fen when we were attacked by the Bogmot."

"The what?" asked Owen, thoroughly confused.

"There was something in the fen, at the Crooked Spire. Kegin knew one way through the Ellerhorn, but Findlin and Lorimen knew of this old settlement. The Bogmot was there."

Owen concentrated, tyring to piece together all that had happened while he had been trapped in the Olgnite spell. "How long have I been this way? Under the spell, I mean."

"Two days."

"It seems like forever. I keep having dreams and nightmares. The Olgnite blood is still there. I can feel it sometimes."

"You're safe now. The Lame Parson and Twig helped Gillerman pull you back."

"More strangers! It seems I missed all the most important events."

"You *were* an important event. If it hadn't been for you, Deros would still be captured by the spidermen."

"It was Gitel and Seravan. I remember both of them trying to control the spell when it was overpowering me. I couldn't fight it, and they kept me from falling under it completely."

"But you didn't, and now you're all safe. We are making arrangements now for our journey to the coast. We're trying to reach White Bird."

As Linne finished speaking, Emerald and Kegin paused at the entrance of the small tent with the two Archaelians. "May we come in, Linne? We'd like to acquaint Owen with our friends."

"We were just speaking of them," she replied. "Have any of you seen Famhart?"

"He's with Chellin. They're trying to draft a plan to get us safely to White Bird. I think we've decided on the old Green Road, if it's still passable."

Owen's eyes widened. "No one's used that way for as long as I've known of it! Is it safe?"

Kegin laughed. "It was closed for a time because of a feud between White Bird and Clover Hill. A marriage gone sour, I think. The road was never dangerous before the raiders came. Our main obstacle now—if the Olgnites are gone, and I feel they are—would probably be that the woods have overgrown the trail."

"Couldn't we just go down the river to Great Bend and along the coast from there?" asked Owen.

"Too open, and there are not enough boats for all of us. It will be faster to travel overland, even if the Green Road is hard to find."

"Our scouts are at it now," added Emerald. "We'll be ready to move as soon as you're fit."

"I'm fit now," replied the youth, struggling to rise but growing dizzy and sitting back down suddenly.

"You've had a wery close call, youngster! You'll be lucky to get your sea legs back in a week. We'll hoist you aboard a horse and pack you like cargo until you can hold your own."

"I am Findlin at your service, and this is my friend, Lorimen," said the Archaelian, bowing. "Wery pleased to see you with the wind in your sails again."

"And he promised to find a boat and crew," prompted Deros, pushing her head inside the tent.

"Now, my lady," began Lorimen, holding out his hands to try to placate the determined young woman, but she continued, shaking her head defiantly.

"We shall find a way, I know. We must go soon, for the Hulin Vipre will report that I'm alive, and they will return here in force."

"I'm going too," Owen announced. "I've decided that."

Deros raised her eyebrows questioningly. "You're the new Elder here! They will need you to help rebuild the Line."

"My father is rested now, and all the old Steward squadrons are here. They can carry on well enough without me. We'll call a council fire and settle it," said Owen. "If there is a boat to be found and you go, then I shall be aboard too."

"Well said, lad." Stearborn laughed. "Those are the heart's words if ever I heard them! You can't let the lass slip through your hands now."

Deros blushed but spoke firmly. "I welcome anyone who wishes to aid my father."

"Aye, it's your father he wants to help, I can tell you! The sprout has grown some since we've been riding with him, and I see he's learned his eye for a woman as well as his father." Chellin Duchin hoisted himself stiffly to his feet, clutching his injured leg. "If we were all so smart, as we once thought we were, we'd soon take this to heart and try to live a safe and snug life somewhere quiet, growing cabbages."

"You needn't make a jest of me," shot Owen hotly.

"I make no jests, my boy! Chellin Duchin has never been known to make light of anything! I wish I were young again and full of that fire that consumes you."

"He's in no shape to go anywhere until he's rested," announced his mother. "Now you louts can all clear out and let him sleep." Linne drove the gathered friends from in front of the tent and sent them on their way. She walked to the fire with Stearborn and asked him to talk to her son. "I don't think he'll listen to me," explained Linne. "But you're someone he respects and admires, my old friend. You and his father have seen enough of war and death, and all that goes with life. You wouldn't lead him wrong."

"Famhart should be talking to him, my lady. I once felt
the same sting. There were those who were sincere and who
meant to set old Stearborn onto the right course, but he was
a stiff-necked young bull, and he went on and did what
he'd meant to do all along."

"Were you sorry for it?" asked Linne, sensing a softening
of the old warrior. "Were you happy?"

The old Steward's eyes brimmed with tears. "I hardly
knew what the word meant, growing up in the world I came
to manhood in. I was satisfied, and I loved, and I sat down
by the banks of soft waters and held her close to me, as a
man might take a drink after a long walk through a heartless,
cruel desert."

"Then I am foolish to try to keep him here."

Stearborn nodded. "He'll go, anyway. The chart is already
laid out, and his course is clear."

"In a way I'm glad," said Linne quietly. "A mother wants
her child to be happy and to do what he feels he must. I have
never really wanted Owen to have to be burdened with the
role of Elder. It has made Famhart old before his time."

They were interrupted by a messenger. "It's for you, sir,"
the youth reported, saluting smartly. "There's movement
beyond your perimeters, sir. No spidermen, but it's the
others who raided through Sweet Rock. They're moving on
the other side of the fen."

Stearborn turned to Deros, who had waited at the fire,
warming her hands. "Do you think they have boats at the
coast, girl?"

Deros nodded.

"Then we might take them for our own use if we could
catch them." He paced nervously about, formulating a quick
battle plan. "I shall have a patrol formed within the hour and
be behind them, as quiet as mice." He turned to the young
woman. "The good Archaelians may find their 'wessels'
sooner than they had bargained for." Stearborn winked and
nodded.

Deros hugged him. "You've always been a wonderful
friend, Stearborn. I shall have my father make you an Elder
in his realm!"

The gruff old commander laughed, tyring to fend the girl off. "None of that now, lass! I have enough of a rub trying to keep after these smart young pups that call themselves Stewards. But look to your kit and see that you're ready, in case we find a boat that will launch you toward your homeland."

Deros hugged him again, in spite of his efforts to escape, and gave his grizzled cheek a peck.

You are young, child," siad Linne, smiling sadly, "and I have no hold on you, other than as a woman who asks a favor of another, if you have the wisdom to grant it."

"What is that, my lady? I owe you and Famhart more than a favor."

"Tell Owen he must not go," whispered Linne. "Not yet. He is still too weak to travel, and his father is counting on him taking the mantle of Elder." Linne heard the words coming from her mouth but could not help herself.

"I will tell him, my lady," answered Deros, her eyes full of compassion. "Yet he will do what he pleases, that much I know of him."

"Yes, he will do what he pleases," echoed Linne, reaching out to pat the young woman's hand.

Stearborn reached out to her, and took her hand clumsily in his own. "You shall have a tall tale, Linne, and maybe somewhere along the end of it, we shall have Famhart make us up one of his famous stirrup stews, like he used to make in camp, when we were on the march for Portiban, in the Middle Islands."

Linne's eyes welled with tears, and she watched the young girl walk away toward the camp kitchens, looking for Elita. She turned to her son who lay against the soft boughs of his crude pallet. Owen's eyes were shut, and he rested uneasily, one arm crooked over his face, and the other holding the sword from Skye firmly to his chest.

"He is so young," she said under her breath, intending it for no one, but Stearborn replied, shaking his head.

"I was two seasons younger than he is now when I saw my first battle with the Stewards. It has a way of making you old, even if you have not many turnings to your age."

"Yes," said Linne. "It always falls too soon upon us, and there is never enough time in the end to wonder about it all."

"There may be more time than you think. If we find these boats, it will take us some doing to unravel their contrary quirks, and then there's the weather! Seamen like the Archaels will have the good sense not to try sailing them off the face of the known seas in an autumn gale, in boats they don't have a feel for." He smiled. "That could take quite some time, my lady."

Linne hugged him then, setting off another serious patch of bright crimson color spreading to his ears and his face above his beard, and causing him to cough nervously in rapid succession. Kegin's return with the stew, and more news of the scout's reports saved him from further embarrassment, and he went gladly, leaving Linne alone in the tent with her son.

A clear, powder blue sky hung above the fen as she set about her task of clearing away the meal Owen had taken, and as she watched through the flap of the tent, two great birds, a hawk and a white falcon, wheeled upward into the early morning sky, rising up higher and higher still, until she lost their disappearing forms in the dusky shadows of heaven's eaves.

A Familiar Face

Owen Helwin's recovery was nothing short of miraculous. In the space of a week, his color had returned, he was walking about the large encampment, accompanied by Kegin and the now ever-present Gortlanders, Lofen and McKandles, who were never more than an arm's length from the youth, ever ready to steady him on his feet if he seemed tired, or to run some errand, or to bring refreshment. The young Stewards—Judge, Jeremy, and Hamlin—spent all their free time with him.

Owen's eye followed Deros as she went about her daily affairs, which now found her much in the company of the Archaelians, Findlin and Lorimen, and their young charge, Enlid. He was a shy, athletic youth with dark red hair who seemed mostly intent upon finding excuses to engage Deros in conversation. The older men found this amusing, but Owen was infuriated and baffled, so he tried to impress this new suitor with the importance of his being Elder. Enlid was unimpressed and too smitten with the beautiful young woman to take notice of Owen's behavior.

Kegin, however, did observe his young friend's cocky appearance, and tried to save Owen further embarrassment, since all the others in the camp were making fun of the young man's poses. "You are wise to take note of my words, my lad," warned Kegin. "I never was able to teach you much about the art of weaponry, but I do have a few choice pieces of advice where it comes to the warfare of love! Never show an enemy your hand, and let the other man make the first play!"

Owen reddened and pretended ignorance. "You speak riddles, Kegin. I'm doing nothing save preparing for the journey to White Bird."

"If you had been healthy enough, we should have sent you with Stearborn's patrol. It would have saved you the spectacle you're making of yourself."

Owen went on parading about in the mail shirt and insignia cloak of an Elder that his father had set aside for him, ignoring the stern looks of Kegin and the amused glances of the others in the settlement. Deros took no notice, now that he was beyond the danger of the illness from the Olgnite curse, which drove him to further desperate measures. She had informed him that he was welcome on the journey to her homeland, along with any other able-bodied men who might bring aid to her father. That she lumped him in among all the others crushed Owen. Her coolness and indifference toward Owen baffled him, and finally he asked his mother if he had somehow offended Deros.

"I'm afraid I made a mistake in asking Deros to try to convince you not to go with her. I think she sees that as an obligation to me to try to dissuade you by making you believe she has no interest in you."

Owen was angry at first but softened as he listened to Linne describing how Deros had sat with him day and night while he was under the spiderman's spell, fighting for his life. "We all have our roles to play, and it seems that Deros is as bound by her own as we all are. Your father is very disappointed that you have chosen to disregard your responsibilities. Deros is holding to her own, even though you don't see that right now."

"I haven't said I won't take my place as Elder," protested Owen, stung by his father's disapproval. "All I have said is that I want to go with Deros to make sure she reaches her father safely. When I return, there will be plenty of time for me to learn all there is about this business of Elder. I am still too young to fill that post now."

"Those were my words, as a mother," Linne said softly. "You are my son, and I have seen the great toll this role has taken of Famhart. Yet he knows there are those who depend on him and who can rely on his judgment and courage."

"There are a dozen others who should stand in line for Elder," persisted Owen. "All of them have the experience and would fill the post better than I right now. Kegin is the first I would select, based on everything that counts in a man."

Linne nodded. "Kegin is an old friend and a brave man. He knows the order of things and would not be willing to go against your father's wishes. It has always been understood that if the Elder has a male child who grows to manhood, then the office will pass from father to son."

"We shall see about a new law," argued Owen. "I know I was prepared in a way, but I never thought it would come to pass so soon. And there are other things as well. I love Deros, and I can't let her just disappear! I might never see her again!" He had spoken before he thought, and his face colored. He turned and stalked from his mother's tent, confused and unable to continue.

Kegin found him walking furiously away towards the borders of the camp. "What have we here? You look as though you've eaten stew without letting it cool!"

"Leave me alone! I don't feel like talking!"

"That much I can see. I think you might change your mind, though. Stearborn has sent a man back to report that they've taken two of the boats of the Hulin Vipre. They were downriver and prepared for a long voyage. Lorimen and Findlin are on their way now to help oversee the fitting out. They asked if you felt like coming along."

Before he thought about it, Owen asked, "Is Enlid going?"

"Of course. He is to be the new Carinbar for Fionten."

"Then I will surely go. I don't want Deros left alone with him."

Kegin laughed before he could stop himself. "Then we

shall have a nice trip. Nothing whets the appetite like good salt air and two young bucks in rut, fighting over a doe."

"That's not the case, Kegin! You jest too much on a sore subject. If you were truly my friend, you'd give me rest from all the pointed remarks about my long looks and lost breath over Deros. Does it never occur to you that I might be concerned for her safety?"

Kegin managed to hold his laughter and tried to respond kindly to Owen's serious glance. "I'm sure you are, my young friend. We are all concerned with her welfare."

Owen bristled, but slowly calmed, for looking over Kegin's shoulder, he saw Deros coming along toward them, arm in arm with Elita. Kegin called out to the pair. Owen blushed.

"We are looking for the Chamberlain of Fionten," said Deros happily, blithely ignoring Owen. "He has agreed to say Elita's betrothal vows. All we have to do is reach the coast, and they will finally be together! Don't you find that exciting?"

Kegin agreed with a nod of his head. "Those Archaelians are good for their word. Are you ready for a boat trip, my lady? We have had word from Stearborn of the two vessels he has captured from the Hulin Vipre."

Deros grasped Kegin's hand, and with an intensity that cut Owen to the quick, asked, "Are they ready with the ships now? Are there crews who would be able to sail these vessels?"

Kegin held up his hands, trying to slow the girl down. "They have only just sent me word, my lady. There is still a bit of work to be done by the Archaels, and some small details to be attended to. I, for one, am glad they haven't left again."

"Are they going with us?" asked Owen, braving the cool glance Deros shot him.

"All are welcome," she replied coolly. "They haven't said whether they will or won't."

"If we are to try to make a passage back to your homeland, my lady, two small boats and crews don't speak well for a well-armed expedition. I hope there will be vessels enough to take a squadron or two with us, but unless things change when we reach White Bird, it looks to be just the barest of parties to make such a dangerous voyage."

"I know other ways to reach Eirn Bol," said Deros. "The Hulin Vipre are cunning, in their own manner, but they haven't discovered all the secrets of the Order of The Thistle."

"Which order?" asked Owen, glad to find a way to enter the conversation again. "I thought you told us much of Eirn Bol, but I don't remember you saying anything about orders."

"The Order of The Thistle," repeated the girl. "It is an old sect that is the sworn protectors of the Alberion Nova. I shouldn't even tell you this much, but you might as well know something about the place you wish to try to aid."

Elita spoke then, her eyes very distant, and her hands were clasped tightly together before her. "It was an old order. There was one in Trew, when I was a girl. They came back from the wars one year with the king, and he was greatly taken with them."

"Were they still there when we were in Trew?" asked Owen.

The woman shook her head. "They had gone long ago. The Rogen drove out all but the children of Trew. I think the Order of The Thistle could have stayed, for they were powerful, and knew many things, but I think they were called away."

"They may have been called to defend Eirn Bol," replied Deros. "There have been many sieges laid to our island by the Hulin Vipre. It always seemed we were under one attack or another, ever since I was a tiny child. My mother was killed in the fighting of one of those invasions. I was only five." Her eyes misted, and she fell into silence, alone with her thoughts for a time. "The Order of The Black Hood brought ship loads of krates from the lands beyond Gilniven."

"Brought what?" asked Kegin. "Were they tribes from below those boundaries, like the Olgnites?"

"They were snakes," answered Deros. "Deadly snakes. A bite would be fatal in the time it would take to breathe. They covered our beautiful island with the asps, and tried to poison our rivers."

"How did you manage to rid yourself of the snakes?" asked Owen.

"We read of their natural enemies in an old volume of one of our librarys, and found how to bring them to the island. The rivers we let clean themselves, for we have an underground stream below Cairn Weal, so there was water enough for us. In the end, the poisoned rivers killed more of our enemies than we would have, for there were other tribes the Hulin Vipre had landed to try to overpower us. They forgot to tell them what they'd done."

"The Black Hood doesn't sound as though they would be good allies," said Kegin, grimacing.

"They hold to nothing, except the overthrow of all the islands in the Silent Sea, and the capture of the Alberion Nova. They live for the conquest of my father, and Cairn Weal."

The companions were interrupted by a signal arrow flying over the wood, which whistled a high pitched note as it fluttered down somewhere behind them.

"It's Stearborn! I wonder what he wants?" said Kegin, a frown darkening his features.

"He may need help," said Deros.

"He'll have it," replied Kegin. "Look!"

A squadron of Stewards was already mounted and thundering away toward Stearborn's position.

"We'd better go too," said Deros excitedly. "I don't want anything to happen to our boats."

"There's not a lot you could do that the Stewards can't," teased Kegin. "I'm sure they'll find some way to hold the boats for us."

"I don't think he's under attack," pointed out Owen. "There were no horns, and I've heard nothing that sounded like a fray."

"The Stewards will see to it," assured Kegin. "I think our next move here is to find a chart, and have Deros plot a course."

"I can remember all the important things," replied the girl. "I only wish we could find the ship that brought me.

The captain was a friend of my father's. He'd have the charts, and all the news as well."

"The Hulin Vipre ships will have charts," said Kegin. "If they come from the same waters, they will have all the same charts."

Another troop of Stewards rode out, and Kegin called out to one of the men as they passed. Drawing up, he replied shortly. "They've found one of the horse-riding gobs, one Ulen Scarlett, down by the ships. He claims to know the whereabouts of the other Hulin Vipre."

"I knew it." muttered Owen. "As if we didn't have trouble enough already."

"Lofen and McKandles will be glad to hear he's alive," said Deros. "They don't seem to really like each other, but I think they feel that truly they are family."

Kegin smiled briefly. "That pair has kept me amused with their antics. I've never seen anyone any more eager to please than the two of them."

Owen's voice sounded bitter as he spoke. "We'll have to leave the horse-master here under guard. I don't want to have to worry about what he's up to while we're away."

"Maybe we should take him with us," said Deros, purposely baiting Owen.

"We'll wait to hear his story," said Kegin. "He may be able to give us fresh news of what's been going on in the other camps."

"He was ready to sell you out to save his hide," sneered Owen. "Why would you want him along now?"

"Anyone would have done the same," said Deros lightly, watching Owen's reaction carefully.

"They wouldn't have," he argued. "If it had been any one of the Stewards, they would have fought to the death to keep you safe!"

Elita tried to calm the waters by saying that no one would know what he would do, until he was in that situation.

Emerald arrived at that moment, looking for his bride.

"Ask Emerald," insisted Owen. "He can tell you what the horseman is really like!"

The minstrel smiled, looking about at the strained faces. "Why ask Emerald when he has news to tell. We are to meet with Ephinias this afternoon. He is to give us instruction in our binding vows."

"I hope you have better luck this time," said Kegin. "After all the broken heads and ruined homes you caused last time, we might be better off if you two openly declared war on each other."

"Who is going with me to the boats?" asked Deros. "I want to find Stearborn."

"I'm going," announced Owen. "I would like to see Master Scarlett. I still owe him a punch in the nose for his bungling attempt at taking care of you, my lady."

"Wait," said Kegin. "He may or may not deserve it, but we need to know what he knows first. You never can tell, my hotheaded young friend! He may have had a change of heart since you last had words with him."

"I would like to see that," glowered Owen. "His pride was a size larger than his cap!"

"Things have a way of changing," went on Kegin. "I remember a day not too long back that I would have thought nothing about cutting the throats of two Archaels. I'm glad I was prudent enough to stop."

"They would have made it exceedingly rough on you, if you hadn't," put in Jeremy, who had joined the strolling group, peeling a pale green apple with a sheath knife at his belt. "That lot may look to be a bit soft, but they wear like iron. I wouldn't want to put them in a cross way with me."

"Where would you have seen them?" asked Owen.

"All through this business! I fought alongside the young one. He's not polished enough for a Steward's saddle yet, but he would certainly be, if he keeps his training up."

Hamlin saw the look that played across Owen's face. "I think I smell perfume here, lurking in the shadows," he said. "This all looks to be something other than our old stock and trade."

Judge, not heeding any of the signals, blundered on. "Why would anyone question Enlid? He's a good lad, and the Archaels are a jolly lot. I like hearing their sea chanties, and stories of sailing boats."

"Not a good subject now," warned Jeremy, but too late. Owen had reddened further, and without excusing himself, strode on before the others. He whistled for Seravan as he went, although he didn't wait for the big animal to catch up with him. He only paused further down the trail when he heard Gitel and Seravan coming along behind him, and heard Deros speaking to the horses, and laughing at something one of them had said.

"You will be more comfortable riding," she called out lightly to him. "It is still a good way on to the boats."

"I'm enjoying the walk," Owen snapped, a little more harshly than he had intended. "I need to think."

"What were you thinking of?" she asked, and pulled Gitel up so she could dismount and walk beside Owen.

Owen's anger dissipated before her questions, and he grew more confused than ever, looking into her eyes. "I was wondering if we are going to be able to take our friends here aboard the boats Stearborn has found."

"You don't have to worry about us," assured Gitel. "Gillerman and Wallach will be able to bring us to you."

Owen was concerned then. "You aren't going with us?"

"We shall be with you, but our old friends have a journey to make as well, and we must help them."

"Who will go with us? We will need someone to help us too."

"Ephinias is the one to make this voyage with you. He has wanted to see those lands for quite some time."

"I don't like this," murmured Owen. "You and Gitel will be gone, and the rest of us are to depend upon Ephinias for all our guidance and protection?"

"He has done that for you all along."

Deros made a face. "I hope that doesn't mean we are going to be spending more time in his animal spells."

"He's fond of those, but you forget that he knows much, and has been to the Sacred Well in Windameir. He may seem like a doty old man to you sometimes, but he is still a master, like Gillerman and Wallach."

"I would feel better if you two were along," admitted Owen. "You've been so close to us, and I was hoping they were going to leave you with us always."

Seravan snorted, and dropped his head over Owen's shoulder. "You are warm-hearted, little one. My great-grandsire told me when I was but a foal that I would have a charmed life, and that I would carry many strong hearts for the Light. If I were able to choose where I would stay, you know I would be with you always."

"And we shall be with you once you reach Eirn Bol," added Gitel.

"That will be hard to do, without you," argued Owen.

"You will have your friends, and Ephinias. You won't be beyond our ken, should you need us. You still carry the sword that can reach us, if the need arises."

"It won't be the same. I know you must go with Gillerman and Wallach, but we shall miss you."

"You said you would be with us on Eirn Bol. Are Gillerman and Wallach going there?" asked Deros.

"There seems to be a lot of interest in that island. The Order of The Black Hood has come to the attention of the Council again, and Wallach has already been there for a look. It seems to be the next place where we may be needed."

"There are many things needed on Eirn Bol," conceded Deros. "I'm glad someone has finally taken notice of my father's plight."

"There has been a great many things to occupy all the Guides down here below the Boundaries, little one." Seravan paused, shaking his bridle. "I feel like we've been down here so long, I've almost forgotten my way home."

"That will be the day," snorted Gitel. "When the time comes, we'll know it, right enough."

Seravan laughed. "He talks of it all like something we'll be doing in a turning or two! I wish that were the case."

"We'll be closer to it, once we get to the boats, and find out what Stearborn knows. There may be other news, as well. Findlin and Lorimen may have sailing orders, and that means we'll be ready to ship out for Eirn Bol the sooner." There was a note of hope in Deros's voice. "We must find stores and arms to take, and a sturdy crew to steer her with! It is a full month's sail to reach the Straits of Horinfal, and then at least two weeks more on to Eirn Bol. And that's if we have a fair wind."

"There they are," said Owen, excitedly, as they neared the

wide landing where the two Hulin Vipre boats were anchored in the shallow water, laying amid the steady hustle and bustle of the Steward squadron, and overseen by Stearborn, who stood conversing with the two Archaels, Lorimen and Findlin, who watched as the stores were all laid carefully below.

There was another there with the others who had his back to Owen, but even without the man turning around, he already knew by heart the familiar face.

The River
Flows

"Here's a sight for these old eyes," boomed Stearborn, catching sight of Owen and striding over to smother him in a bear hug. "All this talk of sea voyages has gotten my blood up, I can tell!"

"A woyage always has that effect on me," chimed in Findlin. "Ewen as a youth, they always had me up to go, no matter what the weather, or which way the wind was blowing." He shook hands vigorously with Owen. "Do you know Master Ulen? He's been giwing us an account of how the Hulin Wipre forces are disposed."

"I'm sure he has firsthand knowledge of those things," replied Owen, his face expressionless. "He seems to have made himself well acquainted with their doings."

Ulen bowed stiffly. "Greetings, Helwin. I have heard tales of your unfortunate bout with the Olgnite curse. You seem recovered."

"I am in my right senses," returned Owen. "Nothing will slip by me now, and I shall be watchful, I can promise you."

Stearborn interrupted the two bristling young men in a booming voice. "Why is the lass dragging her pretty feet through those carrion on the banks? We've gone through the lot of them, and there's not a piece of information to be gotten from it." He pointed to Deros, who was carefully searching a pile of slain Hulin Vipre, followed by Hamlin and Jeremy.

"I think she's trying to see if she recognizes any of them," answered Owen.

"The one she is seeking isn't there. He's at the bottom of the bog."

Owen turned to Ulen. "How do you come to know that?"

"When I escaped the spidermen, my horse was caught in the mud. Two Stewards pulled me free, and as I was dragged out, I passed over another one of their victims wrapped in that foul webbing they bind you with. I tried to pull him free, but he couldn't hold on. This ring slipped off his hand." Ulen held out the object for Owen to see. "It belonged to Tien Cal, the Hulin Vipre prince."

"Are you sure he's dead?" asked Owen, staring at the ring.

"The bog gives no quarter."

"You've repaid that debt, my young friend, with the information you gave us about their numbers and position. It shouldn't be too much of a stretch for us to round them up before they can escape us." Stearborn waved an arm in a circling motion.

Owen saw Deros rise from examining the last enemy corpse and swim Gitel across the river. His pulse hammering, he left Stearborn and the two Archaelians standing with Ulen and went to Seravan to cover his confusion. "Why couldn't he have just saved all the trouble and drowned in the bog?" he muttered under his breath. "That would have served him right."

The big animal said nothing and contented himself with grazing at the tall grass near the river's edge.

"You don't need to condemn me for thinking it," blurted Owen, sitting down heavily beside the horse. "And now there's this Enlid, with his pretty lisp. 'Oh, its wery good to see you, my lady. How lowely you look today!' "

Seravan raised his head and spoke softly against Owen's ear. "Jealousy does strange things. I've seen it spark wars and crack friendships that had endured for turnings. The worst of it is that no one ever knows that's their trouble until it's too late to mend the fences."

"I'm not jealous of these air bags," shot Owen. "They offend my very sense of honor! One is a coward, and the other is a fop who can't even speak properly! He's unproven, and they say they'll take him along on a dangerous voyage, along with another who has proven twice that he can't be counted on and that he's untrustworthy!"

"You are quick to judge, little one. You may not have all your facts arranged in the proper order."

"They are proper enough, and the truth doesn't take many facts to prove it."

"Stearborn is the man to speak with in regard to who goes or doesn't go. They are his ships, for he's the one who has captured them. I don't think you can leave the Archael lad behind, since he is to travel back to Fionten with his two guardians."

"If that's as far as he went, it would be fine by me. Maybe I can convince the Archaels to keep Ulen as well! He can find another fair and show everyone his riding skills. That's where he belongs by all rights! And far away from me!"

Owen sprang to his feet suddenly, glowering as he watched Deros join the others. She nodded to Ulen coolly, which pleased him, but he did not like the way the Archaelian youth kissed her hand or engaged her in conversation, and when he led her on to one of the small rafts they used to load stores and poled her out to the first of the Hulin Vipre craft, Owen could stand it no longer. "Come on, Seravan! We've stood here long enough! I can't leave her alone with that dandy!"

Seravan followed his young friend, amazed at how far gone the young man was and how little he knew of what went on within the human heart. "I'll never begin to fathom all this," he mused aloud. "I have been with you two now long enough to know you and Deros better than you know yourselves. The more you fight each other, the more obvious it becomes that you are meant to be together."

Owen colored, and stammered out a reply, which the big animal missed, and their attention was called back to the group at the river's edge by Stearborn calling out his name in a deep, resonant voice and beckoning him to come back.

"I'll go back," Owen mumbled, "but I won't be nice to either of them! Look, Hamlin and Jeremy aren't buying it, either," Owen said, gloating. He was watching as the two young Stewards followed Deros and Enlid aboard the vessel. Owen could not determine what they were talking about but could tell from their animated gestures they were disagreeing with the young Archael. "Well done, lads," he said half aloud. "Maybe you can correct his speech as well."

Seravan heaved an exasperated sigh. "You shall have need of all of these clans before this is all said and done. You have not learned your father's tact yet."

Owen fell silent then, and he thought of his father's disappointment at his decision to make the voyage with Deros, instead of staying on as the new Elder of the Line. "I have some things to learn," he conceded. "There is much to this game I don't think I shall ever comprehend."

Seravan softened his tone and slowed, so as to have more time to speak before they reached the others. "Your father didn't have time to learn all he should have before he was thrust into a role he never asked for. His father was a hard, cruel man who ruled Boghatia with an iron hand for many years. Gillerman always said that we didn't dare do anything against him, for fear one who was even more cruel might come to power. And he and Wallach knew that young Famhart was to come from the trouble there, and that would be worth all the problems that plagued that part of Atlanton in those turnings."

"It destroyed Boghatia," remarked Owen. "That was a high price to pay."

"Not so dear as it could have been," corrected Seravan. "You look at events as tales, but when you see things as Wallach and Gillerman do, then you see the whole adventure." The horse drew up suddenly, his ears flickering forward, listening intently to something beyond Owen's hearing.

"What is it?" he asked finally, after waiting in silence for a few long seconds.

"I can't be sure. It was a signal, but I lost it in all the racket they're making at the boats."

"A signal? Whose? Is it one of ours?"

"No. It was too faint really to make out, but there was something in it that worries me. I hope Gillerman and Ephinias are back. I would like to hear their report. There are Hulin Vipre still about and won't be happy to lose their means of getting home."

"The Gortlander said he knew where they were," said Owen. "If that's true, then all's well. But we can't be sure of him. And he has that ring."

"It's a Rhion Stone," explained Seravan. "Gillerman and the others of the Council wear something like them. They have great powers if they are used properly."

"Should we let him keep it? Shouldn't Gillerman take it?"

"When he returns, we shall see. In the meanwhile I don't think it would do any good to antagonize the young horseman by trying to take it. He seems to be making much use of it, by all appearances."

Owen looked up to see Ulen Scarlett holding the ring up for Deros to see, making broad gestures with his hands. The girl nodded indifferently but still stood very close to the young horseman. Enlid stepped forward, and the three of them passed from view, going down the companionway that led below decks.

"They seem to have much to discuss," said Owen bitterly. "I guess we should leave them to it."

"You will need to know their plans. Go aboard. I'll talk to Gitel."

Seravan left Owen at the water's edge and went to join Gitel. Owen helped pole a raft loaded with supplies to the Hulin Vipre craft. He found the three in the captain's quarters, a small, comfortable space with a large bunk, a chart table in its center, lit by a rush lamp swinging on a brass chain. The wood was brightly polished and shone in the sunlight that spilled down the companionway. Owen stopped while still on deck and listened.

Ulen Scarlett was speaking. "It would be a simple thing, and it wouldn't hurt anything in the effort to help your father."

"That's not the way he has held rein, Ulen. We have never fallen to using tactics our enemies use!"

"Then it may be time to forget your high-and-mighty ideas! Look where it's gotten you!"

Owen heard Ulen's snort of disdain. "What do you think, Enlid?" asked Deros. "Are you with Ulen?"

"Would the Hulin Vipre accept an outsider?"

"They would if the outsider was dressed in Hulin garb and outfitted as a common soldier," Ulen insisted. "We have enough of their dead outside here to equip a small group that could gradually find their way into the Hulin Vipre homelands."

"It sounds like a workable plan," agreed Enlid. "It might give you a wery big edge in your fight against them."

Deros remained unconvinced. "Who would you ask to try something so dangerous? You won't be able to find takers for this enterprise so quickly."

"Ah, but you're wrong! I, Ulen Scarlett, would be willing to go. Or perhaps brave Helwin will be up for another adventure. He seems to have gotten very handy with the taking on of disguises. Maybe Ephinias could outfit us all as Hulin Vipre and turn us loose inside their lines without anyone being the wiser."

"If you ask Ephinias, he might attempt it, but I am still not sure it is wise."

"You would object? Even if it proved to be of help to your father?"

Owen entered the low cabin. "She would object to a plan that had no hope of success," he said, enjoying the looks of surprise that greeted him.

"Ah, Helwin! I should have known to look for an appearance like this from you! Ever one to create the best impression."

"I was listening at the door. It seems to me that the turncoat of Gortland might be fishing about for ways to return safely to his new masters."

Ulen's jaws clenched. "I can rely on your jealousy to make a speech like that. You pride yourself on your foolish Steward's code, but the truth of the matter is that your precious Line was routed, and nothing can conceal that fact.

The all-powerful, mighty Line Stewards were sent packing by a horde of barbarians from the Leech, your snug little hamlet was razed, and now you find life on the road a bit precarious, so you talk to me from your pedestal, where all the true and just warriors reside! You have no room to speak to me as a superior! I have heard the story of you and the Olgnite curse!"

Owen's pulse raced, and his temples pounded, but he kept control of his temper. He watched with a certain glee as Enlid backed quickly away from the table, his eyes widening with fear. Deros stopped him with an outstretched arm as she turned to confront Ulen and Owen.

"This will do none of us any good, squabbling like washerwomen over a tub! I think you're both cruel and arrogant, bullying each other like this. If I had my way, I'd leave you both behind and go on with Findlin and Lorimen.".

"My serwices are for your asking," offered Enlid timidly, still not taking his eyes off Owen and Ulen.

"You are most welcome. It would be a pleasure to have peace and quiet on this voyage. There will be enough to worry about at the end, without having to listen to all this hot wind!"

"You may wish you had more of it, my high-handed lady! When you're faced with disaster because you would not take an action that would have saved you, you'll wish you had taken Ulen Scarlett up on his offer of assistance."

Owen was on the verge of speaking again but was cut short by Stearborn's voice. It was not kindly, and it came through the open companionway hatch like thunder.

"You two can stow up your puppy whining and bold talk! These old ears have heard all they need to think you've both gone oversides of common sense and decency, and I won't have another yard of it!"

Owen's anger was dampened by the anger in the old commander's voice, and he was further humiliated by Deros's laughter at his discomfort.

"Wery rightly spoke," agreed Findlin. "I'm glad you hawen't been part of this, my young squirt! It would do my old heart a wery great blow to hear such a commotion from our next Carinbar."

Stearborn eased his bulk carefully through the companionway door, filling the small quarters. He kept his head bent to avoid bumping it as he sat on a chair beside the chart table. "You were speaking earlier about something that made some sense—though it came from a boast, my good horseman. I want to hear more of it and less of this ruffling of hackles and parading of feathers in front of the lass here! She's a prize too great for either of you thundering lunkheads!"

"I wasn't—" began Owen, but he was stopped by Stearborn's raised hand.

"Both of you can stow the mudwargle and tell me more of the scheme you had for going back to the Hulin Vipre! That yammering had some merit, and I'd like to hear it without all the barking and yelping in between."

"It was my idea, sir," said Ulen. "I thought of it when I came by Tien Cal's—the Hulin Vipre prince—ring."

"Aye, the ring! Look at the fire in it! That's no ordinary gemstone!" The ring on Ulen's finger glimmered and cast fiery-red tinted shadows upon the air and seemed to be a live thing on the young Gortlander's hand.

"I don't like the feel of it," said Deros. "It's almost as though that man were here!" She shuddered, thinking back over her ordeal.

"Tien Cal," said Ulen. "His followers were not too keen on my having the ring when they came across me."

"The Hulin Vipre caught you?" questioned Stearborn. "When?"

"On my way to find your camp," returned Ulen. "They were going to kill me, but I managed to steal the black I'm riding now from one of them, and that's when I stumbled on to you at the river."

"It's lucky for you that you did," said Findlin. "It's a wery dangerous thing in these waters now. We'we done for the bigger numbers, but there are still bands of renegades."

"You said something of going into the heart of the Vipre nest," Stearborn said. "Do you think it could be done?"

Ulen studied the old Steward, sizing him up before he answered. "With the right people, yes! My old companions would go with me without a doubt. There may be others

who would volunteer their services if they have the brass."
Here Ulen looked directly at Owen.

"It wouldn't work," argued Deros, shaking her head vigorously. "The Hulin Vipre clans are too alien for you to
understand, and they would spot any strangers before you
could reach Hulingaad."

Stearborn pulled out a chart from the rolls beneath the
table and spread it out before him.

"How long would it take to teach someone enough of the
Hulin way to let them go undetected for a time? I don't
mean to have them perfect, just enough so they could move
about undetected for a bit and slip away unnoticed."

"That was my general line of thought," rejoined Ulen.
"Enough time to get the lay of the land, and maybe throw a
snag or two to their plans."

"Plant false intelligence," mused Stearborn. "It might be
something to do, putting a fly in their stew."

"The Order of the Black Hood is a secret well guarded,"
insisted Deros. "No one but the initiated know their ways."

"I have had some of those secrets given to me," boasted
Ulen, again watching Owen's face. "The sign and the pass-
words I have by memory. And I also have this now, which
makes the disguise almost complete." He held up the hand
the ring was on.

"Is there a way we could strike a blow at the Vipre?"
asked Stearborn. "I mean, other than through the Stewards?"

"How do you mean? What sort of blow?"

"Follow me," ordered Stearborn, rising suddenly and
making his way up the companionway and back on deck.
The others followed obediently behind him, looking at each
other questioningly. Only Findlin spoke out bluntly. "Where
are we going? Do we have to keelhaul an answer from someone?"

"No such goings on as that, mate. Old Stearborn just
needed a snoutful of fresh air. Those cramped quarters get to
me every time. I don't think I ever would have made much
of a miner or a sailor." Stearborn fell silent, gazing about
him at the late afternoon, now full of a pale, pearl-golden
light that reflected in the water, and off the red and dark
orange leaves of the autumn trees. The wind was brisk, and

the clear sky promised to bring a night that would require cloaks and blankets. The rafts were brought to the boarding ladders, and the old Steward commander led the way down and helped the others as they poled their way back to shore.

Then Stearborn told them of his plan, pointing toward the distant peaks, where the river had its beginnings. "There was a tribe that lived back in those parts in the early days of the Line. Swore they'd never open their borders or have a peace with the Stewards. Kept their word, too, and caused a lot of heartache and grief for some time. Started raiding when they felt strong enough and would sneak over and steal women and cattle when they could. All the time they kept finding more and more reasons to continue being at war with us, and it grew worse as time went on, until finally Famhart hit on a system that worked to bring them about and to finally call it quits with the Line."

"Which tribe are you talking about?" asked Owen, trying to remember if he'd ever heard this tale.

"They were called the Sardin. You wouldn't have known them. This was before your father ever considered a son."

"What did the Stewards do?" asked Findlin.

"Convinced them a plague had struck the Line," replied Stearborn, chuckling softly to himself. "We'd lost some animals to a bad outbreak of the Black Leg. We dragged those poor carcasses up near the boundaries and started our rumors here and there. It didn't take too many days to have the Sardin glad enough to be shed of us. They removed themselves from our borders, and your guess is as good as mine as to where they came to roost."

"It will take more than rumors to frighten off the Hulin Vipre," said Deros, her beautiful features turning hard in the fading light.

"And we shall find a way to do that as well," went on Stearborn. "I think Ephinias may be able to lend a hand there."

"I knew it." Owen groaned. "More of his spells! He'll be the death of us yet!"

"The salvation, my boy! Our salvation from this toil and trouble we've been stirred into all this time."

"Then you think my plan is workable?" asked Ulen, smiling triumphantly.

"I do. We shall call for volunteers tonight at fire. It shall have to wait for the binding vows, though. That rascal minstrel is finally doing the deed."

"I'd forgotten!" Deros gasped. "I've been so busy with this voyage, it slipped my mind! I have to go back now. I'm Elita's handmaiden!" Deros was suddenly mounted and urged Gitel away before anyone could move.

Owen took one last look at Ulen, with his handsome, arrogant face, and led Seravan forward in readiness to leave. "I shall see you at fire," he said to Stearborn. "We'll find our men then and lay out a plan."

"Aye, lad. Go on. I'll bring these sly dogs along in a moment. We'll make sure the ships are secured and ready to sail."

Findlin nodded, signaling to Lorimen and Enlid, and they went back to the rafts for one last look at the vessels before halting work for the night. As Owen looked over his shoulder at the scene he saw one of the first of the evening stars, high and cold, appear above the dark craft as they floated gently on the river, and behind them, the falling gray shadows of the half-bare trees, their fiery colors sleeping in the growing twilight. Out of the corner of his eye he caught a flash from the wood, a sudden spark or the last of the sunlight reflected off metal, but when he concentrated his attention on it, it was gone, and he went back to his thoughts of the young woman from Eirn Bol and the coming voyage.

The White
Falcon

Along the river, the fires from the encampment were reflected as mirror images of the leaping flames in the dark face of the flowing water. The night had grown colder, and a full moon hung low, a burned orange just over the tops of the wood, giving the landscape an eerie look. White wisps of fog hung above shallower parts of the river, and the horses' breath came in white clouds as they grazed or were tethered alongside their riders.

Stearborn had left a guard posted over the Hulin Vipre boats and ridden back with Lorimen and Findlin to find the others at the Council Fire, talking among themselves quietly. Soft music was drifting on the air. The throngs that jammed together there told of a popular event, and all—young and old, citizen and Steward alike—struggled to get in closer to see the proceedings that went on in the center of the excited crowd.

Elita stood blushing next to the minstrel with a wreath of autumn flowers woven into her fair hair. Ephinias was almost unrecognizable in a clean gray cloak that had a high, peaked hood. He droned on in a barely audible voice for quite some space of time, then looked up at Emerald and made a sign for him to speak.

As the minstrel repeated the binding vows Stearborn turned to the two Archaelians beside him, "This young buck has had a long wait for a binding night! She's a lovely girl. Saved by the Elboreal in Trew."

"The waterfolk?" asked Lorimen.

"Aye! She was left for dead by a blackguard there, burned by the dragonfire! They took her with them for a time, and now here she stands, as lovely a woman as you will ever see."

"I would wish them long and happy life! My old heart is touched by all such goings-on!"

"He's a wery sentimental lug," confirmed Findlin. "One of his faworite things is the binding wows that are held on the beach in Fionten when we celebrate the Spring Rites."

"You hawe no room to chide me, Master Chamberlain! I hawe yet to see you with dry eyes on any occasion that smacks of heart or hearth!"

"I wish we could get the two youngsters to lower their guards," observed Stearborn as he watched Owen and Deros skirting around each other as though they were wild animals catching scent of a snare.

The wind that had kicked up in brief, strong gusts all day subsided as the evening wore on, and a few high stars glittered coldly beneath the moon. There were other musicians who had joined the noisy revelry now, and there was a general call all round for Emerald to sing them a ballad of the Stewards that was a popular favorite among the men. He held Elita closer to him, shaking his head, but soon there was such a hue and cry that his bride handed him his harp. The minstrel held up his hand, and began to play, his strong voice carrying the notes clearly, and the calls and talk began to subside as he sang the slow, aching song of lost comrades, and the bittersweet refrains haunted the crowd long after the last strains of the harp had died away.

> And so long have we known you,
> shared your seasons in the sun

with all the summers gone
watching you go swiftly
as the rivers run,
calling like an eagle, longing
to be free,
knowing now your time is done.

A pause fell over the gathered crowd as the music and words died away, and there were no dry eyes among those there, until the fine, high beat of the finger drum sounded in a lively pace, drawing everyone to dance, and then the other musicians joined in, chord on chord, until it seemed all the sprawling camp was whirling and turning, joined in a bright song to the glory of being alive and gathered together in thanksgiving for deliverance from their enemies.

Elita, shining and radiant, was twirled and turned on every arm, and even Chellin Duchin managed to limp a few bars with the new bride. Famhart and Linne were arm in arm among the festive throng, stopping to talk to many old friends. There were a few gaily colored tents throughout the large camp, and the bakers and cooks had gathered enough stores together for at least a small sample of the wedding feast that had been planned. Small children wandered through the crowd giving out baked apples, and the dancers laughed and sang until at last the musicians tired and the great fires began to burn down.

Before the revelers dispersed to their rest, Stearborn stood on a tree stump near the center of the throng and raised his hand for silence. When he was greeted roughly by a dozen or more gruff Stewards, protesting and complaining of his rude handling of the party's end, he blew a short note on his horn. Owen stood beside him, eyeing the exhausted crowd.

"Lend an ear, neighbors! Hear me, Stewards! I've come to ask for the most stout-hearted of you to come aboard on the chance of a lifetime! New country, new faces, and the very real possibility of great wealth! It's not a place for those who would be weavers or woodmen, but if you've had a hankering for some way out of the regular path, then here's your chance to step forward and join the brigade going to help the Lady Deros, whose father is hard pressed in his battle against the Vipre Black Hood clans and who needs any stout heart who can keep his courage up and knows the way of the sweet science of arms."

A chorus of hecklers answered him from all sides, but there were a few of the younger Stewards who made their way to him, in spite of the chiding from their friends.

"What have you got that's such a choice bird, Stearborn? Why are you running away the dancers to prick at our attention with this rebel baiting?" asked one, a friend of Hamlin's named Jermil.

"I have a succulent tidbit ready for the tasting, my buck! Are you man enough to try to sit down at table to try it?"

"He may not be," teased Hamlin, "but I should like to hear what you've got to say. What is it that could be so secret?"

Stearborn's eyes narrowed, and he looked about him cautiously before he spoke. "Quietly, lads! I'll tell you all, but not shouting it out from this public place. Gather yourselves and you can hear for yourselves everything as it stands."

A young man in a Steward's uniform from the Lost Elm Squadron stepped forward then, addressing the older man in a raised voice. "Is it the foreign girl? Is that the job you're offering? Helping that wench get her father's kingdom back?"

Owen and Jeremy stiffened and leaned forward to see who it was who spoke so disrespectfully.

"Aye," replied Stearborn. "Although it's no matter to you."

"It's a matter if you're asking Line Stewards to throw over their code and ride under a foreign flag!"

"You're loyalty to the Line is admirable, soldier. No one shall ask you to forsake your vows to the Line banners. Now leave us in peace."

The young man jumped up beside Stearborn and raised his hand for silence. "Hear me, Stewards! This wench is no concern of ours once she's beyond the Line! We have extended her our hospitality and given her protection as best we've been able, and once more rescued her from enemies. She asks to repay our kindness to her by taking some of your number away in two captured enemy boats, making for some place in the Sea of Silence!"

A muttering of disapproval and surprise ran through the ranks of those gathered, and a few louder voices in the Steward squadrons voiced their approval of the young man's speech. The crowd was on the verge of chaos when Ephinias appeared beside Stearborn, his face clouded by anger, calling for silence.

"What could he be up to now?" asked Owen, looking in surprise at his old teacher.

"I don't know. He just popped up there!" Jeremy shook his head. "What I'm wondering is who was that Steward?"

"What squadron did he say he served with?" asked Port. "Does anyone here know the lad who was just here?"

Negative replies came from the crowd, and though everyone looked for the man, it seemed he had slipped away. Stearborn called out, raising his voice in his battle tone, so he could quiet the growing excitement. "I think we've had a fine trick shown us here," he cried. "We had gathered you here together to outline a plan we didn't want shouted to everyone, and here we have a good example of being caught in our own snare."

Ulen Scarlett stood amid the Stewards surrounding Stearborn, flanked by his old companions, Lofen and McKandles. They were talking among themselves and seemed intent on some point when Ephinias made as though to speak. Unable to gain the crowd's attention by shouting, he raised a hand and shot a blazing blue bolt skyward, which reached a terrific height above their heads in the night sky and burst into a shower of bright red and gold sparklers that drifted slowly back to earth.

"The minstrel finally got his fireworks." Owen laughed. "Only I don't think these were meant to be friendly."

Showers of sparks fell for a few seconds more, dusting the shoulders of the crowd with dying embers, as the old master began to speak. "Listen to me, Stewards! The threat of deception has been pointed out here tonight! It is easy to join our ranks. Anyone other than an Olgnite could join us, pretending to be a refugee or a soldier from one of the other squadrons. This is too open a place to discuss what we have to discuss, so I move we close this now and you fall back to your own individual squadrons. Famhart and Stearborn will see your commanders and draw any volunteers that way, from known Stewards."

"Aye," rumbled Stearborn. "There's the man! That way no one can come up on your blindside."

Deros made her way through the gathering to stand by Ephinias and Stearborn. "I heard what was said, and it may seem as though I have not been grateful to all of you of the Line. It's true you've taken me in, and that on more than one occasion my life has been in your care. You never let me down, and I'm still here to thank you for all you've done for me, by having helped me and my father."

"Three cheers for Deros!" shouted a voice from the rear of the Stewards grouped around her, and the call was taken up by others, until the whole crowd stomped their booted feet in unison, and they gave her the time-honored salute of slamming their clenched fists against their mail shirts in rapid succession.

The young woman was moved and struggled to hold back her tears, to be able to speak without her voice quavering. "Thank you," she managed. "I would understand if no one thought of this voyage as anything but madness. There doesn't seem much hope, and I can't even promise safe haven at the other side, for I have been gone from Eirn Bol a long time now. But I believe Cairn Weal still stands. Why would these Vipre clansmen pursue me, if my homeland were not still free, my father controlling the islands and sea."

"When do we go?" questioned a Steward.

Stearborn roared out laughing, and gave Deros a clap on the back that almost knocked her from her perch. Port and Starboard joined in on the rowdy laughter, and Chellin Duchin, as weakened as he was by the serious wound he had received, called out loudly and banged his clenched fist against his mail shirt until his knuckles bled. "There you go, lass! The true nature of the Stewards is laid out before you! You won't find a laggard among the lot if your cause is true and just!"

Ulen Scarlett who had been standing near Owen, edged

closer to Deros. McKandles and Lofen stayed where they were.

"Ain't them old 'uns a-bustin' a gut! I ain't never seen so much fun in a-whackin' around on mysel' or anyone else, but then I guess they ain't been raised to knows no better! My old pap used to sit upside an old splinter-tailed nag from Leech, just like he had his own good wits still a-rattlin' around in his poor dented old gourd and a-tellin' me how grand it was."

Lofen scoffed and pushed at his friend. "Your old gaffer was slabwise of his common sense when he ever gave a thought to a-bornin' you! That was *his* first kittleburr!"

"You says it were a kittleburr, I says it was the one thing a-keepin' Lofen Tackman from a early conk, 'cause if it wasn't for your old pal here, you woulds already be nothin' but a pint o'wog out in some bleedin' marsh some'ers outsides of the Plain of Reeds!"

"Shush, you two," shot Owen. "I want to hear the rest of this."

"We can't tells you nothin' about what the lass is a-talkin' about, but we can tell you all the plum parts of what Ulen was after a-sayin'," said McKandles. "He has been a-fillin' us up with them highfalutin' plans of his all night. Lofen wasn't a-takin' to none of it, though. Him and his all-fired tarnbobble again' water has us slabsides of a-hoofin' it on out of here!"

"What are you babbling about?" asked Owen, looking around to study his new friend more closely.

"McKandles is full of them fancy kite tales! We isn't no fools when it comes to how the wind is a-blowin', and after Ulen has been a-fillin' our chubs full of what all he's a-goin' to do once we gets to wherever it is we's off to, then he says old Lofen and McKandles will be bloody border gents, set up proper with plenty of gold to pay for rounds at the inn, and maybe even a fair bit o' skirt to wash and do for an old beggar who ain't never been a-carryin' no bad will towards no soul, 'cept them what has wished him harm!"

"So Ulen has promised you land and a wife, has he?" asked Owen, turning to watch the young horseman once more. "That's interesting."

He watched as the young horseman stayed close to Deros, gazing from time to time over the crowd. Their eyes met and locked for a moment, until Ulen broke the contact by motioning his two underlings to him.

"His Highness is a-callin'. Come on, Lofen. Wese'll see what foltrahoo he's a-takin' up with now!" muttered McKandles, carefully cracking all his knuckles as he finished.

Lofen reached over and grabbed his arm. "Will you stow that snappin' up! It are a-goin' to drive me brinkerside one of these here days, and I is a-goin' to tear them knobby fingers right off your hand!"

As the two men fell to arguing, Owen saw Stearborn beckon to him and slowly made his way through the excited crowd. Talk ran high on all sides of him as he went, and more than a few hands were extended to him as he passed. Stewards from his father's squadron, men he had known from childhood, shook his hand and gave him curt nods, each wishing to be remembered to Famhart. That was no different than it had ever been, but it was more deferential now, and there seemed to be a distance to the greetings. He felt a twinge of guilt, for no one outside his inner circle of friends and his family knew that he was turning down his father and going away with Deros and the Archaelians, and now, it appeared almost certain, the young horseman from the Gortland Fair.

Owen joined with Famhart and Linne at a sudden break in the throng and walked the rest of the way with them. They found Stearborn, full of energy and more noisy than ever, signing aboard a young recruit from Chellin Duchin's squadron.

"This will frost his beggerly old soul." Stearborn laughed. "Nothing like a sea voyage, lad! Can you agree, Famhart? Doesn't it bring it all back in a grand way? The excitement, and all the blood rushing to your head, and the thrill of landfall finally on you, standing the early swing watch and seeing the sun come up out of the sea, making the land all shimmery and golden-red."

Linne laughed at the rantings of her old friend. "You shall have to watch your step or you'll have me aboard, going on like that! Only a tin-eared merchant would be able to resist your pitch!"

"Would you think of going, Mother?" asked Owen suddenly, hearing something in her voice that had not been present since before the road had led them all to Trew.

Linne smiled sadly, holding one of her husband's hands in her own. "We have talked of such a journey," she said softly. "We always promised ourselves we'd go back one day to the country we knew as children."

"But Boghatia is gone," said Owen. "You said your home, and my father's, were both lost."

"They were, Owen," replied Famhart. "Yet there is still something there that calls you, even though all has changed, and there may be nothing that remains."

Port and Starboard nodded their agreement. "It was sad in Trew, but there was a part of it that was reassuring."

"Starboard's always been for returning there when we can't peddle a Steward's wares anymore. I think now he may be right."

Stearborn locked an arm around Deros and hugged her to him. "You see, little one? All this planning of your voyage has set off a dozen old warrior's fondest dreams! Going back to a place where they were young and before all the darker side of it got tangled up in a Steward's code!"

"You would be welcome in Eirn Bol," replied the girl. "If we can keep my father's reign strong and drive back the Black Hood clans, then you would all be most welcome to stay. It is very beautiful."

"Does that offer extend to me?" asked Ulen sarcastically. "I'm sure I could find a little piece of ground where I could run a few horses and maybe even settle down to a quieter life than I've been leading! It wouldn't be the first time that the Gortland Fair was offered safe haven in a foreigner's land." He glared coldly at Famhart and Emerald as he spoke. "But then those without means or countries don't weigh much in the policy of those who do, except when they suddenly find themselves without."

"We're without for now," declared Chellin. "The Line is in ruins, and it looks as though it might take some bit of scuffling to piece it back to what it was. I think that shall be old Chellin Duchin's job until he spills out of these parts for easier duty somewhere on the other side of the Boundaries."

"That's the job that requires all the old hands," agreed Port. "Starboard and I were just speaking earlier of taking the squadron back to some peaceful side of the trade, like it was once, when a Steward could be as good with a hammer and saw as he was handy with his sword and bow."

"They were good days," agreed his brother. "It drew us all together."

The crowd parted long enough to let a messenger through, who reported quickly to Stearborn.

"I think this solves our little mystery about who the disappearing 'Steward' was. The news just came from the vessels that a large party of the Hulin Vipre has been spotted, and one of their camps was not far away. All of them, down to the leader, is dressed in Steward uniforms and carrying Steward gear!"

The young messenger addressed the crowd, pointing in the direction from which he had just come. "I was almost lured into their camp when I chanced on them an hour or so back, but I saw some of them taking off their other uniforms and going through a pile of Steward gear. That made me curious, so I kept out of sight and waited to see what would come next."

"What did come next?" asked Jeremy. "How did you spot them for spys?"

"When they tossed all their clothes in a pit and buried them."

Stearborn tugged at his beard. "This is good news, then, for we can let them have some information now if they're sneaking about like rats to get it!"

"What do you speak of, you old wart-rug?" asked Chellin. "A spy is a spy! The nearest tree with a rope is short enough shrift for their likes!"

"We are playing by a different set of rules with these fellows! If we want to stay ahead of them, we're going to have to try to think like they think."

"That snipe spoke well enough in our tongue to pass muster," said Jeremy. "How could that be if they are foreigners?"

"I'll tell you how that might happen," broke in Findlin, holding a cup of steaming tea out in front of him to let it cool. "The lass says she has escaped those who were searching for her, and gotten as far as the Line. The boat that brought her here was found, and the crew either sailed home, or are in Salt Mother's arms. But what if they were followed and a band of the Hulins has been put in ewery settlement, in all the lands, to see if they can't find the missing girl's whereabouts."

"What think you, Ephinias?" asked Famhart.

The old teacher shook his head and stared out over the crowd, smiling slightly. "They have been among us, all right. They need to find the absent link to the secrets of Cairn Weal, and they know they have to find Deros here. With all the cunning of their race, they land small bands here and there to scout and spy, and it doesn't take much of a mind to know that if you are to look for secrets, you must go where they are."

"It would explain those Hulin wessels being so far upriwer," agreed Lorimen. "We'we come and gone on the Riwer Line quite often, and it would take a local, or someone who's made the woyage more than once, to know about all the shallows and tides."

Ulen Scarlett was jubilant. "So my idea is not so farfetched a plan as it was made out to be! If the Hulin Vipre are passing our lines as easily as all that, it won't be such a trick to return them the favor."

Owen and Jeremy groaned.

"This will mean training," exclaimed the old commander. "Deros must tell us all she can about the Vipre and what they are about. All who go on this journey shall be prepared."

"It will give us time to spread the news we want taken back to their leader as well," added Famhart. "We shall camp each night on the road to the coast, and while our students are leaning what they need to know, we'll mount our own play for any prying eyes."

"And while all this goes forward, we shall be aboard our wessels and safely on our way," said Lorimen.

Ephinias nodded slowly, looking over the gathered Stewards and settlers from the Line. "It will be a fresh start," he said, his clear, gray eyes misty as he searched the sky. "It always seems just at the darkest hour there comes a dawn." He smiled to himself, still lost in his own thoughts. "The kingdom of night is not yet drawn to a close, but we are here on the very edge of it, and we are yet hopeful."

Emerald hugged Elita tightly to him as he stood by his old mentor. "This is the story that I shall make next," he said, looking around at the weary, battle-exhausted survivors of the fierce struggle against the Olgnites from the Wastes of Leech, and the Order of the Black Hood, who came from the Sea of Silence.

"Long live the minstrel! Long live Elita!" came the chorus of shouts from the crowd, and the Stewards banged their fists against their mail shirts. "Long live the Line!"

As they stood cheering, the sky was suddenly a brilliant golden-white, with a dazzling array of bright blue and red showers of stars that arced and towered upward toward the darkest vaults of heaven. The great white falcon glided slowly to earth, to land at the feet of Ephinias. There were visions then of stout sailing ships, and green islands in a dark blue sea, with the smells and sounds of the water strong upon them and a lone banner fluttered over the ramparts of a white fortress, roofed in gold and overlooking all from a high ivory cliff that loomed above the sea's edge.

"It's Cairn Weal!" cried Deros, clutching Ephinias by the hand. "It's my father's banner! It still waves!" Tears flooded her eyes then, and she looked about the crowd until her eyes met Owen's. "We shall be in time," she said.

Ephinias lifted the great bird above his head for all in the gathering to see. "It is our sign," cried the old teacher loudly, his strong voice carrying to all the ranks of Stewards and settlers alike, and the snowy bird spread his wings and rose steadily up into the vision of the fortress on the cliff, higher still, circling ever toward the banner that blew gently in the wind there, and as he disappeared from view, the light from the bright golden light flared and died, leaving the expectant faces of the crowd turned upward, where they saw the three brilliant watch fires of the sky, the Three Kings, as they were called, twinkling gently away in the direction of the coast and the invisible sea.

"The steering stars," breathed Findlin quietly. "They have brought me home from many a long woyage."

"And started us on another," reminded Lorimen.

All watched and grew quiet as the camp settled into thoughts of sleep and dreams, and plans were made among the friends, even as they went to rest.

Far away, the unsleeping sea that brushed the cliffs in the vision rolled and thundered on the headlands of the island of Eirn Bol, and deep inside the fastness of Cairn Weal, an old man, worn and frail, paced before a fire on the hearth. Suddenly the likeness of a familiar face appeared in the flames. It was his own long-departed daughter, with tears in her eyes, trying to say something to him, although he could hear nothing but the noise of the fire. When he despaired at that, another sight came that cheered him. A great white bird flew high up above the very fortress that he dwelled in, with a banner of white and gold clutched in its talons, and a tall ship, cutting through the midnight skies with all sails full and pulling, trailing a wake of blazing stars.

The old man sighed and went back to his pacing as the images in the fireplace died away to crackling sparks that jumped out onto the floor before the hearth in the cold still room where he waited. He had been waiting for so many nights for word of his daughter, who had sailed away to seek what help she could find in the vast lands at the sea's edge, where the last clans of the ancient races yet dwelled, left by the Keepers to protect those Lower Boundaries that grew darker still as the long reign of night fell with an icy blanket of stillness over the once beautiful gardens of man.

Yet high above the black silence there was a long, high call of the Pipe of Truth, and it was still heard in the corridors of the heavens that night, and somewhere in the stillest part of the human hearts that yet beat on Atlanton, there came answers, strong and brave. It was destined that all those who heard that call would be swept away in the River as it flowed on its course toward the ending of one life and the beginning of a new, following the snowy falcon, who carried the proud gold-and-white banner of the Line flying on toward the golden east, where the bright rays of the Sun were waiting for a distant dawn that would not be long in coming.

The wood surrounding Sweet Rock was teeming with Olgnite hordes, and the river ran blood red.

• • • • •

Owen was struggling vainly with his comrades to stem the enemy tide at the perimeters of the burning village. He slashed again and again with the sword of Skye while Gitel fought with his hooves. Then, when he raised his sword for what seemed the last time, a great shower of stars with sparkling trails erupted from the sky.

It illuminated the fallen men and dead horses, and the rest of the squadron, many unhorsed, fighting in a last desperate attempt to head off the deadly swarms of Olgnites.

Then all Owen and his comrades could see were flying, dazzling colors, each more brilliant than the last. Just at the level of the trees, a blinding golden burst filled the entire night, and the vague form of a white domed mountain came slowly into view.

With a rumbling noise that shook the ground beneath their feet, a white-hot river of lava began to flow over the lip of the ghostly vision . . . and into the wood and the battle!

•

THE SEA of SILENCE

Also by Niel Hancock

Dragon Winter

THE CIRCLE OF LIGHT SERIES
I *Greyfax Grimwald*
II *Faragon Fairingay*
III *Calix Stay*
IV *Squaring the Circle*

THE WILDERNESS OF FOUR SERIES
I *Across the Far Mountain*
II *The Plains of the Sea*
III *On the Boundaries of Darkness*
IV *The Road to the Middle Islands*

THE WINDAMEIR CIRCLE
I *The Fires of Windameir*